THE RELUCTANT GUNFIGHTER

A wiry man with a hook nose and a long, dark moustache studied him coldly from beneath a low hat brim. "Do you know who you're lookin' at?" he asked.

"I don't believe so," replied Charles Henry Clayton. "I'm a stranger here."

"They call me El Paso," the man announced.

"How do you do, Mr. Paso. What can I do for you?"

"You can get out your gun," the man said angrily. "Because I'm going to get out mine." And with that, the man drew and fired. Charles Henry felt a sharp pain along his left shoulder. He glanced at it, saw a tear in the sleeve and blood beginning to well. He stared blankly at the man with the gun.

"Why did you do that?"

One of the others chuckled. "This here sure ain't that gunfighter, Henry Clay."

"I ain't so sure," another mused aloud. "Shoot him again, El Paso. He don't seem to rile easy."

El Paso thumbed back his hammer. "Might as well," he said.

But the hammer never fell. Charles Henry Clayton had had enough. ...

THE BEST IN WESTERNS FROM ZEBRA

THE SLANTED COLT   (1413, $2.25)
by Dan Parkinson
A tall, mysterious stranger named Kichener gave young Benjamin
Franklin Black a gift—a Colt pistol that had belonged to Ben's
father. And when a cold-blooded killer vowed to put Ben six feet
under, it was a sure thing that Ben would have to learn to use that
gun—or die!

GUNPOWDER GLORY   (1448, $2.50)
by Dan Parkinson
After Jeremy Burke shot down the Sutton boy who killed his pa,
it was time to leave town. Not that Burke was afraid of the Sut-
tons—but he had promised his pa, right before the old man died,
that he'd never kill another Sutton. But when the bullets started
flying, he'd find there was more at stake than his own life. . . .

BLOOD ARROW   (1549, $2.50)
by Dan Parkinson
Randall Kerry was a member of the Mellette Expedition—until he
returned from a scouting trip to find the force of seventeen men
slaughtered and scalped. And before Kerry could ride a mile from
the massacre site, two Indians emerged from the trees and
charged!

GUNSIGHT LODE   (1497, $2.25)
by Virgil Hart
After twenty years Aaron Glass is back in Idaho, seeking venge-
ance on a member of his old gang who once double-crossed him.
The hardened trail-rider gets a little softhearted when he discovers how frail Doc Swann's grown—but when the medicine man
tries to backshoot him, Glass is tough as nails!

Available wherever paperbacks are sold, or order direct from the
Publisher. Send cover price plus 50¢ per copy for mailing and
handling to Zebra Books, Dept. 1663, 475 Park Avenue South,
New York, N.Y. 10016. DO NOT SEND CASH.

CALAMITY TRAIL

DAN PARKINSON

ZEBRA BOOKS
KENSINGTON PUBLISHING CORP.

ZEBRA BOOKS

are published by

Kensington Publishing Corp.
475 Park Avenue South
New York, NY 10016

First printing: September 1985

Printed in the United States of America

*For the best of all partners
and those special corners.
Always be there.*

. . . and to Scott Siegel with best wishes.

On the day when juices flow
and the virgin fires glow
one will come to fan the flame.
Chaos and havoc be his name.

Poor old woman, wring your hands.
You must go to distant lands
nevermore sweet peace to see.
All roads lead to Calamity.

Part One

Chaos and Havoc

I

Pale morning pierced the mists of Boston Bay and danced bright sparkle on the wavelets nearer shore as Jonathan Clayton Powers squinted aging, watery eyes to make out the ship in the distance. Tall sails rosy against the morning sun, squat dark hull beneath, the vessel was more than a mile away, just standing in at the breakwater.

"It's *Falcon,*" Bull Timmons exclaimed with a snort, and turned a smile of cold victory on the old man beside him. "She's here and you've lost. The wager is mine."

The old man's shoulders sagged slightly, and he rested shaking hands on the sill of the wide window, forty feet above the accounting floors. Below and stretching like arms around the inner bay were the seaward faces of the enclave of structures that made up the headquarters of the Powers Company: long ranks of warehouses, transit sheds, fitting lofts, stores and yards interspersed with wagon yards, smithies and roadways—a crescent of structures embracing the shoreline where wagons rolled and men worked in the orchestrated activity of a port in full array.

His face gray beneath a shock of white hair, Jona-

11

than Clayton Powers looked down upon the world that had been his for forty years and had been his father's before him, and the dread that had lived inside him became a knowledge of loss.

"I should never have made such a gamble," he muttered.

Beside him Bull Timmons chuckled. "You never had the choice, old man. If not this way, then another. I've broken you, old man. I need these yards. And now they're mine."

Beyond the busy shoreline vessels stood at piers and docks, busy with the comings and goings of seaport commerce. In the near distance a stubby yacht dock lay between wide launchways, its pilings draped with the hawsers of a small sloop and a pair of beautiful old sailing launches. Barges and steam tugs lay among the masted vessels, and a brig rested at a finger pier. Beyond the ways, long gray ribbons of weathered dock ran both directions around the harbor's crest, backed by careening stages, drydocks, tackle towers, and cargo hoists.

There were five men now at the high window. Timmons's sullen shadow Luther and the lawyer he had brought had crowded in for a view of the incoming ship, and Watson was there beside Powers, raising a glass to his eye.

"I'm afraid he's right, sir," Watson muttered. "It is *Falcon*."

"I've brought the necessary papers, of course," Timmons said cheerfully. "You might as well sign them. I've won."

"If so it is by foul means," the old man rasped. "If your ship has beat my *Sally* it's because *Sally* has been sabotaged. I don't suppose you'll tell me what you've done."

Timmons chuckled again and shrugged. "Coastal

12

waters can be dangerous, old man. Sometimes a ship can be delayed. I expect your precious scow will be along—in a day or so, when they've pumped out her bilges."

Glancing around, Powers saw a smirk pass between Timmons and the one called Luther, a sullen, hard-eyed thug Timmons retained for odd jobs. No one knew much about Luther, but Powers had little doubt of the nature of the man. He had come with Bull Timmons from the west—from Chicago—and Powers knew now that some of the violences—the "accidents"—that had so favored Timmons's dealing in Boston had not been accidents at all.

"You might as well sign the papers, old man," Timmons said with a sneer. "Get it over with."

"Not yet." Powers straightened his back. "Until your ship is docked and her cargo tallied, I owe you nothing."

"Still stubborn," Timmons rasped. "Well, it won't matter. But if it makes you feel any better, my gamble with you was the biggest of all. If I had lost it would have broken me." Timmons smiled. He had known he would not lose.

Sick with defeat, Jonathan Clayton Powers stood in his window and looked again at the bustle of a harbor he had managed and nurtured for most of his life. And even now, losing it all, he saw the beauty of its thriving activity.

Down in the middle yards dockworkers in bright jackets tended moorings. Stevedore gangs and long-shoremen bustled about on the slope between docks and buildings, their busy paths crisscrossing those of carters, draymen, and teamsters fighting their reins.

Close by, just beyond a launchway to the right, a double gang of longshoremen jogged back and forth between the open maw of a warehouse and the deck of

13

a moored timber barge, carrying huge stripped trunks bound for the shipyards of the Chesapeake.

The timber barge belonged to Timmons, as did more than half the vessels in the bay this season. Bull Timmons had descended upon Boston with money and muscle, and had bought, fought and maneuvered his way into control of a vast shipping empire. But the key to monopoly in shipping was the harbor, and Jonathan Clayton Powers had sidestepped Timmons at every turn to retain his yards—until now. Now, it seemed, Timmons would have it all.

Powers had spent a lifetime living and loving the life of the yards. Much of what he held, he held in trust. It was not just his own holdings at stake now. It was the entire family's fortunes: a quarter his and another quarter in trust for his dead brother's kin, and a quarter each belonging to his sisters. Damned old biddies, he thought, not unkindly, as he thought of the two women he had not seen for years. They had assigned management to him more to be rid of his presence, he thought, than out of any respect for his abilities. But manage he did, and through the years the yards had survived.

He loved these yards. He loved the seasons of shipping, the rhythms of commerce, the never-ending dance of seaport activity. Below, the double gang of longshoremen trudged ashore with empty handslings.

The old man timed them as they entered the open shed, were gone for a moment, then reappeared carrying a mast on their slings, twelve men to a side, jogging as they emerged from the shed, almost running as they reached the dock, the timber's weight propelling them along, then dancing across the long, thin-cleated catwalk stretching from dockside out to the barge's deck, its bouys casting ripples as they crossed.

On deck they dropped slings, skidding the log into place, then regrouped and trudged shoreward, catching their wind to run again. One mast every two minutes, the old man calculated. The wide barge was more than half loaded. He shook his head sadly. He would miss such sights as that.

At the yacht dock, topmen swarmed the shrouds of the sloop to unfurl its sails as deck hands hauled line to raise slack jibsails and spanker. A party of carriages had arrived at the dock, and brightly dressed ladies and gentlemen climbed a gangway to cluster on deck as officers and crew worked around them. Holiday gentry, the old man knew, out for a sail on the bay. Cost them a pretty penny, he thought. But they could afford it. For some in Boston there was no shortage of money. Powers knew the sloop's captain, but not its owners. Probably it belonged to Timmons, too.

He had been a fool. Three times he had been a fool, and now he was paying for it as he watched Timmons's *Falcon* easing up the bay with the Indies mail contracts that would secure Bill Timmons's empire and break the Powers Company forever.

First there had been the war loans, credit extended to his government in good faith. He had been commended for that, but as the years passed and there was no repayment, Powers Company had gone deeper into debt. Then had come the Indies mail routes and a chance at recovery. He had spent the last he had to build *Sally*. Sleek hull, steam sidewheels and banked sails, she would make the run and win the contract. Timmons's *Falcon*, the only other contender, was no match for her. He had gambled his last capital on *Sally*. That was his second mistake.

The third was his wager with Timmons. Powers had thought it a gentlemen's wager: Timmons's payment of all Powers's debts against Powers's consignment of the company mortgages to Timmons, depending upon the outcome of the mail contract race. Powers had learned

15

only this morning that Timmons already held the notes on his capital assets. With the mortgages, he would own it all. The man was a scoundrel. And Jonathan Powers had been a fool.

The Boston docks, the Charleston docks, the Richmond yards—Timmons would take it all. The old man tried to imagine how he managed it. He must have had help within the company, but who?

Buntings danced in an offshore wind. The excursion sloop would go out under sail. The sports would have their money's worth.

A slim figure had wandered into view off to the right, a young man, frock-coated and neat, the breeze tousling his brown hair and ruffling the corners of the sheaf of large papers he carried. In the window Jonathan Clayton Powers shook his head sadly. Another responsibility he would have to drop. Even at this distance Charles Henry Clayton looked hopelessly lost, out of place amidst the orderly chaos of the busy shipyards. He watched as his nephew wandered down to dockside, looked around absently, turned and walked a few steps closer to the launchway, started to sit down on the dock's edge then stood again, peering intently at something on the ground. Laying a piece of wood atop his papers to hold them, he walked briskly past the bobbing catwalk, stooped and lifted a length of rope lying there unattached, its outward end trailing into the water.

What now, Charles Henry, the old man mused resignedly. What wonders is that innocent mind of yours evolving? Timmons was gazing out toward his *Falcon,* serene victory on his face. The others were watching the activity about the harbor, all in their ways waiting for the final kill. Powers looked again at his nephew down by the dock.

The young man studied the loose rope in his hand,

gazed around vaguely at the various vessels close in, shrugged visibly, looked around again, and his gaze fixed on the nearest cleat, set in the catwalk's riding beam.

In the window the old man's eyes widened. "Oh, no," he muttered under his breath.

Down at the water's edge Charles Henry reached a decision. He strode briskly to the catwalk, bent and secured the rope to the cleat, then stood and brushed his hands. He looked pleased.

In the window Jonathan Clayton Powers flinched as Watson's elbow dug into his side. "Do you see that, sir?" Watson whispered, and started to turn away. Powers gripped his arm, holding him there. "It doesn't matter any more," he grunted. Bull Timmons glanced at them curiously, then looked out again, satisfied eyes watching the *Falcon* as she came on, well into the harbor now, beginning her turn toward the cargo piers.

The young man below them had retrieved his papers. Now he gazed around again, cocked his head, and set off down the dock, long strides carrying him into the distance.

Directly out from the high window, at the yacht dock, the sailing sloop had found its wind and was turning smartly, seeking clear channel outward. Trim hull crested the wavelets and made spray as set sails filled.

"My God, sir," Watson whispered, and Powers nudged him to silence. Let the damage be done, he thought. Let Timmons pay the repair bill.

The sloop picked up way, her bow wake rising. Suddenly a dangling line at her stern sprang taut, showering droplets along its length. A piece of stern rail shattered, standing out from the deck, but the line held.

At its other end the catwalk slipped, quivered and splintered as it tipped on it buoys and broke loose from its resting stays. Its near end swung away from the dock, ploughing water as it swung to follow the gliding sloop.

"What the hell—" Bull Timmons erupted as the shriek of torn timber reached them, and he saw what Powers and Watson were watching.

Below and to the right the double gang of longshoremen came jogging from the shed, their burden already lending speed to their feet. In an incredible instant they were down the slope, across the dock and toppling by columns of two into the lapping water where the catwalk should have been. The huge, trimmed log arrowed out from its slings to slap the water and race on, a fearsome fish spearheading its own slim wake. The timber barge trembled as the log thudded home in its side, bursting through its thin hull, collapsing braces, piercing it at waterline.

A hundred yards out the sloop, slow to heel, had finally reacted to the tug at its stern. Even as the trailing line parted and sang it veered broadside into the wales of the anchored brig. Rigging tangled, spars splintered and sails collapsed.

The crippled catwalk, still scudding under its own momentum, tugged the pierced barge sideways, and the hole in its side opened wide as the log twisted in its wound.

In the high window five pairs of eyes were round with awe. "Good God Almighty!" Bull Timmons roared.

With a single, eloquent heave of its deck, the timber barge sank by the stern, its load of unsecured masts shooting outward into the water. As a mass they collided with the mooring blocks of a laden drydock hoist. Cables roared and parted, floating piers broke loose, and the whole structure slid outward, away from shore, teetering from the weight of the whaleboat high in its slings. *Falcon* was just completing her turn, and the careening drydock scudded toward her, its cradled whaleboat leaning outward, twenty feet above the water.

From all the rails of the *Falcon* men dived overboard, and *Falcon* leaned with the wind, her unmanned helm coming about to meet the approaching juggernaut.

"No!" Bull Timmons screamed. "Oh, no!"

They met. Overburdened uprights shattered, and the whaleboat took masts and rigging as it dropped with a deafening crunch directly across the deck of *Falcon*. The little ship buckled, splitting wide open, rebounding waters engulfing its holds. Nose and tail pointing to the sky, it wrapped itself around the fallen whaleboat and promptly sank in two pieces. Above it the broken drydock hoist bobbed and nodded as though saying grace.

Long moments passed before there was movement in the high window. Then Jonathan Clayton Powers's shoulders began to shake uncontrollably. Great sobs wracked him, and it was all he could do to look around at the chalk-white face of Bull Timmons, still staring open-mouthed at where his mail ship's stubby jib stood stark above the water. Everywhere, people were swimming, deckhands from *Falcon,* gentry from the entangled sloop, longshoremen near the dock.

Powers tried to speak and choked, almost strangling. Watson thumped him on the back several times, and gradually the wracking sobs grew into laughter. The old man sagged on his windowsill and howled while Timmons and his cohorts gaped at the wreckage in the harbor.

Gulping air, Powers tried again. "Your ship—didn't—make it, Timmons. You lose!"

Timmons closed his mouth with an effort and turned slowly from the window. Wild rage contorted his face, and he towered over the old man. Watson dashed to a sideboard, pulled out a pistol and pointed it with shaking hands. "Let's not be hasty, gentlemen."

Powers had collapsed again. Keeping the gun trained on the other three, Watson got an arm around his shoulders and helped him to a seat beside the desk. Footsteps thundered on the stairs below.

"Get out of here, Timmons," Powers said between convulsions. "First sign the draft you owe me, then get out."

Luther was still looking out the window. "I seen the one that done it, Bull. I seen him tie the line."

There were loud knocks at the door now and shouting beyond. Timmons stared at Luther. "Did you know him?"

"No, but I seen him."

"Then you can find him. I want him dead, Luther. Whoever he is, wherever he is, I want him dead." He looked back at the old man and the nervous Watson, still pointing his gun. "If I thought for a minute you could have planned that . . ." Then he shook his head. With a final glare he marched to the door, shouldering excited people aside as he went out, Luther and the lawyer trailing behind him.

Watson put the gun away and peered in concern at his shuddering employer, who was regaining his breath and his color. Then he stared again from the high window at the havoc still spreading on the harbor. It would take weeks—months—to restore productive order out there. "It looks like a war zone," he muttered.

At the desk Jonathan Clayton Powers took a deep breath and shook his head. Whether by act of God or act of Charles Henry, the Powers Company was still his and now debt free. Now it was time to begin unravelling some mysteries. "Watson," he said.

Watson remained enthralled at the window. "All he did was tie a loose line," he muttered. "He simply found a line and tied it."

Powers moved around to his safe and extracted volumes of transaction records. "Watson," he said again.

At the window Watson stared as the bobbing drydock hoist, its floats taking water, took one final bow and quietly sank. "He was just tidying up," he muttered.

"Watson!"

"Yes, sir?" He turned.

"Watson, go find Charles Henry and keep him out of sight. Those men are dangerous. Hide him until I can arrange to send him away. Far away."

II

He was tall, slim and well tailored in traveling clothes that suggested the comfort wealth could buy and contrasted sharply with the innocence of a face whose twenty-odd years had been untroubled by serious concern. Stepping down from the foot-board of the high coach in Philadelphia's rail yard, he blinked in bright sunlight then turned to give a hand to the matron disembarking behind him. The coach was not close enough to the boardwalk landing to allow stepping across, and it was a good two feet from the foot-board to the ground.

As the plump woman prepared to step down he stopped her, noticing a benchlike stool just beside the high front wheel. With a grin of satisfaction he gripped the stool and dragged it back under the door so the matron could step on it. She smiled her gratitude and let him hand her down. Her husband followed, and another man, murmuring their thanks as he assisted them.

They gathered there, strangers ending a journey together, as the driver tossed luggage down from the top of the coach and another man emptied the boot,

ranking the various cargo along the edge of the boardwalk.

"It has been a pleasant journey, Mr. Clayton," the
matron told the young man, "and I do hope you are
successful with your art. Will we be seeing you in Philadelphia?"

"Unfortunately, no," he told her, hat in hand. "I'll be
boarding the rail train here in a few hours. I must travel
right on through to Charleston."

"Ah, yes," the matron's husband said. "Your business assignment. Well, don't let them work you too
hard, son. Spend time with your drawing. As Clara
said, if a man has the gift it is a sin not to make the most
of it."

The coach behind him rocked as the driver swung
down from its top to the wheel, then to the bench that
wasn't there and suddenly was dangling and thrashing
from the brake lever.

"My goodness," the matron exclaimed mildly.

"Such language," her husband said frowning, and
with a final tip of the hat to Clayton ushered her away
from the swearing driver. The other passenger had
found his luggage and wandered away.

Charles Henry Clayton replaced his hat on his head
and gazed around at the Philadelphia yards with the
eyes of an artist, noting the textural contrast between
the old brick stage depot nearby and the milled lumber
of its newer and larger neighboring structures associ-
ated with the rail depot a hundred yards away. Midway between was a copious travelers' inn of two stories
whose sign proclaimed rooms to let upstairs and meals
on the ground floor. Bright-clothed small tables were
placed on the wide porch in front of it, and people were
eating there.

"The very thing," Charles Henry Clayton told
himself, and looked around for his luggage. The coach-

24

driver and an attendant seemed to be squabbling about something, but it was none of his concern. His luggage was set near the front of the coach, a large trunk, a valise, a two by three foot flat portfolio of strapped leather, and a tall, closed tripod easel lying half off the boardwalk. Signaling a liveried porter, Charles handed him a coin and indicated the trunk. "Can you get this aboard the train for Charleston? Pullman three in the name of Clayton."

"Yes, sir," the porter said, turning to fetch a cart and stepping aside to make way for a party of ladies arriving to board the coach to Baltimore. Charles tipped his hat to the ladies, one of whom carried a smug-appearing large gray cat. Then he retrieved his valise, picked up his portfolio, adjusted it under his arm and stooped to get his tripod and easel, not noticing that the business end of it, with its iron swivel-peg, was lost beneath the billowing skirts of the lady with the cat.

"Ah," he said happily as he straightened and balanced his load. He tipped the tripod level for carrying.

Immediately behind him there was a piercing scream, followed by another piercing scream as the gray cat sailed through the air to land, claws gripping in panic, on the rump of the near wheelhorse of the coach's team. Charles looked around in amazement as the wheelhorse reared, the cat clinging desperately to its rump, and the team bolted. The brake was still free from the driver's entanglement with its lever, and the coach sailed high and handsome down the road with driver, attendants, and ladies scrambling after it.

From the suddenly empty boardwalk Charles stared bemusedly, then shrugged and walked away toward the inviting porch of the restaurant. "One would think people would be more careful," he told himself with a certain resignation.

Approaching the large building he stopped abruptly, his mouth dropping open, then hurried to remove his hat, dropping his portfolio in the process. Approaching from across the road was a dazzlingly beautiful young woman followed by a small, aged black woman with a mockingbird hat, and a retinue of burdened porters. Charles Henry stood in gaping awe as the girl approached. Huge dark eyes and small, full lips graced a perfect oval face framed by rich, dark curls and crowned with a wide bonnet of purest white. Everything about her attire, from bonnet to gloves, from lace-front blouse that bulged over a bewitching bosom to bustled skirt that molded fine, aggressive hips to the toes of slippers peeping from beneath its hem, was white. There was annoyance in the set of her brow and determination in the thrust of her chin as she set a pace that made the little black woman and the porters scurry to keep up.

". . . didn't even stop by to get the rest of your things," the black woman said as they approached Charles Henry. "And all them nice gifts—and them gentry folks down there waitin' by the church door, what they goin' to think?"

"I'll send for my things," the girl said, and Charles Henry thought he had never heard a voice so perfectly female. "The gifts will just have to go back. Did you pack the good linens, Aphrodite? We'll need those. And my riding habit?"

The little black woman, plainly irritated, hurried forward, trying for eye contact. "I packed all you said. Miss Emmalee, will you hold on for a minute and listen to me? This the foolest thing you done yet, girl, an' that's goin' some. Mr. Lyle, he ain't all that bad, an' he do have money, Heaven know."

As they passed Charles Henry the girl glanced at him

26

and strode on. Her glance indicated there was nothing surprising about a man displaying round eyes and open mouth at sight of her.

"I do not choose," she told Aphrodite, "to spend my life with a man who prefaces each comment with 'ah-hump-sniff' and whose only subject of discourse is the social register. Do you have our money? Then you go along and see that our things are loaded properly. The train departs at five."

With that the vision in white proceeded toward the restaurant while the line of trunk-laden porters hurried away toward the rail station, their pace dictated by the imperious little black woman berating them as they went.

Charles Henry Clayton closed his mouth, replaced his hat and retrieved his fallen portfolio. The trailing business end of his tripod had drooped among a cluster of postal sacks waiting on the dock, and when he righted it, one of the sacks dangled from its swivel hook. With renewed enthusiasm he headed for the restaurant.

The place was packed with travelers and locals, and there seemed to be a meeting going on inside, but he found a small table with one chair on the porch near the open front door and claimed it. The girl's train was to leave at five. That meant her train was his train. He looked forward to becoming acquainted on the journey.

He set his valise and portfolio by the wall and swung his tripod around to stand it upright. The dangling mail pouch scudded away to rest beneath the chair of a dark-moustachioed man in black coat and spat breeches.

He sat at his table, and a boy wearing an apron appeared beside him. "We got ham or chicken, sir."

"Neither," Charles Henry said smiling. "Just coffee

and a pastry, please."

"We got white bread and honey," the boy said, and hurried away into the shadowed interior.

Charles glanced into the restaurant. It was a large, echoing room with dining tables from wall to wall in random order, all of them occupied. Waiters bustled about, threading their way among them, carrying trays and pots. Just inside the door a long table was set by the window, and a man stood at the near end of it, addressing the double rank of ladies and gentlemen along its sides. He had the rich orator's voice of a politician, and Charles gathered from his remarks that he was just back from a visit to the West and full of opinions about what should be done out there. His voice carried clearly above the general babble of casual diners at other tables.

"There is great wealth in those western territories," the man said, "riches beyond belief that could be exploited with proper civil organization. There are forests and minerals, and open meadows beyond imagining that have never felt the plow. The war has been over for ten years now, and still we struggle to recover. But I say the means of recovery are there, to the west, if we could but agree upon a real plan for exploitation. Yet we remain disorganized. And while we dither, those lands are filling up—not with simple working folk who would accumulate their riches and transmit them back here to civilization, but with scoundrels of every variety who are keeping their riches for themselves. Many of them, out in those territories, even avoid paying taxes. . . ."

Charles stopped listening at that point because the gorgeous young woman in white appeared again, beside him. She had been inside. Now she stood at the door and surveyed the wide porch, her eyes dark with anger. As Charles was nearest to her, he received the

28

brunt of it. Placing small gloved hands firmly on lovely hips she glared at him and demanded, "If this is a place of business why can't it accommodate its trade?"

Bedazzled, Charles Henry jumped to his feet and offered his chair. "No seats inside? Then please permit me, miss."

Without hesitation she accepted his offer and let him seat her in his place.

"Thank you," she said.

With his most disarming smile Charles said, "Charles Henry Clayton at your service, miss." He tendered a gallant bow that brought his posterior into abrupt contact with that of a passing waiter. Erratic, dancing footsteps receded into the restaurant, followed by the distant crash of falling glassware.

The girl looked around at the noise, her pretty mouth drawn down in disapproval. Charles shook his head resignedly. "People can be so clumsy," he observed aloud and looked around for an unused chair. He spotted one just inside the door, retrieved it and set it across from the girl, serenely unaware that the chair's presence would be counted on presently by the proclaiming politician.

The man's voice droned on, ". . . impeding the development of a huge potential tax base in those areas. . . ."

Charles sat down, crossed his arms on the tiny table-top and beamed at the girl across from him. "Your name is Emmalee," he said. "I overheard the servant lady call you that."

"Miss Emmalee Wilkes," she admitted. "Yes, I saw you overhearing."

"I am delighted you decided not to marry Lyle," he told her. "Otherwise we would not have had the opportunity to become acquainted. I knew a person named Lyle once. He had several bad habits. Are you going all the way to Charleston?"

29

"I am going to Columbia, then on to Vicksburg. I live there. Are you always so direct with ladies, Mr. Clayton?"

"I have a theory," he said seriously, "that there might be far less mischance in the world if people would be more direct in their communications. The more precise we are, the less chance there is of misunderstanding, and it may be that misunderstanding is one of the causes of the constant chaos that afflicts our race. Do you see what I mean?"

"Not exactly. Perhaps if you would address your remarks more to my face and less to my bosom things would be clearer."

"I beg your pardon." He redirected his admiring gaze to her dark eyes which also were quite interesting. "I am an artist, you see, and lately I have been concentrating on contour. It becomes a habit, I suppose."

She had been observing him with some mild interest, noting the well-cut clothes he wore, the well-cut planes of his face, the guileless intelligence of his eyes, but now a shadow of disappointment crossed her face. "You are an artist? I understand artists usually starve."

"I suppose they do," he said, "if they manage to spend enough time at it. Unfortunately, I never seem to have enough time. There's always business to attend to."

"Oh?" Her interest returned. "You are in business as well?"

"Shipyards," he said. "I am on my way to Charleston to take a hand in our interests there."

"You have shipyards, then, in various places?"

"We are headquartered in Boston. But I think we have several."

"You think? Do you mean you don't know how many shipyards you have?" Her interest now burned lively in her eyes, and Charles found himself entranced by them.

He was distracted, though, by loud voices approaching. A group consisting of a rail clerk, a portly man, and four uniformed law officers was approaching the porch. ". . . serious federal offense," the portly man was saying. "Postal property in transit is protected by felony laws. There were supposed to be fifteen pouches, Miller. They were listed and accounted."

"Well, I labeled them myself, sir," the clerk argued just as loudly, "and there were only fourteen."

"Have to search the whole area," the portly one continued, uninterrupted. "If your count is correct, then one of them has been stolen."

Charles shook his head and turned back to Emmalee. "You see? If people would just pay more attention to the simplest things—"

The boy in the apron set coffee and a tray of bread and honey between them. Charles broke off a piece of bread, spooned honey onto it and offered it on a napkin. "Sweets, Miss Emmalee?"

"Thank you, Mr. Clayton."

He helped himself, then pushed the plate aside to the edge of the table, the spoon handle jutting from it. From inside the restaurant, the politician's harangue went on and on, ". . . control such an economy, and you control the people, I say . . . have to be taught submission before we can ever hope to raise them to the status of productive citizens."

The law and postal group had arrived on the porch, and the portly one was instructing the officers. "It is about this big, a pouch of canvas with leather mouth and handle, shouldn't be too hard to spot."

One of the officers started through the door, his boot narrowly missing Charles's best hat where it sat on the floor beside him. "Oops," he said, and grabbed it up. "That was close." Brushing it off, he set it down on the

31

other side, fixing his attention again on the enticing girl he had met. As the hat went down beside the table its stiff brim whacked the handle of the honey spoon, which flew into the air, spiraling across to bounce off the bare head of the man in the black coat and falling into his soup with a profound splash. He jumped to his feet and shouted, "Here, now!" All eyes in the area turned to him. His chair toppled backward as he stood and one of the policemen pointed. "There it is! Is that it?"

"That's it!" the portly man said. "Officers, arrest that man!"

"Don't see how he thought he could get away with it," the clerk offered, amazed. In a moment four burly policemen had hustled the sputtering citizen away, trailed by the two rail people carrying the precious mail pouch.

"Why," Emmalee said in amazement, "that man must have been a thief."

"Apparently." Charles nodded. "But I must say he isn't a very good one. I mean, if one steals a mail pouch one doesn't ordinarily stop next door for lunch. Just another example of what I was talking about, though. Even those you'd think should be most careful, like thieves, suffer from chronic lapse of attention. Have you ever thought of wearing a little stickpin or something there on your blouse? About midway between—"

He was interrupted by a thump and an explosion of screams and curses inside the restaurant. Curious, he got up to look through the door. Inside there was a resounding crash. He came back and sat down, his face a study in pity for the human race.

"What happened?" Emmalee asked, looking for a spoon to dip more honey. She knew there had been one a few minutes before.

"A man sat down, and he didn't have a chair." Charles Henry shrugged in resignation. "As simple a thing as that—just determining that there is a chair to sit on—and, of course, when he fell he grabbed the edge of the table and pulled the cloth and that spilled things on some of the ladies and apparently one of them was sipping tea at the moment and she threw it all on some people at another table just as their dinner was being served."

"But what was the crash?"

"That was one of the chandeliers. There was a waiter swinging from it, and it wasn't fixed firmly enough. It really is pathetic!"

"It is an interesting subject," Emmalee admitted, "though it's one I had never considered before. How did you happen to become so keenly aware of this—this tendency toward chaos, Mr. Clayton?"

"Observation, Miss Emmalee. Simple observation. I have seen a lot of it. I suppose, being an artist, I am observant."

A lot of people, including one who seemed to be the proprietor, were rushing madly about by then, and Charles frowned. It was hard to carry on a conversation. He stood, picked up his valise, packed portfolio and easel under his arm and offered his free arm to Emmalee. "May I walk you to the station now, miss? Our train will be leaving soon."

She gave him a pretty smile and took his arm. He was so pleased with the gesture that he repeated his bow. As his head went down the business end of the tripod went up between the legs of the proprietor who said, "Eeep!" He jumped forward and bumped a lady stooping to retrieve her purse. She pitched forward, her head butting a wide man in the stomach. One of his flailing

33

arms cuffed another man on the ear and that one howled, turned and sat on a table, which collapsed under his weight.

From the stairs, Charles Henry and Emmalee turned to look back at the melee. Both shook their heads in wonder.

"You see," he said, "it happens all the time."

III

"My uncle is an unpredictable man," Charles Henry told her as the railroad train clicked southward through the rolling lands above tidewater. "When I was given my position at Boston he told me that if all went well in a few years I might be transferred to another of the company's yards. But that was only three weeks ago, and here I am, transferred already."

"That certainly says something about you," Emmalee said, interested and impressed. Then she frowned. "Three weeks? You have been in the shipyards business only three weeks?"

"Before that I was in school. The reason for the sudden transfer is that there was quite a mess at the harbor, and Mr. Watson says someone named Timmons intends to have me shot on sight. So I have to go to Charleston for a while. And I am thinking that from there I might go out West. I hear there are fortunes out there. Have you noticed that you pull your hand away each time I try to hold it, Miss Emmalee? And by the way, what has become of your black lady? I hope you haven't lost her."

"I certainly have," Emmalee said emphatically.

"You've lost her?"

"No, I've noticed that I pull my hand away. I do that intentionally because I do not care to hold hands with you, Mr. Clayton. Why are you to be shot on sight?"

"But have you lost Aphrodite?"

"Of course not. She prefers to ride in the servants' car. Why does that gentleman want to have you shot on sight?"

"I really don't know. When do you suppose you might be willing to hold my hand?"

The car was not crowded, and they had a pair of seats to themselves. They sat knee to knee on the narrow benches, with his valise, portfolio, and hat and her purse, parasol, and bonnet taking up the remaining space. His folded tripod easel lay on the floor between their feet, its end extending well into the center aisle. Emmalee raised a pretty eyebrow now and peered curiously at him. "Mr. Clayton—"

"I wish you would call me Charles. Or Charles Henry, if you prefer. Or Charley. Or even Hank. I would feel nearer then to being allowed to hold your hand."

"Charles, then. Charles, if you don't mind my asking, have you ever had any—ah—dealing with young women?"

He paused to consider it, then shook his head. "No. I really haven't. You are my very first."

"I see. Somehow I thought that might be the case. But where on earth have you been all your life?"

"Various parts of Massachusetts. For a time at Bedford with my Aunt Samantha because my parents sent me there for a summer after there'd been some trouble with the house and it needed repair—actually it needed quite a lot of repair, as I remember—and then while I was at Bedford they moved away. I haven't seen them for years."

"How very strange."

36

"Not really. My parents were always forgetful. They were from Rhode Island originally. I was well provided for, though. They left me a good trust which Aunt Samantha administers."

"So you grew up at Bedford?"

"Only for a while. Aunt Samantha's jelly burned one day, and she sent me off to school. She believes very strongly in education."

"What school did you attend?"

"Oh, several of them. In fact, quite a few. Looking back, it seems I was always receiving letters of recommendation from one school to another. My teachers felt diversity would benefit me. But we were discussing holding hands, Miss Emmalee."

Emmalee Wilkes looked at the charming young man across from her, and her heart warmed a bit. What a lonely life he must have had, she thought. And what a talent. And what a fortune. "A lady normally does not allow a gentleman to hold her hand on such brief acquaintance, Charles. However, I suppose an exception might be made." She extended her hand, and he took it, his fingers a gentle pressure on hers.

"I hoped it might," he said. "One has to start somewhere. Do you suppose that next time you might remove your glove?"

A car attendant entered from the front, carrying a tray of assorted refreshments. "Richmond in two hours," he announced. "Southbound passengers lay over there until morning. I have tea for the ladies and a drop of brandy for the gents who wish it."

He worked his way along the car, serving people here and there, then came to Charles and Emmalee and stopped. Carefully he set down his tray on an opposite seat, then stepped gingerly over the projecting tripod with its wicked swivel hook and turned to look down at it. He had to tap Charles Henry on the shoulder to get his attention and said, "Sir, this might be a hazard here. Somebody could trip on it. Would you mind if I put it in luggage?"

"Oh." Charles looked at the offending tripod, then nodded at the man. "Yes, please do. Sorry, I guess I wasn't thinking."

The attendant gazed admiringly at Emmalee. "Yes, sir. I surely do understand." With Charles's help he pulled out the tripod, lifted it and turned away.

"Keep that strap tight so it doesn't open," Charles urged, then watched the man as he walked away toward the rear of the train. "Now that's what I like to see," Charles told Emmalee. "A cautious person."

The Philadelphia to Richmond Express pulled six passenger coaches, a luggage truck, a servants' car, and two cargo boxcars, in that order. On this run only four people occupied the servants' car, and three of them were asleep. The fourth was Aphrodite.

She had dozed for a while, then awakened to an awful premonition. "That girl doin' somethin' foolish," she told herself, coming full awake in an instant. "Oh my Lord, she doin' somethin' she ain't ought to do. What she up to now?" With an upward glance she added, "Thankee, Gabriel, I 'preciate the message." Then with firm resolve she got to her feet, replaced her mockingbird hat firmly atop her grizzled head, wrapped her shawl about her shoulders and started forward to find Emmalee.

In the luggage car her path was blocked. A complicated contrivance of polished wood with spreading members at both ends was braced crosswise between a pile of boxes on one side and the wall of the car on the other, and a train attendant was trapped against the wall, pinioned there by triangle braces so that he couldn't move.

"Thank heaven you're here," he said. "Can you help me with this?"

Aphrodite stared at the contraption in wonder. "What is that thing?"

"It's a tripod easel. It came open. That sleeve there controls it." He pointed at a brass ring around a center shaft, just beyond his reach.

She edged closer, cautiously, and studied the mechanics of the thing. It was vaguely familiar, but she couldn't place it, couldn't quite grasp the workings of it. Then she remembered. It was like Miss Emmalee's French parasol that flowered open at the push of a ring. She understood then the brass collar below the spring on the center shaft. With gnarled fingers she felt around the collar until she found a recessed catch. "Sho' is a good fit," she said. She pressed the catch, the collar released from the spring and the tripod shortened and collapsed, folding smoothly back into a bundle of enameled sticks. She handed it to the trainman, freed of his imprisonment.

"See that strap there?" she asked. "If you keep that tight it won't open."

Aphrodite headed forward, clucking to herself. She had long since ceased to be amazed at the messes white folks could get themselves into. But now her apprehension was much stronger. She shouldn't have delayed like that in the luggage car. Whatever stupid thing the girl was going to do, she was already doing. Aphrodite knew it.

"That child never did have the brains God gave a goose," she announced as she charged through car six, oblivious to the traveling gentry there.

"When the juices gets to flowin' heaven help us all," she told car five.

"Them virgin fires is a-ragin' an' prophecy fixin' to

39

happen," she proclaimed as she streaked through car four, scattering attendants and travelers. One man was slow in getting out of her way, and she pointed an imperious dark finger at his face. "Chicken guts don' lie," she told him. "Step aside!"

The moment she entered car three Aphrodite knew she was too late. Three seats forward on the right Miss Emmalee sat holding hands with a tall young man in tailored clothing. They were not talking, just holding hands and gazing into each other's eyes as the day darkened into purple evening, and the Virginia backlands slid past the car's curtains.

Aphrodite's tongue went dry inside her mouth, and a dread cold slid up her spine. Eighteen years since she had read the signs as midwife at a baby girl's birth, and the angels had warned her of calamity to come. For eighteen years Aphrodite had tucked and tended her charge and dreaded the coming of the prophecy. And for eighteen years she had schemed and connived to somehow thwart the fates, to get Miss Emmalee safely married off before she fell in love and set destiny in motion.

Now she crept along the aisle, the dread certainty growing with each step. Then she knew. Eighteen years of dread dreams had taught her the face of havoc. She knew him. He was the one. Aphrodite saw all her hopes go flying: tranquility, peace, a quiet old age. In panic she stepped between them and pulled their hands apart. "Child, get away from him! He no good for you!"

They looked up at her, startled. The girl said, "Aphrodite, for heaven's sake! I thought you were in the servants' car."

"Good thing I ain't. Don' you know who this is? Trouble, tha's who."

"What are you talking about? This is Mr. Clayton. Mr. Clayton, may I present Aphrodite."

"My pleasure," he said, trying to stand in the suddenly crowded space. "I had thought you might be lost. Will you join us?"

She ignored him. "Miss Emmalee, you was holdin' hands with him. Child, you can't do nothin' like that. You got to get married first. Angels say they gonna be chaos an' havoc 'less you do."

"I see a lot of that," Charles Henry pursued. "It comes of lapse of attention. Let me clear this seat for you."

"Ne'e mind." Aphrodite scowled at him. "Miss Emmalee gone come wit' me an' sit in another car."

"I am not!" Emmalee reddened. "Aphrodite, what's the matter with you? Behave yourself."

Aphrodite was tugging on Emmalee's arm now, trying to pull her from the seat. At the pressure, Emmalee's white glove slipped free, and Aphrodite staggered back into the flailing arms of a passenger who had just entered from car four. The man danced for balance, careening backward, then sat in an empty seat two seats back with Aphrodite on his lap. She looked at the empty white glove in her hand.

"It a sign," she muttered. "Oh, dire! Dire!" Turning her eyes upward she pleaded, "Gabriel, what I do now?" Then she lowered her head in defeat. "Oh." She turned abruptly to the man on whose lap she was perched and scolded, "Watch them hands! Ain't you know 'bout manners?" Then she got to her feet and stepped forward to confront the wide-eyed Emmalee. "You see, child? You see how it gonna be? But Gabriel say all I can do is trust yo' judgement. Gabriel don't know you ain't got any. Here, put this glove back on." She shook her head, perplexed. "Gabriel say jus' leave you alone. Ain' nothin' I can do 'bout it anyways."

"Aphrodite, what are you talking about?"

"Juices," she muttered. "Virgin juices."

41

"Aphrodite!"

Charles Henry picked up his hat and portfolio. "There. Now you can sit down."

"Not if she's going to talk like that," Emmalee pronounced.

"Miss Emmalee, will you stop holdin' hands wit' him?"

Emmalee bristled. "I will do exactly as I please, Aphrodite. Now if you can't behave yourself you get on back to the servants' car." With that she grabbed Charles Henry's hand and clung firmly to it. For a second his eyes widened, then he sighed, smiled and sat down, gazing at her in happy wonder. She returned his gaze, clung to his hand and smiled. By the time Aphrodite could think of a retort they had both forgotten she was there.

Shoulders stooped in resignation, Aphrodite headed back toward the servants' car.

"Turned my back on her jus' that long," she told the rapt crowd in car four, "an' sure 'nuff her juices gone to boilin'!"

"Gonna be hell to pay now," she assured the passengers in car five. "I don' know jus' what come next, but it ain' gonna be good."

"Angels said they'd be distant lands," she confided to car six. "Angels said we headin' for calamity."

In the baggage car the train attendant was pinned again, this time against the pile of boxes. The tripod braced against the far wall held him fast. The man was weeping.

"You think you got troubles," Aphrodite said scowling at him. "It ain't you that's gonna take up travelin'."

At Richmond station carriages waited to take the

42

travelers to their hotels. With small luggage loaded and Aphrodite fussing in the rumbleseat, Charles Henry and Emmalee were wheeled through the gaslit streets of Richmond and deposited hand in hand before the cupolaed entrance of the Hotel Jefferson.

"Come to my room," he suggested to her. "I'll show you my drawings."

"No such thing!" Aphrodite confronted him. "Ain' you no gentleman? This here girl got to go an' have her sleep."

"Actually, Charles," Emmalee said smiling at him, "it would be better if I don't see your drawings just yet. We did just meet today, you know."

"Very well," he said dreamily, lost in her eyes. "Though I doubt I'll sleep well tonight. But then," he said and perked up visibly, "it is still a long way to Columbia, and tomorrow we will have known each other much longer."

"There is that," she assured him. Aphrodite separated them and hustled Emmalee away to the safety of her own room.

From the darkness a sullen, hard-eyed thug watched them enter the hotel, then moved to the doorway shadows and made note of which room on the balconied second floor Charles Henry entered. The man's coat sagged with the weight of a gun in its lining, and his hand touched the rigid length of the sheathed stiletto behind his belt.

Luther had ridden the mail packet from Boston down to Portsmouth, then caught a coach up to Richmond. He was tired, impatient, and angry. Timmons was going to pay well for this job. Luther didn't like to travel.

*   *   *

43

It was past midnight and Aphrodite was exhausted from her worries before she received her inspiration. But when she did, it was worth it. She had sat for hours on the hotel balcony where she could see both doors: Emmalee's and his. She knew about young people. She was a little puzzled at the rough-looking man who kept appearing at the hallway door, then ducking back at sight of her, but her concern was to guard Miss Emmalee, even if it took all night.

But now, finally, she had an idea. If she couldn't avoid the fates, maybe she could delay them a little.

Their train was to leave early in the morning.

The Jefferson was an old hotel, and its solid doorposts had cable hooks on each side for the placement of ropery so vacant rooms could be left open to air. With a quick glance at the two closed doors, she went downstairs.

In the back of the lobby Aphrodite found a night clerk yawning over his books. "I need some chain," she told him, and spread her scrawny arms wide to indicate a length.

"Chain?" He stared at her sleepily.

"You know. A whole mess of little iron rings all hooked together. Chain."

"Oh." He shrugged. The servants of hotel guests were often beyond his comprehension. He led her down a service hall, opened a storeroom door and poked around in darkness until something rattled. He withdrew a length of harness chain five feet in length. "Coach rigging. Will that do?"

"Do jus' fine," she assured him and took her prize upstairs. At Charles Henry Clayton's door she linked the chain onto one doorpost, ran it through the ornate latch handle, pulled it snug and fixed it to the other doorpost.

She would let Miss Emmalee sleep late in the

morning. No reason to wake the child up until just time to catch their train.

Luther, lurking in the darkened hallway off the balcony, had about run out of patience. Between him and Charles Henry's door was a small, aged black woman who wore a mockingbird hat and looked as though she meant to stay there all night. Hours had passed while he waited, the hotel was silent and asleep, and his job would take only a minute. But still she sat there, scowling and alert, perched on a spindly chair.

He had about decided to kill her, too, when he peeked around the corner again and she was gone. Faint sounds came from the lobby below. Voices, and the rattle of chain.

Luther sighed. Now he could get on with it. Ducking back into the hallway he checked his arsenal. He wouldn't need the gun, but he checked its loads just in case. Then he drew the stiletto and tested its edges. It was razor sharp. Soundlessly, then, he left the hallway, padded across the balcony, fumbled for a moment at the lock on Charles Henry Clayton's door, and entered the dark room, closing the door behind him.

IV

It was past midnight when Charles Henry faced the fact that he simply couldn't sleep. Visions of beauty swam about him when he closed his eyes, drowsing, and his fingers tingled with the ghost touch of a soft, small hand.

With a sigh of resignation he got up, dressed himself and repacked his valise. That and his portfolio were all he had brought from the station. Carrying his belongings, he blew out the lamp, left his room quietly and went down the elegant stairway. There was no one in the lobby at this late hour, but he heard voices and rattling sounds from a back hall.

Beyond the puddles of lamplight in front of the hotel, the streets of Richmond were ink and silver, deep shadows below a serene high moon. Tapping his hat firmly onto his head he chose a direction, hoisted portfolio and valise and started walking.

Upper Richmond was silent and asleep at this hour, but as Charles strolled generally southward he came into other parts of town. Beyond a section where all was closed stores and echoing silence, the character of the streets changed, became older and closer and somehow more nocturnally alive. Here and there were

47

people, quiet clusters of them dim in lamplight outside of places from which merry sounds arose.

Passing one such place he nodded to the rough men lounging there and thought for a moment that some of them intended to visit with him, but when he looked around at them they all looked away.

He went on, and behind him, after a moment, one of the men detached himself from the others and padded after him on quiet feet.

Charles Henry enjoyed the night. The air here was different from that of Massachusetts—richer somehow, with a perfumed quality that tantalized the nose and filled the lungs with promises. In the distance somewhere he heard the rhythmic sounds of people at work, and he headed in that general direction. The quality of the sounds reminded him of the longshoremen loading casks in his uncle's shipyard, although he didn't remember loadings taking place at midnight there.

Once or twice he had the feeling he was not alone, and once when he looked back a furtive figure disappeared into shadows. Charles shrugged and went his way.

He was walking beside a high wood fence when he realized the sounds he heard were coming from the other side, and he noticed a latched gate ahead of him. He also noticed the shuffle of quiet footfalls approaching him from the rear, but he did not know anyone in Richmond and didn't trouble to look around again. He quickened his pace at sight of the gate, and the footfalls behind quickened, someone running quietly.

He hesitated, not comfortable with intrusion. But, then, it was only a gate, not a door. With his decision he caught the latch, swung it open wide and stepped through.

Behind him the gate reverberated to a heavy impact,

then slammed shut. Charles Henry looked around, peering at the portal. He wished there were more light. He would have liked to see the mechanism of such an authoritative self-closing device. Gates of his acquaintance usually were equipped with simple springs or counterweights that did not slam and crash as they performed their function. Outside the gate someone groaned, but he could not tell from inside who it might be.

He was in a small field between buildings, and beyond was light and activity. The area opened into a wagon yard, and gangs of men were working there, loading a string of freight wagons at a lamplit dock behind a warehouse.

The freight was barrels, row upon row of them. Charles went down to the loading dock to watch. Lamps and lanterns gave good light to the scene. Freight wagons stood lined into the darkness, coming forward as each was loaded and the next rolled into place. From the dock, the dancing lights illuminated the warehouse entrance behind the ranks of waiting barrels and the ordered, systematic movement of the men moving them. Off to one side a landau wagon stood, its team hitched, and two more barrels stood beside it, separate from the rest. He noted that all the barrels bore the imprint of Powers Enterprises on their rounded sides. But then most of the barrels he had ever seen did.

Charles walked to the two barrels beside the landau and hoisted himself up to sit on one, started to open his portfolio, then frowned and changed his mind. He got down, set his burdens aside, carefully tipped the heavy barrel so it could be rolled on its rim and moved it forward, near the end of the ranked barrels on the dock, then got his belongings and sat on it again, this time pleased with the viewpoint it gave him.

49

He opened his case, got out his pencils and set to work. It would be a good picture. Strong emphasis of lights and darks, strong shapes of building and shapes of barrel, the line of teams and boxy wagons, the close-order drill of sweating handlers, their muscles rippling and sweat gleaming in the lamplight. It was a fine scene.

It was almost completed when a beefy man in shirt-sleeves and booted breeches arrived, looked around and then made his way straight to Charles.

"Who might you be?" the man asked, suspicious and belligerent.

"Charles Henry Clayton." He removed his hat, started to replace it then set it aside on a nearby barrel. "I'm with Powers Company."

"So what are you doin', then?" The man eased a little.

"I'm traveling to Charleston, to work at the ship-yards."

"I mean what are you doing around here, right now?"

"Oh. Well, really, I am taking a walk. Tell me, have you ever been in love?"

The man backed away a step, looking more closely at Charles Henry's fine clothing, his handsome face, his artists' hands.

"I think I probably am in love," Charles pursued, glad to have someone to discuss things with. "But I couldn't sleep so I came out to have a walk and do a little sketching. I didn't get your name."

The man had backed further away, his eyes wide with negation. "Not me, fella." He shook his head firmly. "You better find somebody else. I'm not interested."

When he hurried away Charles Henry shrugged and returned to his drawings.

The man completed his inspection of the docks and made his way to the landau, a pair of burly handlers trailing after him. He made a wide circle around Charles Henry, eyeing him suspiciously. Then from the landau he roared, "Where's the other damned water cask? There's supposed to be two of them here!"

Charles Henry turned. "This must be your water cask here." He gestured vaguely. "I moved it."

One of the longshoremen approached, and Charles, absorbed in his sketching, lifted his hat from the cask next to him so the man could take it.

"Don't get too close, Benny," the booted one called. "The pansies are in bloom." They laughed and the handler hurried away with the barrel. A few moments later the landau rolled away into darkness, two barrels resting on its demi-bed and the booted man at the reins. Charles asked a handler, "Why does he haul water?"

"Them's the water casks for the *Pallas Athene,*" the man explained. "Understand her captain is particular about water. He won't take on the brack at Portsmouth if he can get good upland water from here."

"He must drink a lot of water," Charles said.

The man looked at him curiously. *"Pallas Athene* is a ship," he explained. "That's the water for the whole ship. It's two days' sail to Charleston from Portsmouth."

"I see," Charles said, adding a few precise shadings to his drawing and holding it up to the light. "There. What do you think?"

The man looked closely at it and his eyes widened. "Hey! That's good. Looks just like everything, don't it?"

Charles was pleased with it. He had truly captured the scene. The structures, the wagons, the people, the barrels with their markings, the painted sign on the warehouse, even some of the faces of the men, were there in clear detail. It occurred to him that this was a picture Uncle Jonathan might enjoy having.

But the scene had shifted now. The last freight wagons were being loaded, the ranked barrels were down to a few, and the handlers were shifting them into position.

"We're gonna need to move that cask you're sitting on," the man said.

"That's all right." Charles Henry stepped down and set his hat on his head. "I'm through here."

When he got back to the hotel it was nearly dawn, and all was still. At his room he found a sturdy chain across the door and tried to puzzle out the reason for it but gave up.

He pressed his ear to the door and heard a sound beyond: someone cursing in a monotone that went on and on.

He backed off and looked again at the number. Yes, it was his room. But then, he had taken all his belongings with him when he went for his walk. Possibly the room had been considered vacated and someone else had moved in.

It was almost morning, anyway, and he still wasn't sleepy. Carrying valise and portfolio, he went back downstairs and out of the hotel, looking for a place to have breakfast and a post office where he could mail his drawing to Uncle Jonathan.

With first light the draymen and ship's crew completed stowing *Pallas Athene's* cargo below deck and sealed the holds. Capt. Cornelius Finch paid off the draymen, with a healthy bonus for their silence, then took the helm and ordered rowers out in the ship's two launches. From the secluded, ramshackle wharf where *Pallas Athene* had stood this past day and a half in a forest inlet southeast of Richmond, there would be six miles of tow before she had water enough to take a wind in her jibsails and creep toward sea under sail.

"Time comes a man must sail creeks for a livin'," Captain Finch muttered dourly. "It's a sad pass." He shook his head in memory of times when there were far easier ways to turn a dishonest dollar.

Pallas Athene crept between forested banks, her stained old wood hull grumbling with the awkward stresses of being under tow. First sunlight danced along the waters between narrow bends and made his eyes water. Finch wiped them with a dirty sleeve. "You, Mr. Thrumm," he called. When Thrumm came trotting back along the deck Finch said, "Go below and roust the cook. Mr. High and Holy will be awake directly, and he'll want his tea an' toast an' fresh linens." He glanced around covertly as Thrumm headed for the companionway, then added under his breath, "Sanctimonious fart probably pisses holy water."

Finch was still boiling from the regal descent of Evan Egmont onto the lowly decks of his ship three days before. No love had passed between the two since the moment Egmont had clapped the captain on the back with a condescending hand and pronounced, "Wouldn't want this load to go astray, would we? Just have your fellows stow my things somewhere—good thing for a man to mingle with his subordinates now and then, eh? Gives them the feeling they're appreciated."

For the past three days Evan Egmont had instructed Captain Finch in the proper handling of his ship, disrupted his crew, tutted endlessly over the condition of his cargo holds and the need for dressing up his top-work and dressing down his decks, and elaborated at length on how much money Finch stood to make from this venture and how grateful he should be for the opportunity.

It was the prospect of the money, pure and simple, that had saved Evan Egmont from being mysteriously lost at sea a dozen times on the cruise from Charleston up to the hidden dock above Portsmouth.

Finch sighed and leaned on his helm. It could have been worse, he supposed. Of the brothers Egmont, who ran Charleston operations for the Powers Company, Evan was the easy one to take. He could have been saddled with Edgar.

The sun was an hour high, and they were past the three mile bend when Evan Egmont, stiff and unsmiling in today's fresh topcoat, spotless linen shirt and striped breeches, came on deck and cast a disapproving look over the ship and the world that contained it.

"We seem to be moving very slowly," he commented.

Finch didn't respond. The man could see perfectly well that the ship's motive force was two boatloads of sweating rowers.

"I told your cook to serve my breakfast up here," Egmont said. "The smell below is perfectly awful. Do you suppose you could have one of your fellows bring a table and chair for me?"

Finch ground his teeth but kept his tongue. "Mr. Thrumm," he called, "would you please bring up a table and chair?"

"Table and chair, sir?"

"Table and chair, Mr. Thrumm."

"Aye, sir." With a shake of his head the baffled man took a pair of crewmen and went below. With much sweating and mashing of fingers they managed to hoist a galley table up through the companionway, followed by a chair. They set them on deck by the stern rail.

"And a tablecloth, please," Evan Egmont added.

"And a tablecloth, Mr. Thrumm," Finch said with a sigh.

The sun was high and Evan Egmont was having his

54

tea when *Pallas Athene's* jib cleared tight waters, and she crept into the widening stream above the harbor channel. Finch looked to his buntings, then called out, "We'll have some sail now, if you please, Mr. Thrumm. Jib and tops. And call in the rowers, secure launches and let them have some of the fresh water in the deck cask."

"Aye, sir."

Evan Egmont cast a disapproving eye over the ensuing turmoil as boats were brought up and secured, shrouds climbed, topsails and jibsails set, and *Pallas Athene* took a rising wind and cruised sedately downstream toward Portsmouth and the sea. "We won't be needing these old tubs much longer," he said. "Steam's the thing nowadays. These stinking sailboats are history."

If Finch hadn't hated the man before, he did now.

In wide waters above Portsmouth they put on more sail, and Finch had buntings run up.

"How do you expect to avoid the patrols?" Evan Egmont frowned, for the first time seeming uncertain. "They do inspect cargoes, don't they?"

"Not often," Finch told him. "And that yellow flag up there says we have fever aboard. They'll just wave us by."

"I hope you know what you're doing, then. It would be embarrassing for me to be passenger on a ship that was found to be carrying contraband."

Finch turned away and spat expertly across the rail. You bastard, he thought. You unredeemed hypocrite. In other words, if you're caught, friend, you're on your own.

They passed Portsmouth with a wave and a flutter of flags. *Pallas Athene* dipped her nose in the breakers beyond, and mainsails and steering sails snapped into place, spars turning to take a quartering wind. Captain

55

Finch gave his orders, spun his helm and set course downcoast for Charleston. *Pallas Athene* rose proudly on her bow wake and took the spray in her teeth, homeward bound.

Eighty barrels of contraband whiskey were secured in her holds, eighty barrels that would disappear into the private warehouse of Edgar and Evan Egmont and where it went from there Finch didn't want to know. He would have his pay, and the crew theirs, and then they would think about tomorrow.

"There seems to be a great deal of loitering about your water cask," Egmont commented, pointing amidships. "I don't recall your fellows being so thirsty before."

Finch cocked his head. There did indeed seem to be an unusual traffic to the water cask, and some of the glances of crewmen as they looked back toward the stern were furtive.

"Mr. Thrumm," he said, "please go forward and see what is going on there."

"Aye, sir."

"We're to be paid off at dockside?" Finch asked Egmont, wanting confirmation again. "As soon as we dock?"

"That was the arrangement, captain."

"And no company scrip or letters of credit," Finch pursued, enjoying the slight demeaning of his passenger. "Real money."

Egmont frowned. "Real money."

"Fine. Just wanted to be sure we understood each other."

A seaman wandered near, and Finch said, "Mr. Jones, please go and get me some tobacco."

The man looked at him, eyes oddly out of focus. "Get it yourself," he said, then giggled and wandered away.

Finch's mouth dropped open and Evan Egmont came upright in his chair. Beyond, at the water cask, someone seemed to be giving Mr. Thrumm a drink from a dipper. Others were holding his arms.

"What the living hell—" Finch threw a sling on the helm's high spoke and charged forward, Evan Egmont at his heels. Elbowing crewmen aside, the captain forced his way through what had become a good crowd at the rail. "What in blazes is going on here?"

"Hey, cap'n!" a cheerful, slurring voice sang, and a large friendly hand clapped him on the back. "Come join us! By God you done right by us this time, you did!"

Before he looked, he knew by the rich breaths of those about him what had happened. The open barrel held fluid, but it wasn't water. It was pure, high-test whiskey. He looked around at the happy, vague faces of his crew. *Pallas Athene* was well asea now, far beyond sight of land or other vessels, gliding happily southward through rolling swells.

"What in heaven's name is—eeep!" The voice, trailing into a high screech, was Evan Egmont's. Finch whirled around. Two large, happy sailors held the passenger aloft by his ankles and beamed at their captain.

"Lookee what we got!" Able Seaman Grable chortled. "A fart. A real hones' to Jeezis fart. Tell ye wha', cap'n, le's fling it overboard an' see if fish eats farts."

"Naw," Ordinary Seaman Whipple said with a frown. "Tha'd be a waste of wind. Le's haul 'im up in th' main sheets an' see if he can talk us up to fifteen knots. He's been talkin' for three days now an' didn' have a sail in front of 'im."

Able Seaman Christopher Thelen blinked slowly at his junior, then tapped himself on the head with a callused finger. "Damme, Teddy, I b'lieve tha's the firs' thing you ever said that was smart. Have 'nother drink!"

Thrumm had freed himself and glowered about him, sputtering from the raw whiskey that had been poured down his gullet. He already looked flushed. "I'll have you all strung t' the yardarms for this!"

Thelen turned pitying eyes on the man and wrapped a large arm about his shoulders. "You'll feel better after a bit, Mr. Thrumm. We got plenty of whiskey here."

"Put that man down!" Finch shouted at the beaming sailors who were now swinging a screeching Evan Egmont back and forth over the rail. "No! No! Not out there! Right here!"

"I know a girl in Newport that's got fourteen sisters," someone said behind him. "An' all of 'em has got these big—"

"I never knew any girl that had fourteen sisters," another said and hiccupped dubiously.

"Well, she says they're her sisters. Anyway, all of 'em's got these great, big—"

"There ain't any that big, Homer."

"There is in Newport."

"Which way are we goin'?" someone asked.

"Which way is Newport?" another asked.

Under a flying moon that evening the happiest ship in the North Atlantic scudded its erratic way northward, far beyond the coastal lanes. They took turns at the wheel and took turns at the cask, and when that ran out there were eighty more below.

Far behind them Captain Finch explained again to Evan Egmont that he would either take his fair turn rowing or Finch and Thrumm would throw him out of the boat and let him swim.

V

It was a smaller, cozier railroad train that chugged and puffed its way southward from Richmond toward Greensboro, Spartanburg, Columbia, and points between. It included the same baggage car that had been switched from the Richmond express, two commodity flatcars, two coaches, and a caboose, in that order.

Charles Henry had arrived early and spent a pleasant hour sketching rail yard scenes in morning sunlight, using a heavy coupling pin to ballast his easel in the freshening breeze, then had had to go aboard the baggage car to stow the easel when a train attendant refused to handle it, and had still been in the baggage car doing a sketch of its contents when the train pulled out. With loaded flatcars between there and the coaches, he might have had to ride there the two hours to Wixton Junction except that the train had to stop and back up to retrieve its caboose, which had become uncoupled.

As a result, Charles Henry was the last to board the coaches, and he found Emmalee Wilkes near the front of the second one.

"There you are." She flashed a smile that almost melted him. "I thought you had missed the train."

"Sweet Jesus." Aphrodite gasped and crossed herself. Her eyes were huge with astonishment.

"Good morning," Charles Henry said, and started to sit beside Emmalee, but suddenly Aphrodite was there and he had to settle for the rearward seat, facing them. He looked curiously at the stunned black woman. "You aren't by any chance Irish, are you?"

"What?"

"I mean, I saw you make the sign of the cross, and in Boston a lot of the Irish do that. And they do speak of the black Irish, although I don't think I believe most of what I've heard, so I simply wondered—not that it matters to me, of course. I am very open-minded." He turned his gaze to Emmalee, who now seemed a little flustered too, and took her unresisting hand in his. His smile was open, guileless, intimate, and complete, a smile infinite and just for her. "I missed you so, I didn't sleep a wink. How are you this morning? I thought all night about where we might proceed to from holding hands, and I hope you have some thoughts on the subject—"

"Here, now!" Aphrodite erupted, suddenly catching the drift. She grabbed their two wrists and pulled their hands apart, then crouched between them, shielding Emmalee, glaring over her shoulder at Charles Henry. "You jus' quit that business, right now! Ain' enough you bring chaos an' havoc on this ol' head, you got to get right down to calamity right here in front of God an' everybody?"

"What?"

"You behave yo'self now! Quit feelin' aroun' on this child. What the matter wit' you anyhow?" She glanced around at the various interested faces turned toward them. "Ain' that right?"

"Aphrodite!" Emmalee hissed.

"Amen," a man across the aisle said, gazing at

Emmalee with eyes loose in their sockets.

"I'm sorry," Charles Henry said.

"How'd you get out, anyhow?"

"How did I get out of what?"

"Ne'e mind. You jus' behave yo'self else you gone have to leave."

"Aphrodite!" Emmalee repeated. *"You* behave yourself. What in the world has gotten into you?"

"Chaos an' havoc is what!" Though she was still upset, and still keeping a wary eye on Charles Henry, Aphrodite lowered her voice and regained her seat. "You 'member, child, I tole you 'bout the prophecy, 'bout how we's gone come to calamity an' all?"

Emmalee thought for a moment, then blushed and grinned. "Oh, that! Oh, Aphrodite, for heaven's sake, that is so silly. You can't possibly believe that superstitious nonsense."

"Superstitious?" Aphrodite drew herself up, indignant and imperious. "I ain' got a superstitious bone in my body. I don' hole wit' politics at all. But chicken guts don' lie!"

"Excuse me," Charles Henry interrupted.

"You is excused," Aphrodite said coolly, then resumed talking to Emmalee, "That prophecy was cast th' day you was borned, child. An' now th' angel Gabriel hisself say it fixin' to come to pass, an' that mean chaos an' havoc done come 'long to fan yo' flame, an' I don' see nobody else doin' that so it got to be him."

"What I meant was," Charles Henry said, "excuse me for interrupting but I seem to be missing the drift of our conversation. Did I do something wrong?"

"Wrong?" Aphrodite's voice rose again. "This girl got the virgin's curse on her, an' you done come an' make her juices flow."

"Aphrodite!" Emmalee now had turned bright red. All around them, people gawked. "Hush!"

"Amen," the goggling man across the aisle repeated, leaning closer not to miss anything.

"Miss Emmalee," Aphrodite begged, "why don' we git on back yonder an' marry Mr. Lyle?"

"I really don't understand what we're talking about here," Charles Henry confessed. "Maybe if we held hands, Miss Emmalee—"

"Cut that out!" Aphrodite barked.

"I assure you," he said, "I have been nowhere near Miss Emmalee's juices." He tried to slide further toward the center of the seat and found himself prodded painfully by the tip of Emmalee's parasol. He picked it up, glanced around and then handed it to the man across the aisle. "Would you please put this in the overhead rack? Thank you." Then to Aphrodite: "What exactly is this 'virgin's curse'? I don't believe I know about it."

"It a prophecy! Cast th' day Miss Emmalee was borned. It go: *On the day when juices flow an' the virgin fires glow one will come to fan the flame. Chaos an' havoc be his name. Poor ol' woman, wring your hands. You mus' go to distant lands nevermore sweet peace to see. All roads lead to Calamity.*"

Charles Henry considered it. It certainly did sound portentous. "What does it mean?" he asked, finally.

Aphrodite shook her head. "It mean jus' what it say. It mean long as Miss Emmalee still a virgin—"

"Aphrodite!" Emmalee hissed again and turned abruptly away, her neck fiery.

"If she fall in love wit' chaos an' havoc it gone set the powers loose, an' I got to go to distant lands an' they gonna be calamity. That what it mean."

"I've been thinking of going west, myself," Charles Henry said. "I understand that is fairly distant."

"I been hopin' I could get her past bein' a virgin

62

before all that happen."

The man across from them, his eyes now glassy, was leaning far enough into the aisle to defy gravity.

"Refreshments!" called a train attendant, entering from the car ahead, and the leaning man jerked around, startled, slipped off his seat and tumbled into the aisle, still holding Emmalee's parasol. As he flailed for balance his thumb released the slip ring, and the parasol flowered full open directly under the attendant's laden tray. Plummeting tea service showered half the length of the car, and the teapot, not a drop yet spilled, thumped into the lap of a man three seats back, who promptly handed the hot object to his wife and stood to inspect his credentials. As his head hit the overhead rack, its central support collapsed and deposited hats, shawls, and hand luggage the length of the car. The woman holding the teapot handed it to a mutton-chopped gentleman facing her. He in turn juggled the hot pot for a second and found another pair of hands to place it in. All along one side of the car people struggled with raining personal effects, while those on the other side gawked at the melee and passed the tea.

The train attendant was trapped in the open door, Emmalee's parasol wedging him from one side, his beverage tray from the other.

Charles Henry, facing back the length of the car, stared at the pandemonium and shook his head. "Incredible!" he muttered. Emmalee had come to her feet, trying to see what was happening, and as the car lurched she lost her balance and sat in Charles Henry's lap. She gasped, blinked, started to pull away, then looked up into guileless eyes that were brimming with joy and wonder. His arms around her were strong and very gentle, and the smile that burst forth on his face was the smile of angels.

"This is even nicer than holding hands," he whispered.

Aphrodite was on her knees on the seat, looking over its back at the shambles of the rail coach. "I knowed it," she gasped, wide-eyed. "I knowed it! Chaos an' havoc. I knowed it all along!"

Emmalee Wilkes stared into the eyes of Charles Henry Clayton, and as the people, the car, the train, and the extraneous world dissolved around her, a trace of his smile echoed itself on her lips, and with the tip of her tongue she tasted it there.

"Charles?" she breathed.

"Emmalee," he whispered, and felt himself falling into huge dark eyes that grew and grew as they came nearer. Her hands crept from his shoulders, her arms encircled him, her breath mingled with his and somewhere, far away, he heard a high voice shrieking, "Oh sweet Jesus there goes th' juices!" but it was unimportant, and he was not inclined to wonder about it now.

As Aphrodite collapsed into her seat, defeated and staring in dark dread at the two entwined across from her, someone staggered past, gasped, "here," and handed her a hot teapot. She wrapped its handle with her shawl, caught a cup tumbling along the aisle and poured tea with shaking hands, her thoughts already turning to what she should take on her trip.

Noon whistles sounded along the waterfront at Charleston as Edgar Egmont straightened his tailored summer coat on imperious shoulders, pulled spotless linen cuffs into place, set his silk hat squarely atop his domelike head and strode out into the sunlight of Powers Commerce Company's shipyards. The bounce in his gait was that of a man who has most of what he wants and is on the verge of acquiring the rest.

Looking down his beak of nose he glanced around as he passed the cluster of sheds, hoists, wagon docks, and bale stacks that cluttered the landward portion of the yards. His nostrils twitched in practiced disapproval at the combined odors of hemp, tar, damp cotton, fish, and sweat which were the aura of a shipyard. A large portion of the satisfaction Edgar Egmont felt came from the fact that soon, very soon now, he would no longer be involved in the mundane and demeaning rituals of running a shipyard which should by rights have been his years before, except that the old bastard who controlled it just kept on getting older and didn't have the decency to die.

Edgar had waited long enough. For years he had expected any day to inherit control of the Powers Company—through his wife—and anticipated how he could liquidate its assets and live the kind of life to which he was prepared to become accustomed. But old Jonathan Clayton Powers, Emma's uncle, just seemed to go on and on. Edgar was tired of the indignity of being constantly accountable to an old man far away in Boston.

But that was all going to change now, very soon. Edgar had Bull Timmons's draft locked safely away, and the day he received word that Timmons had taken over Powers Enterprises he would cash it. And in the meantime there was the other thing, a plan ready to set in motion as soon as Evan returned from Richmond with their final cargo. All things fell into place for a resourceful man, and Edgar had the pleasant certainty that very soon he would get his.

At the yard gate a harried attendant scurried to open the portal for him and stepped aside, giving the haughty Edgar a courteous bow. Edgar ignored him.

In the bustling traffic of lower Market Street he

turned left, walked a block along Tremain and then glanced around, casually. No one was watching him. He turned left again, this time into a deserted alley, and hurried along it until he came to a small door in the side of a private warehouse. Still unobserved, he unlocked the heavy bolt, opened it and stepped inside.

Alone in the dim interior, dwarfed by the ranked bales and crates stacked high along both sides of a narrow aisle, Edgar stood and counted his impending profits. Three shiploads of valuable cargo rested in this warehouse, neatly stacked in their three sections. In two of the stacks, all the crates, bales and boxes had been overpainted and freshly lettered with various company names, all of which were paper operations belonging to Edgar and Evan Egmont.

The third stack still bore its original labels, Powers Enterprise consignments, but not for long. When Evan returned with that old tub *Pallas Athene,* they would do once more what they had done twice before. *Pallas Athene* would make one more voyage. The cargo in her holds would be well insured, but it would be fake—containers matching those here in this warehouse, but containing nothing of value. And in one container would be a bomb. *Pallas Athene* would set sail for the Bahamas and never be seen again. It was really amazing how easily a truly brilliant man could get rich.

The ecstasy of anticipation reminded him of other ecstasies, and he looked at his watch. Then he snorted in annoyance. Even if there had been time, he couldn't go to the Liberty in midday. Too much chance of someone's seeing him, and lately there had been a lot of talk. He was going to have to do something about Absynthe. In recent months the woman had become far too ostentatious, and there was active gossip in all the best circles. Everybody knew Absynthe was being kept, but he didn't like to hear such active curiosity about who was keeping her.

It was necessary to Edgar Egmont's ego that he have a relationship with—in fact that he own—the most beautiful woman in town. But it was equally necessary to his ambitions and his standing in the community—all of which resulted from his wife's being a Powers—that it never become known. Yet Absynthe tended to flaunt the wealth he gave her. And that always set tongues to wagging.

Tonight, he decided, after the Board of Elders meeting, he would "work late." And while he was enjoying Absynthe in her room at the Liberty, he would caution her again about being too visible in the community. She had been wanting a new bed. Maybe he would reward her with that.

He looked around the packed warehouse, and his mind raced with his plans. Evan should return tomorrow with *Pallas Athene*. Two nights' work would clear her cargo into this warehouse and reload her with fake cargo and a bomb with a four-day clock mechanism. Then she would sail. And very soon now, within a few days, he would be notified that Bull Timmons had acquired Powers Enterprises. Then the draft could be cashed.

Within a few days—two weeks at the most—Edgar Egmont looked forward to being a very wealthy man. All he had to do between now and then was to keep things going smoothly.

The sun was shining upon Edgar Egmont as he locked the secret warehouse behind him, made his way unobserved to Market Street and then strolled along that busy thoroughfare, soberly accepting the salutations of the citizenry that recognized his eminence and considered him a very paragon of honor, sobriety, and impeccable integrity. He did not notice the dark clouds building up on the horizon. Edgar Egmont had horizons of his own.

At that moment, though, ninety miles inland, it already was raining, and the steady drizzle that shrouded the station house at Columbia was appropriate background for the gloom that had settled upon Charles Henry Clayton and Emmalee Wilkes.

With the imminence of their parting—she for Vicksburg and he for Charleston to report to his cousin Edgar—the attentions of the two had turned from the immediate delights of hand-holding and kissing to necessary discussion of future plans. And abruptly the bright fires of new romance were doused to sodden ash by the uttering of a cold, wet word. The word was money.

"What do you mean, you have no money?" Emmalee pulled away from him, her expression suddenly becoming haunted. "Of course you have money, Charles. All those shipyards—"

"But those aren't mine," he explained. "They belong to my uncle Jonathan Powers. I told you that."

"Of course, but surely one day you will inherit?" There was real dread in her voice, the pleading note of one who has stumbled upon perfection only to find it imperfect.

"I really don't see how." Charles Henry shook his head, puzzled and disturbed at this sudden bleak turn in their romance. Things had gone beautifully until the subject of money came up. And he had raised the subject himself, because before they parted he wanted some idea of when they would meet again and how they might progress from that point. First he must go to Charleston, because Uncle Jonathan expected him to do that. And she was going on to Vicksburg. It might be prudent, he felt, if he acquired a fortune before joining her there, and he understood fortunes were being made in the West. Charles Henry had no clear concept of *the*

West as such. It was not a subject one considered in Massachusetts. But he was not hesitant to go there if that was what fortune required.

"My uncle is not really my uncle, you see. Actually we are more like third cousins, but that gets very confusing. And my cousins in Charleston aren't really cousins. Cousin Edgar's wife, Emma, is Uncle Jonathan's niece, so that makes her my fourth cousin—or maybe cousin four times removed—but since Cousin Edgar is her husband I find it convenient to refer to him as my cousin, and since the other Egmont, Cousin Evan, is Edgar's brother, well, I think of him as cousin too. Sometimes it is difficult to keep things like that straight.

"As to the Powers Company, that belongs to Uncle Jonathan and his sisters and his brother except his brother died so I suppose that share will go to Emma. Edgar's wife. I think that is why Edgar and Evan manage things in Charleston. I've never met any of them, but I'm sure that's how it all works."

"Then where does that leave us, Charles?" Her eyes were moist now, large and tragic. "Where does that leave you?"

"I hope Uncle Jonathan might leave me his Sunday watch."

"Oh, Charles . . ." Disappointment wracked her, like a chill. Her lower lip trembled. "Charles, this is terrible. I can't love you. Without money, you are just—just an artist."

Aphrodite, approaching from the ticket window, had paused two steps away. The wrinkles of her face, which for two days had been set in patterns of hopeless dread, shifted now, and her eyes lighted with renewed hope. She had never considered that this fashionable young gentleman might not be wealthy. He *looked* wealthy. Now she stepped forward, alive with quickening hope, and placed a dark hand on Emmalee's arm. "Ever'thing gonna be all right, child. You jus' tell this gentleman to go peddle his papers an' you an' me, we'll get ourselves back to Philadelphia an' marry Mr. Lyle. He got more money'n he know what to do with." She shot a glare of victory at Charles Henry.

They both ignored her.

"Is it so important to you, then," Charles Henry said, gazing at the lovely, tragic Emmalee, "that I have a fortune?"

"Oh, Charles, I know it shouldn't matter. But you see, I have promised myself that the man I marry must be handsome and kind and intelligent and brave and sensitive—and rich."

"I'm not rich," he admitted.

"So you see . . ." She spread her hands in futility.

"But after I go west and make my fortune—"

Aphrodite's attention was distracted. A coach had pulled up outside in the rain, and a rough-looking man was going from window to window of the station house, peering inside. She was sure she had seen him before.

". . . just dreaming, Charles," Emmalee was saying. "I don't see how you can be certain of acquiring a fortune. You are a delightful person, but as I understand it in order to become wealthy one must be able to *do* something . . ."

"I can draw."

". . . something of value."

"Emmalee, you are being awfully pessimistic. I have it on good authority that in the west. . . ."

"Whose authority?"

"A man in Philadelphia. He sounded very authoritative."

"In Philadelphia everyone sounds authoritative. Charles, it just won't work out."

70

"That's the spirit, child," Aphrodite said, offering encouragement. "Tell him to move along."

A porter appeared at the door. "Boardin' for Atlanta, Anniston, Tuscaloosa, Jackson, and Vicksburg," he called. "All aboard!"

"But, Emmalee." Charles Henry was near to panic now. "You have to give me a chance."

"Why she have to do that?" Aphrodite demanded.

"Because she loves me."

"There is that," Emmalee admitted. "But Charles, your prospects are so—uncertain."

"Nothin' uncertain 'bout Mr. Lyle's prospects," Aphrodite pointed out.

"Aphrodite," Emmalee exploded, "Hush! Go put our luggage aboard the train. I'll be right there."

"It just means we must wait a bit," Charles Henry said, pleading with her. "I can find fortune out West. I know I can."

"You have never even been to the West."

"I've never been in love, either, until now."

"And this isn't working out very well."

"It will when the other does."

"You're confusing me. What other?"

"When I go out West and get a fortune. It shouldn't take all that long. Will you wait for me? Please?"

Passengers waiting in the station had filed out, following the porter. Aphrodite, burdened with hand luggage and glancing back over her shoulder, went out onto the covered portico, letting the door slam behind her. The ticket agent closed his window and went out through the side door to help with the loading. They were alone then.

"I can't make any promises to you, Charles. I just can't."

"You don't need to promise, then," he urged. "Just say you will think about me."

71

"Oh, all right, of course I will think about you."

"Until I make my fortune, then." He brightened.

"Oh, Charles Henry." She lost control of her will for a moment and tears formed in her eyes. "Oh, it is so impossible!" On quick impulse she squeezed his hand, then turned and fled from the station, into the gray pall beyond the portico. In the instant of her departure a sullen-appearing man outside the door lunged forward, through the door and into the station, drawing a long knife from beneath his coat. Inside he hesitated a moment, then strode toward Charles Henry, who was staring after Emmalee in a daze.

The man was two steps away and closing on him when Charles Henry noticed that he still had Emmalee's parasol under his arm. "Emmalee!" he called. "Wait!" And turning, he stooped to pick up his tripod easel. The attacking man lunged, swung downward with the knife and doubled over the projecting point of a parasol with its handle braced against a bench. The knife, deflected, thudded into the wooden bench as Charles Henry, parasol in one hand and easel in the other, turned and sprinted across the room.

"Emmalee!" he called as the door slammed behind him, cutting off the gagging sounds of the man in the station. "Wait!"

She was just stepping onto the boarding ladder. At his call she turned, saw him there in the rain, her parasol held high and a bright smile on his face, and stepped down again.

"Boardin', miss," the porter urged.

"Wait just a minute, please." She hurried across the gravel apron.

"Is this worth at least a kiss?" Charles Henry asked.

"Oh, Charles Henry."

The water tower spout had been swung aside after filling the locomotive's tanks, and it loomed over them,

72

its valve rope looped below it. Charles Henry opened the parasol, handed it to her and reached for her, burdened by the awkward tripod easel upended across his shoulder. The station house door slammed behind him, and a pale, groaning man limped toward them, one hand tight against his belly, the other holding a gleaming knife.

"Board, please!" the porter called through the haze of rain.

"Just a moment, please!" Charles Henry called back. Then noticing movement behind him he reached around and thrust out the upright easel.

"Hold this," he said, and as a hand took it he took Emmalee full in his arms and kissed her.

The surprised attacker stared at the contraption in his hand, lowered it and its swivel hook snagged the spout's valve rope. As the cascade thundered down on him, completely hiding him, its mass seething and splattering about their feet, Charles whispered to Emmalee beneath her parasol, "It's raining harder. You had better board."

"I will miss you, Charles Henry," she whispered, then turned and ran for the train.

Charles Henry sighed as he reached without turning to retrieve his tripod easel from where it rested in a hand protruding from a column of water. Immediately the water cut off. Charles Henry glanced at the half-drowned man standing there.

"Thank you," he said.

Then he looked again. The man was incredibly wet. His hat was gone, his pouring coat was around his elbows and his pants were around his feet. Though his eyes and mouth were wide open, there was no sign there of perception.

"This weather can be violent," Charles Henry said to himself, then he shook his head, bundled the man's sodden clothing about him as best he could, took his elbow and helped the staggering soul toward the train. The porter was just raising his ladder.

"This man seems to have been caught in a downpour," Charles Henry said. "Give him a hand. He is not feeling well."

Between them, they got Luther aboard the train. "I'll make a cot for him in baggage," the porter said. "Looks as though he has an attack of the vapors."

Having seen what South Carolina weather could do to the unsuspecting, Charles Henry watched from the shelter of the portico as the train pulled out. He felt terribly lonely, and for the first time serious doubts crowded his thoughts. Emmalee was right. He had never been out West. He had no idea what was out there, and the making of a fortune might not be that easy despite what the man in Philadelphia had said. Still, she had made it clear. Wealth was required to win her.

With the vision of Emmalee Wilkes firm in his mind, Charles Henry went forth then full of resolution to find the stage to Charleston. He would complete his obligations there, then he would head west.

VI

Despite the slow-healing scars of war and the more recent and deeper scars of federal reconstruction, the seaport town of Charleston bustled with activity and reeked of honest endeavor. Hot sun baked the battered boardwalks and elegant awning along Market Street and brought wisps of steam from the soupy mud stirred by endless traffic. Recent days of rain had bathed the city, and it lay now in sunlit brilliance.

Charles Henry Clayton perched at ease atop the board seat of a trundling dray cart, unfamiliar reins clasped firmly in his hands, and whistled a happy tune as trace chain rattled in time with the plodding of the dapple horse before him. It was his first experience at the driving of a wagon, and he was finding by observation that there was really nothing to it. One flicked the reins to persuade the horse to go and pulled on them to encourage him to stop.

It was that simple.

And since the store of Messrs. Forsythe and Higgins was directly up the street from the main transit shed at Powers Shipyard, the subject of turning had not arisen. The dapple horse had proven itself capable of negotiating traffic without his assistance, and he was happy to let it do so.

Delivering spools of cable to Forsythe and Higgins was not in the normal course of duty for Charles Henry—it was a little vague so far just what his normal duties would be since he had only been here two days and had not met either of his cousins. But there was a crisis at the transit shed today, and the draymen were busy shoveling spilled tar from the loading floors. So Charles Henry, waiting for someone to tell him what to do, had volunteered to make the cable delivery.

It was no surprise to him that the three vats of hot tar had been spilled in the transit shed. He had seen them there this morning when he wandered through the loft, had breathed their heady reek while he tidied a cluster of loading slings into orderly rows alongside them, moving the heavy webbing from the lip of the sling bay to the open loft floor beyond where they could be spread neatly.

The tar vats had been simmering over their coals, awaiting the arrival of roofers.

The spill had occurred sometime later, possibly while everyone was outside trying to extinguish the flaming web slings dancing below the tackle of their cargo hoists. There had been a great deal of clamor for a time, and somehow the tar vats had all upended.

All in all, the episode had left a frightful mess. It was a particular shame about the bales of imported linen which the tar had inundated.

None of that, of course, needed to have happened, but it did, and Charles Henry stopped whistling now to shake his head philosophically. "I believe it is a natural law," he explained to himself. "Whatever can go wrong, will. Or if not a law, then a statement of the human condition. Good morning!" Eyes going wide at the sight of a stunningly beautiful woman passing on the boardwalk, he raised his hand to tip his hat, neglecting to release the reins first. The dapple horse answered the tug and turned sharply across traffic, proceeding full circle in the busy, muddy street as oncoming wagons skidded and swerved, drivers cursed and a freight wagon slid sideways into a hitch rail, its drooping runboards throwing a sheet of mud across the far boardwalk and into two open doorways there.

Charles Henry replaced his hat, frowned at the sudden chaos behind him and shook a finger at the dapple horse once again plodding toward Forsythe and Higgins. "Except for that, you have done an excellent job of proceeding along the street." Even horses, he decided, were not immune to sudden lapses of attention.

He had lost sight of the gorgeous lady on the boardwalk, but having seen such beauty reminded him forcefully that he must not tarry too long in Charleston. Emmalee Wilkes would be waiting for him as soon as he went west and acquired a fortune.

First, though, he needed to report in here, find out what they needed him to do, and get it done. That was proving difficult. Cousin Evan was not in town, and Cousin Edgar was too busy to see anyone.

So he had gotten a room and spent a day and a morning doing whatever tidying up he could find to do around the yards.

His room was at a boardinghouse just off Market Street. He had got directions from a pleasant gentleman who had told him where to go and then had gone hopping and howling away peeling off his pants as a result of standing on an ant bed while they talked.

He whistled again as fine fancies filled his head: Emmalee's small, warm hands, Emmalee's big, dark eyes, Emmalee's lustrous dark hair, Emmalee's graceful long neck . . .

He arrived at Emmalee's bosom and at Forsythe and Higgins simultaneously, sighed and pulled on the reins.

The dapple horse stopped. Charles Henry tapped his hat firmly in place, swung his long legs over the side and hesitated, frowning. The horse and wagon were stopped nearly in the middle of the muddy street, and it was at least ten feet to the boardwalk. He had no idea how to make the horse move over.

"What is needed here is a plank," he said to himself.

Standing on the wagon seat, top hat tilted and hands on his hips, he gazed around at the busy street. The only unused plank in sight was a long scaffold resting against the second story front of a commercial building directly across the street from Forsythe and Higgins. Its two ends were supported by ropes suspended from pulleys on the roof, feeding block and tackle rigs whose hoist loops dangled to the ground.

Traffic was passing him two abreast in both directions, many of the drivers looking disgruntled. The dapple horse seemed content to stand and wait.

"Stay here," he told it, then stepped across to the bed of a passing buckboard and from there to the tailgate of a jaunty surrey and dropped lightly to the boardwalk. He tipped his hat to a group of ladies. "How do you do?"

"Do you suppose anyone is using that plank up there?" he asked a man standing beside a hitch rail, reading a newspaper.

The man looked up. "Doesn't look like it."

"Then do you suppose I might use it?"

The man shrugged. "It's all right with me."

With that approval Charles Henry walked to the building front, tested the hoist loops and then carefully lowered the scaffold, first one end and then the other. When it was down he slipped the rope slings from its ends, lifted one end of the heavy plank, tapped his hat firmly in place, crouched and came up with the board balanced on one shoulder. It was at least fourteen feet long. The man with the newspaper ducked as he swung

78

it around streetward. "Thank you," Charles said.

Aligning his burden toward his goal he stepped to the edge of the boardwalk, and two approaching teams halted and danced in their traces as the timber was thrust before them. Charles grinned his appreciation at the cursing drivers, moved left a few feet, clambered onto the bed of the first wagon, leapt from there to the next and back to his own rig.

"Thank you," he called over his shoulder as the high cab of a passing coach on the other side clipped the end of the plank and spun him half around. The dapple looked around curiously as he danced on the wagon, keeping his balance. "Whew!" he muttered. Crowds were beginning to gather now on both sides of the street, watching.

Waiting for a break in the traffic, he stood the plank on end, waved the people back on the Forsythe and Higgins boardwalk, and let it fall. It toppled gracefully, its far end landing with a resounding thud on the boardwalk, its near end rocking the wagon. The implacable dapple looked around again. "Don't move," he told it.

"Get that friggin' thing out of the way!" a teamster shouted, halting his team.

"Just be a moment," Charles Henry assured him.

A perplexed-looking man with a starched collar had appeared in the open doorway of Forsythe and Higgins, and Charles tipped his hat to him, calling, "Are you Mr. Forsythe?"

"I'm Higgins. What are you doing?"

"I have your cable," he explained. Then he hoisted the first spool, set it on the plank, aligned it carefully and let it roll. Mr. Higgins disappeared from the door and there were shouts inside. One by one, then, the heavy spools rolled down the ramp, trundled through the open doorway like three-foot juggernauts and dis-

79

appeared into the shadows beyond. When the last one had passed an ashen-faced Mr. Higgins appeared there again. "Is that all?"

Charles Henry brushed his hands together and straightened his hat. "That's all, sir. Thank you for your patronage."

Several of the spectators applauded.

Bracing his feet in the wagon bed Charles heaved at the heavy plank, levered and slid it back to balance across his wagon, crouched and hoisted it high above the traffic, waited for another pair of passing wagons on the downstream side and returned it to the far walk. Carefully, he refitted the end slings, tested the hoist loops and raised it back into place against the front of the commercial building. He was just securing the second hoist when a man stepped backward out of a window above him, carrying a bucket of whitewash, stood on the scaffold, set his bucket there and began to paint.

The man with the newspaper was still standing where he had been, his eyes wide with amazement. Charles Henry tipped his hat to him and stepped to a passing dray and from there to the empty bed of a flatbed wagon. Then he stopped. There was nowhere else to step. The dapple had become bored with standing in mid-street and was ambling off a half block away, the empty wagon following it.

"I thought I told that horse to stay there," he complained, and the flatbed driver looked around. "Here! What are you doin' on my wagon?"

"Just passing through," Charles told him. "Except my wagon seems to have gone the other direction. Do you suppose you might turn around and follow it?"

It cost him a quarter, but he learned from the experience. One does not expect a horse to remain standing. It should, the flatbed driver explained to him, have been anchored. The driver also showed him how to turn a rig, and Charles Henry felt, in all, that his quarter was well spent.

In the storeroom above Forsythe and Higgins, two young clerks who had watched the unorthodox delivery of cable spools were working on an adaptation of methods. The big spools, at one hundred and sixty pounds apiece, were a problem to store. Hoisted from ground floor to second floor by winch frame, they then had to be rolled laboriously—or carried—to their assigned space by the front wall. The clerks had a better idea. They had an inclined plank set on boxes above the trap where the winch frame was set, and they raised the first spool into the loft, aligned it on the plank and turned it loose. "Tallyho!" one commented, and then the blood drained from their faces as the heavy spool shot forward, thundered across the open loft, shattered the frame and sill of the window there and sailed out over Market Street.

A lumber wagon was passing below. The spool thumped down on the end of a long board and the far end of it reared upward, taking the driver's hat with it. It stood for a moment full upright in the mud of the street, then canted outward and fell sedately across the withers of a milkwagon horse, which recoiled in its traces and lashed out with startled hooves, catching the vibrating board and sending it into another somersault, still wearing its hat. A woman across the street screamed and backed into a passing man who clutched at a secured rope, releasing its slipknot. Above them a scaffold canted crazily. A painter clung desperately to a windowsill, and a bucket of whitewash cascaded downward and over the head of a man holding a newspaper.

Charles Henry Clayton, approaching on his way back to Powers Shipyard, hauled the reins to stop short of the pandemonium and gaped at tangled teams, somersaulting boards, and whitewashed citizenry.

"You see?" he told the dapple. "You see that? It is incredible the trouble people can get themselves into." He turned into a sidestreet to avoid the mess. "It comes of not paying attention," he told the horse. "It is probably the greatest affliction of the human race, but no one ever seems to do anything about it." He shook his head and flicked the reins. "It is so sad. It really is."

On Baker's Way, just a block off Market Street, all attention was focused on Stanfield's Emporium at this moment. A variety of men peered wistfully through the windows or leered openly at the door, and a trio of goggle-eyed clerks stood in breathless wonder as Homer Stanfield himself consummated a sale. The attention of an admiring public was not for Stanfield, nor for his emporium, but was centered on his customer and what she was buying.

There was that about Absynthe Malloy that made young men dream and old men drool. Compact and voluptuous, with eyes that promised ecstasy and lips like lingering lust, Absynthe Malloy had reached the epitome of note in Charleston. Every woman within a hundred miles hated her.

Today Absynthe Malloy was buying a bed. Nor was this just a bed. It was a work of art. From tall headboard to tall footboard, from wrought springs to lush comforters piled high and sheathed in velvet, this was a regal rhapsody in vermillion and brass. Brazen cupids cavorted among shining vinery interwoven in the sedate brass bars of its headpiece, which was taller than Absynthe. Satisfied satyrs smiled from the ornate corners of its barred footboard, which was almost as tall. Sinuous serpents and stalwart stags slithered sensuously and stalked suggestively along the siderails, and the feet were eagle claws of polished bronze.

It was a monumental bed, a unique bed, a bed for champions. Few in Charleston had not gawked at it during the month Homer Stanfield had it on proud display, and more than one sermon had been inspired by it. That it should be bought by Absynthe Malloy bordered on poetry. Who else, in all the rampant imaginings of Charleston manhood, could have been a match for it?

The subject of intense wonder now, as always, was who would share such a bed with Absynthe Malloy. Who else, of course, but the mysterious cohort whose funds were such that she could afford to buy it.

It was common knowledge that Absynthe Malloy was being supported in lavish style, and few men in Charleston did not secretly wish that it could be themselves doing so. But no one knew her benefactor. Neither the spies of the ladies' clubs nor the eagle eyes of the ministry had been able to find out. As for Absynthe, she went her way in Charleston, dressed always in the finest and always doing it justice, a gorgeous and glamorous mystery whose only answer to inquiring eyes was a secret and satisfied smile.

Today The Woman was buying The Bed, and crowds gathered to drool and speculate.

"I shall expect appropriate delivery," she told Homer Stanfield with a smile that made his carnation wilt. She stroked the smug, overfed tabby that was her trademark and companion.

"By all means, Miss Malloy," he said gulping. "Would Tuesday be convenient? I'll come and measure your—ah—back stairway myself, of course. These components are quite large."

"Oh, come now, Mr. Stanfield." The eyes that flashed at him knew secrets Eve could never have

83

imagined. "It would be a sin to deliver such a piece as this by way of a back staircase. I would like it delivered through the front."

He blinked. "Of course, I understand. But you see, I don't believe there is room to get it through the lobby at the Liberty—the way that hall turns at the stairs, and then there is the landing—"

"Mr. Stanfield." Her eyes went wide and soft, helpless in their femininity, and he gasped for air to keep from drowning in them. "It would be such a nice favor if you would arrange a suitable delivery."

The cat in her arms yawned and gazed about owlishly.

There were scrabbling sounds at the open front door, and a woman's piercing voice shattered the moment. "John Fletcher, you come away from there this minute!"

"But Lucrecia—"

"I said come away from there! Of all the shameful things, you here ogling that . . . that . . ."

The voices trailed away.

"Anything you like, Miss Malloy," Homer Stanfield said surrendering.

Absynthe was gazing at the front door. Her delicious chin had risen, and her formidable eyes were hooded. She turned back to the proprietor and favored him with a smile that made his knees go weak. "I would like it delivered fully assembled, Mr. Stanfield, with the scarlet draping in place and several of those fluffy pillows; let's say two of the magenta and two in peach. Fully assembled, Mr. Stanfield. And please deliver it from Market Street, shall we say about four o'clock tomorrow."

It was one block from Stanfield's to the Liberty Hotel where it fronted on Market. The cluster of dazzled men in front of Stanfield's watched in silence as

Absynthe diminished along that block, and the sway of her skirts, the arch of her back, the fluffing of her tabby, would be the stuff of dreams for them for many a night to come.

"Block and tackle," Homer Stanfield muttered as he finally turned away. "We'll have to cut through the wall—rig winches—have to talk with 'em at the hotel first—cable hoist, maybe, with a gin pole on the roof. . . ."

VII

"I don't know what you're talking about," Edgar Egmont said, gaping at the dour, uniformed man standing before his desk. "One of my ships?"

"Yes, sir," the man said, thumbing through a sheaf of papers. "An old sailing sloop, identified as the *Pallas Athene*, and registered to this company at this location. We would appreciate some verification, sir."

"Nonsense." Edgar thumped his desk. *"Pallas Athene* is on a routine commodity run to Norfolk. What would she be doing at Baltimore?"

The uniformed man turned more pages, his brow knitting in stern disapproval. "Quite a lot, sir. According to these dispatches, that ship sailed into Baltimore habor at a high rate of speed, narrowly missed collision with several other vessels, did a stern-about some fifty feet from the exchange docks and demanded directions to Newport."

"Newport? You mean in Rhode Island?"

"That was the understanding of the people at the exchange docks, yes, sir."

"Ridiculous." Edgar snorted, though a pallor began to spread across his cheeks. *"Pallas Athene* is on her way back here, due here at any time now. You have the wrong ship, commander."

"One would hope so, sir," the guardsman answered. "Although the description does fit registry. Unfortunately, the Coast Guard at Baltimore was unable to detain the vessel for investigation. Pity about that." The man's eyes narrowed. "There are some very severe charges to be lodged when she's found."

"Severe charges?" Color had returned to Edgar's face at mention of the ship's having escaped. Now the color drained again. What in God's name was that idiot Evan doing at Baltimore? What if the Coast Guard should find the old ship loaded to the gunwales with illegal whiskey?"

"Quite severe," the commander continued. "When the cutter *Point Groves* attempted to approach her, the *Pallas Athene* ran up what appeared to be a tablecloth at the masthead, then came about smartly and attacked the *Point Groves.*"

"Attacked?" Edgar's mouth hung open, his face chalk white.

"Yes, sir. The sloop was tacking outbound when the cutter approached, then she turned downwind and made to ram the cutter."

"Rammed? A revenue cutter?"

"Not quite, sir. At the last moment the sloop veered off and passed so closely that some of the cutter's portside stays were damaged. Then, as they passed, a number of the sloop's personnel stood on their railings and . . . relieved themselves upon the cutter's deck, sir. *Point Groves* was unable to open fire because a thrown dining table was wedged across her swivel gun and unable to pursue because someone aboard the sloop threw a grapple into her rigging with a skiff anchor at the other end of its line, and when *Point Groves* attempted to make way she careened hard aport and sailed in a circle, taking water over her gunwales. In the meantime the sloop escaped to sea."

"Incredible." Edgar managed a frown of distaste and took a deep breath, getting control of nerves that threatened to betray him. "But what has that to do with me?"

"Well, sir." The officer shook his head. "It would be a benefit if you could just corroborate that the *Pallas Athene* that did all that is the same *Pallas Athene* that's registered to your company."

"Which, of course, it is not."

"Which means you can't tell me where the sloop might be found before those people get into more mischief. You did say that *your* sloop is due here?"

"At any time. From Portsmouth."

"Then you won't mind us taking a look at her when she arrives?"

"Certainly not. Not at all. I will be glad to notify you when she docks."

"That won't be necessary." The officer looked at him, speculatively. "We will have spotters waiting, Mr. Egmont. We will meet her when she arrives."

When the officer was gone Egmont paced his office. "Damn!" he hissed. If *Pallas Athene* did arrive, she would be loaded with contraband merchandise. That nitwit Evan insisted upon carrying out his little games despite the danger of something like this, which could snowball into the undoing of their entire scheme. "Damn!" he sputtered again. Whether or not *Pallas Athene* returned (and if she didn't, then where the devil had Evan gone with her?) it was out of the question to consign the bogus cargo (and bomb) to her now. And with the Coast Guard sniffing around, how could he wait for the matter to resolve itself? Until those stores were reloaded in his private warehouse, until their crates and labels sailed away for the Bahamas, he was vulnerable. A cold fear crept up his spine, and he paced the room again, pausing finally by his high window to look out over the harbor.

It was time to change his plans.

He stood for a time, gazing out at the harbor, then went to the door and opened it. "Worley!" he shouted. "Come in here!"

When the harried supervisor of yards entered Edgar glared at him, then beckoned him to the window and pointed. "That old tub out there at the grain docks, what ship is that?"

Worley peered. "That one, sir? With the stub foremast? That's *Lilith.*"

"Is it one of ours?"

"Yes, sir." Worley blinked. "We use it to haul hides and tallow. We dock it away from the other vessels because of the smell—"

"Is it seaworthy?"

"Well, yes, sir, after a fashion, I suppose. It's nearly thirty years old, but I suppose—"

"Does it have a crew?"

"Yes, sir. They stay rather far apart from the rest of our crews because of the smell, but—"

"Does it have a cargo at the moment?"

"Ah, no, sir, I don't think so. You see how high she rides."

"Very well, Worley, have that ship brought to A Dock to receive cargo. *Pallas Athene* is still out and we can wait no longer. One old tub is as good as another. We will consign the Bahamas load to *Lilith.*"

"The Bahamas load?" Worley blanched. "But sir, that is extremely valuable cargo, highly insured—"

"You said the vessel is seaworthy."

"Yes, sir, but the smell—"

"Never mind the smell, Worley. I want that ship loaded and under way by noon tomorrow."

"But, sir." Worley's eyes were huge, his pallor more pronounced. "We can't load that quickly. We would have to pull longshoremen off other schedules."

"Then do it."

"And besides—"

"What?"

"Well, sir, I don't know where the Bahamas load is. It hasn't arrived at the sheds yet."

Edgar lowered his head to curse beneath his breath. Transferring the cargo from private stores to the yard was to have been Evan's job. Where the hell was Evan? "Make arrangements, Worley," he growled. "The cargo will be at dockside first thing in the morning."

"Yes, sir." Looking perplexed, Worley started to run away, but Edgar stoppd him and pointed down into the yards. A tall, well-tailored young man in a top hat was working with a puzzled gang of longshoremen, moving bales from dockside to sheds.

"Worley," Edgar asked, "who is that?"

"That?" Worley grew more perplexed than ever. "You mean him? Why, that's your cousin, sir. Mr. Clayton."

It was Edgar's turn to be baffled. "My cousin? What cousin?"

"Mr. Clayton, sir. He came two or three days ago. You were busy at the time, and of course Mr. Evan was away, and, well, he has been here since."

"Here? Doing what?"

"Why various things, sir. He just came and went to work, that's all."

Edgar stared at him, then stared out the window again.

"By the way, sir," Worley added, "the telegraph lines are up again, and there are several messages for you."

"Well, send someone for them. And meanwhile, send

91

my . . . cousin . . . up here. I want to talk to him."

"If you are my cousin, why have I never heard of you?" Edgar drummed his fingers on his desktop and frowned at the serene face across from him. It had startled him to learn that J.C. Powers had sent the young man to work at the yards. But now, after several minutes of searching inquiry, Edgar was more at ease. Charles Henry Clayton, he had decided, was a simpleton.

"We are not really cousins," Charles Henry explained. "Or rather I suppose we are, but only distantly. You see, my grandfather was your wife's father's cousin—and therefore also your uncle's cousin. And your wife's father was my father's second cousin, so your children—do you have children, Cousin Edgar? No? Well, if you did, then they would be grandchildren of your wife's uncle's first cousin's cousin whose mother was my great-grandfather's sister. But the Claytons, except for your wife's grandmother, remained firmly in Rhode Island until my father moved to Massachusetts before I was born because he had received a kind letter from Aunt Samantha, who of course is really your wife's aunt and not mine except that I began calling her that after I went to stay with her. You see?"

Edgar's eyes had glazed over. Now he licked his lips, breathed deeply and endeavored to penetrate the logic of it. "You referred to my wife's uncle as 'Uncle Jonathan'."

"Well, yes, because it follows that if he is Aunt Samantha's brother then he is Uncle Jonathan, although neither actually is either."

"What I am getting at, precisely, is, do you, ah, have any claim on any portion of the Powers Enterprises?"

"I can't imagine how. And even if I did, I don't think the Clayton family has ever been forgiven for being from Rhode Island. I know Aunt Samantha always encouraged me never to mention that in public."

"So then you have no, ah, shares in the company."

"I don't think so. As far as I know Uncle Jonathan's family has all the shares. He told me to come and work for you." He indicated the letter he had brought, which was a simple introduction, nothing more. "If you will tell me what you want me to do, I'd like to get right on it and get done as soon as possible."

"Are you in a hurry to get back to Boston, then?" Fleeting suspicion crossed Edgar's mind. Simpleton or not, it was possible the old man had sent a spy.

"Oh, no. I don't think I will go back to Boston. But you see, since I left there I have decided to go west and make my fortune. I met a young lady, and—"

Edgar's doubts eased again, and an idea began to form. "That being the case, I expect you will want to get started as soon as possible. I happen to have a special job that needs to be done right away, some cargo to be moved from a warehouse to the docks for loading. You look strong enough, and I suppose I could pay you an amount adequate to start you on your way to the west. Can you drive a wagon?"

"I certainly can. I learned just recently."

"It would mean working all night."

"Oh, I don't mind that, Cousin Edgar. I get some of my best ideas at night."

"What kind of ideas?"

"For pictures. I am an artist."

"An artist." Edgar was beginning to understand why the old man had dumped this particular "nephew," and he resented the old bastard even more. Well, he would dump him, too. Few people who went west, he had

93

heard, came back. But in the meantime, there was a tasty subtlety about the idea of old J.C.'s own assignee being the one who deposited the false cargo that would make Edgar rich, at the exact time that Edgar's manipulations pulled the rug from beneath the old man in Boston. The more he thought about it, the more he liked it.

"Very well, then, let's get right to it. We'll have Worley issue you a wagon, and I'll show you the warehouse and the cargo to be repacked and hauled. You can sign the dock warrants yourself, when you're done."

That way, he thought, if ever a question arose, there would be no doubt who delivered the phony cargo for the Bahamas run. The entire blame could be placed on this simpleton. Edgar felt very good about the whole matter. He would, of course, take no chances. Let the job be done, and a few odds and ends cleared up while it was becoming known that Charles Henry would depart shortly for the wild west. There were many ways of making certain that, after his departure, the young man was never seen again.

"These stacks right here." Edgar pointed out when they were in the warehouse. "First you will remove the inner packing and contents from each container and put all the contents in that corner over there. Then you will repack the containers with the materials you find in that stack by the wall—they are already packaged and numbered so you know which bundle goes where. Then you reclose all the containers."

"That looks like a lot of work," Charles Henry said, skeptically.

"Do you want the job or not?"

"Oh, I certainly do. But it may take all day."

"That's perfectly all right. The rest of it, the transfer and loading, can be done tonight. You will haul the containers to the docks. From there the longshoremen will stow them aboard ship in the morning. Are there any questions?"

"Only one. Why replace all the contents of the containers?"

"Frugality, my boy," Edgar intoned. "Shipping containers cost money. So, rather than buy new ones, we will simply use those that are here for another shipment."

Charles took off his coat, folded it carefully and draped it on a bale. "I had better get started, then. And I want you to know, Cousin Edgar, how much I appreciate your understanding. Why, I expect I can be on my way west within the week."

"You certainly can," Edgar assured him. "Certainly within the week."

He left him there and started back for the yards, then paused at Market Street. Up the street, crowds were gathering and there was the sound of hammers and saws, and a growing babble of voices. What now, he wondered, and turned that way.

The Liberty Hotel was three stories tall, with a false front rising ten feet above that. Now the face of the building swarmed with workmen, and when Edgar saw what they were doing his eyes went wide. A gin pole was being studded in at the top of the building and winches assembled. Scaffolds clung at second-floor level, and people with saws and mallets were removing a large, square section of the wall, about six by eight feet, containing two large double-hung windows. Edgar gaped at the scene. He knew those windows.

They were Absynthe Malloy's windows.

He grabbed an onlooker by the shoulder. "What is all this about?" he demanded. "What are those people doing?"

"You wouldn't believe me if I told you," the man said and chuckled, then turned. "Oh, Mr. Egmont. Sorry, sir, no offense meant. As I understand it, sir, they are preparing to deliver a bed."

"A—a bed?" Edgar went white about the lips. He had forgotten about his agreement to buy Absynthe a new bed in return for her promise to be more discreet. "But why are they taking the wall out?"

"When you see the bed, sir, you'll understand. It's over there, under those tarps. You can see by the size of it, sir, it is quite a bed." The man took a deep breath and turned away, his eyes glassy at thought of the bed being delivered and what uses would be made of it by its new owner. Everybody in town knew where Absynthe Malloy lived. "Somebody," the man muttered, "is fixin' to have one hell of a romp."

"Here, now!" Edgar's nose went up. "What kind of talk is that?"

The man turned toward him again, embarrassed. "Sorry, sir. Forgot you was standing there." Then he hurried away.

Edgar watched from a porch across the street as the project unfolded, unwilling to be seen here but too fascinated to leave. As the workmen finished cutting away the wall section, laying it outward to be lowered on slings, the interior of Absynthe's apartment was opened to view. On the street below the crowds went silent. Men climbed atop hitch rails and wagon beds and crowded in windows across the street.

The wall opened wide, and daylight flooded a bedroom like no bedroom most of those in Charleston had seen. Rich brass and bright crystal gleamed in settings of deep velvet. Scarlet drapings were tied back with gold ropery to reveal the alcove where the bed would rest, just inside the big windows.

"My God," someone muttered. "She has mirrors on the ceiling."

And as they watched, Absynthe herself entered the exposed room from an adjacent parlor, walked to the cut-away wall and looked out at them, smiling sweetly, scratching the ears of a large, satisfied tabby. She was there only a moment, but the effect on the Market Street crowd was profound. Men discovered new depths of longing, and women reached new heights of hatred. Even Edgar, lurking in the shadows and trembling with outrage at the spectacle she had created, found his breath going ragged at sight of her. Whatever else Absynthe might be—stupid, vengeful, intractable, and unpredictable—she was lovely.

The porch roof above Edgar thumped and creaked as a man fell from a window above it and scrabbled at its shingles to keep from falling to the street.

"When I die," a man told any who were listening, "you can have heaven. I just want to go in there."

Then movement began again. Hoists were lifted and fitted, slings were lowered and tarps laid back, and within moments the glorious bed, huge and regal with its gleaming brass and lurid trappings, rose slowly from the ground toward the opening in the second floor wall, as tacklemen hauled on their cables and workmen played a guy line attached to the base of the great head-frame to keep it from turning during ascent.

Throughout the charmed crowd, awed men removed their hats and frantic women removed their men.

"My God," Edgar told himself over and over, "she didn't understand a word I said."

An hour had passed before the bed was in place, slings removed, and the wall section was raised for restudding. As it went up, Homer Stanfield and the owner of the Liberty stopped squabbling over the amount and manner of damage reimbursement to hold their breaths as the section closed into its hole, then stopped. Someone had left the guy rope dangling. Workmen inside the room quickly pulled it in and coiled it beside the bed. Then the section fit smoothly into place and carpenters went to work sealing the joints, with plasterers and painters awaiting their turns.

Absynthe's bed was delivered. Charleston had been suitably entertained, and Edgar Egmont was angry enough to spit nails. "I'll make her regret this," he muttered as he turned away. "Discreet! My God." And yet, sight of the bed, of the familiar room, of Absynthe, had left other ideas firmly implanted in his mind.

He would have no chance to initiate that bed tonight. There was too much to do, too much to worry about: the Bahamas shipment being recrated for loading, the special crate that he would have to rig and handle by himself, after that idiot "cousin" of his had finished hauling—the crate with the explosive device—and a missing ship to find before the Coast Guard found it, not to mention a missing brother who could stay missing for all Edgar cared. And while he was thinking about it, what had been going on at the yards these last few days? The place was one disaster after another.

It was late evening when Edgar returned to the private warehouse, and he was impressed despite himself. Charles Henry had completed all the repacking, exactly as instructed. The containers were ready to load and haul to the docks. Edgar checked every item carefully. All the crates held their proper false cargo. All the valuables were stacked securely in their assigned alcove.

Edgar, meantime, had already delivered the bomb crate to the docks. He would not set the clock fuse until his final inspection, just before the stinking old tub sailed.

Through the night he supervised Charles Henry as the young man struggled to load his wagon, haul cargo around to the docks, stack it there for loading aboard ship and come back to reload. They had the docks to themselves. Between the fact it was night and the reek of the old hide ship moored there, no one else ventured near.

As morning light colored the harbor's waters, Edgar sent Charles Henry away to bathe and change with the admonishment that he be at work at eight o'clock. He would keep the young man busy for a time with odd jobs, long enough for the hide ship to be well at sea, then he would pay him off and send him west. And between now and then, he would arrange an accident on the road. In his office, the work was piling up, but he would get to it later. Timing was critical now to get the ship loaded, set the bomb and send her away on the noon tide.

As Charles Henry strolled toward his rented room, exhausted and exhilarated at the job he had done, a nagging puzzle bothered him. Observant by nature and methodical on occasion, he had counted the crates and containers as he repacked them, and counted them again as he delivered them. There were one hundred and seventy-two containers in all. And yet, when he counted them one more time for good measure—at the dock—there were one hundred and seventy-three. The more he thought about it the more it worried him. Cousin Edgar was paying him well, and was most understanding of his desire to finish his work and go west. He wanted to do his job exactly right, with no mistakes.

He was glad it had occurred to him to mark all the crates he had delivered. They would be loading the ship this morning, and he would stay out of the way. But there would be time before she sailed, he was sure, to slip aboard and count the parcels one more time. If, by some mischance, he had taken something to the dock that didn't belong there, it would be easy to find and return to the warehouse. He would just look for one that did not have his mark on it.

VIII

Lilith barely made the noon tide. Though her cargo was stowed by mid-morning and stores had been tended the day before, it was difficult rounding up a crew for a ship that smelled so bad. Thus she sat, alone and unattended, at the dock for three hours before making way. During the first of those hours Edgar Egmont went aboard alone, a cloth over his face, to make final inspection. Deep in the stinking hold of *Lilith* he opened an odd-sized crate, reached inside and wound a clockwork mechanism, then hastily resealed the crate and climbed on deck gasping for untainted air.

During the third of the waiting hours Charles Henry Clayton approached the noisome vessel, covered his face with a cloth and entered the hold. Within minutes he was wrestling the same odd-sized crate on deck, to the dock and into the bed of his wagon. He was grateful there was no one around. He was acutely embarrassed that he had somehow miscounted and delivered an unconsigned crate. He hurried to return it to the warehouse.

"Harm corrected," he told the dapple horse, "is no harm done."

On the outbound tide *Lilith* set sail for the Bahamas, her unhappy crew holding cloths over their noses. And all of those at Powers Yards, for various reasons, breathed sighs of relief when she was gone.

During the afternoon Charles Henry, casting about for constructive ways to spend the day, made a few deliveries and practiced his skills at wagon driving and the anchoring of horsedrawn vehicles. His preferred method was to find a rope attached to something solid and tie it to the tail beam of the wagon.

The stock tender at the yards had assigned the dapple to other duties, so Charles Henry was using a newly acquired horse, a tall sorrel recently traded in from a stage line at Richmond. The horse was well trained and strong, but the stage line had traded it off after it developed a livid fear of cats.

He had not seen his cousin since dawn. Edgar was not in his office, not at the yards, and no one was sure where he might be. But Worley, the supervisor, handed Charles Henry a stack of sealed messages. "When you find him, give him these. Telegraph lines were down for awhile, and they're up now. These are what was waiting."

Charles Henry delivered a load of imported linens to a commodity house on upper Market and an order of milled castings to a miller in Sethbridge, four miles out on the Santee road. Then he gave a lift back into town to a man who carried a worn rifle and had the look of far places in his eyes.

"Where you bound from?" Charles Henry asked as the sorrel paced the dusty road eastward.

"West," the man said.

"Aha!" Charles Henry reined the sorrel to a halt and turned to the startled man beside him. "Just the fellow I want to talk to. I am going west, you see, and since I have never been there I need to know all about it."

102

The man studied him, narrow-eyed. "Where west?"

"Just . . . west. I'm going to make my fortune. I've heard that is where one goes for that sort of thing, but they never speak of that very much in Massachusetts, so I could use some sound advice from someone who has been there."

The man spat over the side of the wagon, wiped his whiskers and stared at Charles Henry again. "You're going west? To make your fortune?"

"Most definitely. Miss Emmalee expects it."

"What? Gold? Cattle? Land speculation? Snake oil?"

"Oh, whatever is quickest, I imagine. I don't want to keep Miss Emmalee waiting too long. She is a virgin."

"She is?"

"Yes, and her black woman seems to blame me for that. What can you tell me about the west?"

The man seemed to be having a hard time keeping up, but finally he spat again and gave Charles Henry a quizzical look. "I don't suppose you can listen and drive at the same time, can you? I'm supposed to meet someone in Charleston."

"Oh, certainly." Charles Henry flipped the reins. The sorrel regained its easy pace.

"The West," the man mused aloud. "Well, son, I reckon it's just like you heard. There sure are ways to get rich out there all right. Man with a good gun and a fast horse can put himself up a fair stake if he keeps his wits about him. 'Course, there's some drawbacks. There's blizzards and droughts, and outlaws and Indians, and there's places out there that everything that lives has horns, thorns, stingers, or fangs, includin' the human complement that has all of 'em. But, then, if a man can keep from getting gored, stomped, knifed, shot, roasted, throwed, dragged, hanged, froze, drowned, gutted, scalped, snakebit, robbed, or bamboozled long enough, he just might make hisself a fortune at that."

"You make it sound somewhat dangerous."

"Dangerous? Aw, no, son, it's a regular tea party most of the time. Only reason I ever come back east is sometimes I find myself just havin' more fun than I can really say grace over. Yep, all a man needs is a bedroll to keep the frost off him, a good gun to keep the Indians off him, and a good horse to keep the law off him, and he can go far out there. That's something the West has got a lot of. Far."

"Horse, gun, and bedroll," Charles Henry recounted. "That seems simple enough."

"And money. Money helps."

"Well, I expect I might have about two thousand dollars left after I buy a horse, a gun, and a bedroll. Would that be enough, do you think?"

The man brightened perceptibly and fingered his rifle. "Oh? Oh, yeah, that's quite a bit of money. Have it on you now, do you?"

"No, but my cousin is supposed to pay me this evening, and I'll wire along the way for the rest of my trust. I will then."

"And when do you suppose you might leave . . . ah . . . for the West?"

"Right away, I suppose. No sense dallying, I always say."

"Well," the man said, speculatively, "I suppose you'll want some direction, best roads to take and such."

As he drove into Charleston with the smoky sunset at his back, Charles Henry listened carefully to the man's instructions: stage connections to Memphis, provisions for the trail to Fort Smith; the instructions became vague from that point on. "Fort Smith is the jump-off," the man explained. "After that, you got the whole West in front of you. You just make sure you get to Fort Smith. And save all the money you can."

"Be pretty useful out there, will it?"

"Right useful." The man rubbed his whiskers. "Right useful."

After Charles Henry let him off in upper Charleston, the bearded man limped painfully a few blocks north off Market and ducked into a lighted shed. The two men waiting there, playing cards by dim lantern light, looked up and one of them nodded.

"Howdy, Jed. We waited for you. Some of the boys got a bank lined up down in Savannah."

"You go along," Jed said, rubbing his whiskers. He sat down painfully on a cot and began struggling with his foot in the shadows. Perspiration beaded on his face. "I had a change of plans. Soon as I can hop a packet I'm headed for New Orleans, then up to Memphis and over to Fort Smith. I got to be there to meet somebody."

"Oh." The men looked at each other and shrugged. "Well, I guess we'll go without you then." The taller of the two peered at him in the gloom. "Jed, do you mind if I ask you a question?"

"What question is that?"

"What is that thing on your foot?"

"Damned if I know. Sort of a gear wheel seems like. A milled casting. I was riding on a wagon and I got my foot stuck in it and I can't get it off."

Edgar Egmont was waiting at the shipyards when Charles Henry arrived there, and Charles Henry was sent up to see him immediately. Egmont sat at his desk, across from a dark-eyed, slender man whose suit, shirt, and face were a uniform shade of somber gray. Egmont did not introduce the man but favored Charles Henry with a hearty smile and produced a packet of bills for him.

"Finished those few last chores, have you, Charles

Henry? Well, young man, it is a pleasure to send you on your way west with my best wishes. I trust you are leaving soon."

"Well, yes, sir," Charles Henry answered. "As a matter of fact, I thought I might pack and leave on the late coach if that's all right with you. I was talking to a man who has been in the West, and he gave me directions, to a place called Fort Smith. That's where I will be heading first."

Edgar glanced at the gray man, who seemed to think something over for a moment, then nodded almost imperceptibly.

"Excellent choice." Edgar nodded. "Fort Smith. That definitely is west. Well, Charles Henry, you'll find there is a good sum of money there. I trust you will guard it well and use it wisely. It's more than I normally would pay, but since you are my cousin, and since I am an abnormally generous man—"

"Not cousin, exactly," Charles Henry pointed out. "Actually my great-grandmother was your wife's father's aunt, which means that you and your brother— I'm sorry I didn't have the opportunity to meet Cousin Evan by the way—would have been second cousins by marriage twice removed to my father because it was his great-aunt who was your wife's father's mother—"

Edgar's eyes were starting to glaze. "Yes, we've discussed that before," he countered. "And I'm sorry I must be abrupt, Cousin Charles Henry, but I have business with this gentleman." He stood and reached across the desk. "You had best be on your way now. Thank you for coming, and I wish you luck in the West."

Before Charles Henry could recover, he had been escorted from the office, patted on the back, and sent on his way.

Edgar closed the door and turned to the man still

seated at his desk. "You see, Mr. Dooley? He should present no problem to you. And now that you know where to find him—"

"Fort Smith," the man muttered. "Yeah, it'll do. No law past there. You said two thousand dollars?"

"Maybe more," Edgar said and nodded.

"When do I get paid?"

"When the deed is done. You saw the money I gave him. That will be your fee. He will have it with him."

"You know something, Egmont?" the gray man said and scowled at him. "You are a sorry bastard."

"See here!" Edgar erupted, then subsided at the cold gaze of killer eyes regarding him. "Well, it makes no difference to me what you think, anyway. You know what's to be done, and you know where your money is."

"What's to keep me from taking him out right here in Charleston? Save me a trip."

"Well," Edgar purred, "as you said, there's no law past Fort Smith."

The gray man stared at him a moment longer, then got up and left the room. Edgar noticed with a chill that he made no sound when he moved. He shivered, then put the whole affair from his mind. *Lilith* was on her way to oblivion at sea, and the sequestered valuables of three cargoes were securely locked in his private warehouse. Anytime now, he would have word from Bull Timmons that the Powers empire was destroyed, and then he could cash Timmons's draft, a sizeable fortune in itself. Evan still had not been heard from, nor the *Pallas Athene* with her illicit whiskey, but Edgar had arranged a cover for that. If the Coast Guard caught the ship and Evan, the whole thing would rest squarely on Evan's shoulders. Edgar would never be blamed.

By and large, Edgar was pleased with himself. More than pleased, he was elated. He had set out to divest himself of his wife's uncle's control and gain a fortune in the process.

He had done so. And all his tracks, he felt sure, were covered. It was time to celebrate.

With rising enthusiasm, Edgar let his thoughts turn to the pleasures of life. A passing vision of his wife's narrow face and stern eyes crossed his mind and he wrinkled his nose. Emma Powers Egmont was not a devotee of connubial bliss. She had tried it once and didn't like it. Edgar shook his head to clear away the dour image. The vision that replaced it was altogether different. Absynthe Malloy. Absynthe Malloy in her lush bedroom. Absynthe Malloy in that preposterous but nonetheless tantalizing new bed. Edgar was still outraged at the spectacle she had made with that bed, and he would punish her in due course. But first, he might as well find out if the bed was all the bed it looked to be. It had certainly cost him enough.

Edgar picked up his hat and turned the lamp wick down. He had long since worked out several back-street routes to the Liberty that would take him there unobserved.

In the yards, in last light of evening, Charles Henry said exuberant good-byes to a dozen draymen and longshoremen and found Worley and a pair of tired swampers loading bales of Connecticut machine parts onto the wagon Charles Henry had been using.

"Mr. Worley, I'm on my way west to make my fortune," Charles Henry said, pumping the man's hand. "It has been a pleasure working with you."

"And I'm sorry to see you go, sir," Worley said. "Things won't be so interesting here when you're gone."

"Does this load go uptown by any chance, Mr.

108

Worley? I'm going that way to pack my things and meet the night stage."

"Matter of fact," Worley said with a nod, "it does. Dolph Meyers has an assembly crew waiting for these parts at his shop. Would you like to make one last delivery?" Worley had become fond of the young man, taken by his enthusiasm, his readiness to pitch in and help. He was definitely weird, but a nice young man for all that. "Meyers's shop is just behind the Liberty Hotel. You know where that is?"

"Of course. Would it be all right? I mean, it would be a nice parting, to make one last wagon haul before I go west. And the Liberty is just a block from my room, but I don't know if there would be time to return the horse and wagon."

"Oh, that's all right. You could leave the rig there. When we finish up here one of the boys can go and get it. Go ahead. Make the haul, Charles Henry. And remember us back here when you are making your fortune in the West."

The horse was not his favorite dapple, but it was the same tall sorrel that had been traded in from Richmond, and Charles Henry felt a certain kinship toward it, almost as though they had met in some previous time. With final handshakes around, he tapped his hat firmly onto his head, climbed up on the seat and flicked the reins. "Tallyho!" he told the horse.

The lamps were lit along Market Street, and evening crowds were accumulating along the boardwalks, Charleston's gentry out in the cool of day for their evening promenade.

Tipping his hat to ladies and gentlemen strolling by, Charles Henry eased his rig into the alley alongside the Liberty and drove the forty yards to Meyers's shop. He had just begun taking off his coat to unload bales when he noticed a bulk in the inner pocket and snapped his fingers. Cousin Edgar's telegraph messages! He had forgotten them.

Then he noticed furtive movement in the deepening shadows of a footpath alongside Meyers's shop, and a moment later a familiar figure appeared there, walking carefully, looking this way and that. Charles Henry stepped from behind the wagon.

"Cousin Edgar! What a fortunate coincidence! I have messages for you that I was supposed to deliver, but we were so hurried at your office that I quite forgot them. Here they are."

Edgar stood there with his mouth open, startled and guilty, but Charles Henry asked no questions. He simply handed him the bundle of messages and turned away.

"I have to get this unloaded, Cousin Edgar. Thank you again for all your courtesy, and I promise I will write. Have a nice evening." And with that he was gone, vague in the dusk, carrying a bundle toward the machinery shop entrance.

Edgar faded back into the shadows, letting minutes pass while he assured himself that his simpleton cousin was gone and no one else was around. Then he hurried away through a dark lot toward the back gallery stairs of the Liberty.

Climbing these stairs, furtive in the darkness, was the worst part of Edgar's periodic nocturnal ventures into Absynthe Malloy's sanctum. It was here he was most exposed, most likely to be seen. But this time, as before, no one saw him. He made his way up the steps, across the dark gallery and slipped through the rear door of Absynthe's private suite.

"Ah, there you are," she said and came to him, arms going about his waist, breathtaking face raised to him in that way she had that drove all other thoughts from his mind. "My new bed is just gorgeous, Edgar. Come,

110

let me show it to you." She smiled, and the suggestion in it rolled through him like thunder.

Like one in thrall Edgar let himself be guided to the lavish bedroom, where he goggled at the magnificence of the huge brass bed, now enclosed in its proper setting. It dominated the erotic hues and subtle fabrics around it. It was a monumental bed, a bed suggestive beyond subtlety. Its invitation was a royal decree. Edgar barely noticed that Absynthe was removing his clothes and had already removed most of hers.

"Doesn't it just make you want to cavort?" she whispered, draping his shirt over a chair.

"I've never seen anything like it," he admitted, and now his attentions were torn between the commanding presence of the bed and the bewitching unclad presence of Absynthe. Gingerly he sat on the edge of the luxuriant feather mattress, which yielded cloudlike beneath his posterior. Absynthe leaned—his breath went ragged—to pull off his boots. Between them now only one garment remained, and he stood to remove it.

Playfully in the dim lamplight she backed away, and Edgar, neck swollen like a stag in rut, went for her, then stifled a curse as he fell to his knees and rolled upright, whistling obscenities as he lifted his right foot in both hands to stare through tears at a violated toe. The spell was broken.

"Oh, shit!" He stifled a shriek of pain. "My God, I think I broke my toe! What the hell is that?"

Naked, on hands and knees, holding his injured foot high off the floor, Edgar groped in shadows and pulled forth a large coil of heavy rope. "What the hell is this? What's it doing here?"

Absynthe stood wide-eyed and startled. "I certainly don't know. What is it? A rope? Maybe one of the workmen left it when they delivered—"

"I intend to talk to you about that!" Edgar waggled a

111

finger at her, then winced as his stubbed toe connected with the carpet. "Oh, crap!" With a whimper he crawled to the window at the bed's headboard, raised its lower sash and flung the offending coil of rope out into the night.

In the tumult his preparedness had subsided somewhat, and Absynthe sighed. She would have to start all over again. Edgar Egmont really could be a nuisance at times. With the drapes back in place she helped him stand and supported him as he gingerly tested his sore foot on the floor.

"Maybe it isn't broken," he admitted. "But that hurt like hell."

"I'm sure it did," she soothed. "Poor thing."

"Well." He relaxed a little. "Where were we?" Then his glance fell on a bundle of folded paper on the floor. "What's that?"

"I don't know. Something that fell out of your coat pocket."

He picked it up and remembered. The telegraph messages. His attention momentarily diverted from Absynthe, he broke the seal on one of the sheets and unfolded it:

> *TO EDGAR EGMONT STOP CHARLESTON SC STOP HAVE RECEIVED DETAIL DRAWING OF POWERS BARRELS LOADING AT RICHMOND WAREHOUSE NOT OUR CUSTOMER STOP NO RECORD OF TRANSACTION STOP MR WATSON ENROUTE CHARLESTON FOR AUDIT STOP REQUIRE IMMEDIATE EXPLANATION STOP BETTER BE GOOD STOP SIGNED JONATHAN CLAYTON POWERS*

His chin had dropped so far he felt his jaws beginning to cramp, and he snapped them shut. Bewilderment, confusion, and dread roared through him. What was this all about? What drawing? What barrels? Evan's whiskey shipment? But how—

"Oh, come on, Edgar," Absynthe scolded. "Look at you. You're drooping again. Can't you read your mail some other time?" With a shrug she molded herself against him and began renewing his enthusiasm. "Sometimes you can be a real twit," she said under her breath.

Without knowing how he got there, Edgar found himself sitting on the monstrous bed again, this time with Absynthe warm and willing in his lap.

"Ooh," she whispered, squirming as his attentions began to focus again. "Now isn't that all better?"

Absynthe's overfed tabby cat sauntered unnoticed across the room and jumped onto the sill of the open window, perching itself behind the drapery to stare disdainfully at the street scene below. People were strolling along the boardwalks, greeting one another in muted voices, enjoying the cool air of evening, the bright lights of the street lamps. Directly below the open window a young man in a top hat backed a horse-drawn wagon to the boardwalk beneath a lamp, looked around, then walked to the near curb and picked up a length of rope. He tugged on it, looked upward to follow its length where it dangled from the window, and the cat purred as the rope's bristles moved against her. She dipped her head to rub her cheek on it where it lay across the sill.

The young man tugged again, shrugged his shoulders and stooped to tie the dangling end of the rope securely to the tail beam of his wagon. "That should anchor you sufficiently," he told the sorrel horse. "Now you just wait there until someone comes for you. Good-bye." With that he walked away, up the street. On the drape-darkened windowsill the tabby cat began washing her paws.

"Ahhh." Edgar Egmont sighed as Absynthe's practiced hands proceeded with his therapy. "Ah, you do have the art, my dear." Then he paused, sat bolt upright. "Art? Detail drawing? Artist? No. No, it couldn't be. Could it?"

"Edgar!" Absynthe sounded exasperated. "You come back here!"

Sitting now, he unsealed the second of the telegraph messages, and as he read it his eyes widened:

> *TO EDGAR EGMONT STOP DISASTER STOP WHOLE DEAL IS OFF STOP PAYMENT ON DRAFT STOPPED STOP WILL BE THERE SOON TO DISCUSS YOUR SHARE OF MY LOSSES STOP DO NOT LEAVE STOP SIGNED TIMMONS*

"Oh my God," he wailed and unfolded the last of the telegrams:

> *TO EDGAR EGMONT STOP CREW MUTINIED STOP SHIP WHEREABOUTS UNKNOWN STOP MY WHEREABOUTS WILMINGTON STOP WIRE FUNDS FOR MY BOND STOP HAD NO CHOICE BUT TO EXPLAIN TO COAST GUARD STOP DO YOU KNOW SOMEONE NAMED CHARLES HENRY CLAYTON STOP FIRST MATE SAYS HE SWITCHED KEGS AT RICHMOND STOP SIGNED EVAN*

"Edgar, for heaven's sake," Absynthe scolded. "Lie down. Come on, now, Edgar, are you breathing? What's the matter with you? Edgar, why do you look so strange?"

Suddenly the room shook, mirrors and glassware crashed and drapes flared inward, and there was the rolling shock of a large, distant explosion.

The horse in the street below shied, took up slack on the rope attached to its wagon, and rough rope burned across the sill above, startling the snoozing tabby cat who arched, screeched and sailed outward to land claws-scrabbling on the horse's rump. The horse screamed and bolted. The wagon veered behind it, and the heavy rope sprang taut, its upper end still fastened to the frame of the great bed it had been used to guide. Windows exploded outward, hotel wall bulged and parted, and the bed sailed out over Market Street.

The bed absorbed the impact of the fall. As its towing rope burst free it thudded into the dirt street, legs penetrating deep into the surface. Springs sang and parted like rifleshots, and the mattress thudded against the ground. The frame collapsed. High headboard and footboard folded in and down to pin the naked Edgar immobile between feather mattress and overlapped brass bars.

As the dust settled he lay spread-eagled there in all his glory as Market Street crowds gathered around in stunned silence. People ran from all directions to elbow through the crowd for a look at the man in the fallen bed. Only his nose and his sagging pride protruded above the bars.

Then hundreds of eyes turned upward and there were gasps of shock and sighs of admiration. Above them, beside the shambles of the Liberty's wall, Absynthe Malloy, stark naked and kicking, clung to the stump of the hotel's jutting flagpole and screeched at the top of her lungs.

Emma Powers Egmont and two of her friends, fresh from a meeting of the Charleston Temperance League, gawked at the spectacle, and Emma leaned over the bed to peer at various visible parts of the man inside.

"Edgar? Edgar, is that you?"

And still others came running. Worley, out of breath, pushed his way through the crowd and stared at Edgar, then cleared his throat and pretended nothing was amiss.

"Mr. Egmont, sir, there has been an explosion near the docks. One of the men thinks it may have been your warehouse."

Edgar managed to push one hand through the mesh of ornate brass. The hand held a crumpled telegram. "I'll kill him," he wailed, his voice rising from his damning cage. "If it's the last thing I do, I'll kill him."

The explosion that had rocked uptown Charleston was a more distant roar at the stage station on the Columbia Road.

Charles Henry Clayton looked up from tying his tripod easel and portfolio firmly onto the stagecoach boot. "What do you suppose that was?"

"No tellin'," the driver said. "Just ain't no tellin'. You got that tied on proper, young feller? Hop aboard, then. We got miles to make, an' it's a pleasant night for runnin'."

Part Two

The Distant Lands

I

"I don't know how much mo' I can stand," Aphrodite declared, flinging open the pantry door so that Lazarus, bent almost double under a huge sack of dried beans, could enter. "You know what that girl doin' now?"

Lazarus, edging into the crowded pantry with his burden, muttered an inquiry.

"She readin' books, is what!" Aphrodite declared. "There I thinkin' maybe we's shed of that havoc man, an' we ain' even get the whole way home afore she change her min' an' decide he don' have to be rich. An' now she in yonder readin' books. Oh, it a bad sign. Terrible bad."

"I said," Lazarus said more clearly from the shadows of the pantry, "where you want these beans?"

"In th' bean place!" Aphrodite barked. "Where else?"

From the shadows came the thump of a heavy sack hitting the floor, then Lazarus emerged, wiping sweat with a shirt sleeve. "What all this you rantin' about, old woman?"

"You listen, you'd know." Aphrodite withered the tall black man with a scowl. "Ain' I done 'splain it

119

to you?"

"Lordy, you was in full 'splain afore I ever come in wit' them beans, old woman. I ain' heared but jus' the tail end of it. You 'spectin' sperrits or somethin'? How's come you got witch wards on all th' doors on this place?"

"Keep out chaos an' havoc is why." She began pacing the floor, shoulders bent in deep worry. "I didn't want to take no chance on him turnin' up here."

"Who chaos an' havoc?"

"Lordy, Lazarus, you don' listen atall! Chaos an' havoc th' one th' angels say gone come an' set off th' curse on Miss Emmalee."

"That ol' sperrit story? Is you mean th' man done actually turn up?"

"More'n turn up. He done got Miss Emmalee's juices to boilin' when we's on th' train. Then when he got off I thought maybe we's shed of him. Hadn' been for that man as wanted to kill him, maybe Miss Emmalee would have forgot about him eventually. But no, oh no, here he come wit' that gun in his han', an'—"

"Here who come?" Lazarus' eyes widened. "Chaos an' havoc?"

"No, this was after he got off. We was on th' way home an' here come this wet gentleman chargin' through th' train askin' ever'body where Charles Henry Clayton was so's he could shoot him dead."

"Who Charles Henry Clayton?"

"He th' chaos an' havoc one. Pay attention." She reached high to waggle an imperious dark finger under his nose. "Anyhow Miss Emmalee heard who he lookin' for an' what he want to do—the gentleman wit' th' gun, that is—an' you jus' ain' gone b'lieve what that sweet young thing do then."

"What she do?" Lazarus was all ears.

"Why, she politely got up, marched herself through

that train car out to th' couplin' stage 'twixt it an' the nex' car back, open th' boardin' gate on one side an' laid two dollars on the floor in front of it. Then when th' wet gentleman come back through an' seen th' two dollars he naturally bent over to pick 'em up."

"Naturally."

"Well, Miss Emmalee was waitin' right there. When th' gentleman bend over she jus' naturally grab on to th' guardrail an' put both her feet on th' gentleman's rump an' kick him off th' train."

Lazarus's eyes were almost popping from their sockets. "Miss Emmalee? Does you mean *our* li'l Miss Emmalee? She done that?"

"She do. He drop his pistol when he fell off, an' Miss Emmalee got it an' been readin' up on how it shoot an' all."

"That the book she been readin'?"

"That jus' th' first one! Name of *Lady's Home Guide to the Discharging of Firearms, volume three: The Revolver.* Then this letter done come from Mr. Charles Henry sayin' he on his way west to get rich, an' now Miss Emmalee got herself a whole stack of books in there, an' she ain' stick her nose out from th' parlor in three days now."

"What kin' books is they?"

"Fearful bad ones. They's *The Lady's Compendium of Aborigines of the Southwest,* an' one name *A Genteel Review of Western Outlaws,* an' *Merits of the Western Saddle,* an' she also got a book 'bout stagecoach schedules an' hotel accommodations, an' one call *Proper Attire for Western Travel.* Ain' you see what she fixin' to do?"

Lazarus took a deep breath. "I sees, all right. Ol' woman, them witch wards on th' doors ain' gone do any good. You needs to go find yo'self a witch woman. Soun' like prophecy fixin' to happen."

"I been down to see ol' Mama Cujo already. She ain' no help."

"I ain' mean no Mama Cujo. I means you better go right to th' top. You best go find out where ol' Mama Trevalier stayin' these days."

Aphrodite backed off a step, her hands before her. "What you sayin' Mama Trevalier for, Lazarus? That ol' woman died twenty year ago."

"Oh, I knows that. But I hears she done got over it an' she ain' died no more lately. Las' I hear, she ain' even feel poorly."

When Lazarus had gone, Aphrodite paced the floor, arms wrapped about her scrawny frame to stifle shivers of dread. Mama Trevalier! If Lazarus said Mama Trevalier was alive then she probably was. But that just made her all the more formidable. And even when she was alive before, folks had to be powerful desperate to go to Mama Trevalier. Aphrodite raised her eyes heavenward. "You hear all that, Gabriel? How you feel about it?"

It was a subdued and fearful Aphrodite who labored that afternoon in the wash shed, put up a mess of preserves that evening and prepared brooms and dusters for an attack on the house tomorrow. She would get the work caught up, make sure Miss Emmalee's needs were attended to for a time, then she would go in search of the dread Mama Trevalier.

She was abashed and somewhat disappointed. She had never expected Gabriel to agree with that bone-headed Lazarus.

Emmalee had quickly exhausted the limited resources of the Vicksburg Trust Lending Library, but between the half-dozen legitimate books available to her there and a pair of smuggled dime novels that dealt luridly and tantalizingly with the customs of the unorganized territories, she felt adequately equipped to cope with the West.

Completing her studies late in the evening, she went once more through her notes and then retired to an extended sleep filled with assimilation and codifications of all that she had learned. The West was located, obviously, to the west. It seemed to have no very precise boundaries but was rather a sort of patchwork of loosely organized states and unorganized territories covering a surprisingly large area.

She had concentrated particularly upon the routes and modes of travel and upon the dangers inherent therein. Criminals seemed to be very prevalent out there: robbers, road agents, and so on, as well as did wild Indians, rough terrain, and unreliable weather. One required, it seemed, a good horse and a good gun in order to make very much progress in such places.

It was customary, when confronted by outlaws, to either shoot them or arrest and hang them. It was customary with wild Indians to retreat from them as gracefully as the situation might permit.

Emmalee had decided to travel to the West and take charge of Charles Henry Clayton. She was not at all sure Charles Henry was qualified to take charge of himself, and the encounter with a soggy armed villain on the train toward Vicksburg had made up her mind for her. There had been no doubt of that man's intent to find and kill Charles Henry.

She tossed in troubled sleep, dreaming of Charles Henry being confronted by an armed man. In slow motion she saw the attacker, water dripping from his clothing, draw a gun from his pocket. She saw Charles Henry, his handsome chin squared in brave resolve, drop to a deadly crouch as his hand flicked to the holster at his hip and whipped upward again—holding a container of oil paint.

She dreamed of Charles Henry explaining genealogy to a Kiowa war party; Charles Henry standing bravely before a buffalo stampede, wielding a tripod easel; Charles Henry lost and thirsty in endless desert, pausing to draw pictures of interesting cacti. She awoke drenched in sweat.

Someone was knocking on the door. The knock came again and she waited, expecting to hear Aphrodite scolding whoever was there. But there was no sound in the house. Quickly she drew on her housewrap and hurried to the front parlor.

The teenaged boy at the door wore a billed cap, held an envelope and notepad in his hand and seemed to lose his voice at sight of Emmalee. She said good morning to him and waited for him to regain control of his pubescent libido. Emmalee was accustomed to such reactions and had long since stopped trying to fathom their cause. They simply were a fact of life.

The boy gulped several times, then removed his cap. "Good morning, ma'am," he managed in a voice that traded octaves at intervals. "Telegraph message here for a Mr. Clayton?"

"Clayton?" Emmalee was startled. "There is no Mr. Clayton here. What Mr. Clayton is it for?"

The boy looked at his pad. "Mr. Charles Henry Clayton, it says. Says to come to this address. You sure there ain't a Mr. Clayton here?"

"No, he isn't here. Mr. Clayton has gone west. What does the message say?"

He gulped again. "Sorry, ma'am, I can't give this to nobody except the addressee. You see, it's th' rule."

Emmalee shook her head. Then she gave the boy her prettiest smile. "Please?"

Back inside, Emmalee opened the copied message. It

124

was addressed to Charles Henry:

GOT THIS ADDRESS POST OFFICE CHARLESTON STOP HOPE YOU ARE THERE STOP IF SO WAIT FOR ME STOP URGENT I FIND YOU STOP DO NOT GO TO FORT SMITH STOP YOUR LIFE IN JEOPARDY THERE STOP CORDIAL BEST WISHES STOP WATSON.

Emmalee sat down abruptly in a parlor chair. Fort Smith—that was where Charles Henry had said he was going. Suddenly all her nightmares flooded back to her. Outlaws, Indians, buffalo stampedes, thirst, rattlesnakes, all coalesced into a single name. Fort Smith.

"Aphrodite!" she called. "We must pack! We are going to Fort Smith!" Then in the echoes of her voice she heard the silence of the house again and realized why it seemed silent. The normal background noise she had heard all her life—a mixture of Aphrodite's lectures, Aphrodite's admonitions and Aphrodite's complaints—was missing.

The hall door opened quietly, and the gleaming dark face of Sister Mae Wallis, who lived out on Pinmoney Road and cooked for the Eppersons, was thrust into the parlor. "Oh, Miss Emmalee, you is awake. Good mornin'. That Aphrodite, she say to tell you she be gone two-three days an' I's to stay here an' look after you."

"Gone? Where did she go, Sister Mae?"

"She don' say, Miss Emmalee. But she lef' early this mornin' wearin' her mockin'bird hat an' carryin' a satchel. She got a hitch wit' that Lazarus to somewhere."

"Two or three days?" Emmalee frowned and tapped

125

an impatient bare toe on the carpet. "Well, I certainly can't wait that long if I intend to rescue Charles Henry. Sister Mae, will you help me pack my luggage? I have a trip to make."

"But, Miss Emmalee, that Aphrodite, she tol' me stay here an' take care of you."

"That's all right, Sister Mae, you can stay here and take care of the house until Aphrodite returns. It will do her a world of good to have the place to herself until I get back. And she does dislike travel so. Come now, I'll get dressed and you can help me pack."

By midmorning the parlor was full of trunks, valises, and bags, and a drayman had been sent for to haul the luggage to the rail depot. Sister Mae was distraught and a little stunned at the amount of baggage Emmalee would take with her. Emmalee was making one final rummage through the house to see if she had missed anything that the West might require when she snapped her fingers, hurried upstairs and came down carrying a large revolver.

Sister Mae's eyes went wide. "Miss Emmalee, what you doin' wit' that thing?"

"According to the best authorities, these are used quite a lot out West. Don't worry about packing it. I can carry it in my handbag."

Fire burned in a ring of seven stones on the packed-earth floor, dancing red highlights off the dim, close walls of what, at least on this side of the fire, seemed to be just what it had appeared from outside: a tiny, smoky hut. Aphrodite sat upright in a straight chair before the fire and tried hard not to look too closely at anything around her, particularly the moving darkness beyond the flames. For back there, where the fire seemed not to cast its light, sat Mama Trevalier. She had

126

not seen the witch-woman clearly, nor did she want to. Some things were better unseen. Glimpses told her that the back side of the hut was deceptive. The darkness there seemed to go on, as though it were a cave extending deep and down in dimness. And the movements there, beyond the fire, suggested many things: random dark flashes, suggestions of sullen embers burning, repetitive motion as of a large woman shelling peas in the murk, except that the things she was shelling writhed and curled and were larger than peas.

"I ain' never come to you before," she said in quavering voice. "But I needs help, Mama Trevalier."

"Hee, hee, hee." The cackle that rasped from the darkness was like wind in swamp grass, distantly heard. "Sooner or later, everybody needs help. Sooner or later folks come see Mama Trevalier. Sooner or later." The voice came as a wisp of sound, accompanied by vague impressions of unseen light, unheard laughter, scents of ozone, gangrene, and dark spices. "And when they come, folks pay Mama Trevalier's price."

"I come prepared," Aphrodite whispered, trying not to look. "What I needs is—"

"Hee, hee, Mama Trevalier knows what you need. Hush. The virgin's curse. Hee, hee, nobody lift the virgin's curse. Prophecy made is prophecy done. That cannot be changed."

"Then you can't help me?" Aphrodite's dread was tinged with relief. She wasn't at all sure how it might go to bargain with Mama Trevalier.

The voice was more distant yet but harsher now. "Mama Trevalier can always help. Aphrodite needs a charm. A fine juju for Aphrodite. Look beside you, Aphrodite. See what is there."

She looked at the floor beside her chair. A small thing rested there, smaller than a thumb.

"Pick it up, Aphrodite. It is a juju for you."

Hesitatingly, she picked up the object. It was a small bag, laced closed at the top. Its contents . . . she didn't care to think about what it might contain. The feel of it suggested unpleasant things inside.

"Keep it," the voice that was no voice breathed. "In its time it will help you, but only once. Now pay my price, Aphrodite. Say words."

Aphrodite closed her eyes and gulped. She knew the price.

"You said you come prepared to pay the price," the swamp-wind voice insisted.

"I said I come prepared." Aphrodite squared her shoulders and dropped the juju safely into her coat pocket. "I didn' say nothin' about no price."

Darkness extruded toward her, rolling to the fire. "Say words!" a shriek of foul wind ordered.

Aphrodite shivered and raised her eyes. "Now?" she asked, then hesitated a moment and nodded her head. "Mama Trevalier," she announced coolly, "Gabriel, he say tell you to go to hell."

When Aphrodite exited the foul hut she was moving faster than she had moved in fifty years, but she had the juju tucked safely away, and she did not look back at the anger roiling behind her. Four hundred yards away, Lazarus waited with the wagon. He had refused to go closer.

"Whoo," Aphrodite gasped as she climbed aboard the wagon. "It do pay to have influential friends."

"You got it?" Lazarus whipped the pair of mules into motion.

"I got it. A juju. Now all I got to do is stay with that girl an' keep the juju handy."

II

By the time the letter reached Emmalee Wilkes in Vicksburg, Charles Henry had made his way past Memphis by stage and rail, his path marked by emerging local legends. He had completed his historic passage of the Mississippi River and was on the Arkansas.

"Get off the boat," Captain Horatio Lawton ordered, pointing a trembling finger at the side rail where sweating crewmen and passengers were laboring to jury-rig a footplank across a mat of driftwood to the forested bank.

Charles Henry squared his shoulders. "I paid for passage to Little Rock," he pointed out.

"I'll refund your money," the captain said. "Now get off the boat."

"This is infamous," Charles Henry maintained. "As I see it, all you need to do to get the *River Belle* afloat again is—"

"Say no more!" Lawton shouted, fumbling coin from the tail pocket of his coat. "Not one more idea! Here, take this. Take it all. Your fare is hereby refunded in full. Now get off the boat!"

The *River Belle* lay canted in a mass of drift near the

north bank, her nose deep in the shoaling water, her wheeled stern high and dry atop a tangle of tumbled floating logs. The great paddle wheel which drove her was a rat's nest of fouled cable and accumulated flotsam. Lawton, on the verge of apoplexy, steadfastly refused to look in that direction. All along the rails, crewmen and passengers—those not involved in rigging the plank—stared open-mouthed at the shambles around them.

"Properly executed," Charles Henry observed aloud, "it might have worked beautifully. You know, you could have saved a day of negotiating around this jam, simply by conversion of your wheel to serve as a drawing winch. In Massachusetts they—"

Lawton forgot his resolve then and glanced sternward at the rearing mess that had been his propeller. Tears formed in his eyes. "I never heard such a stupid idea in my life," he breathed.

Charles Henry shrugged. "Well, if you didn't like the idea, I don't understand why you even tried it."

"It did sound . . ." Lawton began, then the crimson crept up from his collar again, and he clenched his teeth and pointed. "Get off the boat!"

Shaking his head, Charles Henry assembled his belongings, shouldered trunk, satchel, portfolio, and tripod easel and walked across the slanted deck to the shoreward rail. Passengers and crew stood aside to let him pass. Burdened by his load, it was awkward climbing onto the rail, but he made it on the second try and stared skeptically at the narrow plank jutting outward twenty feet, ending abruptly five feet above the end of another plank resting on the mat of fouled drift.

"This doesn't look very safe," he pointed out. "This first plank needs to be braced so it won't bend under my weight. Otherwise when I reach the end and step off, this first one will spring back into place and probably

130

damage your railing."

"Put an angle brace under this plank!" Lawton shouted at waiting crewmen, who hurried to comply, while Charles Henry waited, balanced atop the side rail, dwarfed by his luggage. In moments the jutting plank was securely braced. Lawton nodded and pointed again. "Get off the boat!"

"Welcome to the West," Charles Henry told himself, and paced carefully out along the plank. As he neared the end of it, the leverage of his weight twenty feet out caused it to lower slowly until its end rested on the next plank.

There were shouts behind him and a piercing wail from Captain Lawton. Charles Henry turned carefully. The low hull of the riverboat had tilted, and the *River Queen* was shipping water over her portside gunwales. Captain Lawton, at the rail, stood ankle deep in froth and waved his arms. "Get off the plank! Get off!"

"First the boat, then the plank," Charles Henry muttered. "There is no pleasing some people."

Turning again, he stepped carefully onto the shoreward plank and headed for the wooded bluff beyond the jam. There was a crash and more shouts behind him, but he did not again look back.

"I really should have done as that man Jed suggested," he told himself as he heaved his luggage, piece by piece to the top of the riverbank. "It would have saved time if I had simply crossed the Mississippi at Memphis rather than choosing the scenic route.

"But the riverboats really are fascinating," he went on, as he climbed the bank to join his luggage. "They remind one of palaces on the water. Or possibly swimming volcanoes.

"Well, at least I am now in the West," he said, reminding himself. He stood, stretching his long legs and working the kinks out of his spine. Behind him was the river, ahead a forest of hardwood and brush. "At least the early part of it. And I do have some good sketches to develop when there is time."

Hoisting valise, portfolio, easel, and trunk, Charles Henry Clayton tapped his hat securely onto his head and began walking. Following the river's wooded valley upstream, whistling a tune now and then to the rhythm of his stride, he put the miles behind him one by one and thought serene thoughts of western adventure, of being rich, and of holding hands with Emmalee Wilkes: a vision which conjured other, progressively more stimulating ideas which he lacked the experience to pursue very far.

Somewhere ahead, a hundred or a hundred and fifty miles, lay Fort Smith, and it was there Charles Henry intended to begin his great adventure. Beyond Fort Smith was unorganized territory. He felt certain that the real opportunities for wealth must lie in unorganized territories. Once a territory became organized, history indicated, it tended to fill up with people. And once an organized territory filled up with people, it tended to become a state. Charles Henry had spent his life in states—mostly Massachusetts, but of late in several others—and had yet to encounter any real opportunities for wealth. Not that he had looked for them, until Emmalee Wilkes came along, but looking back he could remember none.

In Massachusetts it was possible to become wealthy, but only if one were wealthy to begin with. There seemed to be no route from rags to riches in the settled climes, except those routes that required long years of endeavor and accumulation of pennies at a time. Charles Henry was not averse to hard work, but he didn't want to take that much time. There was no guarantee that Emmalee Wilkes would wait for him beyond an appropriate number of months. Getting rich he saw as a necessary requisite to getting back to the priorities of the moment, most of which required that he be in proximity to Emmalee.

He supposed that he might find a gold mine, or strike it rich in the timber business, or become a land baron if he could get in first on a promising development, and it was a continuing concern that most of the plans he could come up with required a certain amount of capital with which to begin. He understood what his uncle Jonathan Clayton Powers had meant when he said, "to make money, one must invest money," and this thought led him back full-circle to the dilemma of the organized states. To become rich, one should be rich to begin.

If that were a natural law, then, what was the lure of the West? According to the man he had heard in Philadelphia, people went west to get rich and succeeded in doing so. And it stood to reason that not all of them were rich to start with. Possibly the trick to the West was in the degree to which . . . he had been so wrapped in his thoughts that he hadn't noticed his surroundings.

He was no longer on a forest trail but had emerged into open fields, and the path he was following had widened into a cart road. Furthermore, he was not alone. A man on horseback was beside him, the horse pacing along abreast of him, the man looking down curiously, eyes shaded below the brim of a flat hat. The man wore sailcloth leggings and homespun shirt and carried a long rifle across his saddle.

Charles Henry stopped, set his heavy trunk on the ground and tipped his hat. "How do you do?"

"Do what?" the man asked.

"It's on the order of a salutation," Charles Henry explained. "I wonder if I'm still on the right road." The sun was high now, and he had no clear sense of direction. He had walked far enough into the open land that the river valley was out of sight.

"To where?" the man asked.

"Fort Smith, eventually, although I am sure there are points between. I understand Little Rock is somewhere ahead, if I am still going west."

"Could be," the man said.

Charles set his other luggage on the trunk, removed his hat, wiped his brow, then stuck out a hand. "My name is Charles Henry Clayton, sir."

"Do tell," the man commented, ignoring the offer to shake hands. Charles Henry noted that the man's hand rested on his rifle, which was pointed disconcertingly at Charles Henry. The man peered at him closely. "You a Gittings?"

"A what?"

"Gittings. You a Gittings?"

"No, not that I know of, though several of my ancestors on my father's side had some rather odd habits. They were from Rhode Island."

The man's eyes went dark and slitted. The rifle barrel twitched. "You funnin'?"

"No, they really were. Do you know anyone from Rhode Island?"

"You ain't a Gittings, you say you a MacLootie?" the man suggested, frowning.

"Not that I know of." Charles Henry pursed his lips and scratched his head. "I believe there was a Maclamore in my mother's lineage somewhere, but I don't recall any MacLooties."

"Nobody but Gittingses and MacLooties comes this way," the man growled. The frown was menacing now, the aim of the rifle pronounced. "Declare y'self, stranger. Which are you?"

Charles Henry backed away a step, real concern washing over him. "Which would you like me to be?"

he asked.

The man glanced toward a hilltop ahead, back of the road. The remains of a burned house stood there. "See that?"

Charles Henry looked at it and nodded.

"Virgil MacLootie's place," the man said. "It burned."

"That is a real shame . . ." Charles Henry began.

"I burned it."

"Good for you. Look, would you mind pointing that gun somewhere else?"

"Who's askin'?"

"Charles Henry Clayton."

"That's the same thing you said before. I never heard of you. What are you doin' here?"

"As I told you, sir. I'm on my way to Fort Smith."

"Walkin'? Carryin' a steamer trunk an' them other things? And no gun? How come you're out here without any gun?"

"I haven't had the opportunity to acquire one yet, though I intend to. That, and a bedroll and a horse. How do you know I don't have a gun?"

"You didn't put your hands up when I pointed ol' Meat-In-The-Pot at you. People with guns always raises their hands when a gun's pointed at them. People without just don't think about it. What's your name?"

"Charles Henry Clayton," Charles Henry told him for the third time.

"Well, at least you're consistent." The man nodded. "Maybe you are just passin' through."

"I certainly am. And may I ask your name?"

The man's eyes went narrow again, and the hand tightened on the rifle. "Who wants to know?"

Charles Henry took a long breath and sighed. "Charles Henry Clayton."

"Howdy, Charles Henry Clayton," the man said,

turning the rifle away. Then he leaned from his horse to shake hands with the surprised traveler. "My name's Virgil MacLootie."

"I thought you said you burned the MacLootie place," Charles Henry said.

"I did. Burned it after some Gittingses ran me out of it an' moved in. Caught some of 'em in there, too. Shot one whilst they was gettin' out. Abe Gittings it was, ol' Papa Bill's nephew, one of Papa Bill's brother Samuel's boys, from over to Brisket Hollow. His mama—Abe's mama, that is, Samuel's third wife—she was a Jones, one of th' Joneses from up around Big Roche an' thereabouts, about fourth cousin to my sister Mary's husband's brother Harold. Harold Jones. My sister Mary married Hobert Jones, is why we're kin. You got any kin?"

Charles Henry's eyes had begun to glaze. "Not right around here." He replaced his hat, lifted valise, portfolio, and tripod easel and said, "I'd best be on my way. I'm going west."

"I could tell that by the direction you was walking," the man said. "Mind if I ride along with you?"

"Not at all." Charles Henry glanced expectantly from his heavy trunk to the strong and unoccupied rump of the horse, wondering . . .

"Come along, then," Virgil said, and led off up the road. Charles shrugged, hoisted his trunk onto his back and followed.

A mile passed, and then another as Charles Henry plodded along in the wake of Virgil MacLootie's horse. They were cresting a hill when MacLootie turned in his saddle. "Like me to give you a hand with some of that there?"

"I'd appreciate it," Charles Henry said. He started to shrug the trunk off his shoulders, but MacLootie reached down and took the easel. "I can carry this.

Won't be too much of a bother."

"Keep a good hold on that strap there," Charles told him, "so it doesn't come open."

They had gone another mile, and Charles Henry had returned to his interrupted thoughts of riches when he heard a sudden, metallic snap and looked up to see Virgil MacLootie somersaulting backward off his horse, which was now occupied by a fully flowered tripod easel. The man shrieked as he hit the ground, and Charles Henry dropped his trunk.

"I told you to keep a hold on that strap!"

From there to the cotton settlement of Hibley, it was Charles Henry's turn to ride. With a broken arm and a concussion, Virgil MacLootie was in no condition to navigate a saddle.

Charles Henry had seen a drawing—an excellent drawing, the techniques of which he had studied—of plains Indians using travois. Inspired now by circumstance, Charles Henry had fashioned a travois of willow branches and soaked rawhide from MacLootie's pouch. The travois was adequate to carry Charles Henry's trunk, valise, portfolio, easel, and MacLootie.

Charles Henry carried MacLootie's rifle and kept an eye out for Gittingses.

Hibley was a tiny place, a cluster of cabins, a store, livery shed, and two churches where the citizens met once a week to praise God and twice a month to cast bullets. The local doctor was a shell-deaf veteran of the War between the States.

"That there is Virgil MacLootie," he shouted as he helped Charles Henry unstrap the injured man.

"I know," Charles Henry said.

"What?" the doctor shouted.

137

"I said I know! He has a broken arm!"

"What's he ridin' this thing for?" the doctor shouted. "His arm broke?"

"Yes!" Charles Henry shouted. "That one there, with the splint on it!"

The doctor looked where Charles Henry was pointing. "This arm has a splint on it!" he shouted judiciously.

"I know." Charles Henry shook his head and hoisted Virgil MacLootie onto his shoulder.

"What?"

"I said I know! I put it there!"

By the time Virgil MacLootie was bedded and tended in a cabin bunk Charles Henry had a headache. He had a meal of pork belly and beans at the doctor's table, served by a woman with cotton stuffed into her ears, then was given a corner by the hearth where he could sleep on a pallet.

Morning brought a breakfast of pork belly and grits. Virgil MacLootie sat on his bed, his rifle beside him, and glared wordlessly at Charles Henry throughout the meal. Finally he thumped his empty coffee cup down on the bench and said, "I reckon I am obliged to you for fetchin' me here. Ma Darcy says I fell offen my horse."

"You certainly did," Charles Henry agreed.

"Don't see how I could have done that, but I reckon I did because iffen you had walloped me you wouldn't have fetched me here afterwards. Where'd you say you was goin'?"

"West," Charles Henry told him. "I'm on my way to Fort Smith."

"Far piece for a man walkin' and totin' a steamer trunk. What you need is a horse."

"I certainly do. I had thought I'd get one at Fort Smith, but that was before I had to leave the boat. Do you suppose I could purchase a horse here?"

138

"More'n likely. Folly Brisco keeps a stable, though he'll cheat you iffen he can. Mother's uncle was a Gittings, one of the nephews of ol' Wiley Gittings from up around Potter's Knob, little brother to Hathaway Gittings that robbed the Stuttgart bank ten-twelve years ago—all of which reminds me, I'd best be ridin' out this morning. Word likely already out that I'm here, and Hibley be no place to fort up ag'in Gittingses." With considerable sweating and swearing Virgil managed to put on his shirt and coat, his injured arm paining him as he did. "Tell you what," he said, standing and picking up his rifle. "Iffen you will saddle Buckeye for me, I'll go along to Folly's with you and see you get a good horse for a fair price. Can't abide cheatin'."

Folly Brisco's livery shed was the largest building in the settlement of Hibley, a rambling, much-expanded structure combining livery stable, tackle stores, a smokehouse, and smithy with two storage barns, one of them a small log structure set aside from the rest for the storage of gunpowder.

Folly himself was a surly, barrel-chested man with a full beard and no liking for Virgil MacLootie or anyone who traveled with him. He did, however, have a few horses for sale and after some dickering punctuated now and then by the sound of Virgil's rifle being cocked, he agreed to a reasonable price on a good blue roan complete with a comfortable saddle, short-bit halter and trappings, and a set of copious saddlebags.

"That steamer trunk be in your way from here on," Virgil advised Charles Henry. "Best you pack what's necessary in them bags and leave the rest. Man travelin' far does best to travel light."

Charles Henry led his saddled roan across to the doctor's cabin. The doctor was away this morning, tending a family with pox, but the cabin was full of people, mostly women. They looked up guiltily from where Charles Henry's portfolio was spread open on the table, and the doctor's wife blushed. "Didn't mean to pry," she shouted, then blushed again and removed the cotton from her ears, continuing in a normal voice: "You do them drawings freehand, do you?"

Charles Henry beamed. "I don't mind you looking at them. Most of them are just sketches. I'll paint them later. Do you like them?"

"Oh, Lordy, yes." An aging woman near the wall nodded.

Another chirped, "I swan, I never seen the like. There's a feller lives way up by Jonesboro that paints pictures a lot, but his is mostly blobs an' swirls. These here, they look like folks and places."

While the admiring public of Hibley oohed over his works, Charles Henry set about unpacking his trunk and transferring clothing and effects into the two saddlebags. When the bags were full there was a lot left.

"I don't know what to do with all this," Charles Henry said.

"Leave it," Virgil said from the window. "We best move out. I'm gettin' a fidgety feelin'."

Charles Henry shrugged. "Why don't you ladies see if there is anything here you can use." With their attention diverted now to the trunk, he reclosed his portfolio and carried bags, valise, portfolio, and tripod easel out to stow aboard his roan. The horse endured the packing and strapping until it came to the easel. Charles Henry tried to lay the contrivance along the animal's starboard rail for lashing, and the horse danced away, a pained expression in its eyes.

"Come back here," Charles told it. "This isn't heavy. It won't hurt you." He tried again, and the horse sidestepped again. People crowded in the doctor's doorway to watch Charles Henry and his horse going 'round and 'round the hitching post.

"He don't like it," Virgil called. "He thinks it's ugly."

"How am I going to carry it, then?"

"Well, you might have to strap it on yourself because that horse sure don't want it strapped to him."

Charles Henry gave up. Carrying the easel under his arm, he took up the reins and started back toward the livery, Virgil falling into step beside him. From the house there was the chatter of enchanted women: "I believe these is the finest britches I ever seen." . . . "Land, wouldn't my George look likely in this here bib and cravatte." . . . "Lord, George would die before he'd wear the like." . . . "Then I'll bury him in it. Martha, do you have any idea what a body does with one of these?" And so on.

They were approaching the livery where Virgil's horse waited when the mountaineer tensed and shaded his eyes. Beyond the stable a close-riding bunch of men with slouch hats and rifles had turned the bend and were coming in.

Virgil hissed, "Gittingses!" and ran for the stable. Charles Henry tied his horse and followed.

The men had seen them and spurred their mounts, rebel yells rising on the morning air. Doors and shutters slammed.

Virgil MacLootie was in a dark corner of the stable, behind hay bales, his rifle in his good hand leveled at the open door. Folly Brisco was gone. "I knowed he'd lead 'em down on me," Virgil barked. "Find cover!"

A running horse thundered past the open door, and a rifle flared. Charles Henry dived for cover behind the smithy forge. Another shot from outside showered splinters from the doorframe.

"Why was it you don't have a gun, again?" Virgil yelled irritably from the hay bales.

"Guess I probably should," Charles muttered, rising to look, ducking again as a ball spanged off the anvil beside his head and howled away through the roof.

Another rider appeared in the doorway, and Virgil's rifle roared. A riderless horse veered away and ran.

"Yee-Haw!" Virgil shouted, struggling for a fast one-handed reload in the gloom of the stable. Then, "Hot damn, I cain't see a thing back here. You, what's your name! Grab up that lantern and fetch it here, quick!"

Charles Henry grabbed the bale of the coal-oil lamp and scurried across the stable as another shot thudded into an upright, and horses bolted through the back double doors and out into the corral.

With light, Virgil completed his reload and got off another shot. Outside, someone howled.

"Yee-Haw!" Virgil roared. "Got me another'n! Be still with that lamp!" He reloaded again. Then he peered out through the smoky doorway across from him. "That ought to hold 'em a minute or two. You take a look yonder in the store. Folly ought to keep a gun around here some'ers."

Taking the lamp, Charles Henry ran to the interior door and into the storage rooms. He looked hurriedly around, saw tackle and supplies but no guns. Beyond was the smokehouse, and he found nothing there, either. Thirty yards from the far door of the smokehouse was a little log building, and he ducked and ran for it. He heard a shout, and a rifle ball thunked into the logs as he heaved the door open and rolled inside, closing it behind him. Again, there were no guns to be found, just a stack of squat kegs. Outside there was more shooting.

Shaking his head in frustration, Charles Henry edged the cabin door open, saw the path clear and sprinted for the smokehouse. He ran through that, through the store rooms and skidded to a halt in the livery shed just as a yell sounded from outside, and a man spurred his horse directly at the open doorway,

142

leveling a rifle as he came.

The doorway had bar hooks on either side. Charles Henry sprang to one side of the arch, extended the folded tripod easel across and wedged it in the top hook on the far side. The charging horse went under it. The rider didn't. The shock of impact threw Charles Henry backward. The tripod easel, released, fell on the dismounted rider, sprang open and bounded forth into daylight, directly in front of two more riders.

Their horses had never seen a spring-loaded tripod easel in action. In an instant one of the riders lay stunned on the ground and the other was clinging to a bounding, crow-hopping mount careening off into the distance.

"Yee-Haw an' Godalmighty!" Virgil shouted from the shadows.

Then there was silence. Gunsmoke hung heavy in the stable, curling upward from the open doors, morning sunlight slanting in the dancing vapors. One Gittings lay moaning in the doorway. Two more were outside, one bleeding and one out cold. Beyond in the yard a fourth was crawling away, dragging a limp arm.

"Let's light a shuck," Virgil suggested, hurrying past Charles Henry, pausing only to kick one of the injured Gittingses in the ribs and take something off another.

Charles Henry retrieved his easel, inspected it quickly for damage, found none, folded it and ran to climb aboard the roan. Virgil was already on his Buckeye, circling and twisting, looking for further trouble.

As they pranced past the cabins of Hibley, heading west, Virgil lay his rifle across his lap and reached across, reins in his teeth, to hand something to Charles Henry. It was a revolver. "You hang onto that," Virgil said when his mouth was free again. "Man never knows when he might need one. Hot damn, I never saw nothing like that thing you done with that . . . that

143

thing. I was in bad because I was unloaded and couldn't reload without the lantern. By the way, where did you put that lantern?"

"I must have left it in that little house," Charles said.

"What little house?"

"That little cabin with all the kegs stacked in the middle of it."

Virgil stared at him, his face going white. Then he sank spurs into Buckeye. "Let's move!" he shouted.

III

The wagon road wound through forested hills and lush valleys, climbing into that area of mountains and streams that Charles Henry's tattered almanac told him had been named *Aux Arcs* by the French. Charles Henry tried several times to persuade the blue roan to carry the tripod easel tied to its saddle, then gave up and strapped it on his own back. The horse was willing to carry him, but he must carry the easel.

"Pride goeth before a fall," he explained to the horse.

Virgil reined back to squint at him above his whiskers. "Do you always talk to horses thataway?"

"Only when it seems appropriate." Charles Henry adjusted the easel on his back and remounted. "I think I will name this horse Captain Keech."

"Where'd you fetch a name like that from?"

"Captain Keech was a great-uncle of mine on my father's side. He sailed a packet out of Newport, but he went bankrupt after a while because he decided he would not carry anything wrapped in oilcloth and all the mail packings were oilcloth so he refused the contracts."

"Why did he decide that?"

"Because oilcloth was made out of muslin, and he

had a brother in the textile business, and he didn't like his brother and decided not to encourage the use of textiles."

"Sound to me like you come from a strange family," Virgil declared.

"My aunt Samantha thinks so. I don't mean *aunt* as in an actual aunt, you understand, since she really is more on the order of a fourth cousin, but I find it convenient to refer to her as my aunt. Do you see what I mean?"

"No."

"Why not?"

"Because I don't know what an *ahnt* is. I thought I did up 'til now. When you said a while ago that we *ahnt* makin' very good time up this hill I thought you meant like we *ain't* makin' very good time and was just talkin' funny like you do, but now I reckon *ahnt* means like your fourth cousin that you told me about is your *aint* Samantha, like my *aint* Pearly June except that she really is my *aint* an' you said yours wasn't. What you say that there horse's name is?"

"Captain Keech."

"How come you want to call a horse somethin' like that?"

They came up to Little Rock on the evening of the second day from Hibley and found space for their animals in a commercial barn. Charles Henry off-saddled both horses and stowed their gear. When he looked around, Virgil MacLootie had kicked up a bed of straw near Buckeye's head and was trying one-handed to spread a blanket there.

"What are you doing?" Charles Henry asked.

"Makin' a place to sleep."

"Don't be ridiculous. There is a good hotel just up the street. We passed it on the way in."

"I don't hold with hotels. Folks shouldn't pay for a

place to sleep."

"Nonsense. A good night's rest in a real bed will do you a world of good. I shall pay."

"In that case," Virgil said, tossing him the blanket to roll and picking up his rifle, "let's go."

The hotel was a three-story structure with a chandeliered lobby which fairly swarmed with people. Charles Henry edged his way to the desk while Virgil strolled circuitously around the room, rifle in his good hand, scowling at faces in the crowd. He nodded to ladies, squinted at men and kept his thumb on the hammer and his finger in the guard.

A bald man scanned Charles Henry from behind the registry book, practiced eyes taking in the well-cut traveling clothes, somewhat dusty but still elegant, and he managed a tight-faced smile. "Yes, sir?"

"Accommodations." Charles Henry tipped his hat to him. "Do you have two rooms?"

"Only one left, sir. Sorry."

"Well, then, one will have to do. The names are—"

Suddenly Virgil was beside him, glaring at the desk clerk, edging Charles Henry away to hiss into his ear, "Don't say my name in here!"

"Why not?"

"Gittingses!"

Charles Henry looked around the room, saw no one paying them any attention, and shrugged. He turned back to the desk. Virgil was beside him, leaning casually on the desk, facing the lobby crowd, hat low over his eyes.

"In my name," Charles told the clerk.

"Very well, sir." The man raised his pen.

The room was noisy, and a group of men wandered near, arguing in loud voices. " . . . say the market's gonna fall an' we best sell futures on th' whole dang . . ."

147

". . . Henry," Charles continued, and the man dipped his pen.

" . . . drought over in Tennessee," a man explained loudly. "They won't make a bale to the acre. Why, if we's to tie ourselves to . . ."

"Clay . . ." He was drowned out by another haranguer demanding his say, something about "adjustable futures."

Virgil shook his head and spat. "Ain't any of them a-going to get rich lessen they get their facts straight."

"Very well, Mr. Clay," the clerk said. "Room two forty, up the stairs and to the right." He held out a key.

Clay? Charles Henry looked at the upside-down ledger. Then he grinned as the argument increased by decibels behind him. He said something to the clerk, but the clerk just put his hands on his ears and shook his head.

Charles tried again, stabbing a finger at the name written their, first to the right, then to the left as he shouted, "Charles . . . ton!" The clerk thought a moment, then picked up his pen and nodded. *"Charles* Henry Clay-*ton,"* Charles said again, but it was lost in the dispute over cotton futures.

Charles Henry reached to his waist, extracted a flat wallet and opened it, bright currency revealed in the lamplight. Virgil MacLootie reacted instantly, shoving hard against Charles Henry, hiding the wallet, barking at him in the din, "Ye damned fool, don't show that here!" With a quick glance around, MacLootie hissed, "Quick, three dollars an' put the rest away!"

Surprised, Charles did as he was told. Then Virgil moved aside, and Charles handed the clerk three dollars and took the key. Virgil hovered near, his eyes wide and his rifle ready. Again and again he shook his head. "Knothead," he proclaimed, the word lost in the din.

Three other pairs of eyes had seen the flash of currency in that unguarded moment. Midway across the lobby two men glanced at each other, then began maneuvering separately for better proximity to Charles Henry. And to one side of the desk, near the stairs, a small, splendidly attired individual sitting on a carpet-bag came to his feet, blinked furiously, then looked away quickly and began pacing in thoughtful circles.

A pair of hillmen had entered the front doors, grunting and panting as they carried between them a new-shaped stone grinding wheel. Bent to their efforts, they side-stepped across the crowded lobby, jostling people aside, and brought the heavy stone to the desk. "Where you want this?" one of them demanded. The clerk stood on tiptoe to look over his desk at their burden.

"What is that?"

"What do you mean, 'what is that?'" one of them said panting. "What you think it is, bear sign? It's a grindstone. We was told to deliver it here."

"Well not in here," the clerk admonished. "Take it around to the back, you idiots!"

The older of the men dropped his side of the stone, leaving the other to juggle the angled disk and wrestle it upright, bumping Charles Henry as he did so. "You mind your mouth," the older told the desk clerk. "They said bring it to this hotel, and here it is. All I asked you, politely, was where you wanted it."

"Well, I don't want it in the lobby," the clerk shouted.

Virgil MacLootie had edged aside to make room for the men. Beyond them Charles Henry straightened his hat, picked up his valise and reached for his saddlebags. "Come on, Virgil," he beckoned. "Let's go find number two forty, then we can wash up and look for something to eat."

His saddlebags seemed stuck to the floor. With a

shrug he crouched and heaved, then swung them across his shoulder and headed around toward the stairs.

Virgil MacLootie's eyes bulged as he watched the big grindstone, propelled by Charles Henry's saddlebags, shoot away from the desk and thunder across the crowded floor. It hopped across the toes of a gentleman smoking a cigar, and that gentleman howled and danced away, bobbing and hopping, people caroming from him on all sides. The rolling stone meanwhile attacked a gowned lady from the rear, rolling into the trailing edge of her gown, folding the cloth about itself and throwing the lady into a back flip as it shucked her out of the garment and headed for the door, a thundering, thrashing monster in blue velvet, wild with flailing hoops. Smashing a chair and throwing a porter's bench aside it leapt out the doorway, careened across the porch and down the wooden steps to rampage into the dim street. Women screamed out there, horses reared in panic, bullets pierced the blue velvet and ricocheted off stone.

The two hillmen diverted their attention from the desk clerk to stare at the empty floor where their stone had been, and Charles Henry turned at the foot of the stairs.

"Come along, Virgil," he said, then stared at the pandemonium in the lobby. The middle of the room was littered with recumbent people, including a screaming lady in pantaloons. Outward from center a wave of ricocheting people swept to the walls. "My Lord," Charles Henry said. "What have they done now?"

Outside, out of sight, there were more shouts and curses, shots fired and the panicked neighing of horses tangled in their traces. Then there was a crash of splintered wood, cascading sound of broken glass and more screams, distant now, as from inside a distant building.

150

Charles Henry dropped his burdens at Virgil MacLootie's feet and hurried to help the shucked lady to her feet. He tipped his hat as she gained her equilibrium and ran screaming for the back of the hotel. Charles went to the open front doors and looked out at the shambles in the street. A hitch rail lay flattened; and there seemed to be a wild party going on in a broken-fronted shop across the way.

He returned to the stunned MacLootie, picked up saddlebags, valise, and MacLootie's pouch and said, "Come on, Virgil. Let's get washed up." Climbing the stairs he confided to his speechless companion, "You know, this place is just like other places. People are so careless sometimes, it's unbelievable."

Behind them two men in separate parts of the lobby untangled themselves, one from a mass of fallen citizenry, the other from an overturned chair, and regrouped in time to watch Charles Henry herd Virgil MacLootie into number 240, upstairs. And a small, elegant individual crawled out from beneath the stairway, dragging a carpetbag behind him, in time to watch the same thing.

The desk clerk stood frozen behind his desk, his bald head draped beneath a thrown linen kerchief, and two hillmen wandered about the lobby looking for their missing stone.

In room 240 Charles Henry filled a wash basin, then helped Virgil MacLootie get his coat and shirt off over his broken arm. MacLootie seemed unusually thoughtful, and Charles Henry had to remind him twice that it was impossible to get either coat or shirt past his right wrist unless he laid down his rifle.

Later, as they strolled along a side street, Charles Henry asked, "What did you mean, 'Gittingses'?"

"What about 'em?" Virgil's rifle lifted, and he glanced quickly around.

151

"Back there in the hotel. You told me not to say your name. You said, 'Gittingses'."

"Oh. Couple of folks there in that lobby looked familiar, like they might have been Scruggses. You seen one Scruggs you seen 'em all. And if they was Scruggses they was Gittingses. It's all kind of one and the same."

"Related families?"

"Yeah. Old man Waldo Scruggs is second cousin to Mammy Lou Gittings, and then Marvin Hulsopple—he's a Scruggs on his mother's side—he married—"

"I understand," Charles Henry cut him off. "Did they see you, too?"

"I don't reckon. They weren't any Scruggses that I personally know. But iffen they had heard the name MacLootie there'd a-been hell to pay. Most folks around here is either Gittingses or kin to Gittingses or owes money to Gittingses. Little Rock ain't no place to speak of MacLooties. I'm goin' to breathe easier when I get up around Stonebridge. Most of them'uns is Mac-Looties. I can lay up there a bit 'til I get the use of this arm again."

They found a place near the river that served up pork belly and beans. It was full dark when they headed back toward the hotel, and Virgil had begun to fidget. The barrel of Meat-In-The-Pot swayed this way and that, following the quick shifting of his eyes under his hat brim. Charles Henry, for his part, strolled along the climbing path and chattered happily about moonlight, monochromatic gradations, and the nuances of shadow on paper until Virgil suddenly blocked his path with his rifle barrel and hissed, "Git your gun out!"

"Why?" Charles Henry pulled up short and peered around. "What's wrong?"

"Gittingses. Git your gun out."

"I don't have my gun." Charles reflected. "I may have left it at the hotel."

152

"Well, my land!" Virgil swung around to confront him, disbelieving. "What good will it do you at the hotel? We ain't at the hotel."

"I'm not sure I left it there. It might be in my valise, but then again I may have left it in my trunk at the horse barn. It is an awkward thing to carry around, you know, Virgil. I tried putting it in a pocket, but this coat has very shallow pockets and it kept falling out. Then I pushed it down the front of my pants but that really became uncomfortable. Don't you remember? Every-time I took a step the gun sank a bit lower, and finally had to work it all the way down my pantleg and then remove my boot to—"

"Hush!" Virgil whispered, and spun around, Meat-In-The-Pot swaying one way and another in the dark-ness, its length balanced in his strong hand. Voices, subdued but distinct, came from ahead of them. Voices and the sound of footfalls on the path.

"It might be in my saddlebags," Charles Henry sug-gested. "Of course they are at the hotel, too. Maybe we had better go and look."

"Will you shut up?" Virgil hissed angrily. "I think we got Gittingses!" Then he squinted in the darkness. "What is that in your hand?"

"This? A piece of rope. Someone left it dangling from a post back there and when I pulled on it it fell, so I just brought it along. Do you want it?"

Virgil shook his head and muttered in his beard. Then he ordered, "Stay behind me." The approaching men were nearer now, and a muffled voice came clear: "There's somebody, Jake. Is that them?"

As if in response a man's voice shouted from down the path, behind them, "I see you, Jake! Head them off! It's MacLootie!" A gunshot flared from down the path, echoed by hoofbeats—a running horse, closing on them. Charles Henry had no sooner spun around than

153

Virgil was beside him, leveling his long rifle one-handed. With a crack like a bullwhip its muzzle spat white flame, and a riderless horse loomed above them, its hooves churning the dust of the path.

"Here!" Charles Henry waved his arms, and the horse skidded aside, the whites of its wild eyes aglow in the murk, hooves prancing.

"You can't run about untended," Charles said, and stepped toward the horse. Virgil MacLootie was on his knees beside him, trying to reload with one hand. From up the path came the sound of men running toward them, and another shot. Charles heard the bullet whisk past. The horse shied and started to bolt, and Charles Henry, in desperation, threw the coil of rope at it, retaining one end. He was almost dragged off his feet when the rope caught somewhere on the horse or its trappings. "Whoa!" he shouted. "Stop that!"

The men were almost upon them, but Charles Henry had his hands full. He dug in his heels, and the horse pranced at the end of the rope, then bolted again, cutting across the path, stretching the rope as it began to run in circles, Charles Henry pivoting to keep from being pulled off balance.

The taut rope sang over the bowed head of MacLootie, taking his hat as it went. Behind him as he spun Charles heard a bull voice, high with victory. "Pray, then, MacLootie, for it's the last thing you'll . . . ark-k-k!"

The racing horse had come full circle, and its taut rope thumped and twanged as it took Jake Scruggs off his feet, bowled him into another man and flipped a third to land head-down on the path. The sudden pull of three men's weight turned the frightened horse, and it charged down-path, its dragging loop throwing the men into further gyrations.

Charles Henry yelled, "Virgil, jump!"

From a squat, MacLootie leapt into the air as the horse thundered by him and its rope whisked below him. "What the livin' hell are you doin'?" he flared at Charles. "I'm tryin' to set a load!"

At the end of its rope and running flat-out, the horse jerked the line from Charles's hand and bounded off into darkness.

"Now where the ever-lovin' is my ramrod?" Virgil fumed, casting about in the darkness.

Charles looked after the horse. "That animal is likely to hurt somebody," he said. Then he walked to the jumble of fallen men on the path. One lay peacefully atop another, who was groaning and thrashing about under his weight. There was a pistol in the man's hand, and Charles Henry took it from him carefully. "You'll hurt yourself with that," he said. The third man was crawling off into brush, moaning pitifully. As Charles approached him the man turned, brought up a gun and pointed it at him. Charles had forgotten the gun in his hand, had never realized it was cocked, but as he raised his hands before him the pistol roared and flared and the man screamed, his own gun flying off into darkness. Then he got to his feet and ran.

Virgil MacLootie came running, then skidded to a halt as he saw Charles Henry. He looked at the young man, looked at the injured pair on the ground, took a deep breath and roared, "Yee-Haw!"

They didn't find Virgil's ramrod but started back for the hotel without it and were within a stone's throw of the place when two men stepped out of shadows, knives flashing. "Give us the money," one of them said to Charles.

Without hesitation Virgil charged, his arm thrust forward, Meat-In-The-Pot's five-foot length held sideways. He took one man in the throat, the other full in the face with the buttstock and bowled them over, then

155

spun to deliver judicious thumps to their skulls.

Charles stood stunned, then tapped his hat on his head firmly and squinted at Virgil. "Well, are you going to Yee-Haw?"

"Shoot no." Virgil panted happily. "These'ns ain't Gittingses. Just a couple of thieves is all."

As they strolled away a small man in elegant attire watched from the shadows across the way, nervous fingers pulling at his lower lip. Weldon Hempley had decided that this was not a good time to approach the young gentleman in the top hat. Perhaps tomorrow.

Workmen scurried about the lobby of the hotel, working late into the evening to clean up some of the mess that had somehow occurred there.

By the time they reached the top of the stairs Charles Henry was walking in a decidedly odd fashion, stiff-legged, feet spread and bending to grip one leg about the knee. Virgil peered at him. "What's the matter with you?"

"Oh, it's this pistol. I'm going to have to work it down into my boot, then retrieve it from there."

"I thought you didn't have your gun with you!"

"Well, I didn't. This is another one. I didn't know quite how to return it, and I didn't want to leave it lying out there."

Later, when the hotel was quiet and only a dim lamp burned at the registration desk, two men in rough hill clothing crept through the front door, looked around, then marched across to the desk. They were bearded men and heavily armed but had the look of hunted men.

At the desk one of them thrust a gunsnout into the face of the clerk, and the other peered at the register, deciphering enough of the writing there to identify the number 240. Then he turned the book and held it before the clerk. "Who is this?" he whispered, pointing a large finger at a name there.

"Mr. Clay, sir," the clerk said nervously. "Henry Clay. From Charleston."

The two hillmen looked at each other. "I know that name," one said. "Don't recollect from where, but I've heard of Henry Clay, sure enough."

"Reckon you prob'ly have at that," the other said and nodded. "Cousin Will's got a hole in his wrist like nothin' I ever seen. He says he ain't never saw a man draw an' shoot like that'n. Man that good with a gun is bound to be known."

"You mean Virgil is a-travelin' with a famous gun-fighter?" The second one looked incredulous.

"Bound to be," the first answered. "You said yourself you knowed the name. Henry Clay. My land! What you suppose a man like Henry Clay is a-doing in these parts?"

IV

As days passed into weeks other legends were in the making.

Though few knew his name and few cared to ask, Jedediah Pike's notoriety spread steadily westward as more and more bystanders became aware of The Man in the Iron Cast. Rail passengers on the Tallahassee Special gaped silently at the man who occupied two facing seats in car four, swearing creatively and unrelentingly as he labored with files and saw over the ten-inch gear wheel around his ankle. A few, early in the journey, had offered assistance and found the man quite surly.

Aboard the little steam sailer out of Tallahassee, passengers and crew whiled their time watching Jed's continued labors. For four days as the vessel fought an opposing current Jed Pike ate a lot, slept a little and sweated copiously over a hand-cranked grindstone on deck, throwing showers of sparks and streams of profanity as the little wheel wore away at the metal casting which imprisoned him. Regularly, twice to the half hour, he would shout and a deckhand would come running with a bucket of water to pour onto his ankle, clouds of steam rising from the heated metal. Then Jed would begin again.

A surgeon aboard the *River Rebel* churning upstream from New Orleans took a look at the predicament, pondered alternatives and suggested, as gently as possible, "That heel may have to come off."

They fished the surgeon out of the river relatively unharmed, and no charges were filed against Jed Pike. There was a certain sympathy generated by his predicament.

The captain of the *River Rebel* even had a grindstone rigged on deck at the stern, geared and pulleyed to take power from the main drive of the vessel, and a pallet set there where Jed could lie in comfort while the grinding proceeded on his propped ankle. Crewmen came in relays to douse him with water.

When he transferred to the smaller steamer *Larkspur* for passage up the Arkansas, there was no such accommodation. It was back to files and saws and sweat.

Jed had one consolation. Despite his troubles, he was sure he was ahead of Charles Henry Clayton. He paused in his filing to check the loads in his repeating rifle, lick his lips and think about money.

Luther never knew who kicked him off the train. All he knew was when he dragged himself into the town of Vicksburg after five bad days on the road he was tired, miserable, weaponless and had a bad cold. He was ready to kill somebody.

From Vicksburg he sent a telegram to Boston. While he was waiting for a response he lurked in back alleys and bars, occasionally flashing the little money he had left. His best ploy was the simplest one. He would enter a saloon, sit sneezing and coughing at a lighted table long enough to drink what passed for beer in these

160

parts, then he'd pull out a roll of bills and peel one off to pay for his drink. Then he would sneeze again, lurch to his feet and stumble out into darkness. Usually, within a minute or two, someone would follow.

In this manner, in the course of two evenings, Luther acquired a pair of stilettos, a lead-weighted sap, a fairly good revolver, and more money than he had had when he started.

The response from Boston was negative. Bull Timmons was no longer there. Luther sent a message to Chicago and got a response within twelve hours. Bull Timmons had not returned to Chicago. There was a possibility he was in jail in Charleston—several people were in jail in Charleston—then again he might have left Charleston, but his associates did not know where he might have gone.

Luther sneezed his disgust, and the sneeze sent him into a coughing fit.

Luther's memory was hazy on some points, one of them being how he had come from cornering a victim in South Carolina to finding himself wet and cold in the baggage car of a train crossing Alabama. Then, shortly afterward, he had found himself again, bruised and dazed, in a ditch beside a railroad.

But he seemed to be heading west, so he had continued in that direction.

He had lost all track of the young man Bull Timmons had sent him to kill. But now, armed and supplied with funds, he began his stalk anew. Luther prided himself that he had never failed to find anyone he had gone after. In the process he made up his mind that, when this job was done, his next target would be Bull Timmons himself for sending him on this miserable journey.

Luther went to the post office.

"By dame id Claytod," he told the clerk there. "Id

dere ady bail for be?"

The clerk stared at him. "What?"

Luther pulled out a kerchief and blew his nose profoundly. "I said, my name is Clayton. Is there any mail for me?"

"Clayton?" The clerk sorted through stacks of general delivery. "No, sir, I don't see any Claytons addressed here. Sorry."

"Shid," Luther muttered, turning away.

The clerk was still looking. He glanced up. "Clayton, did you say?"

"Claytod." Luther nodded, his sinuses closing again. "Chahles Hedry Claytod. Did you fide sobtig?"

"Well, yes. There's a letter here with your name on it, but it's not to you. It's from you."

"If id's frob be . . ." Luther blew his nose again. "If it's from me, where's it from?"

"Looks like it's from Memphis, sir. Could that be?"

"Bust be. Who'd id to?"

"What?"

Luther swore and cleared his nose again. "I said, who is it addressed to?"

The clerk looked at him skeptically. "I don't think I can duscuss that, sir. If it is from you, then you know who you sent it to. Otherwise, it must be from another Mr. Clayton, and we can't reveal information about people's mail."

Luther glanced around. There was no one else in the building. Casually, Luther leaned on the counter, beginning to cough, and the clerk came closer. "Can I do anything, Mr.—"

Luther's arm shot through the grillwork, strong fingers closing on the clerk's neck, and he pulled the man against the grate. With his other hand he grabbed the letter, pocketed it, then pulled out his lead-filled leather sap.

In the afternoon he found the address on the letter. He knocked three times before a round black woman came around the house from the back and said, "Ain' nobody to home."

"W'ere did dey go?"

"What you say?"

He blew his nose. "I said, where did they go?"

"Lawsy," she said shaking her head, "nobody tell me nothin'. All's I know is, Miss Emmalee pack up ever' thing she own an' go off some'eres on th' riverboat, then that Aphrodite, she come back two-three days later and fine th' chile gone so she head off some'ers an' all's I know is, they ain' back yet."

Eventually Luther opened the letter and puzzled out its contents:

> *My Dear Miss Wilkes;*
> *I hope this letter finds you in good spirits and splendid proportion, just as I last saw you. I leave Memphis this day bound for Fort Smith, where I trust I shall begin accumulating wealth without delay. As they say, the early bird gets the worm, and I do so look forward to returning to you at the earliest possible opportunity.*
> *My best to Aphrodite and, to you dear lady, my undying anticipation.*
> *Y'r ob't s'vt,*
> *Charles Henry Clayton.*

Luther crumpled the letter and cast it aside. Fort Smith. He was going to Fort Smith.

At the waterfront in the evening Luther accosted a man hauling fishbox lines. "'Ow do I ged to Ford Smid?"

*　　　*　　　*

The gray man did not have to pick up Charles Henry's trail from Charleston. He had never lost it. He was tempted several times, as he dogged the Bostonian through the Appalachians and across the quiet plains, first by stage and then by rail, to put an end to the farce Edgar Egmont had begun: to simply close on the young man, kill him and take the money he had coming. It amused him darkly that he was, in fact, doing exactly what Egmont had intended. He was following along, letting the young man get a long way from Charleston before he completed his task.

But then, Egmont had been right on one point. There was so much structure of law in the East that any murder was chancy, whereas in the West almost anything—if done professionally—could be hidden forever.

And the gray man was a professional. He had many names, none of them traceable. He had many skills, all of them lethal. He never acted without thought and planning. Emotion was the mark of the amateur in his field. Emotional action led to complications, and the gray man never, in more than twenty years of plying his trade, had problems with complications. The people he was sent after simply disappeared, neatly and permanently with a minimum of questions asked later.

His price was high, but he was worth it. And his willingness to follow one young numbskull halfway across the country to collect a paltry two or three thousand dollars was born of a second motive. Dooley—the name by which Edgar knew him—had been in the East too long. Instinct told him it was time to try new places. And good intelligence told him the fields of the West were fertile for one competent at his trade.

So he followed Charles Henry, keeping him often in sight and always in reach. Twice they rode the same train, once the same stagecoach. And once the gray man had stood over Charles Henry's undefended back as the young man knelt to drink from a spring in the wooded hills of Alabama.

Dooley was in no hurry. Somewhere, when he was ready, he would kill Charles Henry, take his money and simply vanish. He thought of East Texas as a good place to set up shop after that. He also was considering the growing market for his skills in California.

Dooley had no concern about losing Charles Henry. The young man was naive to the point of nincompoopery, open and visible, noticeable in any setting by his manner, his dress, and his speech, and by some of the bizarre things he tended to do. Dooley had seen several odd occurrences along the way, as well as several mildly eccentric actions by Charles Henry, but there were no sure connections.

No, it was unthinkable that he might lose his quarry.

The unthinkable happened outside Bryson, where the rail crossed from Alabama into Tennessee. The wood-burner, chugging through backlands, stopped for water at a place where sluice gates fed a flue with water impounded above a high field.

It was the third occasion for Dooley to be on the same train with Charles Henry, and caution dictated now that he remain in a different car. The young man might be dimwitted, but he had eyes.

The halt was leisurely, the day bright, and Dooley watched the young man step off the car ahead, set up his easel, set a portfolio pad in place and begin to draw, obviously entranced with the intricacy of the wooden flue structure descending through pristine forest to the waystop.

The ground where the tripod stood was sloping, and Dooley watched as Charles Henry tried to adjust his easel to accommodate it. First he moved a rock into place for one of the legs, then looked around vaguely,

165

walked out of sight for a moment and placed a smaller object under a second leg. Then he resumed his drawing.

Dooley got off the train to stretch his legs, staying beyond and behind Charles Henry so as not to attract his attention.

For a half hour the artist worked as people from the train strolled back and forth along the roadbed or gathered ahead to watch the crew take water into the boilers. Then it was boarding time. From ahead, Dooley watched Charles Henry fold his equipment and reboard his car. Satisfied that his quarry was safe, Dooley strolled back toward his own car. He paused near the coupling, then stooped and picked up an object lying on the ground. It was an odd contrivance, like a short shepherd's hook made of heavy guage steel. It looked vaguely familiar.

Carrying his find, Dooley boarded his car and settled into his seat. A porter came through from the rear, stopping at each car to release the wheel locks. Dooley felt the train lurch and begin to move, heard the engine's whistle and the emission of steam. He turned the heavy metal object over in his hand, puzzling over it.

There was hurried, startled conversation in the car around him, and he glanced up, puzzled, then looked out the window. They were going backward!

With an oath Dooley dropped the metal thing, got to his feet and ran to the front of the car. He threw open the curtain and looked ahead. The rest of the train was gone. Ahead was just a forested rise, ribbon of rails receding rapidly as the car he was in—and those behind it—trundled downgrade and backward, heading for the Alabama line.

Dooley the professional, Dooley the competent, gray killer with the flawless record, stood with his

166

mouth open and watched the forest pass. Then he pursed his lips, made his way carefully back to his seat and picked up the object he had left there.

He knew what it was now. He had seen coupling pins before.

At Little Rock on a bright morning Weldon Hempley slicked back his hair, gave an ineffectual brushing to his sparse moustache and shrugged his small shoulders to perfect the alignment of his elegant coat. His boots were blacked and shined, his cravat flawless, his linen spotless.

With a nod of approval for his own irresistibility, he retrieved a leather case from his carpetbag and opened it to reveal a set of documents, which he leafed through carefully. He made some notes on a pad, inventoried the checkmarks and notations on a list of written descriptions, then closed the case and went down the hall to room 240.

He knocked carefully, then stood aside. He remembered vividly the reaction of the other man—the one with his arm in a sling—to sudden confrontation.

There was no response. He knocked again, then tried the door cautiously. It was unlocked. Inside was an empty room, no personal effects and no luggage. Hempley closed the door and hurried downstairs. The desk clerk was supervising a team of workmen repairing furniture. From across the street came the ring of hammers, the whine of saws.

"Excuse me." Hempley tugged on the clerk's coat-sleeve. "I was trying to find Mr. . . . ah . . . Clay. Mr. Henry Clay? Do you know where he might be?"

The clerk scowled at him. "About half of Little Rock seems to require that information. All I know is, he and his companion departed very early this morning."

"Oh." Hempley's shoulders sagged, his hopes fading. "Then I don't suppose anyone knows where they went?"

"Enough people have inquired about that this morning," the clerk said, "that the information seems to have filtered through. As I understand it, they went west on the Stonebridge Road. And I suspect they have quite a following by this time."

Hempley trudged back up the stairs, returned his case to his carpetbag and sat on the edge of the bed. He had been so close. Only one parcel left. All these months, traveling and pushing, doing his best, and one left, and he had felt such a strong hunch last night. The man was well dressed, he was a stranger, he was going west, and he had cash money.

"So close," Hempley muttered to himself. Then a feeling of resolve began to grow. One does not come that close to a likely score and then just give up.

Weldon Hempley stood, squared his shoulders again, picked up his carpetbag and went to find and harness his buggy. He was a long way from St. Louis now, a long way from the people who made decisions for him. He would make one of his own.

He had intended to end his circuit at Little Rock, then circle back by way of Springfield and Jefferson City, to St. Louis.

But no one up that way had any money. He had made the route before.

When Weldon Hempley headed out of Little Rock, he was westbound on the Stonebridge Road.

V

As the sternwheeler *Merriwether Lee* belched and thrashed its way northward along the sullen river, its plume of dark smoke drifting aside to subdue views of the east bank in the distance, Emmalee Wilkes stalked the promenade deck impatiently, twirling her parasol.

Somewhere ahead and to the west Charles Henry stood alone against the wild land, facing unknown terrors and hostile elements for which he had no defenses. Somewhere out there he needed her—needed her level head to think for him, her assurance to guide him, her presence to get him out of whatever predicament he currently was in—yet this boat proceeded at a stately creep, and there was nothing she could do to speed its pace.

She had already visited the Texas deck, where her presence had left the captain and three officers goggle-eyed and willing to risk their ship and their livelihoods for an opportunity to gaze again into her dark eyes. But a sternwheeler is a sternwheeler, and the boat could only go so fast.

Male passengers tipped their top hats to her as she passed, stumbling over one another in hope of a glance or a smile. The morning was barely two hours old, and already she had declined invitations to four companionable strolls on deck, five tea-and-sweets in the saloon and two visits to private cabins. She had begun to regret the absence of Aphrodite. For all her eighteen years of worldly experience, Emmalee knew little of the nuances of dealing with pleasant gentlemen with hungry eyes. Aphrodite had always run interference for her, before.

The boat rode heavy in the water, loaded with cargo and passengers. The gentlemen aboard seemed to divide roughly into four groups: those who were following Emmalee; those who stared after her with soulful expressions but were constrained by the presence of their wives; those who were busy running the boat; and a smattering of hard-eyed individuals who seemed to have no interest in the bright morning, fresh sunlit air, birdsong, and the sounds and smells of the river, but rather who kept themselves to smoky tables in the fore end of the saloon, playing cards. She had the impression they lived there.

In slate-gray traveling attire with pale lemon blouse that matched her gray-trimmed bonnet, carrying parasol and handbag, Emmalee paced the decks of the *Merriwether Lee* and stewed at the slowness of travel.

She paused at the port rail, crossed lemon-gloved arms on the varnished mahogany and gazed at the west bank creeping past. Here the bluffs softened, stepping down toward the river in a series of swells, and much of the forest had been cleared for planting. Tiny across the expanse of brown water, men worked in their fields, hoeing and chopping. There a wagon rolled on a distant road, angling down toward a village ahead. There a man on horseback jumped his mount across an obstacle and turned it to trot away into the forest. And there a woman walked across a barn yard followed by a half-dozen children, all carrying pails.

170

Emmalee smiled to herself. It would be pleasant to walk across a barn yard followed by a half-dozen children carrying pails. She envisioned their young faces, bright and inquisitive and trusting—a bit like Charles Henry.

And with that thought she began worrying again. It was taking a long time to get to somewhere from where she could begin finding Charles Henry, and who knew what trouble he might be in even as she stood here admiring the scenery.

She turned from the rail and bumped into a gentleman standing directly behind her.

"Excuse me," she said. She started around him and was stopped by his hand, gently commanding, on her arm.

"Whatever for, my dear?" He tipped his hat and smiled knowingly into her eyes. "I have not been so honored in a very long time. Permit me the liberty, my name is Crouch. Col. Dyson Crouch."

"Miss Emmalee Wilkes," she told him, trying to shrug off the suggestive hand on her arm.

"Yes," he said with a smile. "I know. I had a look at the passenger registry, you see. Oh, please, I didn't intend to pry. It is just that a young lady—such an exquisite young lady, if I may—and traveling alone— well, a man must be forgiven a certain curiosity in such matters, don't you think?"

"Not necessarily." The pressure of his hand was somehow unpleasant and she shrugged it off. He was a fairly tall man, handsome in a knowing way, but his eyes said he knew distinctly too much. Emmalee decided she didn't like him.

"Of course." He chuckled. "The protocols, by all means. Perhaps we should walk along the deck for a time, let all the passengers see us becoming acquainted— quite innocently and casually, of course. Perhaps then

171

we might take our noon meal together, then climb to the observation deck and gaze at the scenery for a time. Chance encounter, so to speak, developing into a lovely relationship. I assure you, Miss Emmalee, Col. Dyson Crouch is a man who knows how to be discreet."

Emmalee's eyes widened as she began to catch the drift. "See here, Captain—"

"Colonel, my dear, if you please."

"See here, Colonel, I believe you are making an improper advance. If my woman servant were here she would know how to deal with you."

He pursed his lips, still holding her eyes with his knowing gaze, then he chuckled. "Ah. That is a pretty touch. A pretty touch by a pretty young lady. Yes, I like that. And we shall play the game that way. We shall pretend at innocence and discretion right up to the—unh!"

Emmalee had given up trying to shake off the cloying, commanding hand and resorted to poking him in the belly with her parasol. He turned her loose and backed away.

"Now that," he snapped, "was uncalled for." Just for an instant the urbane humor dropped away, and Emmalee shivered at the ugly hunger that showed through. She backed away, started to turn but he took two long strides and blocked her path again, his eyes now inventorying her body as though it were merchandise.

"Don't do that again," he said. "My patience is limited. Now, name your price."

"My—my price?" Her lip trembled in consternation. Suddenly she realized what she was hearing and felt the warmth of a blush creeping up her neck.

"Certainly. I am prepared to make a generous offer—possibly even to bid for the entire journey provided we have certain understandings between us."

"Captain Crouch!" She felt as though she were going into shock. She glanced around in panic but there was no one else near at the moment.

"Colonel," he insisted. "Well, name your price, my dear, and the game can begin."

"Oh!" She turned away, hurried from him to the stern quarter of the deck where chairs and frilly tables decorated the platform high above the water. He followed her, and again the insistent hand was on her arm, sliding around this time toward her bosom.

She twisted away, shaking her head, thinking furiously—all those books, all that study, wild Indians, outlaws, blizzards, stampedes, but nowhere had she found instruction for dealing with Colonel Crouches.

"Well," she said, raising her chin and looking at him squarely, "I suppose we all do what we must." Then she set her parasol and handbag on a table and began peeling off her gloves.

"Ah," Crouch said, a delighted smile on his assured face. "Now we are getting somewhere." He leaned against the railing, crossed his arms and watched her contentedly.

"Yes," she said. "We are about to." She pulled out a wrought-iron chair, testing its weight delicately as she did so. Then she turned and charged.

Chairlegs bracketed the man's face, rungs collided with hat and starched collar, and Emmalee braced herself and pushed. The man's arms went wide, wind-milling for balance, then he was no longer there. A glimpse of spatted feet above the rail and he was gone.

Emmalee took several deep breaths, trying to calm herself. She returned the chair to its place by the table, pulled her lemon gloves on again, picked up her handbag and parasol and marched to the gangway leading down to the cabin decks. On the lower decks people were shouting, and there was the creak of davits and winches as lifeboats were lowered overside.

On her deck a purser ran past, shouting, "Man Overboard!" She watched him pass, fury in her dark eyes, then turned to unlock her cabin.

"Nonsense," she muttered. "Such a fuss. It was only Corporal Crouch."

For a time she paced her room, until her breathing became regular and the flush of anger subsided from her cheeks. Then she opened one of her trunks, the one containing all the reference books she had not yet the time to study, dug through them and came up with one. It was a small, discreetly covered book with its title embossed in self-effacing sans serif characters: *Genteel Recourses for Social Situations*.

She sat, opened the book and glanced through its table of contents, then turned to chapter three: *Dealing with Lewd, Lascivious and Lecherous Behavior*. She retrieved a pad and pencil, and as she read she made notes.

Fortified finally against further such frustrations, she returned to her consideration of how to make the time pass until she reached the Memphis crossing and could head west in search of Charles Henry. She didn't want to stroll on deck anymore. One Colonel Crouch was enough. She went back to her trunk of books, rummaged through them and came up with *Popular Pastimes of the Western Frontier—A Lady's Reference to Rituals, Rules and Strategies*.

She found the correct chapters, read them, thought for a while, read them again, made a few notes, studied her notes and then picked up her handbag, locked the cabin behind her and descended to the main deck.

In the saloon, three tables were occupied by hard-eyed gentlemen absorbed with their games. She selected a table, pulled up a chair and slapped down a

174

thin stack of bills.

"Deal the cards," she told the startled gentleman next to her. "I'll cut."

On a serrated mountainside where pines whispered in the spring breeze, Charles Henry Clayton sat on a ledge and applied suggestions of magenta to the rich depths of valley tones emerging on his pad. Top hat cocked at a rakish angle, linen sleeves rolled up and his tongue sticking out of his mouth, he dabbed bright color with his brush, touched in a quick water-wash, then switched brushes to capture and outline the tints with a mix of rich umber and royal purple. He gazed at the result critically, then nodded and looked out across the wide valley opening before him.

The rolling mountains in the distance, carpeted with forest and increasingly hued in rich azure as the sun quartered above them, reminded him of those he had sketched but never painted in the Carolinas. Yet these were different, richer somehow in texture, less abrupt in form—more comfortable mountains than those but with a certain wildness that was all their own.

The mountainside dropped away below him, down and down to a deep valley whose depths looked cool and secret. Then the forest spread up and away, rising into the swell of mountainside beyond.

He looked back to his painting, was tempted to modify and amplify, but constrained himself. It was complete. It was the scene before him, complete with suggestion of the passage of time involved in its execution.

"Ah." He smiled, setting the pad aside to dry. "As Master Dubois always said, the essence of art is knowing when to stop." He turned to Captain Keech, grazing nearby. "Well, what do you think?"

175

The horse looked up curiously then resumed its munching at the rich mountain grasses.

"What do horses know, anyway?" Charles Henry stood, stretched his arms and rolled his shoulders. Nearby, a pan of coffee sat beside the coals of a small fire. He strolled to it and refilled his cup. "When I am wealthy I may bring Miss Emmalee here. We might even decide to stay here. Do you see that knoll down there?"

The horse ignored him.

"What a lovely spot for a house. We could have a cistern just about there, and I could devise a method of pumping water right into the house so that she wouldn't have to go for it with buckets."

Distantly he heard the sound of a horse approaching, scrabbling gravel at a steep place on the trail.

"And a barn. We would need a good barn. I probably could devise a lift of some sort so that she wouldn't have to pitch hay into the loft. A lift for the loft." He turned again to the horse. "This is a pretty good conversation, Captain Keech. You should pay attention."

The sounds of approach were nearer now, and Virgil MacLootie appeared around a shoulder of the slope. His wide hat was pulled low over his whiskered face, long rifle across Buckeye's saddle, and he wore a fresh sling on his arm.

"Got back as soon as I could." He dismounted, dropped Buckeye's reins and clapped the horse on the rump. Buckeye wandered off to join Captain Keech. Meat-In-The-Pot was sporting a brand new ramrod. "Cousin Millicent said to say howdy to you."

"Cousin Millicent?"

"Millicent McGrath. Sweet little thing—need to stop and visit her now and again or she gets lonesome. She ain't a close cousin, more a kissin' cousin, so to speak. Here, I brung you this."

176

He tossed a large piece of cured leather to Charles Henry. "Get out your gun," he said.

Charles stiffened. "Gittingses?"

"No, just a chore to do. Douse some water on that there leather. Soak it good, so's it's soft. This coffee still hot? Good. You can work on this flat rock here. I'll show you what to do."

"What am I doing?" Charles Henry inquired, wetting the leather.

"You're fixin' to make yourself a holster for that there gun."

"Which one?"

"Doesn't matter. They're both navy thirty-sixes. They're just alike. Now spread that leather on that rock, take out your knife an' I'll show you where to cut."

With Virgil instructing, Charles Henry shaped a piece of leather twice and a half the length of one of the pistols, trimmed its two ends to the shape of spades, cut horizontal slots at one-inch intervals down one end and shaped the other around the pistol, trimming it so it made a neat sleeve.

"Doin' good." Virgil nodded. "Now set the gun aside an' fold the whole thing over in the middle. Now, all you got to do is lace the sleeve end through the slotted end—that's right, in one slot and out the next, all the way down. Now pull it tight and lookee there what you got."

Suddenly, the leather was a completed holster, self-contained and self-fastened, its centerfold forming a broad loop to hang from a belt.

Virgil grinned broadly. "Ain't that something? Up in these hills, folks have to figure ways to do what's needed with what's at hand. That there's a way somebody figured to make a holster iffen you don't have no rivets or yarn or a needle and awl to sew with. Makes a fair fast holster, too, once it's oiled up.

"Now," he continued, his expression turning severe, "you put that thing on your belt and put that there loaded gun in it and don't never let me see you runnin' these hills without it, ever again!"

Startled at the command, Charles Henry did as he was told. The holstered gun at his hip had a comfortable feel to it, and its butt was just where his hand would be if he should want it.

"Leather be dry pretty soon," Virgil said, the severity gone from his tone. "And when it is, it'll fit that there pistol like a glove. What's this?" He set down his cup and picked up Charles Henry's pad.

"It's a painting. I did it while you were gone."

"Dang sight better'n anything I ever seen," Virgil said. He looked from the painting to the scene across the valley and back at the painting. "Reckon a man might hang this up if he wanted a picture on his wall."

He looked more closely at the picture, eyes narrowing as he picked out details. "Lookee here! You even got people in it."

"Where?"

"Right here—see, about where the trail breaks out on that mountain yonder. See these dots? Why, for all the world that's a string of men ridin' along there. Must be ten or twelve of 'em." He looked up. "When did you paint this?"

"While you were gone. I didn't see any men."

"Well, they're here. What I mean is, when did you paint this here part right here?"

"Probably an hour ago. Why?"

Virgil dropped the pad and picked up Meat-In-The-Pot. He turned to stare at the shoulder where the trail came down. "Run bring in them horses, fast as you can," he ordered.

Charles Henry scrambled to oblige. When he

returned to the shelf with the saddled mounts, Virgil had their possessions packed. The fire had been doused and scattered.

Charles Henry lashed their various luggage aboard the two mounts, had another argument with Captain Keech about the tripod easel before slinging it on his own back, then swung into his saddle. Virgil was already mounted.

"Come along now," he told him. "And you might as well get your gun out."

"Gittingses?"

"Right. Gittingses."

Far across the valley, where the trail broke out on the slope of distant mountainside, there was a flicker of color, a tiny hint of motion suggestive of a small, elegantly attired man aboard a spring buggy, traveling as fast as the mountain trail allowed.

VI

From the ledge clearing the trail swept downward in a slow curve around the flank of the mountain, and their horses fairly flew. Forest shadows flicked past, here pines like sentries, there scrub oak and walnut. The trail was a broad path here, and the mounts took to it with glee.

Charles Henry clung to his hat, eased his reins and let the blue roan have its head. The tripod easel clattered against his back and wind whistled in his ears. Virgil was in the lead for a time, leaning low over Buckeye's neck, flogging with heels and reins, a wilder sight than Charles Henry had seen in years of academy riding. Then as the path dipped through a hollow, the horses sheeting water from a stream as they bounded across, Captain Keech surged ahead, and Charles put heels to him, enjoying the sport.

Out across a high-grass meadow they raced, startled wildfowl bursting from cover before them, deer and smaller game fleeing from their path. Charles Henry held onto his hat, leaned low into the flying mane and rode. He heard the drumming of Buckeye's hooves just behind, keeping pace. Thin through the wash of wind came Virgil MacLootie's shout, "Let 'er rip, Johnny

Reb!" And a moment later, "Sorry 'bout that!"

The meadow raced by them, a wall of forest looming up ahead, Virgil flapped his heels and Buckeye leapt into the span between the two, slowly drawing abreast of Charles Henry.

"Be climbin' shortly!" Virgil shouted. "Run him out, then rein him in!"

Charles nodded, slapped his hat firmly down atop his ears and took the reins in both hands. "John Brown's Body," he howled, "lies a-molderin' in the grave!" The meadow slanted downward toward a meandering brook. Charles flicked his reins, tightened his knees and set his heels, then rose slightly in the stirrups. As Captain Keech bore down on the stream he raised the reins, just a touch to bring the horse's head up, then reached back to deliver a resounding slap to its rump. Captain Keech became airborne. "Yee-Haw!" Charles shouted. The touchdown on the far bank was flawless, forefeet finding the turf, hind legs thudding down to recapture the momentum, and Charles touched reins to lean the roan into a right veer onto an uphill trail. Immediately behind him he heard a shrill whistle.

As the upgrade became pronounced and forest overshadowed the path again, Charles eased back on the reins and brought the exultant Captain Keech down to a steady lope. Virgil pulled alongside again, grinning through his beard.

"You can ride, sure 'nough."

"Part of a gentleman's training, as they say in Massachusetts. But they don't have many horses like this in Massachusetts."

"Prob'ly got the sap bred out of 'em. Let's go left at the fork, the Bald Knob trail."

The path now led up and ever up, winding around shoulders of steep rise, sometimes bordering sheer precipices that made the horses cling to the bank. "Old Indian trail," Virgil told him. "Not used much now 'cept for special occasions."

The forest thinned and moments later they came out above it. Virgil looked back over his shoulder. "Just ahead we'll pull up, take a look-see."

The peak they were on was not the highest around, but its top was bare rock, an age-molded crest of granite. "This here's the original Bald Knob," Virgil lectured as they reined in on a wide ledge, letting their horses stamp and blow. "They got one up in Missouri they called Bald Knob, but it ain't the original one. It's just another one."

Two miles back and far below was the hollow they had crossed, its central meadow a bright fan of apple-green surrounded by dark forest. Moments passed, then a line of riders appeared at the far side, moving fast across the grassland.

"How many you make 'em?" Virgil was leaning from his saddle, intent on the scene below.

Charles Henry tipped his hat down to better shade his eyes. "It looks as though there are ten. No, I think eleven."

"They're Gittingses, sure enough," Virgil spat. "That there is Samuel Gittings hisself. Abe's daddy. The one in front. An' them two with the straw hats—see 'em? Them is Curly Joe and Sidney, two of ol' Papa Bill's boys. Can't make out the others just yet. Let's wait a bit."

Charles Henry glanced at him nervously. There were a lot of armed men down there. "Shouldn't we be moving along, do you think?"

"Won't do any good," Virgil said sourly. "They know we're up here and if some of 'em takes the Hickory Creek fork they'll be waitin' for us whichever way we come down."

"Well, for heaven's sake, Virgil, why did we come up here then?"

"So's I can see who we got down there, figure out what to do about it."

Charles Henry chewed his lip, pondered the situation and sighed. "Virgil?"

"What?"

"Back there when your arm was broken—as I recall, you fell on your head."

"Could be. I don't recollect."

"Virgil?"

"What?"

"Are you sure you're all right?"

Virgil was still squinting at the riders below, his whiskers working rhythmically as he chewed on a stick. Now he straightened, rubbed his eyes and squinted again. "Well I be a—do you know who that is ridin' with them Gittingses?"

"Which ones?"

"The last four." MacLootie pointed with his rifle. "The first one's Will Heath. Outlaw from up in Missouri, broke off from the James bunch because he couldn't get along with Dingus. Bad news, that's what Will Heath is. Bad news. I don't rightly know the next two but you can see how they ride—sort of like soldiers? They're some of Heath's bunch, sure enough. And that last one—by heaven if that don't look like Jamie Haak!"

"Hake?"

"Haak. It's a Dutch name. Jamie growed up in these hills, wildest young'un anybody ever seen, then he got hisself a gun an' went to killin' folks an' finally run off. Last I heard he was over in Texas, runnin' with a real bad bunch. Wonder what he's a-doin' here?"

"If those men aren't Gittingses, why are they after you?"

"Well." Virgil tipped his hat up and scratched his head. "Far as I know, they ain't. Them ain't feud folks. Mainest thing ol' Will Heath is interested in is robbin' banks an' trains. And as for Jamie Haak, mostly what he looks to do is build up his reputation as a gunfighter. He's mean as a snake already—an' fast as one, too. An' he just keeps tryin' to get faster. But they don't none of 'em hold me any grudge that I know of." Virgil sat back in his saddle, visibly worried. Then he turned a speculative scowl on Charles Henry. "Boy, is there anything you ought to tell me about?"

Virgil dismounted, walked out to the edge of the cleft and squatted there, watching. Charles followed.

"I never heard of any of them." He kicked at a pebble, then at a larger rock. It rolled off the ledge, bounced off a rock below, bounded off another and arched far out to the left to rebound off yet another, larger stone resting precariously against a tree trunk. The big rock wobbled, slid askew to the very edge of a lower bluff and lodged there, teetering.

"One reason these trails is dangerous," Virgil mused aloud, "rain and frost loosen up the rocks an' sometimes they just go a-slidin'."

The men below had reached the near edge of the meadow and gathered there, milling around. From up here, Charles could see that the trail forked there, one path leading upward to the crest where they stood, the other bending around the base of the rise. Distant faces turned toward them, then the party divided, five men turning right, six to the left.

"Virgil," Charles Henry ventured, "why are the Gittingses trying to kill you?"

Virgil mulled it over. "Kind of a long story, I reckon. Goes back to before I was borned. MacLooties and Gittingses settled out here, and after a while they didn't hit it off so there got to be some feudin' and finally the

185

two families just sort of put space between them. Th' MacLooties backed off up this way, an' the Gittingses backed off to the east. That settled things for a while."

"But then they started again?"

"Three year ago. Me and my cousin Frank—he was my mother's baby sister's oldest boy—we decided to settle us some bottom land, picked some out over past Hibley and built ourselfs a house. Gittingses didn't like that, so they come and run us off one night an' shot Frank right through the back of his head. So I laid up for a while 'til some of them moved in, then I just naturally burned 'em out an' got me one an' winged another 'n whilst I was at it."

"You told me about that part. Why were you out there this time?"

Virgil looked at him as though he lacked good sense. "I got to check my crops now and again, don't I?"

He got to his feet again, and they mounted their horses. "You want to lend me that extra pistol?" Virgil asked.

Charles Henry dug it out of his saddlebag and handed it over. Virgil checked the loads and thrust it into his belt. "H'yar we go!" he shouted and heeled Buckeye into a lope. Charles Henry wheeled the roan to follow.

"This is the way we came up!" he shouted. "Why are we going down the same way?"

"Because there's only five of 'em down here and six t'other direction! Why else?"

The horses danced down the rocky incline, their hooves throwing stones off the shelf. Then the path widened and Virgil gave a war whoop and kicked Buckeye into a dead run.

As Charles Henry raked Captain Keech, he heard rumbling sounds somewhere in the flanking forest.

Virgil had slipped off his sling and was riding now

186

with the reins in the splinted left hand, Meat-In-The-Pot held high in his right. Charles Henry clung to his hat and his reins and tried to stay close behind the hillman. The running trip up the Bald Knob trail had been an experience. The thundering trip down was a nightmare. Hard curves, sheer ledges, and beetling bluffs of rotten stone spun past. Vines and brush whipped at legs and loose gravel scudded from under blurring hooves. The trail wound and veered, and Virgil held Buckeye to a dead run.

At a tight bend to the right Buckeye skidded tail-down, put on a surge and disappeared around the turn. A second later Charles Henry heard a rifle bark. There were shouts. Then he was into the turn, Captain Keech wheeling and leaning to make the cutback. There were men and horses there. A man clung to a rearing steed in mid-path, another flopped loose aboard a horse pitching off into the brush, a third clung half dismounted to a skittish sorrel that was dancing on its toes and spinning in circles. In an instant Charles Henry was through them, past them, and just ahead was the flying back of Virgil MacLootie, waving Meat-In-The-Pot. "Yee-Haw!" floated back on the stinging wind.

A moment later MacLootie reined Buckey hard, turned and disappeared between cedar clumps beside the path. Charles Henry reined the galloping Captain Keech to follow. He pulled up.

In a tiny clearing Virgil MacLootie had dismounted and ground-reined Buckeye, and was squatting to thump a load into his rifle.

MacLootie said, "Come on," and jumped a deadfall to sprint away on a barely visible footpath, angling back up the trail. Charles Henry crammed his hat on tighter and followed. His long legs brought him up with MacLootie as the hillman rounded a broken shoulder of rock and clambered toward the top of a ledge.

At the top MacLootie eased forward, squatted and waved Charles Henry down beside him. They were atop a ridge bluff. Before them was scrub wood and past that was the trail. A man was just picking himself up from the ground there, another struggling to fight free of a stand of nettles. Two others were on horses, working to calm the skittish animals.

MacLootie watched them for a moment, then stood and raised his long rifle, using his splinted arm to brace its barrel. "You, Samuel!" he shouted. "Sam Gittings!"

One of the men on horseback stiffened, then swung around leveling a rifle.

"Don't shoot," Virgil said. "For iffen you do I'll surely kill you. Let's talk."

Sam Gittings hesitated but did not lower his gun. "I see you, Virgil MacLootie. What do you want?"

"Was it another Gittings I wanted, Samuel, you would be a dead man now. You've come a long way from home, Samuel. Why have you followed so far?"

"Blood demands blood, MacLootie. There's been killin'."

Virgil stood rock-still, in plain sight. "And that means it must go on, then? If you'll have it that way, Samuel, I can kill you this minute. And then some other Gittings might kill me, and there's a God's plenty of MacLooties to find him out, an' it will just go on and on. Will you let it end here and now, Samuel? Speak your piece!"

A man had come out of brush just below the bluff and stood now looking back and forth from Mac-Lootie to Gittings. He was a thin, nervous-seeming man with a gun worn low. Will Heath, Charles Henry guessed, because the man did not look like a Gittings.

"Where's the honor in lettin' a thing like this drop?" Samuel Gittings called.

"Where's the honor in not?" MacLootie snapped at

him. "There's better use for strong blood than to soil the hills with it!"

In silence then the two hillmen gazed at each other across a span of fifty yards, their rifles leveled at each other, fingers on hair triggers.

The other man on horseback, a nondescript man in tattered homespun, had edged back toward the cliff beyond the path. The two on foot, both younger models of their uncle Samuel, stood still and never took their eyes off Virgil. Their hands were on their guns, but they had not drawn them.

"Who is that with you, there?" Sam Gittings called.

"Just a feller travelin' through." Virgil's voice turned to a sneer. "I don't need ask who you're travelin' with, Sam. I know Will Heath down there an' his kind. You may be a Gittings, Samuel, but I'm surprised you'd associate with trash. What do you say, now? Will we let this drop, here and now?"

Again Samuel hesitated, then his rifle barrel dipped. "Maybe we will think on it again," he said.

The man below the bluff, watching in open-eyed amazement, suddenly crouched, teeth bared in a snarl. "Well I'll be damned," he hissed. Then with a motion Charles Henry barely saw, he drew his low-slung gun and fired.

Charles Henry heard the bullet hit Virgil MacLootie, saw his friend stagger back, saw the gunman turn to aim at him. In shock, reflexes took over. Artist's fingers found the butt of his revolver, artist's eyes directed it, and he painted a hole dead center in the canvas that was Will Heath. Even as the man began to crumple he thumbed the hammer and fired again but missed this time, and the bullet spanged off rock at the pathside.

The man on horseback had a gun out and was shooting at him. He fired back, and the man's horse sidled against the rock ledge. The man leapt from the

189

animal, hidden beyond it, then clapped it away and leveled his gun with both hands. Charles fired again, his shot high, and suddenly there was that rumbling again and a piece of the cliff sheered off, a huge wedge of shale that took the outlaw edge-on and buried itself in the ground. Gravel thundered down to veil the scene in dust and falling rock.

The Gittingses had not moved. Samuel sat his horse, rifle lowered, and the two younger men stood frozen, hands still on their guns. Charles Henry had one shot left.

Slowly Samuel Gittings raised his rifle, stared over it at the top-hatted young man on the bluff, then extended it to point. "Is Virgil MacLootie dead up there?"

"I don't know. I haven't looked."

"Well, if he is, it be God's will. If not, though, I'll keep the word I gave him. We will think on this again."

He kneed his horse and trotted away down the trail, not looking back. The younger Gittingses glared at Charles Henry for a moment, then went to find their horses. Mounted, they followed their uncle and were gone.

Charles Henry Clayton carried Virgil MacLootie down from the bluff on the shoulder of Bald Knob, cradling the lanky hillman like a child. He draped him over Buckeye's saddle, mounted Captain Keech and took the other horse's reins. "Yee-Haw," he muttered, then slouched in his saddle and leaned to the side to be sick.

When it passed he started down the back trail, looking for a path that would skirt the meadow below and bend away to the north.

Early in the evening he found a place tucked among hills. A pretty woman tended sheep on a knoll, and there was a cabin and barn below.

She watched him approach, ready to run, until she recognized the horse he led. Then she dropped her long stick and lifted her skirts to run to him.

"Are you Millicent McGrath?" Charles Henry asked. "Because if you are, I've brought Virgil Mac-Lootie to you."

He stepped down, eased Virgil off his saddle and cradled him again, walking toward the cabin. He felt as though he would cry. Then a faint sound came to him and MacLootie stirred, groaned and raised his head feebly. "You got out your gun," he whispered.

The woman gasped and ran to open the cabin door.

"You'll need to watch out for Jamie Haak now," MacLootie whispered again. "Will was bad, but Jamie's worse."

In the cabin Charles lay Virgil on a soft bed and the woman brought water and cloths.

Virgil stirred again, looked Charles Henry squarely in the eye. "In the territories, they call him Powder," he said and fainted.

VII

Fort Smith was a sprawling settlement a mile or so from the unorganized territory. It had seven stores, three hotels, a school, two churches, and a hanging judge. From here was administered what passed for law in the territory beyond, and its streets were alive with the traffic of the frontier. Belted men strolled the boardwalks, hard-eyed and silent, aloof from the townspeople about their daily business. The purposes of the belted men lay to the west. The trade of the townspeople lay to the east. Some went west from here for reasons of their own, and others went west to bring them back, dead or alive.

In such a place the unusual was expected, the odd was normal and only the bizarre was worthy of note.

Jed had done his best to attract no attention to himself, but it is difficult to be inconspicuous when one is wearing a gearwheel on his foot. Jed fumed and made dark plans as he sat on a nail keg in a blacksmith shop, hour after hour, while the smith's two assistants worked on his impediment with stone saws, and the smith charged admission for people to come and look at him. With crowds gathering for market week, he had a lot of takers.

193

"I may kill that son of a bitch before this is over," Jed muttered, glaring across at the enterprising artisan.

"We ain't in business for our health," one of the assistants pointed out. "You want to pay for this?"

"Stop talking and cut."

"I ain't never seen anything like this," the assistant said. The casting had been cut through on one side, a wide V-cut that made of it a closed crescent rather than full circle, but still it clung as the stone saw loops droned away, working now from inside out, making a second cut on the other side. "Be a lot easier if we could put this in the forge and soften it. Get a good cherry glow on it, we could bent it right off."

"I wouldn't have anything to bend it off of," Jed told him.

"Yeah, there is that." The assistant shifted his loop for a better cut. Steel dust filtered down in a continuous small rain. "I bet the first thing you're gonna want to do is get out of that boot. I hope you don't take it off in here."

"From now on I stick to banks," Jed muttered.

"What?"

"I said shut up and keep sawin'!"

The noon stage from Little Rock rolled past the smithy and on down the hill to the square. Several passengers alighted, dusty and cramped from the journey. One of them was a grayish man who debarked quietly, collected his luggage and blended quietly into the crowds gathering for market week. Of the several badges who stood around eyeing the newcomers, one or two glanced at him but paid him no further attention. Dooley was easy to ignore. It was part of his stock in trade.

He stood for a time beneath an awning, mild gray eyes missing nothing, then strolled away to find room at a hotel. "My name is Smith," he told the clerk. "John

194

Smith. I'd like a room in the front, overlooking the square."

The badges around the stage stop paid more attention to the heavy-shouldered, sullen man who had come in riding the boot. People picked up between scheduled stops tended to arouse their curiosity. But a thorough once-over of the man and a hasty checking of wants and warrants revealed nothing they could pin down. The man looked like trouble, but they had nothing on him.

A badge approached him. "Nice day for traveling, isn't it?"

The sullen one looked at him. "Shid," he said.

"Beg pardon?"

Luther blew his nose. "What's good about it? You seen a young fellow around here gode by de dabe ob Claytod?"

The badge squinted at him. "That's a bad cold you got. If I was you I'd put on a asfetidy bag. Onions will help, too. Onions and plenty of mustard."

"Neberbide." Luther shrugged, picked up his pack and started away.

"Pretty good mineral springs over by Burley," the badge called after him. "They got a place there that you can lay on a rock, and they'll cover you up with hot mud and let you breathe camphor. Some folks swear by it."

"Who was that?" another badge asked, sauntering over to stand with him, watching the sullen man cross the square.

"Pilgrim with the vapors. What he needs to do is run over to Burley and get plastered."

"See anybody on the stage that we need to think about?"

"I guess not. Usual crop. The real ringtails don't take the stage, anyhow. They might rob it, but they don't

195

very often ride it. What was that name the marshal said we was to look out for?"

"Clay. Henry Clay. Fast-draw artist from back East someplace. They say he's gunned down a dozen men, most of 'em real gunslicks. They know for sure he plugged Will Heath last week, out in the hills."

"Is that who done Will Heath? I heard about that. I never figured anybody'd get the drop on Will Heath."

"Way I heard it, Will Heath had the drop on him. Had his gun pointed right at him, and this Clay, he drew and fired before the hammer could fall."

The other whistled. "Man! Clay, huh? Henry Clay— come to think of it, I have heard that name."

In a second floor window behind them there was a movement of gray. Dooley the hunter set his bag on the lumpy bed, opened it and extracted a long, sleek weapon with a swing-load breech and telescope. The gun was neither rifle nor pistol, but a little of both. Its barrel was fourteen inches in length, and a slender, custom-made telescope was mounted atop it. The breech was single-shot, milled to chamber the new brass cartridges, but much deeper than the usual .44s and .45s brought out by Smith and Wesson and Colt. This was a custom gun and its cartridges were .41 caliber and a full two inches in length.

The walnut grip was massive and had been shaped precisely to Dooley's hand.

He rubbed it with oil, rewrapped it and replaced it in his bag. Then he pulled a chair to the window and sat there, crossing his legs comfortably. From the window he could see the two roads entering from the east. A lot of people were coming into town, bringing their live-stock, crafts, and produce to market. He watched until it was too dark to see.

*   *   *

The weather remained fine along the Mississippi, so the deck passengers aboard the cotton steamer *Molly* traveled in comfort. No floating palace was *Molly* but a squat barge with every inch of deck space given over to the hauling of livestock and a few passengers upriver, and of cotton bales downriver. The few passengers rigged awnings on the foredeck and cooked their meals over fires set in tubs of sand.

Aphrodite chewed on a drumstick and turned the juju over and over in her hand, as though the featureless little leather pouch might tell her something important.

"Wish I knowed what this thing do," she muttered, and Lazarus looked around. His eyes bugged when he saw what she held.

"Woman, you put that thing away," he ordered. "Law, they ain' no tellin' what kine sperrits an' haints gone leak out if it gets open."

Aphrodite put the juju away. "Wish I had got some instructions with it. Feel a whole sight better if I knowed what I was supposed to do with it whenever I wants to use it—if I knowed what I was supposed to use it for."

"Maybe Gabriel tell you when the time come," he offered.

"Maybe so. If he payin' attention." Aphrodite knew from eighty-four years of observation that the attention span of angels tended to be acutely limited. She would trust Gabriel implicitly, but she would never count on him.

Lazarus stood to stretch his legs. Afternoon sun gleamed on his dark skin, the folds of his homespun shirt and canvas trousers, and the tight salt and pepper of his hair. Aphrodite looked up at him. "You a good man, Lazarus, even if you is a bonehead. Ain' ever'body would have carried me to the boat, then

197

come along this far to make sure I's got my comforts."

He smiled at her. "Shoot, ol' woman, I don' mind. I jus' wish you'd change your mind an' git on back home where you belong. You ain' got no business traipsin' aroun' the country lookin' for that girl. You too old for travelin'."

"Ain't I, though!" She shrugged in ancient resignation. "But you knows th' curse, Lazarus. If I don' catch her up an' git her back home they gone be calamity, an' I gone have to go to distant lands. I'll travel a long way to keep from doin' that. If I has to go clean to Fort Smith, then I'll go clean to Fort Smith."

"What if you catches her up there an' she ain' want to come back?"

"I ain' gone ask her. I's gone tell her."

Aphrodite got to her feet to stand beside him, watching the river laze by. At four feet eight inches, she was dwarfed by his towering six feet six, but there was no question who was in charge. "Man say we be at Marvel 'bout sundown, an' that's where I get on the boat goin' up to Fort Smith."

"You want me go on up th' river with you, old woman?"

"No, you come far enough. I won't have no trouble gettin' the rest of the way."

"You got some money to get you by?"

"I got some. Don't you worry about it. You jus' get on back home an' keep a eye on the place 'til we gets back."

The old boat chugged around a long bend and in the far distance, on the left bank, was a stream of reddish water converging into the stream. Above it was a settlement, and there were small wheelboats there.

"That it." Aphrodite pointed. "That Marvel."

Lazarus stood in frowning thought as the boat crept toward the mouth of the Arkansas. Then he squatted, unrolled the long pack in which he carried his belongings, and pulled out a big, double-barreled shotgun. He handed it to Aphrodite, with a sack of powder, wads, and shot. "It loaded," he said. "I want you to take this 'long wit' you. Ain' no tellin' when you might need it, an' I never uses it, anyways."

The gun was almost as big as Aphrodite, but she looked in the tall man's eyes and did not have the heart to decline.

"You jus' catch up that girl an' get on back home," he said. "Serve her right if you was to whale the tar outten her when you do."

When Aphrodite boarded the little timber barge at Marvel she noticed a familiar face. A timid-looking man with gray side whiskers, spectacles, and a round hat was among the upriver passengers. He had also been one of the passengers on the cotton steamer. She had noticed him because of his peculiar manner of speech. He sounded a little like Charles Henry Clayton.

Samuel Gittings, with his nephews Curly Joe and Sidney, waited at Yoakum's Mill for the rest of the party. Of the six who rode in, four were of the Gittings tribe.

"Virgil MacLootie may be a dead man," Samuel told them. "And I'll not mourn him iffen he is. But he made some sense there before Will Heath shot him down. There has been enough feudin' betwixt the Gittingses and the MacLooties, and I'll see an end to it now. It's over."

One of the outriders, a Missourian with an eye patch, stared at him. "I don't give a damn about your feudin'. We found Will Heath up there, stone dead with his gun in his hand. One shot, dead center. I don't reckon it was Virgil MacLootie that done him."

"Feller with him," Gittings said. "When you boys throwed in with us at Little Rock it wasn't to find Virgil MacLootie. You was after that there notorious gunman you heard about back there. You wanted to try him out, you said. Well sir, iffen that was him with Virgil, I believe you all made a bad decision. I ain't ever seen a body shuck leather that fast in all my life."

Jamie Haak had said nothing. He stood apart, just listening. But now his pale eyes glowed with excitement.

"I don't believe it was done fair," the man with the patch said. "I never seen anybody could outdraw Will Heath."

"I could have," Jamie Haak muttered.

"It was fair," Gittings said. "We all seen it. Will had his gun in his hand and pointed at that feller before he ever went for his'n. Next thing, Will Heath was dead."

"Well, where's Luke?"

"He's dead, too. That same feller brought the mountain down on him."

When the seven Gittingses had gone, the man with the patch chewed at his lip for a time. Then he said, "I'm through, Powder. I reckon those boys told it like they seen it. Will was all for tryin' out this new feller, and Will's dead. I'm headin' for Texas."

Jamie Haak, the man called Powder, gazed at him for a moment and a smile played around his thin lips. "So you're through. I think you are a coward, Cory."

Cory stiffened and turned, his hand at the six-gun low at his hip. Hard as bad winter he was, tough as the hills that had spawned him, yet now he hesitated. Cory had faced down many men in his time and had killed more than even his legends would tell. Yet now he looked at Jamie Haak, slim and relaxed, smiling, moon-blond hair falling long and straight below his hat, and the cold fires of hell playing in his fierce, pale eyes, and he hesitated. In that moment Cory decided he did not want to die. He took a long breath, his shoulders slumped and he turned away. "Maybe I am," he said.

But Powder wasn't through. "I kill cowards, too," he purred. "Front or back, Cory. Your choice."

Cory spun then, crouched low, and his gun was in his hand. But that was as far as he went. Powder's arm blurred, and agony exploded in Cory's chest—once, twice and again, dully.

Powder holstered his smoking gun, looked for a moment at the fallen Cory, then called to the people by the mill, "You saw it. It was fair. His gun and boots will pay for his burying."

His pale eyes glowed coldly as he mounted his horse, took Cory's in tow and turned upriver. With Will Heath gone, Powder had time on his hands. He had trailed with Will for a time, as Will's reputation grew, so that he could kill him and take his reputation. But now Will Heath was dead and the reputation was added to that of another man, a stranger from the East. Powder was not displeased. It was better this way. Will Heath would have been too easy. The reputation he could gain now, by putting the stranger under, would be the kind that made legends. Somewhere upriver was Henry Clay. Powder went in search of him.

Fort Smith slept in the dark of night. A few saloons were open, but no traffic was on the streets. Only a dog and a few straying cats noticed the light that bobbed and swayed into view where the east road topped a rise to descend into town. The light moved steadily, rhythmically, side to side and up and down, as it came closer.

"That arrangement works very well, if I do say so myself," Charles Henry Clayton commented to the man beside him in the buggy. "I think it is interesting that I haven't seen it done before."

"You're right," the small man holding the reins answered. "And it is such an obvious device, too."

The horse pulling the buggy had long since recovered from its own amazement and plodded along, now resigned to the startling extents of human innovation. It had a pillow strapped to its head, fluffed and molded about its ears, and atop the pillow, secured in place by leather thongs, was a lighted lantern. Its glow as it bobbed and dipped with the horse's movement was feeble, but it provided enough light for the horse to stay on the dark road. Ahead were the scattered lights of Fort Smith. Behind the buggy a tethered blue roan followed in darkness.

"You have made a very wise decision, Charles," Weldon Hempley said for the eighth or ninth time, reinforcing that decision. A sale could not be considered closed until it was consummated and the money in hand. "Parcel nine is the last piece of land we had in the Colorado territory, and I'm sure the asking price already has been raised. It's a good thing I ran across you when I did. If I had gone back to St. Louis with the papers still unassigned, I imagine my company would have tripled the price on it and had customers banging on the door at that."

"Tell me again about the pre-development sale," Charles said enthusiastically. "About the value escalation and all that."

"Well, it's simple. Forbish, Walker, and Boole—the people I work for—are land agents with a contract to represent the railroad grants through Kansas. Big pieces of those grants are put up for sale to raise money for building railroads, and it's our job to divide those pieces into parcels that people can afford and go out and find people to buy them. So when this federal land came up in the Colorado territory, they assigned it to us

202

to do the same thing. It's the only one of its kind out there so far, so it really is a prize. Pre-development means the asking price during the time the pieces are being sold. Price generally goes up when it's all sold, because then the federal restrictions go off and the owners can begin to develop it. All sorts of good things are likely to happen out there as soon as your title is filed. There's just no telling what it will bring. That's why the price of the last piece is usually a lot more than the other pieces."

"But I am buying at regular pre-development price?"

"Yes, because they can't raise the price until I get back to St. Louis."

"What I'm wondering about," Charles Henry said, "is whether it wouldn't have been better for you to go back and let the price go up and then sell it to somebody. I mean, I certainly appreciate what you're doing for me, but it seems like you could make more money if—"

"I'm not doing this for you," Hempley admitted. "I'm doing it for me. I work for Forbish, Walker, and Boole, but only on a commission basis. If I go back with parcel nine unsold, they will raise the price and sell it. But it won't be my sale. They won't pay me a commission on anything sold in St. Louis."

"That hardly seems a decent way to do things," Charles Henry said.

"My sentiments exactly. So you buy parcel nine and I'll get my commission and we'll let Forbish, Walker, and Boole go hang. They made the rules, not me."

They rolled into Fort Smith, the headlighted horse plodding dark ways toward the sleeping square.

"There is a decent hotel over there." Weldon pointed. "We can get some sleep, then go over to the federal land office first thing in the morning. You have made a very wise decision."

203

"My uncle Jonathan always said a man must invest money to make money. I am just delighted to have made this decision. All the way west I have been wondering how I would get rich when I got there. Now that's settled and all I have to do is go and find parcel nine and start accumulating wealth. Miss Emmalee will be so pleased."

"I have an uncle Jonathan, too," Weldon said. "He has a store in Illinois."

"My uncle Jonathan has shipyards," Charles Henry related. "Of course, he really isn't my uncle. You see, my uncle Jonathan's father married a Clayton who was my grandfather's sister, which makes Uncle Jonathan's mother my great-aunt. But I never knew her, so the person I really think of as my aunt is her daughter, which makes her not my aunt at all, actually, but more of a fourth cousin if you see what I mean. But since I think of her as my aunt I think of Uncle Jonathan as my uncle although he really is about the same category of relative as Aunt Samantha, I suppose. . . ."

Weldon Hempley's eyes had begun to glaze by the time they stabled their rig and horses and found the decent hotel.

VIII

Thursday was the beginning of "market week" in Fort Smith, and the big annual event had drawn people from all over western Arkansas. Craft stalls were set up around the square, tents were pitched in every available open place and acres of holding pens had been erected in the hayfield just off the square for livestock to be shown, sold and traded.

Because of hostility between local merchants and the craft and produce stalls, only one day's set-up time was allowed. Thus everything that needed to be done to get ready for the big week had been done the day before, with the tools at hand and without noticeable pre-planning.

As dawn touched the sky Jed Pike rolled out of his blankets under a tarp at the edge of town, stretched his muscles, cursed roundly at the never-ending ache and humiliation of the battered gearwheel on his foot and started for the blacksmith shop. A few more hours, they said. Another inch of cold-cutting and they would be able to remove the thing. At this point Jed was about willing to give up all his other ambitions in favor of just one: to be once and for all rid of his gearwheel.

In weeks past he had acclimated to it. He had

developed an unusual style of walking that tended to draw curious stares from people, but at least it kept him from walking in circles because of his imbalance. He had noted, too, that his left leg was becoming substantially stronger than his right one.

As he plod-clunked along the first of the boardwalks that would lead him across the square, a man hurried up to him, grinned and held out a hand. "Give me a dollar," he said.

Jed stopped. "You found him? He's here?"

"Big as life," the man said, "and just like you described him. Young, tall, nice-lookin' feller, dark hair an' fancy-lookin' clothes. Wears a top hat. He must have come in last night, because he sure is here now."

Jed breathed deeply. At last. At long damned last. Now he would have something to show for his pain. The eastern nitwit with the money had made it to Fort Smith. It was collection time. He handed a dollar to the man. "Where is he?"

"Probably still over at Piney's Eatery. I seen him there just a few minutes ago. Him and another feller—one of them land drummers that comes through—was havin' their breakfast. They was talkin' some kind of a land deal, talkin' about goin' over to the federal land office to register a title. Land office never opens before seven-thirty, so I guess they'd still be there."

Jed's heart went cold within him. Land deal? Register a title? The money the easterner was carrying, in Jed's opinion, belonged to Jed. He had come a long, hard way to steal it. It would be disastrous if some land drummer got to it first.

One bright thought, though: if the land drummer was interested in the dimwit, that meant the dimwit still had his money. Jed's greatest fear had been that he might lose it somewhere along the way before Jed could intercept him and retrieve it.

Jed hitched his rifle higher under his arm, swung his gearwheeled foot carefully off the boardwalk and set his course for Piney's Eatery, hardly noticing anymore the peculiar, self-correcting pace that had become habit to him.

Behind him the man pocketed his dollar and shook his head in wonder. "Damnedest thing I ever seen," he told himself.

Jed had to take a long detour around the pens of cattle and sheep that had been set up the day before, and another detour around ranks of open wagons with their tall slat cages full of chickens, turkeys, and guinea-fowl.

He ducked under the rope between the cage hasps on two wagons—the wagons, pens, and stalls formed most of a circling corral the size of the square, with ropes run along the nearsides to fence off the big enclosure. In most cases the ropes had been secured to the easiest things at hand: the cage hasps.

At Piney's Eatery, Luther already had Charles Henry Clayton in sight, and he sat half turned away at a back table, trying to keep an eye on Clayton and the man with him without being seen. He sneezed, blew his sore and fiery nose and waited for the first, best chance to kill Charles Henry so he could go home and get even with Bull Timmons. Luther was out of patience. If the room had not been so crowded, including a collection of badges who wandered in and out, he probably would have killed the young man at first sight. All he waited for now was an unguarded moment, a moment when the witnesses were all distracted. Under his coat, he already had one of his stilettos out and ready to throw.

"I'm sure I have seen that man somewhere," Charles Henry commented casually to Weldon Hempley as they finished their coffee.

207

"What man?" Weldon glanced around.

"Over there by the back door. The big man with the bad cold. Can't for the life of me remember where I've seen him, but I have a distinct impression of dampness."

"It's a small world," Hempley commented. He pulled out a pocket watch. "Well, it won't be long now. As soon as the land office opens, you will be on your way toward fame and fortune. You plan to leave today? For Colorado?"

"Just as soon as I own that land." Charles Henry nodded. "I shall go out there, see what needs to be done to make my fortune, do it, and then get back to Miss Emmalee just as quickly as possible."

"She must really be something."

"Oh, she is." Charles nodded eagerly. "She most definitely is something. I intend to start off immediately by holding hands with her, then see what else develops."

Hempley glanced at him, started to ask a question, then decided not to. It was his business to sell land, not to pry into the private fantasies of other people—no matter how peculiar they might seem. "What say we go walk around the square, then head over to the land office?"

"Tallyho," Charles Henry said. He stood, tapped his hat onto his head and added, "Be careful of that—" But it was too late. As Hempley arose his leg brushed the folded tripod easel which leaned against the table. The easel slid, tipped and fell clattering to the floor to rebound gloriously, high into the air as its strap slipped, and its spring-loaded members shot open. It landed upright in the center of another table, one of its legs in a coffee cup that was in the process of being picked up by the farmer who sat there. The farmer went one way, the easel the other, and the contrivance had

208

no more than touched the floor than it was up and heading for the door, its easel-arms astraddle the back of the hound dog that had been sleeping there.

"Come back here!" Charles Henry shouted, bounding after it.

Hempley stared after him, his mouth hanging open. Beyond him, near the back door, Luther's table crashed to the floor as he stood, raising his stiletto, his expression similar to Hempley's. He almost gutted himself puting the knife away as a curious badge looked in through the open door to see what all the commotion was about.

Weldon Hempley exited the place at a high run, in pursuit of his prospect, and Luther sat down again to ponder his changing situation. "Wad I deed id a rifed," he told himself. When he glanced up again another man was entering the eatery, a man who walked oddly, wore a gearwheel on his foot and carried a rifle.

"A rifed," Luther told himself. He pulled out a large handful of currency to display carelessly before stumbling and lurching out the back door.

In the square, market week was coming alive. With his easel retrieved and slung securely on his back, Charles Henry waited for Weldon Hempley to catch up, then they strolled around looking at the sights. In the second-floor window of a hotel, a custom-designed telescope atop a custom-designed firearm followed their every move.

"I need to get the strap fixed on this easel," Charles commented as they stopped at a produce stall. "They have carrots. Would you like a carrot?"

In the window Dooley squinted through the fine scope, his brow creased in puzzlement. He was not surprised at finding Charles Henry again. He had known he would. Dooley always found his man. But he was puzzled at the small, elegant man walking with him.

Obviously a drummer, but what kind of drummer?

It remained only for him to lure or follow Charles Henry Clayton away from town, away from witnesses, and he would complete his task. He would have his money and Edgar Egmont would have his way. Yet the fact of the drummer bothered him. It was in the nature of traveling salesmen never to miss an opportunity at money, and this one was sticking to the Clayton youth like a leech. Dooley squinted and worried, waiting for a clue.

"Seven-thirty," Weldon Hempley said, reading his watch. "Shall we proceed to make you rich?"

"Tallyho." Charles Henry nodded, crunching a mouthful of carrot. The remainder of the bunch of carrots protruded from his shallow coat pocket, and a gray mule had taken up with him, following closely behind, trailing its lead. As he turned to follow Hempley the mule nudged him, and he noticed it. "Well, hello. Who let you loose?" He stooped, picked up the trailing rope and looked around. No one seemed to be aware of missing a mule. With a shrug, Charles Henry led the animal to one side of the square and tied the lead securely to a convenient rope strung between chicken wagons.

"That should keep you until your owner shows up." He scratched the stiff ears, stroked the probing muzzle. "Here. Have a carrot."

Hempley was waiting. Charles hurried to join him, and the salesman pointed. "The land office is right over there."

In his window, Dooley saw the point, swiveled his sighted gun to follow it and gasped. "The land office!" he whispered. "He's buying land!"

In the instant of realization, as he saw his money slipping from his grasp, Dooley made a complex professional decision. Charles Henry and his money must not

210

be parted until Dooley could get him alone and unwit-
nessed and take it from his body. But Charles Henry
was on his way toward the land office with a salesman.
The land office was there for the recording of titles. It
was there the money would change hands. The salesman must not get to the land office.

Dooley braced himself, brought his custom gun to
bear on the glass-enlarged back of Weldon Hempley,
and began to ease the trigger. Then he stopped. All he
could see through the glass was a fury of feathers and
hurtling forms. The entire far side of the square was
obscured by an eruption of chickens.

At the southeast side of the square Luther emerged
from behind the bank next to Piney's Eatery carrying
Jed Pike's rifle. He didn't have to look for Charles
Henry. He saw him immediately and threw the rifle to
his shoulder. A striped chicken flew squawking past his
head and startled him. The rifle twitched upward and
roared, and an airborne red rooster crumpled in flight
and fell into a holding pen full of dairy cattle, bouncing
off the nose of the herd bull. The bull shook its head,
looked at its feet and went wild.

At the sound of the shot a battle-scarred gander,
released from its cage as wagon hasps popped methodically along a widening wake—the point of which was
a mule looking for more carrots—took to the air and
homed in on Luther, its beak open in a raucous honk,
strong wings flailing and flogging him. Luther dropped
his rifle and ran.

Charles Henry and Weldon Hempley turned in the
door of the land office. Pandemonium was spreading
through the square. "That must have been the opening
gun," Charles Henry said. "They really know how to
stage a fair here, don't they?"

A sleepy clerk greeted them in the little office. "Good
morning, gentlemen. What was the shooting about?"

211

"They seem to be showing their chickens," Charles Henry told him. "We want to record a title. I'm buying parcel nine from Mr. Hempley here."

Hempley pulled out his sheaf of legal papers and handed them to the clerk. "I've done all the entries," he said. "This is the agent's authorization, this is the grant order: binder on the company, parcel description, and the substantiating documents from the federal district court in Denver, all signed and notarized."

The clerk thumbed through the papers, checking signatures and seals. He got out a file of federal authorization notices, pulled one and compared it with the grant order Hempley had handed him, and nodded.

"All in good shape," he said. "Fees and notarization come to five dollars."

"Who pays that?" Charles asked Weldon. "You or me?"

"You pay that."

"Oh." He dug out his wallet. "I'm not going to have much money left. But then again, I'll be wealthy soon." He handed the money to the clerk.

"All right," the clerk told him. "You pay him now, the agreed price of the property, so I can witness it."

What changed hands now was almost all the money Charles had. It was his two thousand dollars from Uncle Edgar, plus a thousand from Aunt Samantha, plus most of what he had picked up in Memphis, wired from his trust. "That just about cleans me out," he mused aloud.

When Weldon had the money in hand, the clerk nodded and signed a form. He walked over to a man sitting at a telegraph key. "Wire's open, Joe. Go ahead and put this on to St. Louis."

Turning back to Charles Henry, the clerk said, "Congratulations, Mr. Clayton. You are now the rightful owner of one parcel of land in Colorado, for better or worse."

A man opened the front door and called to the clerk, "Hey, John, come out here. You wouldn't believe what's going on." The sounds from outside were deafening: a cacophony of shouts, howls, squawks, roars, snorts, neighs, and honks, punctuated by the thunder of running hooves and flapping wings. "Good God!" someone near at hand screamed. "Those cows are breaking down the sheep pens!" A terrified chicken bounded flapping through the open door and came to rest on the head of the teletype man.

"Office is closed," the clerk declared, and shooed his customers out the door.

Weldon Hempley still had the money in his hand. Charles glanced at it. "You aren't going to carry that around with you, are you?"

"Good Lord, no," Hempley said, stuffing the cash into a pocket. "I'm heading for the bank, right now."

"I'll go with you." Charles touched the butt of the navy Colt hanging at his hip. "This town gets a little rough, it seems to me."

Through a melee of running livestock, fluttering and screeching domestic fowl, and howling people hurtling to and fro, they started across the square. "I don't think I've ever seen anything like this." Hempley gazed around in awe. Violent motion was everywhere and a thickening haze of dust.

"I don't think I ever saw a busier town," Charles Henry said.

A gray mule plodded behind them, dragging new disasters in its wake. Two men with badges ran past, one shouting at the other, " . . . haven't the vaguest idea. But we damn well better arrest somebody. Good Lord, look at . . ."

A flailing citizen whizzed past, pursued by a dairy bull. The two men with badges veered and followed,

213

scattering chickens, turkeys, and geese before them.

"I have a theory," Charles Henry told Weldon Hempley, "that most of the trouble people get into is the result of absentmindedness. And unless this is a planned activity, there is an awful lot of absentmindedness here.

In the second-floor hotel room Dooley's eyes were wild with frustration. With an oath he brought up his gun, sighted on Charles Henry, squeezed the trigger and shot a flashing stiletto out of the hand that was sweeping toward the young man's back. Luther fell and rolled in the dust, while the bent stiletto arced high in the sunlight to fall point down, slashing across the haunch of a boar hog straining at the bars of its pen. The hog squealed, dug in its heels and splintered wood flew. The hog leaped to join the fray. Head down, feet pumping and tusks glinting it thundered blindly across the square, clearing a path behind it and a path ahead. The open door of a hotel was in its line of charge, and the hotel's stairs were beyond.

Approaching the bank building Charles and Weldon stopped to let a footrace pass. The event consisted of a flailing citizen, two men with badges, a goose, a dairy bull, and several yapping dogs. A herd of sheep flowed from between two buildings and scattered before the runners.

Charles Henry Clayton, Weldon Hempley, and a bounding ewe entered the bank and closed the door behind them.

In the square Luther got to his feet, gripping his bleeding right hand with his left, and suddenly found himself running at full tilt, caught up in a mass of people fleeing from a rampaging dairy bull. His heavy coat was open to the wind, molded by the position of his arms as he gripped his sore hand, and its billowing folds began to fill up with chickens. "Shid!" he screamed and ran for his life.

Directly ahead of him a gray man bounded from a second-story window while a raging boar slashed the curtains behind him.

In the alley behind Piney's Eatery Jed Pike groaned, put a hand to his aching skull, rolled over and looked into the face of a curious sheep. A line of guineas strolled past, chattering happily and pecking gravel. He closed his eyes again, feeling around for his rifle. It was not to be found. With an oath he got to his knees, wiped some of what he had found instead of his rifle from his hands, and staggered upright. Lashing out with his gearwheel he cleared a path of livestock and went in search of his gun.

At the top of the east road hill a flat wagon loaded high with trunks and assorted luggage halted as the occupants of its bench stared ahead in disbelief. Emmalee Wilkes shaded her pretty eyes with her parasol and pointed. "What in the world is going on down there?"

The teamster shook his head. "Darned if I know. Might be market week. They have that every year about this time. But I never saw a market week that looked like that."

Leaving the bank, Charles Henry almost stumbled over a man who was stooped there, picking up a rifle. The man straightened and Charles blinked at him, then clapped him on the back. "Say now! I remember you. My old friend from Charleston. You know, you were right about the routes to Fort Smith. If I had been smart I would have followed your instructions to the letter. Weldon, this is a man I met outside of Charleston. He gave me a lot of good advice about the West. You know, sir, you were exactly right—about money coming in handy, and all. I have just purchased a parcel of land that will make me wealthy, I am sure. We

215

just this minute completed the transaction, and Mr. Hempley here just put the money in the bank. Isn't that great? Ah, why are you wearing a metal casting on your foot? That looks like the ones I delivered for Uncle Edgar. Possibly I will try that sometime. It certainly is good to see you again. Take care of yourself."

With another clap on the back Charles walked away, trailed by the happy salesman. Long after they had gone Jed Pike stood there, rifle dangling from his hand, oblivious to the havoc that grew and grew around him. Finally he blinked, and a tear coursed down his dusty cheek. The man in the iron cast was weeping.

At the stable Charles Henry saddled the blue roan and stowed his gear aboard—all except the tripod easel which the horse still would not tolerate.

Ahead lay the unorganized territory, lawless and intriguing. And somewhere beyond that lay his fortune. At the edge of Fort Smith he turned to look back. Most of the people were off the streets now, and the livestock had taken over.

"I shall miss this place," he told the roan. "I don't think I have ever seen a more dynamic town. Ah, well." He turned and tapped heels to the horse's gunwales, settled his hat firmly onto his head and set his course for the wilds of Oklahoma.

"Tallyho, Captain Keech! We're off to Colorado!"

IX

Emmalee Wilkes had never seen a messier town. Everywhere she looked were broken-down pens, collapsed pavilions, bits of trampled debris—and animals. There were all kinds of animals, everywhere.

"You'd think people would have more pride in their community," she suggested to the teamster, who stared around awestruck as the wagon entered the square. "Drive over there," she said pointing. "The place with the goats on the porch. The sign says it is a hotel."

Carefully, the driver swung his rig left and circuited around an overturned buckboard to pull up in front of the hotel. Emmalee accepted his hand down, then strode up the steps, across the porch and into the lobby, catching up her tan skirt with the canary trim so that its edges would not catch on the garbage strewn about. A man was trying to coax a cow down from the second-floor landing, and there was a duck on the counter. She rang the hand-bell that rested there.

A disheveled person with glasses appeared from a back hall and asked, "Yes?"

"I am looking for someone. His name is Charles Henry Clayton, and he may have come here. Can you

217

help me?"

"I don't know, miss. We had a lot of people here last night, and then all this happened while ago. I don't know where anybody is. Try the book."

Emmalee opened the book, turned it around, and she and the duck perused its recent pages. The name she sought was the next to last one in the register. "Oh, he *is* here. See?" She gave the disheveled man a smile that fogged his spectacles and pointed out the signature. He came around the desk to look over her shoulder, his breath going ragged at the view from there.

"Ah, yes. That one. Came in late last night with the drummer. Tall, nice-looking young man, very well behaved. Paid in advance."

"Do you know where he is now?" She backed off a pace, not caring to be slobbered on.

"I'm afraid not, miss. I don't even know if he is still here. You see, there was a terrible disruption earlier, and—"

"I could see that when we drove into town. A celebration of some sort, I suppose. Where do you suggest I should start looking?"

The man cleaned his spectacles, his eyes large and sad. "I'm afraid I wouldn't know where to look for anyone right now." His spectacles clean now of their dust and fog, he replaced them on his face and looked again at Emmalee. His eyes grew large, his breathing grew ragged and he gulped several times. "However, if I could see of bervice—ah, I mean be of service, miss—"

"Never mind. I will just look around."

"You might buy the trank."

"Do what?"

"I mean, you might try the bank. People bo to—er, go to the pank—bank—"

"If I have missed him, I shall have to go further west.

218

Are there modes of travel west of here?"

His eyes enlarged even further. "Oh, you mustn't woe guest—go west, miss. That's the torri-tetti-tetor—Oklahoma. It's a plaid base! I mean—bad place! Boutlaws and admen! Cornifators!"

The man was so upset that she put a soft hand on his shoulder. "There, there," she said.

It calmed him somewhat. "If you have to go west, miss, there is a stage line up to Kansas. I can appange ras—arrange passage for you."

"That is kind." She smiled. "I'll let you know." She turned away, her bodice molding her fine back and small waist, her full skirt suggesting the delights beneath it, and the man's tongue knotted itself again. "One picket to Tittsburg!" he told her, then turned bright red and hurried into the back room.

The bank was a serene and quiet place, untouched by the recent festivities except for the two bow-tied men who were stalking a wary sheep across the lobby.

A teller remembered Charles Henry. "Yes, ma'am," he said panting, "that sounds like the young gentleman who came in with Mr. Hempley. He was talking about going to Colorado. He wanted to find parcel nine."

"What or where is parcel nine?"

"Haven't got the vaguest idea, myself. You might try the land office across the square. I guess John would know."

Because of the shambles in the square, Emmalee went around. As she approached a blacksmith shop a bearded, broad-shouldered man stepped from its open front, breathed deeply, then extended his left foot out in front of him and gazed at it lovingly. "Ah," he sighed, grinning hugely.

He turned her way. He saw her, tipped his hat, turned abruptly right and slammed into the smithy wall. He sat down hard on the boardwalk, grunted, then turned his face to heaven and shrieked, "It's too strong! My left leg is too damned strong!"

Emmalee hurried past, glancing back over her shoulder. "This is the strangest town!" she muttered.

As she neared it, the door of the federal land office banged open and a goat bounded out. Behind it a flustered man in the doorway yelled, "Git!" The man regained his composure as she entered. Beyond him, another man was sweeping the floor while a red chicken operated the telegraph key on the desk, pecking happily at its button.

"I am trying to find Charles Henry Clayton," she told the land agent. "They said at the bank that you might know where he is."

The agent's brow wrinkled a moment, then he nodded. "That one. Sure, the land buyer. He was in here just a while ago, maybe an hour or two now. Bought a parcel of land in Colorado. The way he talked, he may be on his way there by now."

Emmalee sighed. "Parcel nine, I gather."

The agent shooed the chicken away and looked through some papers. "Yes, ma'am. Parcel nine, Colorado territory. That's a long way."

She sighed again. "Yes," she said. "Of course it is."

Back in front of the hotel, she asked the teamster waiting with her luggage, "What would you charge to drive to Colorado?"

"I'd sooner eat frogs," he explained. "You might see Farley Underwood, though. He's always talkin' about headin' out into the territories. He might tote you."

While the teamster unloaded her luggage on the hotel porch, Emmalee went in search of Farley Underwood. She found him—had his location pointed out to her—in a reeking outhouse behind a saloon. She waited on the path until he came out, hitching up his pants. He was a scrawny, aging man with peppery chin

220

whiskers and only a few teeth. His bald dome, when he raised his slouch hat in passing, shone within its half-circle of white fringe.

"Go right on in," he invited. "Seat's still warm."

"Are you Mr. Underwood?"

He stopped and turned back, his eyes running up and down her in a querulous inspection. "Say! Ain't you a dumplin', though! Underwood sure is me. Who might you be, dumplin'?"

"I am Miss Emmalee Wilkes," she told him. "I am traveling through in search of someone, and I was told you might drive me west."

"Hee, hee! I might drive you crazy, far's that goes. Done no less fer many a woman in my time. Where you want to go? I reckon I could take you far as Fort Gibson if you pay good and don't talk much."

"I may need to go as far as Colorado."

The grin disappeared from his wrinkled face. "Colorado what?"

"The Colorado territory. It's west of here."

"Thought maybe that was where you meant. Lordy, I always did think it might be just fine to go out there an' see what there is to see. Just never had no reason to go, is all. My, but wouldn't that be something? Colorado!" His sunken eyes misted, his gaze far away beyond her.

"Good. Then you will drive me?"

"Absolutely not!" he snapped, returning abruptly to the here and now. "Fort Gibson, maybe. But not a step farther."

"Well, why not? You said you wanted to go. If it's because of the rigors and perils of the trail, I can assure you—"

"It ain't because of no such thing. It's because you're a woman. You certainly are a woman. And that can't lead to nothing but trouble."

221

"Now see here!" She set her chin. "I have read all about outlaws and Indians and such—"

"I ain't talkin' about outlaws an' Indians. I'm talkin' about me. Just imagine we was to go west together, just you, you little dumplin', and me, all by ourselves out in the big lonelies. Maybe the first day or two, everything be all right. Maybe even three. Then the loneliness would begin to set in."

"Mr. Underwood, mind your manners!"

"Ain't my manners I'm worried about, dumplin'. It's yours." He thrust out his scrawny chest and lowered shaggy brows in a frown. "Three days at the outside, an' you wouldn't be able to control yourself no longer. And I'm gettin' way too old for that kind of carryin' on."

Her eyes went wide, her hand to her mouth. "Mr. Underwood, are you suggesting—"

"Yes, ma'am, I am. Women just can't seem to leave me alone."

As she stalked once again toward the hotel he trailed after her, chattering happily. "Don't you take it too hard, miss. Time was, I'd have jumped at the chance to have a dumplin' like you makin' moon eyes at me. But I had to swear off. It just got to be too much for me. Wasn't for that, though, I'd hitch up my buckboard this minute and we'd head for Colorado. Always did wish I had a reason to go see those mountains out there."

He stopped. A man had ridden into town, directly to the center of the square. Now he sat his horse there and pushed back his hat. Unkempt hair the color of cured straw fell limp and straight to his shoulders. Fierce pale eyes turned lazily to take in all that was around him.

Farley Underwood made a strangling sound, then grabbed Emmalee's arm and pulled her away behind a half-erect pavilion. When she started to protest he put a

222

hand to her mouth and shook his head. "Be still, missy. Just be quiet. That's Powder out there."

The rider in the square raised his pistol partway out of its holster and let it fall back. A smile played across his lips. He raised his head and shouted, "Henry Clay!" The name echoed around the square. People edged toward the boardwalks, toward doors and points of cover. A man with a badge hurried from an alleyway and halted abruptly, his eyes fixed on the rider.

"You, John Law!" The rider fixed him with a pale stare. "I'm looking for Henry Clay. Is he in this town?"

The man stammered, "I—I don't know any Henry Clay."

"Hell you don't." The pale eyes went cold. "Man that gunned down Will Heath is known. I want him. Where is he?"

"Well, he ain't here." The lawman squared his shoulders with an effort. Other men with badges had appeared around the square, but the pale-eyed rider ignored them.

"You might be lyin', too," he purred. "How about that? You lyin' to me?"

"He ain't here. I told you. We want him, too. You think if he was here we wouldn't have him?"

"I'm here, and you don't have me."

The lawman's mouth moved, but nothing came out. He seemed to be struggling with himself. The rider stared at him a moment longer, then turned away, pivoting his horse to face another of the badged and belted men. "You. Even if you don't know Henry Clay you'll have his description by now. Anybody been here that matches that description?"

The man swallowed hard. "You can't do this, Powder. This is a law-abiding town. You can't just ride in here and—"

"I don't see anybody stopping me." He leaned

forward, his pale stare on the sweating lawman. "Ah. You do remember." His hand crept near his gunbutt. "Where is he?"

Without a word the lawman pointed west. Powder looked in that direction, then turned his horse full-circle, hauling the reins, his eyes settling on every lawman in sight, one by one.

"If I have been lied to, I'll be back."

He spurred his horse to an easy lope, turned at a side street and was gone, westward.

Behind the pavilion Emmalee turned a white face on Farley Underwood. "That man was an outlaw!"

"Yes, ma'am. Just about the worst one there is these days outside of Texas."

"Well, he humiliated those law people, and they didn't do anything."

"Oh, they will. They'll get their courage screwed up a little and a bunch of them will take off after him before long. If they're lucky they won't catch him."

"Who was that gentleman he was asking about?"

"Henry Clay? Why, dumplin', from what I hear he probably is a more dangerous man than Powder. That's why Powder's after him, I reckon. Man like him can't afford to share a reputation."

"So this is the West," Emmalee murmured.

"No, ma'am. This is just where it begins. Now like I was tellin' you." He fell into step with her, toward the hotel. "I would be plain happy to haul to Colorado if it just wasn't for your feminine inclinations. But maybe some other time—"

People had reappeared around the square. The lawmen had all gone off somewhere. Beyond the square, a tall stagecoach approached, its team trotting with the heads-up prance of fresh horses.

The hotel man met her at the porch. "There you are!" He pointed out, beginning to gape again. "There is a peat to Sittsburg—I mean, seat to Fitts—to Kansas, if you want it."

She looked at Underwood again, imploringly. He shook his head. "No, ma'am, dumplin'. Three days at the outside, out in the lonelies with me, and you'd probably be actin' just like him." He gazed sympathetically at the hotel man. "You ought to swear off."

"That's easy for soo to yay—you to—oh, go riss in the piver, Wunderwood."

"I shall take that ticket to wherever it is," Emmalee said.

"I've already laken the tiberty of raking your meservation."

The stage driver, though, had other thoughts on the matter. He took one look at the heap of luggage on the hotel porch and shook his head. "Absolutely not!"

Emmalee gave him a pretty frown, then smiled sweetly at Farley Underwood. "You see, Mr. Underwood, your problem is solved. I shall go to Colorado by other means. All I need you to do is haul my luggage."

Hooves thundered and a large party of badged and belted men swept past, their faces dark with anger. A gray mule dragging its rope and munching carrots skipped aside as they passed, then turned to look after them.

In a lockup three streets away a large, red-nosed man under arrest for stealing chickens had watched the departure of most of the local law. Now he removed a shoe, pulled several bills out of it, replaced it and rattled the cage lock to get the guard's attention. "I god sub bore buddy," he taunted, backing away from the door, showing the money in his good hand. A few moments later, armed with the guard's revolver and clasp knife, he crept away from the lockup and began a search for transportation. He was going west.

*   *   *

225

Far down the river, passengers unloaded at the dock at Little Rock and trudged into town. Aphrodite, mockingbird hat firmly on her snowy curls and a huge shotgun cradled in her arm, walked a step behind the scholarly looking man with the funny accent: the one she had noticed several times along the way. The man had seemed unusually interested in the cable-bound steamboat they had passed a day ago and again had taken a wide-eyed interest in the little town where the powder magazine had exploded. Now, as they reached the main street of this town and saw heavy repairs underway on two buildings, the man stopped a workman and asked, "Would you mind telling me what happened here?"

"Nobody knows, exactly." The workman shrugged. "Seems like there was a grindstone in a blue hoop skirt that sort of run amuck."

"Incredible," the scholarly man told himself.

"Ain' no incredible 'bout it," Aphrodite corrected him. "It chaos an' havoc at work, an' I is hot on th' trail."

X

The blue roan loved to run, and Charles Henry Clayton loved to ride. Thus the forested hills of the Oklahoma territory flowed past in bright sequence through the afternoon, and the traveler found himself twenty miles into the land of the five tribes by the time sunset gloried the sky ahead. Its gold hues reminded him of the fortune awaiting him somewhere out West, and the pinks and contours of lovely ray-spun clouds reminded him of the pinks and contours of Emmalee Wilkes awaiting him back East. The far-flung goals of those interwoven images produced in the young man an intense, rich loneliness that demanded capture.

The coach road he followed was well defined and approximated the course of the winding Arkansas River. But now he turned from the road and headed north a mile or more until he found a crest overlooking a tributary valley with the unfurling sunset beyond it. He stripped the roan of saddle and tack and clapped it on the rump. "Eat some grass, Captain Keech. We shall rest here a while."

He set up his easel, got out his paints and went to work.

The sunset proceeded in dramatic sequence to

produce image after image, one complex glory blending subtly into the next, a spectacle of light and hue retelling the day's events at evening for an enraptured audience of one.

With tongue thrust out and brow furrowed, Charles Henry worked to capture it all, to miss no nuance of tint, no shift of shadow, to capture the light show with his brushes, and as he worked a hush came over the land.

He was almost done. The light show was winding down in rich reds and encroaching purples, and a last shaft of pale magenta broke the clouds to herald the end of day. He switched brushes to capture it.

A large red hand speared past his shoulder, its index finger stabbing at the place his stroke began. "That not right. Quick, more yellow."

He dabbed yellow and sidelined the stroke, nodding his agreement. "Just the touch. Exactly. Ah, fantastic!" Then he stiffened and almost tripped over his feet as he spun around.

The man at his shoulder was tall, red-skinned and wore a bright turban and buckskin shirt lavish with beadwork and painted symbols. "'Bout right," he said. "Need evening star, though. Right there."

"But that isn't where it is," Charles told him.

"Where picture needs it to be," the dark warrior said frowning at him. "Not art if it don't improve on nature."

Charles looked closely at his painting and conceded. The evening star did need to be where the man said. Otherwise the climax of the narrative imagery was lost. He dotted it in, pale against the purple of the night. It was just right.

He turned again and discovered he had not just one critic but several. Beyond the tall Indian were several more, all staring in critical appraisal at the picture he had done.

Captain Keech grazed nearby, undisturbed by the silent invasion.

One of the Indians, an old man with long white hair and a face that was a map of fierce wrinkles, stepped forward and delivered what sounded like a lengthy, critical appraisal of the painting. In a sibilant, musical language unlike any Charles Henry had heard, he evaluated the work point by point, the tall warrior occasionally nodding his agreement.

When the elder had finished speaking the tall one told Charles Henry, "Unegadihi say you do pretty good work. Too much like what you see and not enough like what you feel, but that because you are young and stupid. Unegadihi also say what the hell you doing up here? You breaking a treaty?"

For lack of any other idea Charles Henry extended a hand. "My name is Charles Henry Clayton. I don't know about any treaties."

"Bullshit," the warrior answered him solemnly. "White people all know treaties. You make 'em, you break 'em. All the damn time." Then he took Charles Henry's extended hand and shook it. "I am Gunasoquo. Wolf clan chief at two rivers village. I talk damn good English."

"You certainly do," Charles Henry said. "But I really didn't mean to break any treaties. What did I do?"

"You off the road, you break the treaty. You break the treaty, I supposed to break your damn head. See them?" He waved imperiously at the other Indians, who stood watching them curiously. "They wait to see what I do about you. You my problem. Bullshit."

"I'll be glad to go back to the road, right away." He had become very aware of the short axe the man held in his hand. It looked like an excellent head-breaker. "I'm just passing through."

229

"Sure. So is Butterfield Stage Line. So is Missouri-Kansas-Texas Railroad. So is every bluecoat at Fort Gibson. So is every drummer and farmer and owlhoot on the wagon roads. All just passin' through. Not much left of damn treaty anyhow. We don't break a few heads we got no clout at all." Tentatively he raised the axe, and Charles Henry's hand went to the gun at his side.

"Ah-ho!" the Indian said, then stared at him again, curiously. "Damn fast. Pretty good. Maybe we better talk about this."

He stepped to the others and a long conversation ensued, accompanied by some sharp remarks and waving of fists. The old man, Unegadihi, shouted them to silence and walked over to look at Charles Henry's painting again. He ignored Charles Henry. He studied the painting, then went back to the Indians and expounded at length. Charles Henry had the impression a vote was being taken.

Gunasoquo returned to him. "Unegadihi says you no owlhoot. Says owlhoot kill somebody he don't care. Says you kill somebody but you don't feel good 'bout that."

"How does he know that?"

The tall warrior stared at him. "You don't look at your own picture? Picture tell a lot. Unegadihi has eyes. Unegadihi say maybe we widen the road enough so you still on it, then treaty not broken. Damn good idea, 'cept we have to stay here tonight so we can narrow the road again tomorrow when you go back. Lot of damn trouble for one white man."

"I'll be glad to go back right now."

"Bullshit. More traffic on that road right now than ants on a hedge apple. Lot of white people. Owlhoot chasin' a owlhoot, posse chasin' a owlhoot, drummer in a buggy chasin' a posse, wagonload of luggage chasin' a drummer. Everybody chasin' everybody. Somebody gonna get hurt. We stay here with you. Unegadihi say tomorrow you can paint another picture."

"Very well," Charles said. "I'll be glad to do that. Your Unegadihi sounds like a fascinating person. I wish he could speak English so I could chat with him."

"Unegadihi talk English better than me if he want to. He just don't want to. He say if white man want to talk to him white man can damn well learn Tsalagi."

The Cherokee had been hunting in the forest. They had game and shared it with Charles Henry. As night blanketed the hills they sat around a small fire—one top-hatted New Englander and seven stolid Indians—and chewed on juicy venison flavored with a tangy sauce that Charles Henry decided not to inquire about. Captain Keech was the only horse in the crowd, the Indians preferring to hunt afoot, and he grazed contentedly at the firelight's edge.

When the meal was done five of the Indians rose to their feet, packed their provisions and walked away into the darkness. Only Gunasoquo and old Unegadihi remained.

"They go home," Gunasoquo explained. "Sleep with their wives. No sense all of us sittin' out here all night."

With first dawn Charles Henry was awake and boiling coffee in a pot when voices called from down the hillside, and Gunasoquo went to respond. The ancient Unegadihi looked around, then sidled close to Charles Henry. "You want to know something?"

Charles blinked. "You *do* speak English!"

"Course I do. Learned it in Georgia sixty years ago. You want to know something?"

"What?"

"I know the meaning of life."

"You do?"

"Give me some coffee and I'll tell you."

Intrigued, Charles Henry poured coffee in a bowl and handed it to the old man.

Unegadihi blew on it, sipped it and made a face. "Good," he said.

"So what is the meaning of life?"

Unegadihi gazed at him somberly. "Life," he said, "is just one damned thing after another."

More voices floated up the hill, then Gunasoquo came into view, followed by a long file of Indians—men, women and children—more than forty in all. Resplendent in their finest, brightest garb and carrying their best weapons, the men strutted proudly among the assembling flock. Gunasoquo looked around him, caught Unegadihi's nod and nodded back. Then he began herding the Indians into a group near the edge of the bluff, in ranks and rows, the men alternately standing and kneeling, the women and children grouped among them. A beautiful Cherokee woman with blue eyes handed Gunasoquo a fresh buckskin shirt with bright embellishments, and he changed into it. Then he joined the ranked savages. All of them stared stolidly at Charles Henry, and Charles Henry stared back.

"Wolf clan of two rivers village," Unegadihi explained. "Now you paint."

Several hours and many baby-tendings, child-chases and grumbles later, Charles Henry tipped his hat back, took a deep breath and waved them in to see. The painting was a magnificent array of portraiture in copper tones and bright hues. They were all there, and he had perfected their likenesses. They stood about in silence, gawking at the picture, then Gunasoquo whacked him on the back. "Damn good," he said. "We keep this. Let Bird clan and Paint clan and other damn clans eat their hearts out."

When the clan had gone with its picture, Charles Henry saddled and packed Captain Keech, strapped the tripod easel on his own back and mounted up.

Gunasoquo alone remained with him, and the tall warrior trotted ahead down the trail with Charles following, slightly bewildered.

At the wagon road Gunasoquo pointed him west and said, "Stay on road past twin peaks. After that you in somebody else's territory. I don't care what you do then. Damn nuisance. Good artist, though."

"Whose territory is that past the twin peaks?"

The Indian shrugged. "Maybe Cheyenne, maybe Osage. Who cares? Nobody civilized out there. Bullshit." And with that he was gone, back into the forest.

Once again, Charles headed west. He had the feeling he had missed something but couldn't decide what it was. Yet the day was fine, the land beautiful and the spirit of adventure high. "We'll cover some ground today," he said.

He had gone three miles when he saw horsemen coming toward him. It was a large party—tired, gaunt men with badges on their shirts and defeat in their eyes. Several of them were bandaged, their clothing caked with dried blood, and two were draped across their saddles.

They came on, plodding, and Charles Henry pulled aside to pass them, tipping his hat. He was a hundred yards beyond when there was a shout behind him, then another, and someone yelled, "Henry Clay!" Then something whined past his ear, and there were gunshots behind him. He turned and went pale. The entire party of lawmen was thundering after him, guns drawn, eyes wild with the hunt.

"Oh, Lord," he muttered. He tapped his hat firmly onto his head and put his heels to Captain Keech. The horse bounded, then stretched out in a mile-eating run.

"That old man was right," Charles Henry told the roan. "Life *is* just one damned thing after another."

Deep in the hills of Oklahoma Farley Underwood

rode, slouch hat flapping about his ears, chin whiskers abristle as he pushed the borrowed horse to its limits. "Gonna find that son of a bitch and put a hole in him," he swore for the hundredth time, fingering the huge old Walker Colt strapped to his saddle horn. "Ain't nobody make Farley Underwood break his word to a dumplin'."

Somewhere ahead of him was his wagon, its bed piled high with Emmalee Wilkes's luggage, a large, surly man at its reins. Underwood spat downwind.

It had happened so fast: he had loaded the girl's belongings onto his wagon, put in some supplies and helped her aboard the Pittsburg stage. "You don't fret, dumplin'. You just enjoy the ride. I'll be along directly."

She had turned those marvelous dark eyes upon him then, and smiled. "You will follow along behind the coach?"

"Missy, that old wagon can't set near the pace this coach will make. But it can go some places this coach won't go. Your luggage will be there when you need it."

He had watched the stage roll away, then climbed aboard his wagon. Two good horses awaited the touch of his reins. But he had no more than kicked off the brake when suddenly a large, red-nosed man bounded aboard, lifted Farley by scruff and scrapin's and flung him off his wagon. By the time he had his feet under him his rig was on its way west, thundering out of town toward the territories.

There was nothing to do but go after it.

Farley knew these hills. He knew the trails and cutoffs and where a man on horseback could gain himself some time. He would catch his wagon. He would put a large hole in the man who took it. Then he would take a trail he knew that would bring him into

Kansas not too far behind the dumpling's stage.

Jed Pike was not one to miss an opportunity. As a day and a night passed, and then another day, and the departed minions of the law did not return, he practiced walking in a straight line and kept a hard eye on the bank. He needed money. He had come a long, miserable way to get money. And he knew where the money was. It was in the bank.

He had scouted the town and its inhabitants. With sure instincts he had selected four scruffy characters who didn't have a brain among them but were capable of following a leader and had no scruples about robbing banks if someone showed them how.

With the skill of long practice he made his arrangements. Eight good saddle mounts whose owners did not know they were gone were assembled now, near but discreetly apart from the entrance to the bank. All his men had bandanas around their necks, and he had instructed each of them about covering his face. All of them wore guns, and all of them awaited his signal.

In the bank Sam Parker stepped from his desk to peer into a dark corner behind a cabinet, then swore softly and went to get his dustpan. He wondered how long it would take to clear out all the evidences of that damn sheep that had occupied the institution for the better part of a day.

Carrying his dustpan with its burden, he walked to the front door, opened it, tossed the sheep leavings out into the street, then looked around and froze. A few paces away saddle horses were gathered, and several scruffy men with bright new bandanas around their necks glanced at him then looked away guiltily.

"Oh, Lordy," he muttered. He closed the door and

hurried to the teller windows. "Boys, I hate to tell you, but I think we are about to be robbed again."

The other two men in the bank looked up at him. "Whose turn is it this time?" one asked.

"I guess it's mine," Parker admitted. "Get the big money into the hidey-hole, put the petty cash in the number one bin—you know the routine. Be sure and lock the back door when you leave."

"Most of the law is out of town," a teller pointed out. "There isn't anybody we can get to catch them coming out."

"I know. We'll just have to roll with this one. Go on, scat." He took off his coat, slipped on sleeve garters and an eyeshade and took their place behind the teller windows.

He sighed. Such was the cost of doing business in Fort Smith.

Out in the square there was a hush. People who had seen such things before took hint and got off the streets. Jed saw the signs, knew what was happening and was satisfied. No one would interfere. He would take the money, head west, get shed of the four nitwits somewhere along the way, then maybe go to Texas.

He started to cross the open ground, then hesitated. The afternoon stage from down river was rolling in. It pulled up in front of the hotel, and he waited. In a few minutes the newcomers would be off the street, the coach gone off to the barn.

Several passengers debarked. Some of them stood around sorting their luggage, then went into the hotel. Two of them, however, looked around and began walking toward the bank. One was a timid-looking man in a dark suit. He had gray side-whiskers and a round hat. The other was a tiny, aged black woman carrying a shotgun.

Jed leaned against the tailgate of a low-slung milkwagon and waited. There was plenty of time.

"I got to cash a draft," Aphrodite told the man named Watson. "Then we can look 'roun'." She sneezed. "Dang dust gone be th' death of me."

Watson stared around at the slowly healing shambles of the square. Everywhere was sign of recent pandemonium. "He has been here," he said.

"Ain' no doubt 'bout that," she concurred. She sneezed again. The wind was stirring dust from the trampled open ground.

Watson pulled a large kerchief from his pocket. "Here, cover your nose with this."

She took it, tied it around her neck and pulled it up to cover her nose. Then she retrieved her shotgun and satchel from him. "Bank's right yonder," she said. "Won' take me a minute."

At the bank, Aphrodite took a pouch from her satchel, handed him the satchel to hold, opened the door and went inside, cradling the heavy shotgun awkwardly as she fumbled for a draft and pencil.

Watson stood by the door, waiting. A few paces away several nervous men with bright new matching bandanas stood holding eight horses. He stared at them, had an inspiration and started toward them. One of them might have a clue as to the whereabouts of Charles Henry.

Across the way Jed Pike saw the pilgrim step toward his nitwits and frowned. He didn't want them talking to anyone. "Hey, you!" he shouted. "Hold up!"

He stepped away from the wagon and immediately regretted both his choice of words and his action. Forgetting his ambulatory problem he veered sharply right, rebounded off the milkwagon and fell flat on his back behind it, his rifle roaring as it discharged into the sky. The milkwagon horse, startled at the shot, slipped its hitch rein and danced backward, head up. Jed was

237

pinned beneath the low-slung bed, between heavy wheels. He couldn't move. All he could do was watch and swear desperately as his picked crew of nitwits across the way went into action, responding in perfect order to the signal he had drilled into them.

As one, the four men pulled their bandanas over their noses, drew their pistols and caught up the reins of the stolen horses, two per man. The pilgrim, just steps from them now, stared in surprise.

Inside the bank Sam Parker, his back to the teller window, stiffened as he heard the shot outside. Now they would come. He wished it were over. He never enjoyed being robbed.

The voice behind him made his hackles rise. He had not heard the door open, didn't know there was someone already in the bank. "Got to get some money," the voice said. "You can put it in this poke."

Raising his hands, Sam Parker turned slowly. A huge shotgun was pointed at his stomach. The desperado behind it was less than five feet tall, face camouflaged by a bright kerchief.

And she was black.

"Easy," he cautioned, his eyes on the shotgun. "Here's the money." Making no fast moves, he emptied the petty cash bin and stuffed the currency into the pouch she held. The old eyes between mockingbird hat and bandana looked slightly confused. "Don't worry," he told her. "You have it all. Now just go."

"But—"

"No, that's all. Just go."

She shrugged, the shotgun twitching in her arm, and the man went pale. "Well, all right."

Baffled by such strange practices, Aphrodite left the bank. She set foot on the walk and suddenly was caught up in a swirl of horses and masked men. They swept down on her, and someone lifted her aboard a spare horse. In the confusion of the instant she saw Mr. Watson also being handed onto a mount. Someone swatted the horse she was on and she clung for dear life.

"Yah-hoo!" a man yelled. "Let's ride!" And they were off in a thundering pack, out across the square, into a roadway and heading for the no man's land of the Oklahoma territory.

For a time it was all Aphrodite could do to cling to the back of the running horse. Then she began to get the rhythm of it and looked around. There were eight horses, six of them occupied. Four of the five men galloping with her were strangers. The fifth was a wild-eyed Mr. Watson, trying desperately to stay in his saddle.

"Man alive!" one of the strange men yelled through his bandana. "Slicker'n goose droppin's!"

"Just like the man said," another shouted. The one who held the reins to Aphrodite's horse dropped back a step and handed them to her. "Here ye go! Lead on! We're with ye!"

As they careened down the road, through a draw and into the hills beyond one of the men leaned toward another. "Joe, do you mind if I ask you something?"

"What?"

"I don't rightly remember them two. Who are they?"

The other one searched his memory, then shook his head. "I don't, neither. Don't matter, though. All we got to do is take orders."

"Yeah, but who from?"

"The one with the shotgun, I reckon. She pulled the job. She must be our leader.

239

XI

Like wildfire, word spread through the West. Faster than horses could travel, the word went out. Powder was on the prowl and had his sights set on a newcomer, the notorious Henry Clay of Charleston.

Jamie Haak, the man called Powder, was a dark legend in the territories. Ruthless, ambitious, and deadly fast with a gun, it was around him that the stories were growing, stories that spread from saloon to cow camp, from hideout to hideout, wherever the men gathered whose lives depended on their guns. There were many gunslingers, a lot of them overrated but some of them not. And above them all in the whispered construct of legendry stood the bleak, deadly figure of Powder.

Yet, word had it, there was another now who might—just might—be better still. Hard men licked their lips in anticipation. Henry Clay came from the East, and the reputation spreading before him was dim and confusing. How many notches did he have? No one could agree, but each time it was discussed the number grew, fed by one certainty. He had done Will Heath. Everyone knew that.

What did he look like? How did he operate? Where

was he now? It was all a mystery. But the mystery would soon be resolved. Powder was on the prowl. From the badlands to the Cimarron breaks, from the Llano Estacado to the Neutral Strip, from Fort Smith to Waco to Dodge, word spread. Somewhere, one day soon, Powder would find the mysterious Henry Clay.

Among the hard men some, the few who were best at their dark trades, strapped on their guns and took lonely trails. Two reputations were about to be wedded by a bullet, and some wanted to be in at the kill.

High in the western funnel of the unorganized territory, a buffer between the lonely plains of western Kansas and the Comanche haunts and cattle trails of the Texas Panhandle, was the long rectangle of territory known as the Neutral Strip. More often it was called No Man's Land. Law there was the law of the gun. As merging trails closed upon Oklahoma word went out by those mystic means common to underworlds and the killer breed that Powder somehow had missed his mark in the five tribes region.

Powder had been on the trail of Henry Clay. Now, it was known, Powder continued westbound. But now it was Henry Clay who trailed him. Hard eyes glinted over chip fires at the terrible cunning of the eastern gunman. Had Powder met his match? Across the lonely lands trails turned toward the Neutral Strip.

Unaware of any of this, Charles Henry Clayton lay facedown at the lip of a narrow, brushy wash and peered through a screen of shrub at the file of distant savages on horseback, crossing the scrub-mottled flats of western Oklahoma.

For several days he and Captain Keech had traveled through increasingly rising lands, more dry and bright with each sunrise, and had seen no living person. Not since crossing the southbound rail at Waverly Station. There had been a man there, a leather-faced man in canvas and skins, who had told him the "heathen" had arisen in the Washitas and that war parties were out to the west. Then the man had tried to steal his valise. Charles Henry shook his head slowly. It had been a shocking breech of hospitality—particularly after Charles Henry had helped him rig a pulley to make it easier for him to flag the mail. The man would have got away with it, too, except that he became entangled in his pulley rope and involved with his parcel hoist and was abruptly whisked away aboard the highball express.

Charles Henry had gone on west from there, musing again on the disastrous consequences of a simple lapse of attention.

From there he had crossed a wide river valley where sweet water ran in a tiny stream over red sand, then climbed to a plateau that was two days' crossing, then another valley and into broken lands where there were no trails, and one had to follow the sun.

His face had darkened from the glare. Squint-wrinkles appeared around his eyes. He had become leaner with travel, tougher with the hardships of it, and loneliness was a companion. It crept upon him in unguarded moments. How far he was from home. "But where is home?" he would ask Captain Keech, and the roan would turn its ears to his voice. Home—that was wherever Emmalee was. Home was with her.

"I won't leave her again, once I return to her," he told the horse. Then he leaned to pat its sleek neck. "You are a very good listener, Captain Keech. Just don't start answering me. That would mean we have been in the sun too long."

There had been days without food, and once without water, and he had learned some things all the schools in Massachusetts had not taught. He had eaten rabbit killed with his own gun, and had found that a sprinkling of sage improved the flavor. He had shared water from a sandstone basin with his horse and shared the spangled nights with chorusing coyotes. And he had drawn on and killed a diamondback before it could strike the roan.

"Do you know," he told the horse, "sometimes I think that instead of going back to Miss Emmalee, I might prefer to bring Miss Emmalee out here. Just look at this! She would love it. Over there where the green leaves show, beyond the grass—that will be a swale, and there is water there. Yes, you can smell it. But see beyond, that flat hill? There is a rise below it, and a man could build a house there, and pens and a barn. I could put in a well and raise spinach and squash, and I could devise a long-handled trowel so that she would not have to kneel to weed the rows. I could rig hoists and pulleys to help her scald hogs—yes, and a clamp for her parasol to shade her when she plows. Ah, Captain Keech, there is nothing I wouldn't do to make her happy."

The visions thus evoked were more than he could stand. Neck-reining Captain Keech he headed at a lope for a grassy rise from which he would have a view of the mesa with some interesting hills in the background. By sundown his swelling portfolio was ready to receive another painting, this one of a mesa bathed on one side with amber sunwash, its far side in rich and somber shadow. Again, he had captured the element of time and wished he had someone to show it to. The painting seemed to last, to count the minutes and convey the changes of a period of duration. He wasn't quite sure how he did that, but he knew it was unusual and interesting. He missed Unegadihi. The old man probably could have explained it.

He ran his eye over the details before packing it away—the lights and shadows, the hues of rich green and frosty gray, the texture of the sheer stone bluff below the flat top of the hill, the Indians. "Virgil Mac-Lootie was right," he exclaimed. "Things do jump out at you in a painting." There, tiny on the flank of the mesa, was a line of mounted Indians. They were coming his way. And they were looking at him.

That had been an hour ago and several miles east. Now he lay at the lip of a narrow draw and watched the war party on his trail.

It had been a good run. The roan had fled with enthusiasm, and Charles Henry had ridden with conviction—and twice he thought he had lost them. But each time they appeared again, still on his trail. And each time they somehow were closer. He decided he didn't know this land well enough by far. The hills and breaks forced him to travel circuitously. The Indians knew the shortcuts.

Below him, in the brushy bottom, Captain Keech browsed disinterestedly from the occasional leafy plants that grew among the screening salt cedars. Charles Henry eased up carefully to get a look at the lay of the land. It was fairly flat here, ribboned by gullies and washes that meandered through it. To the west, the land sloped slightly downward, and the sun stood on distant misty hills.

The roan had some run left, but not much. More breaks lay ahead, possibly a mile away. He felt he could gain distance that far. But then would be the mazes again, and the mazes were what was defeating him. The Indians knew the shortcuts.

He lay and stared long at the sloping flats beyond the wash and the maze-break beyond that, and thought he saw a pattern to the broken land out there. "If I could paint that," he muttered, then smiled bleakly and tapped his hat tightly onto his head. "Oh, well. A half-witted idea is better than no idea at all."

He scrambled down the side, caught up the horse's reins and mounted. He leaned forward to scratch the roan's ears, then settled into the saddle and swatted its rump. "Tallyho, Captain Keech!"

With a leap and a scramble the horse mounted the left bank, lunged over the top and bunched powerful haunches to bound away across the sloping land. Behind him, Charles Henry heard war cries like the yipping of coyotes, dim on the wind. Leaning into the horse's motion, he raced toward the next maze of breaks.

He hoped the Indians knew the shortcuts out there, too. He counted on that.

Emmalee Wilkes was beginning to worry about her luggage. Farley Underwood had assured her that it would be there when she needed it, but she was three days into Kansas now, and the contents of her suitcase were being stretched to the limit. She even wore mismatched blouse and bonnet on this leg of her journey, and faced the distinct possibility of having to wear the same ensemble two days in a row if her luggage did not appear. She had seen neither luggage nor Underwood since she had left Fort Smith.

Still, Colorado lay to the west, and somewhere out there Charles Henry was undoubtedly in trouble. She kept moving. The stage she rode now was the mail express from Sedan to Winfield, its teams pacing the long, lonely miles between barren waystops, its payload a strongbox, two express sacks, and four passengers. One was Emmalee. The other three were thrilled.

The man with the round belly and gold watch chain had spent the morning slipping nearer to her with each bounce of the coach until the thrust of her parasol's point had driven him to the far side of the coach where he sat carefully apart and pouted. The gangly man with the dark suit and chin whiskers ogled her at intervals, blinking solemnly, then passed long moments in silent prayer. The young man with the bright tweed jacket and red cravat chatted interminably, his face a constant leer, his remarks so often suggestive that Emmalee was very close to putting her parasol up his nose when gunshots rang out and the coach lurched crazily, veered across the road and came to a dust-swirling halt.

There were voices outside, angry and demanding.

"Throw down that strongbox!" a gruff male voice called.

"Keep them hands in the air!" another demanded, and Emmalee wondered vaguely how the driver and guard were going to manage to obey both commands.

The brilliant young man across from her had gone pale. "My God," he said, "we're being robbed."

The plump man immediately began to sweat, and the gangly one lapsed into prayer again.

Emmalee raised a corner of the dust-curtain nearest her and peeked out. Several men with masks on their faces and guns in their hands were there, all mounted and all intent upon the stagecoach. Even as she looked one of them called, "You folks inside, step out here where we can see you!" The three men with her seemed to be trying to sink into their padded benches.

"Come on out," the voice called again, "or I'll start shooting through the sides."

"Do you hear that?" she asked the three men. "That could be very dangerous." With a shrug she opened the door and motioned the men. "Go on, step out."

Frightened and dazed, they filed out of the stage. The plump man's hand brushed across her swelling blouse as he went by, and he suddenly sprang from the coach, his eyes wide, propelled by a parasol point in the posterior.

"I never!" Emmalee fumed. She gathered her skirts and stepped from the door, to the step and then to the ground. As she turned, blinking in the bright afternoon sun, one of the mounted men whistled and another gasped, "Hot damn!"

Emmalee tipped her bonnet to shade her eyes, then peered from beneath it, looking from one to another of the masked men with the guns. Two of them removed their hats, but the guns never wavered.

Up on the box, the driver and guard sat stiffly, their hands held high.

She looked back at the masked men. "Is this a robbery?"

The one nearest her gulped and nodded. "Yes, ma'am. That's what it is."

"Then are you men outlaws?"

Another of them chuckled. "Are we outlaws? Well, yes, ma'am, I guess you could say we are."

"Let me get this straight." She raised a gloved hand to count off on delicate fingers. "This is the West, and you men are outlaws, and you are committing a robbery?"

The nearest one frowned, puzzled. "You got that about right, ma'am."

"Oh," she said. Then she nodded. "Just a moment, please." She opened her voluminous purse and dug around in it. "Ah, here it is," she said. Then she drew the Smith and Wesson and opened fire.

The big revolver blazed and roared and blazed again, .44 slugs screaming from its snout. The nearest outlaw flailed his arms and pitched backward off his saddle. The one next to him shrieked and tried to swing around but was pitched sidewise from his bucking mount and grabbed at the saddle horn as his foot hung in the stirrup. The saddle slipped, the horse bolted and the man was carried howling away, clinging and bouncing beneath it.

The driver roared, "Good God Almighty!" and dived into the stowage tow to come up with a short rifle and begin firing. The guard, meanwhile, had leapt to the ground to retrieve his shotgun. As the horseman nearest him swung toward Emmalee the guard came up with his greener and its roar blasted the man from his saddle. A bullet sang through the stage's siding, and the driver swiveled to pump three fast shots toward the far side. There was a screech from there.

Emmalee's fourth shot took the hat off a large outlaw and sent him racing away, low over his pommel, flailing his mount with the barrel of his pistol. She fired a shot at the final outlaw still before her, and the bullet zipped past his face as he pointed his gun at her. Then he lowered it, saying, "Aw, hell!" and turned to thunder away after his hatless companion.

The area around the coach was a sudden vacuum, reeking of powdersmoke and stunned silence.

The three male passengers stood agape, the plump one still holding a hand to his prodded posterior, the gangly one dazed and open-mouthed, the brilliant one stunned and as yet unaware of the spreading wetness that darkened his britches.

The coach guard, a grizzled and squint-eyed little man, gazed at Emmalee and grinned. The driver climbed slowly down from his box and walked over to her. His face was chalk white, and his hands were shaking so badly he dropped his rifle. The grinning guard picked it up for him.

He stared down at Emmalee. His mouth worked but nothing came out. He started over again, his voice strained down to a chirp. "What in God's name did you go and do that for?"

"Do what?" Emmalee asked sweetly, staring in

249

admiration at the smoking revolver in her hand. It did have an authoritative way about it.

"Why on earth did you commence to shooting at those men?"

"Why did I . . ." She looked up at his pallid face. "Why, because they were robbing us."

"Ma'am," he squeaked, choked and shook his head. "Ma'am, you don't just start—"

"They were outlaws. They agreed that they were."

"When men have guns pointed at you—at all of us—you don't just haul out a—"

"This is the West," Emmalee explained, speaking slowly. "Those men were outlaws. They were robbing this stagecoach."

"Yes, but, God, ma'am, you can't just haul off and—"

"I have it on very good authority that that is exactly what one does in such situations. None other than Miss Jane Falwether-Smythe prescribed it in an essay in *The Lady's Compendium of Western Culture and Habits.*"

"Jake?" the grinning guard interjected.

"Furthermore," Emmalee continued, *"The Lady's Guide to the Discharging of Firearms,* I believe in the second chapter, points out that a firearm is only a firearm when it is used upon necessary occasions. Otherwise it is simply an awkward piece of metal."

"But, Ma'am, you could have got us all—"

"Jake," the guard repeated.

"And besides that," Emmalee concluded, "I am on my way to Colorado to find Charles Henry Clayton, and I do not have time for this kind of foolishness."

"But, Ma'am, in the name of heaven—"

"Jake!" The guard shook his head, took the driver by his shoulder and pushed him toward the front of the coach. "Get up there and drive. Don't you know when you're outnumbered?"

As they proceeded toward Winfield, making good time across the flint hills, the young, brightly dressed man sat in the far corner of the coach, his legs tightly crossed and his hat over his lap. He stared out the window and blushed furiously.

Emmalee wondered again what had become of her luggage. She hoped it would be there when they arrived at Winfield. She really didn't want to have to wear the same outfit twice in one week. What would people think?

XII

Squatting on his heels atop a sandstone ledge, Powder watched the chase across the flats. Eight hostiles, probably Kwahadis from the staked plains, rode in hot pursuit of a lone white man.

Powder was only mildly curious at first. The man rode well but had little chance of escaping. The Kwahadis would catch him in the breaks beyond and he would die. Maybe he would kill a couple of them first, maybe not. Powder could have turned the tables if he wanted to. They would pass below where he sat before entering the breaks. From here he could ride down, intercept the chase and take out enough Indians to end the drama. But Powder wasn't interested in wasting bullets on Indians. So he only watched, whiling away the time as evening came on. He needed provisions and would take them at Camp Supply. But he wanted to arrive there in the dark of morning, when the soldiers were asleep and the sutler's place was shut down. It was easier then.

The chase neared him. The man could ride. He had gained a little distance across the open ground, probably had an idea about now that he was escaping. Powder spat. Damn fool would not escape. The

Indians were taking him just where they wanted him.

Powder toyed with his gunbutt. He could take the man out of his saddle from here, if he wanted to. A hard smile played at the corners of his lips. That would spoil the Kwahadis's fun for them. He was tempted, just to see them prance and howl. But then they would come for him and he would have to waste bullets on redskins. He had better things to do.

As the rider approached, Powder squinted in the evening light to make him out. A traveler. A pilgrim. Too much load on his horse, too much baggage. he wore a gun but wasn't using it, and there was something strapped to his back. A flapping thing like a bundle of laquered sticks. He wore a top hat, was young, lean. Powder tensed and swore. The man could be . . . suddenly he knew him. He had never seen him, but he knew him. Henry Clay. The eastern gunman he meant to kill.

With lightning reflex Powder shifted on his heels and drew his gun. But it was too late. The man was past, his horse thundering by to swerve toward the breaks. Even as the gun came up the man and horse plunged down an embankment and disappeared into a long, angling draw.

The Kwahadis yipped and cavorted in their run.

Powder cursed under his breath. But still he sat and watched. If that was a pilgrim out there, the show was about over. But if it was Henry Clay . . . he wished he could see better, into the breaks.

The Indians split up, four kicking their horses down the shoulder of the draw to follow their prey, the other four crossing and heading out across the diminishing flats toward a distant place where the draw would wind back to their path.

An intense, cold curiosity suffused Powder. He wanted to see what Henry Clay would do. Suddenly the death chase became in his mind an interim thing, beyond which Henry Clay would go on, and Powder would find him out there somewhere and put him down. The image he had of Henry Clay was clear, and Henry Clay would not be stopped by Indians. But what would he do? If he ambushed them, how would he set it up? If he eluded them, how would he manage it? To know these things would be to know the man better. It would add to his advantage sometime soon.

Easing down the backside of the ledge, Powder swung aboard his horse and went to see. He knew about where the two routes would coincide. He wanted to be closer.

In the draw, Charles Henry leaned into his run and counted the rippling thuds of Captain Keech's hooves on the packed-sand bottom. Ahead the draw would bend, and if his eyes had not fooled him there would be a screened cutback just beyond where another, smaller draw joined. The roan was tired. He could feel it in his stride. The bend opened before him, and he watched the right bank. He almost missed it. The opening was narrow and screened by plum thickets. He skidded Captain Keech into a hard turn and burst into the thickets, expecting momentarily to hurl them both against a blind wall. But the thickets thinned, and he was in a tiny wash, tapering away before him, climbing. Easing back, he slowed the trembling roan and brought it to a halt. He swung down, snugged the reins and wrapped an arm around the horse's muzzle to quiet it.

There was no sound. The high walls of the breaks echoed only the wind on the flats above. He peered back the way he had come and chewed on his lip. He hoped the Indians knew some shortcuts here. If so, they might have crossed the draw and gone on, to intercept him a half mile away. Or, they might have divided up to

255

catch him over there between parties.

If I get out of this, he instructed himself, I have to remember to take Miss Emmalee to parties. Ladies enjoy parties. Maybe we can make a list of cotillions and . . . with an explosion of sound a massed party of yipping hostiles racketed by on the other side of the plum thickets. He hoped it was not the entire group. He hoped at least a few had taken the shortcut. Otherwise they would be right back and would find him. He wondered what they were so angry about. It probably had something to do with treaties.

Silence again, and he waited. The evening light was dimming. Still he waited. He wished he could see what everyone was doing, where they had gone. Minutes passed, and no one came. He straightened his hat, tugged the reins and headed on up the little draw, leading the roan.

All he had gained was a little time, a few minutes for Captain Keech to rest. The Indians would discover his trick and would return. He got out his gun and checked the loads, then checked the extra gun in his saddlebag. He wished he had practiced more with them. He had no idea how he had managed to outshoot the outlaw in Arkansas, and he didn't like the idea of counting on an ability that might have been pure fluke.

He had walked two hundred yards since the hostiles went by, and now he listened for their return. Any minute now, they would be on him. They were either in the draw behind him, backtracking, or up on the flats riding to cut him off.

He walked further, up the rising wash, and removed his hat as his head cleared the grassy top. In the lingering evening he stretched for a look around. There was no one there.

Leaving Captain Keech, he climbed to the flat for a

better look. The plains were empty. Then he saw movement in the distance, to the west, and suddenly recognized what he saw. The Indians were a long way off, riding hard away, their dust feathering out behind them. And beyond, just a short distance, was a man on a horse, riding for his life.

Surprised, Charles Henry squinted in the dusk. There was no doubt about it. The Indians had found someone else to chase and were hard on his heels. A distant pop came back on the wind, then another, and two Indian ponies ran away riderless. The six remaining hesitated, then fanned out in two flanking arcs, further now from the rider, and went after him again. They stayed further away now, out of gun range, but still they pressed him, and still he ran. The light was fading.

After a time he brought Captain Keech up from the wash, flanneled him down and scratched his ears. The Indians and their new prey were long gone. The Oklahoma breaks spread lonely beneath a spangling purple sky.

"If we had a lantern, we would proceed," he told the roan. "However, it probably is best if we both get some rest and start again fresh in the morning." He made his way a half mile to a sandstone ledge above the breaks and settled in for a pleasant evening.

The ledge behind him hid the sight of a distant— miles distant—bobbing speck of light that was not a star.

As he made a small, sheltered fire and looked through his packs for something to eat, he thought of Emmalee. How would she react to all this if she were here? "Probably nothing like me," he said to himself. "It seems to me that women are very much different from men." He turned to the horse, grazing nearby.

"Isn't that a delightful coincidence," he proclaimed.

Elsewhere, true to the nature of occurrences, other things had been happening.

When Farley Underwood found his wagon, a bit beyond where he had hoped to catch it, its team was still hitched and restive, its load of luggage was intact and its running gear was mired to the hubs in a seep. There was no sign of the big man who had taken it, and Farley swore with enthusiasm. He had looked forward to shooting the thief.

He unhitched the team, brushed them down and set them out in good graze while he labored to unload the rig. Some of the boxes and containers weighed a ton or at least seemed to. Out of curiosity he opened a particularly massive small trunk and looked inside. It was packed to the brim with books. He stared at them with the wonder of one who does not read. "My land," he mused aloud. "Do you suppose that dumplin' knows what it says in all them?"

When the wagon was empty he re-hitched the team, hauled the rig out of the seep, then loosed the team to graze again while he reloaded the luggage. "Pore little thing gonna be wonderin' where this stuff is," he told himself. Two miles back was a trail he knew that cut north and west through the hills. It came out, eventually, a little east of the town of Winfield in Kansas. Re-hitching the team he turned the rig, avoided the seep and drove to the bend where the trail began. He looked around carefully before making the turn, and from there on drove with his eyes alert. "Them Cherokees is crazy," he told himself from time to time. "Nice people . . . but crazy."

He had gone several miles along his way when three young Indians sprang from a cedar thicket by the trace, all of them puffing with exertion, laughing and looking back to fling derisive birdcalls into the forest, from which came the yipping of Iroquoians in chase. The youngsters skidded to a halt at sight of the laden rig, looked at one another, then in a concerted rush they clambered aboard the moving wagon and tossed Farley Underwood, rifle and all, into the brush at the trail's edge. One of the boys took the reins and urged the team to a run. Another crab-walked along a sideboard to the tail, clung there to untie the reins of the trailing saddle horse and turned it loose. The third clambered to the top of the luggage heap and postured there, laughing and waving a roll of paper. He was doing a precarious dance when the wagon vanished around a turn.

By the time Farley got himself picked up and brushed off he was surrounded by irritated Indians, all adult males. A large, axe-wielding warrior strode to him and scowled down at him. "What you give them wagon for?"

"I didn't give them a damn thing! They jumped me and took it!" Farley had seen where his saddle horse went and started after it. But a large hand on his shoulder restrained him.

"You not in with that thievin' bunch, why you up here? You breakin' treaty?"

"I'm not breakin' anything. I'm just passing through. Now let me go. Them hootin' jays stole my rig!"

"Tough bullshit." The big brave sneered. "Hell with rig. Easy come, easy go. Damn Bird clan pups steal clan heirloom from us. We catch them, we whop their butts."

"Clan heirloom?" Farley's face went grave at the seriousness of the crime. He knew the Indians, knew how deeply they treasured their symbolic things. "Say, that's too bad. Somethin' passed down from generation to generation?"

"Since last Wednesday," the big brave assured him. "Painting of whole Wolf clan. Bullshit. Now we probably have to ransom it back. Damn Bird clan pups. Need their butts whopped."

"I'll do it for you when I catch up. That's my wagon and team they got there, and a dumplin's luggage that she's waitin' for."

"What kind dumplin'?"

"Oh, she's about this tall, got a shape on her make a man's tongue go dry and as pretty a face as ever you did see, and she's on her way to Colorado. Couldn't hardly keep her hands off of me from the minute we met, which is why we're travelin' separately. I don't hold with that kind of carryin' on."

The brave stared at him. Then he nodded. "You go on," he said. "You catch them pups you say Gunasoquo gonna whop their butts if Wolf clan picture not back here by sundown. You tell 'em. Bullshit."

Farley ran to retrieve his horse, leapt to the saddle and jumped the animal into the trail. "I'll tell 'em!" he called. He headed up the trail at a dead run.

"Lot of real opportunities in the West," Weldon Hempley said nervously as his buggy rolled past the twin peaks and into the territories beyond. "All opening up now. Man gets in on a good predevelopment proposition he can be rich in no time. Why, I know of one deal that just closed that turned out to be worth twenty, thirty times what was predicted. Lots of big money heading out there right now to negotiate for it, and the fellow that bought it doesn't even know—"

"Shuddub ad dribe," the sullen, burly man beside him said.

*   *   *

It took Farley Underwood half a day to retrieve his wagon again. The Bird Cherokee youngsters set a hard pace, and when Farley finally overtook them the wagon team was near exhaustion.

He hauled alongside, grabbed the reins and eased them to a halt. Then he swung around, trained his rifle on the three teenaged miscreants and gave them a royal chewing-out which lasted for all of four minutes before one of them, wide-eyed with awe, shrugged and spread his hands in confusion. "Tla no," he said. "Kani gi da, u-duvsanuvhi."

Farley stopped, his mouth still open. "What does that mean?" He turned to one of the others. "Don't he speak English?"

His face a blank, this one shrugged eloquently. "U yo-i." he explained.

The third looked at the second, holding his roll of paper. "Gudei-si u-duvsanuvhi?"

"Well, my land!" Farley shook his head, exasperated. "Why didn't you tell me?" With an oath he pointed to the trail beside the wagon. "Get the hell off my rig."

Obediently the three climbed down. Farley pointed at the rolled paper. "I don't care whether you can understand me or not, you young pups. But if you don't get that thing back to them people, that big one is gonna bust your butts. And he means it, too. Now go on!" He waved his rifle at them. "Git!"

Wide-eyed, the three started back down the trail, whispering among themselves in Tsalagi.

Underwood looked after them, then tied his saddle horse on behind the wagon and climbed to the box seat. The Cherokee boys looked back now and then, glancing over their shoulders. As Underwood headed north, they kept walking south. When they were out of sight one of the boys, near bursting with suppressed laughter, elbowed the one next to him. "Old fart sure can string words together, can't he?" It set them off into howls of laughter made even worse by the antics of the third, dancing around on the path, waving his arms and singing, "Old fart . . . u-duvsanuvhi . . . old fart . . . u-duvsanuvhi . . ."

"I guess we'd better take this back where we got it," the one with the rolled paper gasped finally, wiping his eyes. "If Gunasoquo gets mad enough to tell my father, I'll get whaled for sure."

From that point on Farley Underwood maintained a vigilance he had not before achieved. He was tired of losing his wagon. He was tired of being thrown from his box. He was tired of having to chase after the dumpling's luggage. He was tired of people making a fool of him. And after a few days of such constant vigilance, as he selected a spot for early camp on a hillside half a day south of the Kansas line, he was just plain tired.

The six desperados had ridden hard for three days, making a beeline northwest across the rolling terrain of the territories, following faint trails as they found them, sleeping light and putting the miles behind them. Aphrodite and Watson remained uncertain as to how they had acquired the faithful following of four that traveled with them, but they had sorted out that somehow, inadvertently, they had committed a bank robbery and were now outlaws. They suspected too that the eight horses carrying them across wild country probably were not legally acquired. They had talked it over between them the first evening out, sitting across a campfire from their four faithful fellow felons, but could come up with no better course of action than to proceed.

"At least," Watson said with a shrug and wiping his

spectacles, "we are proceeding in the proper direction. Your Miss Emmalee and my Mr. Charles Henry are westward bound. So are we."

Aphrodite adjusted her mockingbird hat and gazed across at the happy faces of Joe, Jasper, Jesse, and Alexander. "I never in my whole life see a dumber bunch than them," she pointed out quietly. "Here we is, runnin' from th'law, an' they don' have a care in th' worl'. Seem like nice enough folks, but they sure is boneheads."

"When we reach a place with a telegraph," Watson said, "I shall contact my employer Mr. Powers and arrange for the money to be returned to that bank—and any such other compensations as are necessary. I'm sure it can be worked out. I am concerned, though, as to what we should do with these four gentlemen."

And that remained an open question. As the days passed, it became evident that the four had developed an immediate and intense loyalty to Aphrodite. They considered her their leader, and every suggestion that they might turn around and go home brought an immediate shaking of heads. "No, ma'am," they would say. "We're with you, all the way."

Joe had suggested they rob a train. Alexander thought they might hold up a stagecoach. Jesse was in favor of more bank jobs, and it had occurred to Jasper that they might steal a bunch of horses and sell them to the army. But since no such opportunities had yet arisen, they were happy to push on northwestward. They were well provisioned, well mounted and made good time.

Late in the afternoon of the third day they found a distinct trace leading north of west and followed it. Near evening they topped a hill and pulled up. Half a mile ahead a loaded wagon trundled along, going their direction, and Aphrodite squinted at it in the distance.

She rubbed her eyes, looked again and then waved her shotgun. "Come 'long. I needs a closer look at that there."

At a gallop they closed on the wagon, and as they approached Aphrodite's eyes widened. "It is!" she exclaimed. "It sho' 'nough is!"

Farley Underwood barely heard them coming before they were all around him, horses prancing, guns pointed at him. He gaped at them. There was no doubt they were outlaws, but they were like no outlaws he had ever seen: four men with bright, matching bandanas on their faces, a tiny, white-haired black woman, and a school teacher? He had seen some sights in his years, but this cut the cake.

"Put down that gun," the black woman ordered.

He put down his rifle and raised his hands. "Look here, now—"

"Where you get that luggage?" she demanded.

He blinked. "Why, I got this from a young lady back at Fort Smith. It's—"

"What she look like?"

He blinked again. The shotgun she pointed at him was huge.

"You want us to shoot him?" one of the bandanas asked hopefully.

"No! Jus' be still. You, I say what that young lady look like?"

"Well, she was about—ah, she had these nice, round—pretty face, you know, dark hair—real looker, she was, I mean—"

"Tha's her. What you do wit' her?" The shotgun twitched ominously.

"Ma'am, I didn't do anything with her. I didn't give her a chance. She took the stage to Kansas, and I took her luggage. That's all."

"Get down," she ordered.

They left him standing in the trail, disarmed and afoot, and as they rolled away the black woman turned on the wagon box to call back to him, "You ought to be 'shamed of yo'self!"

He watched them dwindle in the distance—masked outlaws, schoolteacher, black woman, sundry horses, and his wagon loaded with the dumpling's luggage. Finally he started walking. He was about ready to cry.

XIII

In Kansas the trail became a road and the road intersected a better road, heading due west. They rolled into Winfield on a bright afternoon, Watson driving, their four fearless freebooters following cheerfully and leading the extra horses.

"Tell me again about that prophecy," Watson said. "It is most puzzling."

"It cast th' day that girl was borned," Aphrodite said. "It a pow'ful prophecy—even ol' Mama Trevalier say they ain' no breakin' it. All's I can do be catch her up an' stay handy wit' my juju, maybe make things better some way. But it say I's goin' to distant lands, an' I don' want to go to no distant lands. I wants to go home."

"Yes, but how does it go?"

"It go, 'On the day when juices flow / an' th' virgin fires glow / one will come to fan th' flame. / Chaos an' havoc be his name. / Poor ol' woman, wring yo' hands. / You mus' go to distant lands / nevermore sweet peace to see. / All roads lead to Calamity.'"

"Strangest thing I ever heard."

"You think that's hard to believe?"

"Oh, no." He shook his head and glanced at her owl-eyed through his spectacles. "No, after some little exposure to Charles Henry Clayton I am prepared to believe anything."

"He sho' fit th' chaos an' havoc part, all right." She looked around at the little town they were entering. There were people on the street, horses at hitch rails, a buckboard in front of a general store. Nothing seemed at all amiss.

"Don' look like he been here," Aphrodite said.

"No, apparently not."

Behind them, following the wagon, Alexander edged closer to Jasper and asked, "We gonna pull another job here?"

"I reckon. Don't know why we'd be here otherwise."

"There's a bank over there. And a Wells Fargo. Western Union across the street. Wonder which it'll be?"

"Don't know. She ain't said yet."

On the wagon Aphrodite pointed. "Pull up over there. They's a telegraph place next to that hotel, you can go get us de-outlawed whilst I checks the hotel an' the stagecoach place. See if that girl been here."

They parked the wagon, and Aphrodite told their four escorts, "You all wait here an' tend th' horses. We got business to do."

Jasper nudged Alexander. "Another job," he whispered.

The four dismounted and watched as Aphrodite went into the hotel. Watson led the wagon team to a watering trough, let them drink, then backed them away to stand in front of the Western Union office. Aphrodite came out of the hotel, shook her head at Watson, and started across toward the Wells Fargo station. Watson went into the telegraph office.

Watering the horses, Jesse sidled closer to Jasper. "It ain't the bank?"

"Don't look like it."

"Man," Alexander breathed in wonder. "See what they're doin'? Two jobs at once!"

Joe looked at him, then at the places Aphrodite and Watson had gone. His eyes lit with understanding. "Wow. Slicker'n goose droppin's."

"What's our signal supposed to be?"

"She didn't say, so I guess it's the same as before."

People passing by glanced in puzzlement at the four roughly dressed men with matching bandanas and far too many horses. An aproned merchant standing before his store seemed deep in thought. Now he turned and crossed the square to the frame courthouse. A moment later he reappeared with a large man wearing a badge. The sheriff held a bulletin in his hand, and the two men read it together, glancing up now and then to stare at the four men down the street. The merchant pointed toward the Wells Fargo office. The sheriff looked again at his paper, prodding it with a finger. The merchant nodded.

Jasper, watching all this, nudged Joe. "Uh-ch. This don't look good."

At the east edge of town, a stagecoach rolled past the first buildings, and the driver turned to the wiry guard. "Hope the sheriff is here. We're gonna have some explaining to do."

"I'll give 'em a shot," the guard said. "Let 'em know we're coming in."

The sheriff handed his bulletin to the merchant and started walking toward the four suspicious-looking characters with the horses. Their bandanas did match the description wired from Fort Smith. And apparently there was a black woman and a schoolteacher with them.

The four saw him coming and started to back away. The sheriff raised his hand. "You there! Hold up!"

A block away the coach guard raised his gun and

fired a shot into the air.

"That's it!" Alexander yelled. In perfect synchronization the four raised their bandanas over their noses, drew their guns and vaulted aboard their horses.

"Shoot that sheriff!" Jasper shouted, and Joe and Jesse blazed away. With bullets singing around him, the lawman turned and sprinted for the cover of a buckboard. He raised his gun, but the arriving stagecoach pulled into his line of fire. Driver, guard, and passengers stared around in amazement.

Watson stuck his head out the telegraph office door, then ran into the street, waving his arms. "Here! Here!" Horses surged past and he was swept up by Joe and Jasper, one on each arm, and plopped into a waiting saddle.

Aphrodite erupted from the stage office, saw what was happening and shouted, "You all stop that! Behave yo'—"

Alexander was ready for her. Grinning beneath his bright bandana he leaned from his running horse, swept her up in one arm and handed her across to Jesse.

"Got her!" Jesse said. With a practiced flip he dumped Aphrodite into the saddle and clapped the horse on the rump. "Yah-hoo! Let's make tracks!"

"Slicker'n goose droppin's," Joe said.

The gang swung into a turn, horses leaning in unison, and thundered past the stagecoach, down the street and out of town. Aphrodite and Watson clung to their saddles, still shouting, their voices lost in the melee.

In the stagecoach Emmalee Wilkes's eyes went wide as the howling, shooting gang drummed past, and a cloud of dust blotted them out. "Aphrodite?"

She stood, bent to open the stage door and stabbed backward with her parasol, deflecting the groping hand of the plump man. She threw the door open, leapt out and ran around the coach to stare at the receding dust column that was the outlaw gang going west. "Aphrodite?" she asked herself again, then put her hands on her hips, stamped her foot and yelled, "Aphrodite!" But they were too far away to hear.

People milled around her in confusion. She saw her luggage aboard Farley Underwood's wagon across the street and muttered, "Well, it's about time." She started toward it.

A large man with a badge fell in beside her. "What was that you said back there, miss?"

"Back where?"

"Just then, when you shouted at those outlaws. What was it you said?"

"Aphrodite?"

He nodded, a puzzled frown on his bulldog face. "Yeah, that's it. I thought it was Afro-something. That's the name on the wanted sheet, too. I take it you know her, then?"

"I should certainly hope so. She is my mammy."

He gaped at her. "She is your mother?"

She stopped and stared up at him. "Well, of course not. Don't be ridiculous. I said 'mammy,' not 'mother.' It means an entirely different thing."

"Do you know the rest of the gang? The men with her?"

"I haven't the vaguest idea who they are. I don't even know what she is doing out here. She is supposed to be in Vicksburg, resting."

"I need to ask you some questions, miss."

"Very well. Is this a good hotel? Do they provide tubs for bathing, do you know? I wonder where Mr. Underwood is. Have you seen him? He is my wagon driver. I'll need that trunk there. Do you mind? And that box. Here, let me help you. Oh, and I'll need those two cases, also. Careful, don't drop any of them. I'll go ahead into the hotel and take a room."

"Miss—"

"This is very kind of you. If I find Mr. Underwood I'll send him to help you with the rest. The hotel people will know where you should put them."

"Miss—" But she was already gone, up the hotel porch stairs and into the shadowed lobby, the admiring eyes of many passing men fixed on her receding backside.

Sheriff Milo Gaines tried to shrug, but his load would not permit it.

Two miles out on the westbound road the notorious Aphrodite gang slacked its speed from a gallop to a trot, and the four bandanas handed reins over to their leaders.

"Close call," Joe said grinning.

"Two jobs at once," Jasper added.

"I'll bet that stagecoach had a strongbox," Jesse reasoned. "Hadn't been for that sheriff we might've—"

"Did you have a chance to send that telegram?" Aphrodite asked the white-faced Watson.

"I certainly did not. I was no sooner in the door when I heard shooting and looked out and then . . . I don't know precisely what happened then. What did happen?"

"I think we is outlaws some more."

"Well, what do we do now?"

She rested her shotgun across her scrawny lap, adjusted her mockingbird hat and looked back at the distant town. "Guess we best not go back there. Guess all we can do is go ahead on. I got to find that girl. This country already gettin' distanter an' distanter."

There were times when Milo Gaines didn't like being sheriff. This was one of those times. He sat stiffly on a sofa in the lobby of the hotel, acutely aware of the vision of huge, dark eyes staring at him disbelievingly, of the scent of fresh-bathed girl, and he ran a finger beneath his stiff collar, trying to loosen it. The posse had gone out and come back empty-handed. He had wired the towns down the line. He had satisfied himself that Miss Emmalee Wilkes knew nothing about any of the charges filed against her servant and guardian. And now he was trying to answer her questions.

"I don't care if she *is* eighty-four years old, miss. She's still a wanted man."

"But it is so preposterous," she pursued. "Aphrodite would never break the law. She is just a sweet little old woman."

"Bank robbery," he reiterated. "Horse theft, malicious mischief, disturbing the peace, unlawful entry into a treaty zone—of course, everybody does that— but those other things, miss, they sure enough are charges, and somebody sure enough thinks she's the one that did them."

"Possibly those other people did those things without her knowledge."

"She did the bank robbery all by herself, is what it says. Eyewitness description. The others stayed outside. And right here, today—she was the one that tried to rob the stage office. Leastways, she went in there. And the schoolteacher went in the telegraph office. The way it looks, they were doing a double robbery!"

"But they didn't take anything!"

"No, miss, but who knows what they might have done if they'd had the chance? Looks to me like the whole gang is a bunch of pretty desperate characters."

She blinked. "Aphrodite?"

"Looks to me like she's their leader."

"But she is—"

"Yes, I know, miss. Eighty-four years old." The soapy smell of fresh-scrubbed girl came to him again, and he felt remorse. "I really am sorry."

He went away more puzzled than ever. Milo Gaines was a methodical man, and nothing about this added up. It was impossible to see the girl as anything other than she seemed: a ravishing, stunning, impetuous creature off on some harebrained adventure—and yet she seemed to know the leader of a notorious outlaw gang. And there was that story the stage driver and guard told, about this same sweet little thing standing off the Colby bunch, driving them away virtually all by herself. And the chance remark by one of the passengers that she carried some sort of secret weapon disguised as a parasol.

"Maybe she's a Pinkerton," he muttered as he walked back toward his office. "That might fit. Then again, maybe she's a federal agent. If so, that sure is some disguise he's come up with. Or maybe a foreign agent? A spy?" He sighed. "Lord only knows. Maybe I better stick with stuff I know about and leave things like that alone."

He returned to the hotel in the morning, carried her voluminous luggage down for her and stowed it back in the wagon still standing by the porch—he had taken it on himself to put the three horses, wagon team, and spare, in the livery yard—and finally asked how she was going to arrange for the luggage to be transferred.

"Oh, that is up to Mr. Underwood," she told him. "By the way, have you seen him around anywhere? I don't know where he is keeping himself. He is a very strange man—but obviously reliable."

When she boarded the morning stage for Coldwater he helped her aboard, and she smiled and waved at him as the stage departed. It was two hours later that a dusty, unshaven old man with a bald head and a few teeth rode into town on the back of a hay wagon, got down and limped across to the luggage wagon, in-

274

spected it carefully and went searching for its team. Milo Gaines met him at the corner. "Are you Mr. Underwood?"

"That's me. Where's my horses?"

"Over at the livery. Would you mind telling me how that wagon—"

"Sure. Bunch of outlaws stole it from me. Looks like everything's all right, though. Them things belong to a dumplin'. You seen a dumplin' go through here?"

Gaines nodded. "She's on her way to Coldwater. You better hurry."

Far to the west, deep into the empty and rising land, the iron rails of the Chicago, Rock Island and Pacific railroad sliced across the rolling shortgrass prairie toward distant railhead in the foothills. The train chugging westward on the line today included a special car, a luxurious private coach leased to Mr. B. B. Timmons of Chicago. Its contents included Mr. Timmons himself and a collection of burly, sullen men, the cream of the Chicago crop.

Timmons sat in a velvet chair, deep in thought, then turned again to the papers and map spread on the table beside him. The papers were sheafs of telegraph messages, handwritten reports, and calculations. The map was of a u-shaped area among mountains, divided by rough grid lines. A penciled x marked one of the subdivisions which bore the number nine. In the crotch of the u was the number seventy-five.

Timmons stared at the map for the hundredth time. It was his ticket to recovery, to recapitalization, to revenge. He picked up a cigar, bit the end, stuck it firmly between his teeth and snapped his fingers. "Light."

The nearest of the sullen men jumped to his feet. "Yeah, Bull." He flared a match and held it as Timmons drew on the cigar.

Timmons stared at the map a moment longer, then scowled as he picked a paper from one of the stacks. It was a message from Forbish, Walker and Boole in St. Louis:

REGRET ADVISE PARCEL NINE TRANS-FERRED THIS DATE STOP TRANSACTION FIRM STOP TITLE RECORDED C CLAY-TON STOP OUR MAN HEMPLEY ENROUTE TO FIND C CLAYTON WITH PURCHASE OFFER YOUR BEHALF STOP PRICE MAY MODIFY ACCORDINGLY STOP SUGGEST YOU PROCEED PARCEL NINE MEET HEMPLEY THERE STOP

Timmons sneered. "Our man Hempley. Well, 'Our Man Hempley' had better have that deed in his pocket, or I'll have 'Our Man Hempley's' hide. No 'Our Man Hempleys,' no 'C. Claytons,' *nobody* gets in Bull Timmons's way on this one."

The disaster of his last venture, the collapse of his plans to take over the shipping interests of J. C. Powers, was a deep wound in Timmons's belly. It had almost ruined him. He had been so close. So close. Then that idiot in Boston had sunk his ship—literally. And the Egmont brothers had collapsed. He still had no clear idea what had happened in Charleston, but suddenly everything he had worked for, schemed for, had dissolved. He hadn't even had the satisfaction of hearing from Luther that the Boston idiot was dead. In fact, he hadn't the vaguest idea where Luther had gone. The man had just disappeared.

But section seventy-five would put him back on top

of the heap. The mountain was the bomb, and parcel nine was the fuse. Section seventy-five gave him the mountain. He would get parcel nine.

He read casually through some of the other papers spread there. Two were of particular interest. One was a detailed and highly confidential report to a mining company from one of the company's field engineers. It had cost Timmons a lot to get hold of that piece of paper. It had cost the price of two men's lives. But it was worth every penny.

The other, and even more interesting, was a private letter to Timmons from a person on his payroll and employed in a secure federal office. Colorado was about to become a state.

He pursed his lips. Colorado was about to become *his* state. He knew how to manipulate it, had it all worked out. All he needed was parcel nine.

XIV

The name of the place was Whiskey Creek. Located in the middle of the Neutral Strip between Texas and Kansas—the area called No Man's Land—it had no legal existence and no legal residents. But for all that it sported a booming economy and did a brisk trade.

The place was a hodgepodge of shacks and tents clustered on the prairie overlooking a narrow creek that sometimes carried water to the Beaver. It was a watering hole for the occasional trail herds now taking the west routes up from Texas, and a watering hole for their drovers. It was hangout and hideout to the worst of men, a place where anything that could be imagined could be purchased for a price—anything from bad whiskey to bad women, from games at a crooked table to games on a dirty floor, from a bed to lie in to a street to die in.

There was no law in Whiskey Creek, except the law of the gun. The Neutral Strip was the dead end of the unorganized territory, beyond the jurisdictions of any except a distant federal court which had learned long since that the officers it sent there seldom came back.

It was to Whiskey Creek that Powder came, and within a day he had killed three men. He selected them

279

carefully, called them out and shot them down. They were the three meanest and fastest that he could find, and with their deaths he stated by example that Whiskey Creek was his for as long as he cared to stay and that no one was to interfere.

It was here that Powder intended to make his play, to put an end once and for all to the spreading legends of the mysterious Henry Clay of Charleston. Since his brush with the Kwahadis, Powder's need to kill Henry Clay had become a burning rage. The man had humiliated him as no other had ever done, and in so offhand a manner that the thought of it produced a blind, black fury.

They had been within a hundred yards of each other out there near the Washitas. And somehow, Powder was now convinced, Clay had known he was there. Somehow the man had sensed him, manipulated him and used him as a decoy to draw off the Indians.

Six Indians had died in the pursuit. Powder had been in no real danger. But in the process he had sweated, retreated and run a good horse to death. He had walked nine miles on sore feet before finding another horse. And somehow, he felt, the man called Henry Clay had been there all along, watching him, gloating.

Henry Clay was still out there, somewhere. But Henry Clay would come to Whiskey Creek—all trails in the Neutral Strip led to Whiskey Creek—and Powder would be waiting.

How fast was Henry Clay? The legends kept growing. But that would end. He would prove once and for all that no one was as fast as Powder.

Still, there was no sense taking chances. What he had heard of Henry Clay was ominous. It would not hurt to have a backup gun, as long as the backup gun didn't live to talk about it.

That was easy to arrange. Anything could be had for

a price in Whiskey Creek.

Charles Henry Clayton almost missed Whiskey Creek. The day was warm, wind steady from the southwest, and he smelled the place from two miles away as he approached along the Beaver Trace. Within a mile the reek had become so overpowering that Captain Keech began to balk, so Charles Henry turned north to go around.

Then, topping a swell in the rolling prairie, he looked off to his left and saw the squalid shantytown—now crosswind from him and far less objectionable. He also saw where much of the smell came from. Hide wagons were ranked east of the town, downwind, waiting there in the sun while their drivers and escorts indulged themselves in various recreations.

From where he sat now, the land dropped off in three distinct shelves down toward the little town overlooking the nearly dry creek. Beyond the creek, which wound around the town in a horseshoe bend, were the surging bluffs that reared a hundred feet to cedared crests separating this valley from another to the south. The sun was quartering, a line of thunderheads trailed into the vast distance of the sky, and he caught his breath. "Marvelous," he whispered.

From this distance the cluster of tents and shacks looked bright and clean, miniatures catching the sun's rays and reflecting soft brilliance.

"Just a sketch," he told the roan. "A quick sketch." But by the time the "quick sketch" was done an hour later he had forgotten the downwind reek of the place and had become interested in the signs of life and movement he saw there. While he sketched, a line of wagons loaded high with kegs and jugs had come into view on the prairie northeast, and now they approached him, angling toward the Beaver Trace.

As the first wagon passed, its driver and swamper

281

stared openly at the neatly dressed, top hatted young man standing out on the plains with portfolio in hand. He waved at them. "What place is that over there?"

"That yonder is Whiskey Creek, pilgrim," the driver called back. "Only place I know of that a man can get hisself flacked, sacked and shellacked and pay for all three privileges."

Charles Henry decided it definitely would be a shame to pass so closely by such an interesting place and not at least take a closer look at it. Besides which he was young, lonely, and could use some civilized conversation.

The wagons went on by while he repacked his belongings. He mounted Captain Keech and started after them. As he neared the town he found the wagons all halted atop the first of the three step-down banks, drivers and swampers standing around them, perplexed. From here it was obvious that the series of banks, each between eight and twelve feet high, were far too steep to go over with a loaded wagon. He saw the friendly driver and reined over to him.

"There is a trail over there," he said, pointing east, "that looks as though it leads right to the town. You could swing around—"

"If you've been over there you know why we ain't going to do that," the teamster said. "Damn buffalo wagons stink to high heaven, and the trail's downwind of them. We wouldn't get these animals within a mile. We thought about comin' in from the west, too, but you can see why we changed our minds." He pointed and Charles Henry looked to the west. The trail meandered gently there, riding the inside of the horseshoe bend, then lining straight west along the creek. Far out in the distance, across the creek, was a dark veil of rising dust, and at its apex the creek bank seemed to be alive.

"What is that?"

"Longhorns," the man told him. "Trail herd comin' up from Texas. Water pools in the creek up there, so the waddies bring 'em there to drink. Most likely while them cattle are tankin' up up there, the drovers are down here stackin' up some hell time."

"I don't see what that has to do with your coming in from the west."

"You don't? Lord, son, you ever seen a herd of parched-out longhorn cows bein' pushed off their water by a bunch of drunk 'pokes? No tellin' how long them boys have been seein' the sights of Whiskey Creek, or when they're gonna take a mind to move on. But when they do, I wouldn't want to be anyplace within five miles of the north end of that herd. They'll be halfway to Kansas before they get bunched again."

Charles Henry gazed at the distant mass of meat with renewed respect.

"I guess we'll just have to carry these things from here," the teamster said, looking dismally at the lined wagons loaded with heavy wares.

"I tried something once that worked fairly well, when I was delivering cable spools," Charles Henry told him. "I set a plank from the wagon bed to the door and just rolled them in. That would be easy enough to do here, if you have some planking. What are those, whiskey barrels?"

"Those two wagons are whiskey. This one here is coal oil, that one over there is salt meat and the last one—with all the honey jugs stacked in it—them kegs there are blasting powder. The way I heard it, some of the tent folks here have got together and plan to blast out some creek bank downstream a ways to make a dam, then charge for the water."

"Well, whatever they are, they are all round except the honey jugs. They should roll nicely if you lay some planks."

The driver was skeptical. He looked at the slope down to the town, at the three stage bluffs, at some of the other drivers. "I don't know," he said. "Maybe we'll tote the honey jugs, then think about the rest."

Down on the east road three wagons had come into sight, plodding steadily toward Whiskey Creek. The wagons were full of dark-coated men with cloths held to their faces. The horses pulling them had sacking wrapped around their noses.

"Well, if that don't beat all!" a teamster beside Charles Henry said. "Will you all look at who's in them wagons? That's Brother Thorpe, there in the lead one, sure as bugs crawl."

Several others squinted. Some nodded. "I believe you're right," one said.

"What's he doin' way off down here?"

"I heard they run him out of Hays. Maybe he decided to save some souls at Whiskey Creek."

"He's crazy. There's folks down there would slice him from Praise Be to Amen just for the fun of it."

"Maybe not," another said, tugging at his whiskers. "They might just decide he's the best entertainment this week."

"'Til one of them yayhoos gets tired of him and commences to shootin'. I think we'd best get this stuff unloaded and delivered before the fireworks start."

Charles Henry tipped his hat to them, slid Captain Keech down the first bluff and headed off to see the sights of Whiskey Creek.

Up close, the cluster of tents and lean-tos was unbelievably shoddy and reeked of whiskey, offal, and unclean men. Yet, it was a bustling place and to a man too long alone it hummed with excitement. Somewhere a piano tinkled out of tune. Somewhere else a quartet was murdering Sweet Molly McGuire. Several hoarse

284

female voices sang in lively disharmony inside a large tent, behind which was a long, rundown shack divided by hanging blankets draped into a series of cribs. Most of them had their draping pulled, but two were open. A fat Indian woman sat in front of one of these, and a weather-hardened woman with a dirty gray shift leaned against a post before the other. They eyed him as he rode by but said nothing.

Just inside the first perimeter he found a common corral and turned Captain Keech into it. "I'll be back presently," he assured the horse.

As he walked through the shantytown he was aware that several men turned to watch him pass. One looked distinctly surprised, but he was no one Charles Henry recalled seeing before. By the time he had made a round of the place, there were a number of rough men more or less following him—though in most cases not quite seeming to. And he overheard pieces of whispers: ". . . Clay." ". . . Henry Clay." ". . . Powder."

He perked up at that last name. Virgil MacLootie had warned him to be on the lookout for someone named Powder. And Virgil had been afraid of him. Was the man here? At Whiskey Creek?

He glanced around. The men nearest him now all seemed of a type: hard-looking men with handy guns. Most were not looking directly at him, but they were there, and they were all around him. And one or two made no pretense of disinterest.

Charles Henry began thinking in terms of Gittingses.

The line of thunderheads he had seen on the horizon was rolling in, creeping eastward, and the afternoon sun had long since disappeared. Gusts of wind now whipped the edges of shanties and chittered through tent lacings. A delicious coolness had come upon the prairies.

Between a pair of rope corrals a group of men

285

labored to lay down planking in a long runway that ended at a sod building with the most substantial doors he had seen in this ethereal place. One of them waved at him, then glanced around at the men keeping pace with him and turned away abruptly.

Thirty yards and three rows of squalor away the missionary wagons had rolled into Whiskey Creek. Someone aboard was playing a drum.

Charles Henry had seen enough. He turned and headed for the corral where he had left his horse. He had gone only a dozen paces when two of the men following him ran to cut him off. They stood there in his path, bleak eyes unblinking, their hands near their holstered guns.

A wiry man with a hook nose and long, dark moustache studied him coldly from beneath a low hat brim. "Would you be Henry Clay?" he asked.

Charles Henry blinked at him. "Sorry, no. My name is Charles Henry Clayton. You must be looking for someone else."

"I don't think so," the man said. "Powder says you're his, but I got an itch to find out for myself. Do you know who you're lookin' at?"

"I don't believe so. I'm a stranger here."

"They call me El Paso." The man emphasized the name, then waited for recognition to manifest itself. But none came.

"How do you do, Mr. Paso. What can I do for you?"

"You can get out your gun," the man said with a sneer. "Because I'm going to get out mine." And with that, in an instant that was barely a blur, the man drew and fired. Charles Henry felt a sharp pain along his left shoulder. He glanced at it, saw a tear in his sleeve and blood beginning to well. He stared blankly at the man with the gun.

"Why did you do that?"

One of the others chuckled. "I guess that answers your question, El Paso. This here sure ain't no Henry Clay."

"I ain't so sure," another said. "Shoot him again, El Paso. He don't seem to rile easy."

El Paso thumbed back his hammer. "Might as well," he said.

But the hammer never fell. Charles Henry had had enough. Stunned and hurt, he let his artist's reflexes take over. Long fingers found and thumbed the navy Colt, quick eyes leveled it and he fired twice. His second shot knocked a fresh-lit lantern off a post into a stack of straw. But that didn't matter. His first shot had killed El Paso.

"Aw, my God," Charles Henry breathed as the man fell full length, facedown at his feet. "I've done it again." He put his gun away, looked dazedly around at the staring, shocked gunmen, then walked away.

A few steps beyond was a large tent with music coming from it. Lanterns had been lit inside against the growing storm-gloom. Its music nearly drowned out the shouting of the man standing in one of the missionary wagons and waving his arms. Charles Henry turned aside and entered the tent. Planks across barrel tops served as a bar. There was whiskey being served. A dozen or so men were in the place, but he ignored them and stepped to the bar. "How much for a drink of whiskey?"

The barman was a short, round man with a dirty apron. "Quarter each."

Charles Henry lay down a dollar. The barman poured amber liquid in a little cup. Charles Henry tasted it and drew a quick breath. It was horrible. "One is enough," he told the man.

With a shrug the barman handed him his change.

The place had become very quiet, a silence that

287

seemed to spread to the streets beyond. Charles Henry noticed vaguely that most of the patrons were leaving the tent, stepping carefully and quietly. He glanced up and saw two men enter. The first, a heavy-shouldered man with a shotgun, walked around behind the bar and gestured at the barman. "I'll take over here," he said. The first barman turned white and scuttled from the tent, in close company with the rest of the patrons.

Charles Henry tasted his whiskey again. It was really rotten stuff, but he felt terrible and decided he needed it.

"Henry Clay." The voice behind him was low and infinitely cold, like dry scales coiling.

He turned. The man there, ten feet away, had long, straight, moon-blond hair hanging to his shoulders. His eyes were nearly colorless, and his face was a sneer. "Henry Clay," the man said again, relishing the name. "I knew you'd come."

"My name is Clayton," Charles Henry told him.

"I know you, Henry Clay. And you know me. They call me Powder."

"I have heard of you. But my name isn't Henry Clay. I am Charles—"

"Shut up and draw."

Charles Henry stared at him. "Do what?"

The words seemed to throw the gunman into a rage. "You set me up!" he hissed. "Made a fool of me. They say you're the best there is. Well, you're not, and I'm about to show you. You shot El Paso out there. He wasn't fast. Neither was Will Heath. They just thought they were. I know you, Henry Clay." The man crouched now, his pale eyes blazing. "You got a gun there. Haul it out!"

Charles shook his head, the hackles rising on his neck. He heard a click and knew the heavy-shouldered man behind the bar had the shotgun pointed at his back. He wanted to look around but couldn't take his eyes off Powder. "My name is Charles Clayton. I told you that. I don't know any Henry Clay."

"I said draw!" Powder hissed.

Charles still held the three coins in his hand. Now they fell from nerveless fingers. "Woop," he said, and knelt to retrieve them. Thunder rolled over him, sudden and deafening. He looked up to see the bloody mess that had been Powder cartwheel backward across a bench.

Charles got to his feet. The tent was full of smoke and silence. He leaned across the plank bar and looked behind it. The other man lay there, his shotgun in his hand and a hole in his head.

Charles stared at him, then looked again at what was left of Powder. "Well I'll be darned," he said.

Two miles west of Whiskey Creek, in the gloom of approaching storm, a buggy edged its way down from the plains to the lower westbound road, and its driver peered ahead. "It's getting dark," he said. "I'd better put on the headlight."

The large man with him paid no attention. He had straightened in his seat, now was looking back along the road as though in premonition. "Turd aroud," he ordered.

Spatters of rain were falling when Charles Henry stepped from the tent. Men stared at him, then stumbled over one another as they backed away. Somewhere nearby a sonorous voice was ranting, ". . . Whatsoever thou hast in this city, bring them out of this place: for we will destroy this place, because the cry of them is waxen great before the face of the Lord; and the Lord has sent us to destroy it . . ."

No one seemed to be paying any attention. A haystack was burning near an adjoining tent, but no one seemed much interested in that, either. Everywhere, people gathered to stare at him. He wandered back the way he had come, and someone behind him shouted, "Dead! They're both dead! He done 'em both! He done Powder!"

And the whispers flanked him. ". . . Henry Clay . . ."

His foot caught a tent rope and he kicked at it, then bent to pull it up and heave on it. There were crashes and curses as the tent collapsed on those inside. He walked on.

The ranting voice had been shouting, ". . . then the Lord rained upon Sodom and upon Gomorrah brimstone and fire from the Lord out of Heaven . . ." But now the voice tailed off.

"I don't like this place," Charles Henry muttered. "I don't like it at all."

A few feet away a whiskey barrel lumbered down a plank ramp and thudded into a jury-rigged catch-trap of knotted rope. Two men lifted it out, set in with several more on the soddy's apron and turned to catch the next one. Charles Henry stumbled over another rope. He started to reach for it, but several admiring men beat him to it. "We'll just get this out of your way, Mr. Clay," one said.

"I've seen enough sights," Charles Henry muttered. He turned on his heel and started back with long strides toward where he had left Captain Keech. The swivel hook on his tripod caught an angled plank-brace as he turned, and he heaved it loose.

The rope the men had pulled had in turn reoriented the final planks. Now, as another whiskey barrel rumbled down from the ledges, it veered off at an angle and took out two tents and a shack before shattering itself against a hitch post. Whiskey flooded from it.

The next one took another angle and bit a corner out of the soddy as it headed for the dry creek. The following one scattered the burning haystack and the one behind that found the hitch post again. Men were shouting now, all around, running wild-eyed to escape the parade of thundering kegs. But the source, at the top of three bluffs, did not hear them. Up there, men began methodically unloading another wagon.

By the time the first coal-oil barrel hit Whiskey Creek, three more were on their way behind it, and a dozen blasting powder kegs were beginning their journey.

"The angel of the Lord done descended!" someone roared.

Coal oil shattered and gushed, and whipping winds spread flame in dancing arcs of violent illumination.

Charles Henry found the corral and kicked down its bars. Inside Captain Keech was still saddled and packed, and he swung aboard, driving the other stock out ahead of him. "Go find a better place to be!" he shouted. "This one stinks!"

Spreading fires provided all the illumination he needed to head the roan out at a gallop. He arrowed past the outer perimeter of Whiskey Creek, into the clean prairie rising beyond, jumped Captain Keech up the first bluff and turned west. Within a hundred yards he had to take the second bluff to avoid a huge herd of stampeding longhorn cattle descending upon the flare-bright town. Far out behind them a light joggled in the darkness in a way no cow had ever seen a light joggle.

He rode a quarter mile, then looked back as the rumble of brooding storm was shattered by repeated explosions. Bright clouds of climbing brilliance billowed from the dust and smoke that blanketed Whiskey Creek. In their glare he could see figures scurrying off in all directions. He stared in awe. Another bright cloud grew and the shock of explosion followed it.

Below him, bright in the glare of the burning,

exploding town, three careening wagons full of people thundered by.

"Don't look back!" someone shouted. "In the name of God, don't look back!"

The spectacle finally shook Charles Henry out of his bleak stupor, and he gaped at what had been the town of Whiskey Creek, now a glow of spreading flames swirling through clouds of dust and punctuated by horrendous explosions.

"Catastrophic," he breathed. "A whole town—and nobody was paying attention."

He had wasted enough time. He turned the horse and headed west. Big drops of rain splattered him, and lightning danced among black clouds. He found his slicker and put it on. Distantly on the horizon was a line of radiance where the setting sun still softened the lands beyond the storm.

Somewhere out there was Colorado. Somewhere in Colorado was parcel nine. And somehow, with parcel nine, he would earn his way back to Emmalee Wilkes.

"Tallyho, Captain Keech," he muttered. "We still have a way to go."

Part Three

Calamity

I

"Assuming the prophecy is valid," Watson reasoned, shifting for a more comfortable position in the saddle, "then it seems fairly simple how it might be countered. The prophecy applies to your Miss Emmalee because she is—and only so long as she remains—ah—untouched."

"She stuck wit' it long as she a virgin," Aphrodite answered.

"Ah, yes. Well, if she were no longer that, then the prophecy would not apply. Isn't that correct?"

The gang was traveling through rising country now, prairie lands that went on as far as the eye could see under a brilliant sky laced with mare's tail clouds and flights of wild birds. The land was slightly rolling but seemed flat in its immensity, bounded by horizons lost in sheer distance.

"That what I been tellin' you," Aphrodite said with a sigh. "I been tryin' ever' way I knows to get that girl paired off, ever since she come of age—an' maybe a little befo' that. She get pas' bein' a virgin, then they won' be no virgin's curse."

"Well, surely there have been eligible young men. So why is she still a—ah—"

"Because she won' have none of 'em, is why. She want to fall in love first."

"I see." Watson removed his hat to wipe his temples, then replaced it, precisely level above his graying sideburns. "Well, it appears she may have done that now. Fallen in love, I mean. After all, I can't imagine a well-bred young lady traveling halfway across the country in pursuit of a young gentleman for any other reason. Possibly if she and Mr. Charles Henry could be brought together—"

"Nosuh!" Aphrodite shook her head violently. "Not him! Don' you see? He the problem. He chaos an' havoc an' he gone be that wherever he go, an' the prophecy don't have nothin' to do wit' that, 'cept to warn about him."

"Oh, but surely—"

"Can you imagine that sweet little thing's life was she married up wit' chaos an' havoc? You seen what he do, Mr. Watson. Ever'where he go, it like Apocalypse done been there. Sooner or later, she get hurt. I ain' gonna have that, no way!"

"But—"

"He *in* the prophecy, not part of it. He don' end when it do. He a . . . a . . ."

Watson thought a moment. "Possibly an elemental force."

"Mos' likely. Anyhow what I got to do is find that girl an' take her home, befo' they gets together."

Watson squinted ahead. The two bandanas riding before them, a hundred yards away, seemed to dance and shimmer in the glare of day. Two more were behind them the same distance. They had been forced to flee from the law three more times before leaving Kansas, and Aphrodite had assigned their happy companions to fore-and-aft guard duty. It kept the men occupied and gave them some mental exercise—

remembering what they were there for.

"My mission may be somewhat more difficult, it appears," Watson said.

"Nothin' difficult 'bout findin' *him*. You jus' follow th' disasters."

"It isn't just finding him. I am supposed to find him and keep him out of trouble."

"Oh." She glanced at him in sympathy. "Well, I's glad I ain' got your problem."

Ahead of them the lead bandanas had topped a swell, halted, and now one of them came galloping back. It was Jasper.

"You want us to tell you when we see somethin'?" he asked.

"Might as well," Aphrodite said. "Otherwise they ain' much point you ridin' lookout like you is."

"Okay. We seen somethin'."

"What?"

"Kinda hard to tell. I guess you better come and look."

From the top of the swell they could see a sod house, a corral, and a windmill. As they came closer the scene became stranger. The soddy was a shambles, half its roof caved in and a corner pushed awry. Its strap-hung door lay open and aslant, and a pair of horses in team harness stared solemnly out at them, only their heads able to clear the doorway.

The windmill derrick was a stubby, sturdy structure. A haywagon rested halfway up its side, one front wheel caught in the cross-bracing. A rope was secured to the wagon's tongue and led up and over the top brace. At its other end dangled a plank bench with two battered men clinging to it. They were just out of reach of the derrick struts and too high to jump.

"Thank heaven you came along," one of the men called down to them.

"We weren't going to rob him, honest," the second wailed. "We were just joking."

Watson pulled up and looked solemnly at Aphrodite. "I think you may have a point. This sort of thing just can't go on forever."

She grinned at him. "He sho' ain' hard to track, though, is he?"

Watson shook his head. "I just wish we had some idea where he is going."

In a ravine some miles away, Charles Henry Clayton was wondering the same thing. Since entering the Colorado territory several days before, he had been lost. The land, except for climbing slowly to the west, remained changeless day after day: wide, rolling hills of short grass, occasional streams usually in deep washes where little forests grew in hidden coves and everything around came to drink.

The summer sun here, up on the prairies at midday, washed the land in a glare that had no color and painted its own pictures of shimmering lakes in the distance. The mirage phenomenon so entranced him that he spent most of a day trying to capture the magic of it in paint: vast lens of sky that seemed to invert itself at the horizons and flow inward, dazzling and dancing, to create things that were not there and obscure the things that were.

Later, studying his painting and using the "see the dots" trick that Virgil MacLootie had taught him, he found much that was interesting. Far off in the dancing myth were riders, and at another point a flow of movement suggestive of a horse and buggy. And there, at the edge of the world, a line of low-rigged ships as though bound for the spice ports of Cathay.

Captain Keech had grown lean and tough with the travel, a horse of high spirit and low humor who enjoyed an occasional prance, run, bucking fit, or nip at an unguarded buttock and would go out of his way to step on Charles Henry's hat if he left it lying around. The hat, as a result, had developed considerable character over the past few hundred miles.

Although a close rapport had developed between man and beast, there was still one chore Captain Keech refused to do. Steadfastly and firmly he rejected carrying the tripod easel. Charles Henry had grown accustomed to the easel being strapped to his own back.

But despite the company of Captain Keech, Charles Henry was lonely. He had come a long way and had no idea how much further he must go to find parcel nine. And with each day Emmalee Wilkes was further from him. "You know what I have done?" he asked the roan. "I have fallen in love." It was no surprise to either of them.

Now he followed a wide ravine which had a little stream in its bottom and listened to the echoes that preceded him. When the echoes began taking on a life of their own, with hoofbeats and voices he had not originated, he stopped and shook his head. "Too much sun," he told the blue roan. But the echoes went on and on, sounds of many horses walking, and there were voices among them. Then a fresh-emptied peach tin clattered down the ravine's wall. "I think there is someone up there," he told Captain Keech.

For another half mile he paced the sounds above him, before finding a ledge that climbed to the top. The ledge rose through a stand of wild plums and piñon which ended at prairie level, and there was a much-used road there, a road that had not paralleled the ravine where he had entered.

Captain Keech emerged into the midst of other horses and riders, reared in surprise, then honored the occasion with a fit of plunging, bucking, and dancing.

Charles Henry clung desperately to his saddle, trying to outlast the roan's latest enthusiasm. He was aware of blue men all around him, all clinging to pitching mounts, shouting and cursing.

At the noise, Lt. Sam Grist swung in his saddle to look back. His eyes went wide. His entire patrol seemed to have suddenly gone berserk. Men clung to pitching mounts, which wheeled and danced. He saw Corporal O'Malley fly from his spinning horse to roll and scramble to his feet. Some of the others were down, and Sergeant O'Shay was among them, lashing out with words and quirt: "Here now! Stop this, Bejaysus! What in th' Holy Mother's name . . ."

There was a stranger in their midst, doing his own wild clinging, but now that all the army stock was in full gyration, the stranger's horse suddenly stopped its pitching, lowered its head and ambled out of the fray where it and its rider turned to watch in fascination.

Sergeant O'Shay's mount had joined the game. Sergeant O'Shay left his saddle at the peak of a crow-hop and came up almost at the feet of the stranger. He got his own feet under him, swore with Gaelic richness and brushed dust from his uniform. The stranger tipped his hat. "How do you do. I'm Charles Henry Clayton."

O'Shay stared at him. "And did you start this, then?"

"Probably so," Charles Henry admitted. "Captain Keech hasn't seen another horse for several days. He failed to contain his enthusiasm. Are you the United States Cavalry?"

O'Shay looked sadly at the remnants of his patrol. "Ask me that sometime when I can answer with pride."

"I was told in Fort Smith—" he began, then stopped to tip his hat to the lieutenant spurring toward them. "How do you do?"

"This gentleman joined us abruptly," O'Shay told his

300

officer. He dodged aside as Private O'Roark cart-wheeled between them.

"Well, do something!" the lieutenant snapped.

"Yes, sir." O'Shay hitched up his pants and waded into the fray.

"I was told in Fort Smith," Charles Henry continued to the lieutenant, "to look up the cavalry when I got to Colorado."

"You might have let us know you were coming," Grist said glaring at him. "We'd have staged a parade." A bucking mount danced past, a soldier clinging to a stirrup. "Corporal O'Toole! Control that animal!"

"Yes, sir."

It took a relatively short time, all things considered, to bring the patrol back into order. Privates O'Hanlon and O'Brien sported visible bruises, and Corporal O'Malley carried an audible grudge, but aside from that the pick of Company B was none the worse for wear.

Charles Henry rode at the head of the column beside Lieutenant Grist, the dour Sergeant O'Shay close behind.

"I really don't expect to encounter hostiles this near Fort Lyon," Grist explained. "A few Arapaho bucks, maybe, but they won't bother us. We'll point west another two days, into the foothills, then sweep to the north and circle back to join the rest of B Company on Sand Creek. The main trail crosses there, and that's where the hostiles will point—if at all."

"What are they hostile about?"

"Oh, there have been a lot of people moving in on a valley past the front range, and a lot of the Indians up there don't like it. They've been complaining to the Indian agents, and some of them think they might get nasty. The valley is a federal parcel that was sold off for railroad capital."

"That sounds like the place." Charles Henry nodded. "Do you know where parcel nine is?"

"Never heard of it."

"They said in Fort Smith the cavalry might direct me when I reached Colorado."

"Well, it might be part of that valley. I guess they'd have sold it in parcels. I haven't been up there, but the word is there's a lot going on. Some people have been building a town, and there are rumors of minerals of some kind. Thing like that draws people."

"I can see how the Indians might be a bit upset."

"More than a bit. The one to worry about is Falling Rock. All the other chiefs have gone to council with the commissioner, but Falling Rock pulled a bunch of hotheads out and moved back into the mountains somewhere. Sent word that he had a vision of some kind of calamity falling on the white men up there, and he intended to see it. That's what has the agents worried. They don't know what he might do. So we're setting up positions on the trails to warn people. Can't keep them out, but we can tell them to be careful."

"In my experience," Charles Henry said, "people are not very good at being careful."

"Do you mind if I ask you a question?"

"Of course not."

"What is that thing on your back?"

"An easel. I am an artist."

"Forgive me for asking."

"Beggin' your pardon, sir." Sergeant O'Shay edged his mount forward. "But are you the artist General Wallace is lookin' for?"

"Not that I know of. I don't know General Wallace."

"What artist is that, sergeant?" Grist asked.

"Well, the word is—you know how word spreads, sir—that General Wallace has asked about in the territory lookin' for some artist that does pictures of ships

302

an' things. I don't rightly know what it's all about."

"Neither do I," Charles Henry said.

"How do you know about that, sergeant?" Grist asked.

"Well, sir, one of th' transfers from Fort Union, a lad named O'Hurley, was tellin' Corporal O'Sullivan about it over in A Company. You know, sir, O'Sullivan is a sort of cousin o' mine, his mother havin' been part O'Shay on her mother's side, an' this new lad O'Hurley is kin to the O'Hare's back in Boston, that is also some of my father's kin. So we got started talkin' about it, an' O'Hurley says his third cousin, Paddy Muldoon, which isn't my cousin, bein' on the other side o' his family an' all, has a brother that married one of th' Pratt girls— Emily, it was; the wild one—and she is sort of kin to the Powers family in Boston, that's close with the Wallace family. So O'Hurley says—"

"Sergeant," Grist said.

"Says there was quite a doin's up in Boston a while back, and old man Powers had this nephew who was an artist—"

"That's me!" Charles Henry swiveled around. "Jonathan Clayton Powers is my uncle! That is, he is not really my uncle—more like a fourth cousin, since his mother was my grandfather's—"

"Mr. Clayton," Grist said.

"Niece—or rather her brother was his nephew, which is the same thing but explains it better—but I prefer to call him my uncle since my Aunt Samantha, who isn't really my aunt but always has allowed me to call her Aunt Samantha although she is another cousin three times removed—or is it four? Which is the one equivalent to fourth cousin?"

"Are you kin to the Claytons from Rhode Island?" the sergeant asked.

"My father was one of the Rhode Island Claytons,

though my family always preferred not to talk about that. Do you know the Rhode Island Claytons?"

"Know 'em? Why, sir, my great-aunt on my mother's side was a Clayton. Her brother was Silas Clayton at Newport, the one that had the whiskey still. My great-uncle Shawn O'Flynn was in the business with him for a while and married his sister—out of spite, they said it was—when they broke up."

"Well of all things," Charles Henry said. "Silas Clayton was my great-grandfather—one of them, at any rate. I had four."

"Gentlemen," Grist said.

"Cousin!" Charles Henry extended his hand.

"Cousin!" O'Shay clasped it. Then he said, "Anyhow, O'Hurley said he heard from one of th' O'Hares that Mr. Powers had sent this artist off—yourself, most likely—and meantime had told Harold Wallace about him. Harold Wallace's father was a cousin to old Major Wallace that is kin to Lew Wallace in Indiana. And Harold Wallace passed the word about him, and now Lew Wallace is lookin' for him because he has gone west—I guess it's yourself that has gone west."

"I certainly have, but I didn't know about General Wallace."

"It's retired general now. He's been visitin' down in the New Mexico territory. And he must be lookin' for yourself. He has a picture of some ships that you drew. But Mr. Powers sent someone to find you, didn't he? Fellow named Watson?"

"Mr. Watson? I haven't seen him since I left Boston."

"Well, maybe we'll get it all sorted out. But I wouldn't want to be goin' to New Mexico right now. Lots of trouble down there. Outlaws an' gunfighters. They say Henry Clay is out somewhere, and nobody knows exactly where."

"I've heard of him."

"It's only about three days south to Fort Union from here. Maybe four. And there's a regular stage between there and Fort Sumner."

"I can't go to New Mexico right now. First I have to find parcel nine. Where did your Lieutenant Grist get off to?"

They looked around. Lieutenant Grist had dropped back to ride with Corporal O'Malley. The lieutenant's eyes seemed glazed.

Charles Henry traveled that day and the next with the cavalry patrol, until their trail turned north along a ridge from which tall mountains were visible in the distance.

"Those are the Rockies," Sergeant O'Shay told him. "Grandest mountains on the face of this earth, but fierce sometimes. Man has to watch hisself up there."

"Take care of yourself, cousin." Charles Henry gripped the big Irishman's hand.

"An' yourself," O'Shay said. "An' when you get the chance, you might go see what General Wallace wants with you."

Lieutenant Grist tipped him a quick salute. "Be careful up there, Mr. Clayton. And remember, when you get into those mountains, watch for Falling Rock."

He watched the patrol off, waving. Then he turned the roan westward again. Ahead, the blue mountains beckoned, rising against a sky that glowed like gold. Out there was parcel nine. Out there was his fortune—his ticket back to Emmalee Wilkes.

He bedded that night by a silver stream, and the following evening and the evening after that among greater and greater slopes. And he was in the mountains. As he rode, he gazed around in wonder. He had seen mountains: the Blue Ridge, the Cumberlands, the Ozarks—but now he knew he had not seen mountains, not really. Landscapes unfolded about him now that

305

humbled the senses. Charles Henry Clayton had come to the Shining Mountains, and like so many before him, he was awed.

Then on a bright morning he topped a wooded ridge and the land fell away before him, sloping out and away into a broad valley lush with forest on its near slopes, grassed and rolling beyond.

The valley spread into blue distance to the west and north, and wings of it curved around the stark base of a huge peak that split it from the south. At the base of the rise, where streams joined, was a cluster of bright color.

There was movement on thread-tiny roads, a bustling of traffic from the south and from the passes west. And up on the mountain flank itself, in the clear areas among forests, was more movement. People were there and they were doing things.

Near noon he angled into a trail, and an hour later the trail joined a road. He heard sounds of logging and waved at a man driving a six-horse hitch ahead of two wagons heaped with straight logs.

Where the road curved toward the cluster of color at the mountain's base there was a sign: Calamity, Colorado; Town Lots; C. Nightingale, Prop.

II

And so Charles Henry Clayton came to Calamity.

The town itself, clustered at the base of Calamity Peak, was barely recognizable yet as a town, though there was much activity there. Where a month or two before there had been no structures, now there were a few, and soon there would be more. The townsite of Calamity occupied most of parcel sixty-one of the newly patented lands. It was the enterprise of one Clarence Nightingale, a retired prospector who had come up from Denver the day his title was vested to plat a site and hawk town lots before someone else could beat him to it.

Having the only land office in town, Nightingale was doing land office business selling twenty-five and fifty foot building lots starting at a hundred dollars apiece. The office itself was a tent with a table in front of it. Streets and lots were delineated by twine strung between stakes.

Wagons and rigs stood around, several saddle horses were tied under scrubby trees to one side, and tents, lean-tos, and cabin foundations were springing up on various twined-in rectangles.

"Line up!" the proprietor of Calamity City shouted at the twenty or thirty people clustering before his tent.

"First come, first served! Get in line! Where you're standing is State Street, main thoroughfare of this here metropolis! And right over there, crossing it, is Grand Avenue!"

Sitting Captain Keech's saddle behind the crowd, Charles Henry looked where the man was pointing. There were four stakes in the ground there, making a square about thirty feet on a side.

"That intersection," the man continued, "is the main corner of the central business district! Prime commercial lots, price negotiable! Only two left! This nearest one," he said pointing toward a twined rectangle where a yellow dog lay sleeping, "is the site of the Grand State Hotel! That one across the corner is Bedlow's General Store! See that man over there, setting tent pegs? That is Mr. Bedlow himself, getting ready to go into business! Get in line, I say!"

"Marvelous," Charles Henry breathed. "I wouldn't have believed there was such a town here." In all the broad expanse of Calamity, as of this day, the only completed structures were twenty-two tents, a dozen lean-tos, and three shacks. But covered wagons stood on several of the lots, and there were people hauling logs, sawing lengths, laying rails, building things.

"Imagination is a wonderful thing," Charles Henry told the horse. "Tell people there is a town someplace, and even if there isn't they will get busy and build one."

"Did you say something?" A man standing near looked up at him.

"I was talking to my horse. We have become very close. Do you know where there is a stable?"

The man glanced around at the large canvas plat hanging on the land office tent. It was a picture of a large square composed of small rectangles in blocks bounded by streets. Two streams converged near the center of it. There were notations on some of the little rectangles. "Two streets over." The man pointed across bare ground where nothing stood but stakes and twine. "Second and third lots on the far side."

Charles Henry gazed in that direction. The stable undoubtedly was there, but no one had built it yet. "I wonder if they have grain," he mused aloud.

"My name's Smiley," the man said. "Most of us are keepin' our stock in a rope corral over in the creek bottoms. Good graze there and a few bins of oats. If you take some, leave the price on the bin."

Charles Henry found the place, rubbed Captain Keech down, bought him some oats and turned him loose. He hung his saddle and travel gear under a tarp where many others hung, then tipped his hat to look up the mountain where other activity was in progress.

Up there, men and teams were at work laying steel rail, a track curving up the side of the mountain to vanish past a swell and reappear in the distance beyond, still climbing. High above where it disappeared in forest, a puff of dust erupted from the mountainside, and a few moments later there were echoes of an explosion.

Where the rails—or their waiting roadbed—came down, almost at the edge of Nightingale's townsite, men were erecting buildings and chutes of hewn timber on the bank of a wide draw through which flowed a good-sized creek. Alongside the rail bed, marching up the mountainside, was a row of strongly built braced uprights anchored in rock.

Mystified, Charles Henry started toward the construction site. But as he approached it a stern-looking man with a shotgun gestured at him and pointed to a sign: T & T Mining Co. Keep Off.

Charles Henry cupped his hands. "What are they doing up there?" he called.

The guard only shrugged and frowned at him. But a

bristle-bearded little man walking up the path stopped beside him and pointed upward. "Big wig from Denver thinks there's gold up there. Aims to mine the ore up there and cart it down here to stamp. Ain't that the silliest thing you ever heard?"

"I don't know. Do you suppose there is gold?"

"Maybe. There's sign. But prob'ly not near enough to pay for all this get-ready."

"Lucas!" the guard shouted across. "If the boss wants you talkin' about his property he'll tell you so."

"Shee!" Lucas swore and ambled away.

A man with a mallet had driven a post in the middle of a twined lot facing on Grand Street. Now he hung a sign on it, fresh-painted letters on whitewashed wood: Smith & Sons Haberdashery.

"Marvelous," Charles Henry said.

At the land office tent Clarence Nightingale was hawking his wares in a loud voice. "Line up! Line up! First come first served! This is the place to buy your lots! Over yonder where the creeks come together, that's Forest Acres subdivision! Across from it, where them trees are, is Rolling Meadows Estates! Fine bunch of lots there! Be the high rent district one day! Line up! Line up!"

This last was shouted at Charles Henry, who at the moment was all the line there was.

"This here is the place!" the man shouted at him. "Get a lot while you're young, I always say! What'll it be, young feller?"

"Pardon me," Charles Henry said. "I'm new here. How do I go about finding parcel nine?"

The man's face became severe. "This here is the land office, son, not the tourist bureau! You want to buy a lot?"

"I can't even afford a little, until I find parcel nine and decide how to become wealthy."

"Well, when you do, you'll need a lot! Come see me then! All right, folks, this is the place! Line up! Line up! Good lots still available on the hill yonder, what we call The Heights District! Mostly upwind from the Tannery section!"

"You need somebody to show you around." It was Smiley.

"I need to talk with a native."

"I am a native. Been here nearly three weeks now. What parcel is it you're looking for?"

"Nine."

Smiley thought about it. "Surveyors laid out the valley in parcels. They did it like sections as nearly as the land allows. This is number sixty-one, that Nightingale bought—good spot. He was a prospector and had been up here and knew how the land lays. Most of us took Hob's choice. I wound up with forty-six. It's a few miles northwest of here. Little dry, but the missus and I can make a crop on it, I expect. But as I understand it they started at that peak off yonder, which is sort of the northwest corner, and they numbered the parcels from west to east in the first row, then from east to west in the second coming south, and so on. Nine must be in the first row, way over there in the hills somewhere north or northwest of here. They got corner cairns with numbers."

"That's a long way."

"Sure is. May be up in the rough country, too. Those low-number ones were about the last to sell, because they're all above the valley, up in the hills. Now this mountain here," he said waving a hand upward at the giant peak climbing from the town's south side into blue distance, "is where the town got its name. This is Calamity Peak. I don't know why it's named that. Personally, I'd rather call it Bald Knob. Kind of a homey name, if you're from Missouri, like the missus and I

311

are. The original Bald Knob is in Missouri."

"Arkansas," Charles Henry corrected.

"What?"

"The original Bald Knob is in Arkansas. The one in Missouri isn't the original one. It's just another one."

"Where in heaven's name did you get an idea like that?"

"From Virgil MacLootie." Charles Henry shrugged then changed the subject. "What did he say the name of that hotel is?"

"What hotel?"

"That one right there." He pointed at the vacant lot at the intersection.

"Oh, that one. That's the Grand State Hotel. Old Nightingale plans to build it himself with the money he makes from selling lots."

Charles Henry tilted his hat, folded his arms behind him and strolled back and forth past the hotel, lips pursed in thought, studying the imaginary building. "Interesting architecture, as one might view it. What do you suppose that is next to it?"

Smiley gawked at him. "Where?"

"The next building. Right there."

Smiley squinted at the vacant prairie with its twine enclosures. "I don't know. Maybe a barber shop?"

"Maybe so." Charles Henry unslung his tripod easel, sprung it open and set his portfolio on its arms. "Let's find out." He got out his tools and began to sketch.

He did the Grand State Hotel first, complete with fluted columns, gingerbread trim and cupolas. He made it three storeys tall with a false front on the State Street side. Its porch was imposing, its windows narrow and fusty. "Eclectic gothic," he pronounced.

"Wow," Smiley said in admiration.

He added a barber shop next door, a handsome

beanery next to that and followed with a millinery store that sported a dry-goods poster in its window. There was a board walk, hitch rails, and elegant people passing by. Beyond it rose the imposing mass of Calamity Peak. Beyond the hotel, looking down Grand Avenue, were several small shops, a professional building, and a bathhouse. Across Grand were Smith and Sons Haberdashery, a saddlery, a feed store, and another millinery.

"Now what did you do that for?" a large woman at his shoulder snapped. "There ain't hardly enough business here for one millinery, let alone two. I ain't even in business yet, and already you're runnin' me out."

"Sorry, ma'am." He drew boards across the door of the second millinery and put a For Sale sign on it.

"I could expand into that," a man said. "Feed stores need room. I might add a line of farm equipment."

"I think I'll run for mayor," someone else pondered aloud.

Mr. Bedlow was leaning on his shoulder. "You ain't got my grocery store in there!"

"I can't see it. It's behind me."

"Well, you can't see none of them others, neither, but you got them."

"Where's the bank? You can't have a town without a bank."

Clarence Nightingale pushed through the sizeable crowd that now surrounded Charles Henry. "What is this! What's going on h . . . ah?" His eyes widened. "Ah!" He gazed raptly at the drawing. "That's it! There she is! Calamity! You see there?" He turned to shout at those crowding around. "That's what I been tellin' you!" He turned back to Charles Henry. "Where's the courthouse?"

"What courthouse?"

313

"Right there!" Nightingale stabbed a finger at the end of Grand Avenue. "Right there, that's a courthouse."

"I don't see any courthouse."

"Well, there has to be a courthouse! How much you want to put a courthouse right there?"

Smiley pushed forward to whisper in his ear, "Don't settle for less than the price of a lot."

"A lot," Charles Henry told Nightingale.

"Don't quibble! How much?"

Smiley got Nightingale's attention. "How much do you want for that lot over in Rolling Meadows Estates? The one with the trees on it."

"That's my best residential lot! It's a fifty-footer! Hundred and fifty dollars!"

Charles Henry looked around at him. "A hundred and fifty would be—"

"And you'll throw in the lot?" Smiley asked Nightingale.

The man sputtered, then nodded. "Done!"

"Draw the man his courthouse," Smiley said.

Charles Henry was astonished. "You mean he is going to pay?"

"Shut up and draw!" Nightingale ordered.

By evening, Charles Henry had a prime lot and three hundred dollars for two street scenes and a pair of building designs.

"Just what this place needed," Smiley remarked. "A good fast draw artist. I've got four more commissions lined up for you tomorrow. I'll take ten percent."

"But I was planning to leave tomorrow, to find parcel nine."

"You can leave in a day or two. Lord, son, there's people here with more money than good sense. Strike while the iron's hot!"

They walked together toward Smiley's covered wagon, where Mrs. Smiley was preparing supper.

"I feel a little funny about charging money for pictures," Charles Henry said.

Smiley turned to him in the dusk. "That's about the dumbest thing I ever heard. Shoot, didn't you see how bad old Nightingale wanted that picture? He *needed* it."

"Well, he can use it to sell more lots. That's fair. But the others . . ."

"Yeah. Smith wants a picture of a store he hasn't built yet. Bedlow the same. The Stanleys want a picture of a house that isn't there yet on a piece of ground they just bought. Shoot, son, don't you know why we're all here? We didn't come buying land. We came buying dreams. And we're not fixing to build houses and stores and things. We're fixing to build dreams. And if we can see a picture of our dreams, something to look at and show around while we work toward it, why, that is worth a lot. Money is only money, son. Dreams are a whole lot harder to come by, and a devil of a lot harder to hang onto. Come along. Sarah will have the soup on. Don't forget my ten percent."

Again there was the distant sound of explosives on the mountain, which Charles Henry had heard several times during the day. He looked up. With the appearance of stars beyond Calamity's bulk, other lights had appeared on its face. Lanterns moved and paraded as whatever work was going on up there continued, and there were two large clusters of lights.

"That looks like whole towns up there," he noted.

"Camps. Two of them, on separate sections of land. There's a dispute over who owns the mine they're working on. Solomon Trask founded it and opened it up, and it's his money—or his backers'—that is being spent up there. He's T and T Mining. But just lately another bigshot showed up and claimed section seventy-five which is about half of where the minesite

315

is. Claims Trask has a faulty title, and seventy-five belongs to him. Now there's two armed camps up there. T and T is going on with the mine development, but claims have been filed with the governor, and there's supposed to be a mining committee on the way to settle the argument. T and T claims the whole strata is its, and that the new fellow has falsified the records. The new man, Timmons, says seventy-five is his, and he intends to buy out or push out Trask."

"I don't suppose they ever considered sharing," Charles Henry said. "What are the explosions?"

"Blasting powder. Trask is trying to bring in a mine, get ore down here to sluice and separate and get a smelter in operation so he can record a strike before the mining committee gets into it. I've heard there has been some shooting up there, but I don't know that for sure. Don't see much of those folks down here, except that man Timmons and one or two of his thugs come down about every other day to look at the sales register on town lot deeds. They expect somebody, seems like."

The Smiley wagon was one of nearly twenty—overlands and prairie schooners—laden with the worldly goods of as many families and parked tongue-to-tailgate in a double circle on a campground established on a rise between the creeks. Sarah Smiley had put on a supper of stew, and several families came to join them at the fire. Men, women, and children; they were diverse people, but they all had the look of far travel and the excitement about them of wanderers finally arrived at the promised land.

The talk was of land, of crops, and conditions, and of the future. Just as with the town that was not yet a town but soon would be, these were farmers who had come to farm, and soon would be farming.

"Too far into the season to make a summer crop," a man said. "I'm going to break out as many acres as I

316

can the next few weeks and plant wheat and oats. That way I can make two cash crops next summer while we're clearing more land for truck."

"We brought corn," another said. "I got plenty if somebody wants to try for a fall harvest with me. I'll trade for nails and plankin'. We aim to have a cabin snugged in before snow falls."

The patented valley was broad and fertile. Those who had bottom lands were wasting no time putting them to use. The valley floor held more than eighty land parcels. Some of these parcels, the ones with water and deep soil, would support as many as four families. Others, higher and drier, might support only one. Most of those present had found and claimed their lands, then had come to Nightingale's townsite to buy and barter what they would need to settle in. Some were also buying town lots.

"We're here to stay," a tight-lipped man with a quiet wife and five noisy children commented. "We been bumped and pushed off too many places that wasn't ours. This place is ours and we ain't goin' no farther."

Charles Henry sat apart and listened to the good talk as night settled on the valley. He found he liked these people. As Tom Smiley had said, they had their dreams. And the dreams were good to share. He dozed by the fire and dreamed of life here as it might be—as it should be. He saw farms across the valley, fields of corn and wheat, garden plots, sturdy cabins snug against the winter, water diverted from the flowing creeks to serve the needs of families. He saw the distant land, and it was no longer distant. It was here. He dreamed of Emmalee.

"Would you look at that," a woman whispered to her husband. "That young fellow is sound asleep where he sits. What do you suppose he's smiling about?"

The man looked, and a smile played on his own face.

He put an arm around his wife. "That's a fool question, darlin'. Only one kind of idea makes a man look that-away."

When Charles Henry aroused himself to set aside his easel, hat, boots, and gun, then curled sleepily by the fire with his head on his valise, Sarah Smiley came with a blanket to put over him. "You do find the strangest people," she told her husband.

III

Having found his own cash crop, Charles Henry made five more drawings of imaginary buildings on newly purchased sites. And through the morning his eyes turned upward to the giant mass of Calamity Peak. The mountain stood aloof from the bustling valley at its foot and offered vistas to be seen for those who would climb it. The near approaches, two adjoining patented sections of mountain, were guarded and posted against trespass. These were section seventy-six, where the rails were being laid and the smelter and stamp mill were being built—with the rolling thunder of mine blasting high above them—and section seventy-five, next to it on the west, where the Timmons camp lay a thousand feet above the town and a mile or more by path.

But beyond, a pair of miles west of where the creeks joined and curved to flow as one around the mountain's eastern shoulder, a road came down from some distant pass, and there was traffic on it.

So in the early afternoon he retrieved a rested Captain Keech, stowed his portfolio and tool pouch, added a sack of thick sandwiches donated by Sarah Smiley, strapped his easel on his back and headed for high ground.

The west road wound and curved around the flank of Calamity, climbing toward a pass due west of the great peak. He had gone several miles and was angling up the mountain itself when he met a string of freight wagons coming down, and the lead driver hailed him. There were five wagons, loaded to their limits with squat casks of a type he recognized. His eyes widened, and he backed the roan away a few steps. Blasting powder.

The drivers of the wagons had a gaunt and haunted look about them.

"How far is it to the Timmons camp?" the lead driver called.

"Just a few miles." Charles Henry pointed back the way he had come. "This road doesn't go there, though. It goes to the town. The camp is above, up on the mountain."

"Well, how do we get there, then?"

"I'm new here." Charles Henry shook his head. "This is my first look around. How far have you come with that load?"

"Three days." The man spat. "Three friggin' days of no smokes, no lights and campin' a half mile from these bombs if we wanted a fire to cook on. Crap. I won't never take a job like this'n again—if I live through this'n. Hold that horse, mister. Don't let him dance like that. He could strike sparks with them iron shoes."

"Sorry." Charles Henry reined in the skittish roan. "What in the world are they going to do with all that blasting powder?"

"We don't ask questions," the man said and sighed. "We just haul. But not ever again. Nosir! Anyhow, two of these loads goes to the Timmons camp. The rest goes on up Covey Creek, place in the hills yonder." He pointed north.

"Sorry I can't help," Charles Henry said. He didn't

want to pass the wagons on the narrow track, and this was as good a place as any to cut back. "Drive carefully." He swung the roan to the left and spurred up a steep bank, coming out on a sloping crest that angled back east, climbing away above the road.

"They should look for another line of business," he confided to Captain Keech as he put distance between them and the train of explosives.

The sun was past its zenith, and the view to the north was spectacular when he reined in on a high slope that topped a precipitous ledge. He had no idea how far he had come, but as he looked down past the drop-off he could see the entire valley, spreading away to the north where hazy hills encircled its high end. Directly below him and distant with the slope of the mountain was the townsite of Calamity City. Off to his right, and not very far away, thunder erupted with the contained bark of mine blasting.

"I didn't mean to come this far," he muttered to the roan. "I hope those men don't mind us being up here." He dismounted and walked to the edge. Directly below was a large camp of tents and lean-tos, and armed men moved about. Among them were several of a type Charles Henry remembered seeing before, distinctive by dress, actions, and general form. These were, it seemed, all of a kind: burly, sullen-seeming men who wore dark suits and carried no visible weapons. They all looked familiar to him. Then he remembered the sodden, half-drowned individual he had assisted that time when it rained in South Carolina, and he had kissed Miss Emmalee beneath her parasol. These men looked like that one, the man he had helped aboard the train.

Thoughts of Emmalee Wilkes flowing like honey through his mind, he backed away from the ledge, set up his easel and portfolio and looked again out across

321

the valley. There was a picture there, just waiting to be painted. And as the fleecy clouds drifted their shadows across the distant rolling floor, he went to work, his brushes attempting once again to capture that subtle sense of passing time.

Voices drifting up from below blended into the background of mountain song. He caught a word here and there, a phrase, but they meant nothing and were not part of his preoccupation until one voice rose above the rest, a man panting and shouting, "Bull! He's here, Bull! Found his name on a deed!"

There was the crunch of feet on gravel. Then another voice, deeper. "Did you see him? Where is he?"

"I didn't find him. He'd gone off somewhere. But he's here. Bought one of those town lots yesterday. Nightingale says he's a young fellow, tall and dresses fancy, and he has a picture of the town that he drew. Got it hangin' on a plank for people to see."

There was a pause. Then the deeper voice ordered, "All right. Take two of the boys with you. Find him and talk to him. If he'll sell parcel nine, buy it. If not, you know what to do. I don't have time for extended negotiations."

It was several minutes before the impact of what he had heard filtered through the Emmalee honey in Charles Henry's mind. But when it did, he stopped painting. They were talking about him.

The painting was nearly done. Shadow-brushed rolling lands extended outward from the tiny townsite—complete with courthouse and Grand State Hotel —away past neat farms and tilled fields into blue distances that he painted as he saw them because that was how they would always be.

The two creeks curved away across the land, flowing from what seemed to be a single source in the northern hills to spread twin arms of bright water southward

322

across the valley until they merged into one at Calamity City. The larger creek was almost a river, flowing wide and deep through the heart of the patented lands. The smaller, east of it, was also a good stream, clear waters leaping and laughing in the sun. He looked more closely at his painting. Somehow the place where the creeks originated, seemingly at a single point, gave the impression of people present. Yet it was many miles away.

The traffic on the roads was as he had seen it as he painted—more covered wagons coming in from east and south, over the old trail he had followed and up the Denver road, a band of riders topping the ridge far to the east, a buggy plodding along a trail, three freight wagons loaded with blasting powder starting north from the town, families moving out in search of deed parcels—people coming and going.

It was a good picture. He would finish it before heading back.

Far away to his right he heard again the ritual shouting of things he could not understand, followed by a brief silence, and then the thunder of mine blasting. Each time the thump came, the mountain seemed to quiver beneath his feet.

The picture was finished. He gazed at it in admiration. Again, there was that subtle something that suggested time passing. He wished he knew how he did that.

The voices from below had been indistinct, routine voices for a time. Now the deep voice came again, and he listened: "Look out there. Is that my powder wagons?"

"Those three going north?" someone else asked. "Yeah, that looks like them."

"Well where's the other two? They're supposed to be up here. Damn it, we're running out of time. If Trask gets pay dirt down this mountain, we lose. I want that mine closed!"

"I dunno, Bull. I guess they're down on the road somewhere. Do you want me to go find them?"

"Yes, I want you to go find them!" The deep voice was angry. "They should have been here yesterday!"

"You goin' into town, Bull? Where do you want us to put the stuff when it gets here?"

"Out there on that hump." Charles Henry glanced over the edge. The man was pointing east. "Right where it slopes down. Dig a hole and bury it deep with fuse to the surface plus four feet."

"Yeah, Bull," the other said, dutifully. "That's gonna be an awful lot of powder in one hole."

"If I need to bring that hump down, I want it all down," Bull said.

From where he stood, above them, the place the man had pointed to was concealed. But in the distance Charles Henry could see a hump in the mountain's profile, maybe two miles distant. It was the only hump he could see.

With his painting finished, he folded his portfolio, strapped it on the blue roan, put the remains of his lunch in a saddlebag, went back and got the tripod easel and approached the horse again. Captain Keech looked wide-eyed at the easel and danced away, sidestepping partway up a gravel bank at the base of the cliff behind them. Gravel rolled and clattered. Charles Henry shook his head and strapped the easel on his back. "I wasn't going to put this on you," he told the horse. "You have made it very clear how you feel about that."

There was a shout from below. "Someone's up there! Who is that?"

"Dunno," another said. "I guess we better go see."

Charles glanced over the ledge, and a pair of sullen men with dark suits were looking at him. "Hey!" One pointed. "Who's that?" Then they both pulled hidden guns from their coats and ran toward a path that led up to the shelf where he was.

"Aw, Mercy," Charles Henry breathed. Their path would bring them up between him and his escape route. He grabbed Captain Keech's reins and ran. But the men were already ahead of him, and one came into sight as he rounded a shoulder. The man saw him, leveled his pistol and fired. The bullet sang off rock behind Charles Henry. He turned, started the other way, and Captain Keech balked. The ledge was narrow here, and he refused to turn. Another bullet whined past him. "Well, have it your own way!" he scolded the horse. He dropped the reins and ran, back around the shoulder, going east.

Behind him he heard a sudden thunder of hooves, a shout and a sound of someone rolling down a steep slope. "Ow!" someone shouted. "Get off me!" Then there were scrambling feet and rattle of gravel and one said, "Go get that horse!"

"Hell with the horse," the other said. "Come on. Let's get that trespasser!"

Charles Henry ran along the sloping ledge where he had stopped to paint, danced across a narrow ledge between a rock face on his right and a hundred feet of straight down on his left, leapt to another sloping shelf and then angled up a rise where the shelf disappeared. As a grove of trees swallowed him he glanced back. The two men were behind him, after him, and had seen where he went.

Charles Henry climbed, crawled and ran, angling east and uphill through cedar forest, and came out on the other side on a sharply inclined slope that tailed off ahead into a ribbon of pathway curving around another rock cliff.

Feet sliding, arms windmilling, he reached the foot-wide ledge and skipped along it, hugging the rock. Another bullet whanged above him, and gravel showered him. He flung himself around the outcropping.

Close now, and just ahead, he heard the singsong voices again, and this time he could hear the words. "Fire in the hole!" the first voice shouted, repeated by others lower down, like echoes. "Fire in the hole! Fire in the hole!" Then the nearest voice: "Clear the slope!" And those below: "Clear the slope! Clear the slope!"

He dodged past a jutting stone ledge and suddenly was in a wide, clear area, a gentle slope where crushed stone was piled in great heaps, and the trees had all been cut. There were rails here, a narrow-gauge railroad leading into a hole in the mountain at the top of the cleared rise. Steel-wheeled carts stood on the rails, anchored with stay-poles. Far ahead, through intervening forest, he could see corrals and a camp.

"Fire in the hole?" he said. Then he looked at the hole and understood. He turned, but the two men with guns were approaching the ledge he had crossed. Ahead was the wide clearing and beyond it a sheered rock face. The mine was to his right, and the slope plunged downward to his left.

The tracks at the very mouth of the mineshaft ran between stubby towers of heavy timber, with ropes dangling from them in long loops to studded wheels at the base. From these other ropes fed waist-high along the tracks, out to where the mine carts were lined. These ropes had iron grapples attached at intervals. With a leap that was pure panic Charles Henry reached one of the towers and flipped loose its dangling rope. Then he ran to one of the grapples and tugged at it, but it was secure to its cable. Wildly he looked around for a tool, spotted one, retrieved it from the nearest mine car and thrust it into the grapple's sling. The tool was a long, tapered iron pin. With its leverage, he freed the grapple, looped his loose rope through its eye, snugged it and sprinted to the edge of the mineshaft. He whirled the grapple, swung it and threw it over the top of the ledge, then climbed as it snugged. He had just pulled himself over the ledge when thunder roared below him, and the clearing was hidden in a gush of dust and debris. The shock almost threw him off the shelf.

He stood, dusted himself off, pulled the rope up after him and coiled it neatly. Then he climbed. Below him were shouts and shots. "Look! Those men! They're Timmons's men!" Shots fired. "After them! Don't let them get away!" More shots. Charles Henry reached a forested slope and disappeared into the cedars.

It was nearly an hour later when he came down off the high peak onto lower slopes, nearly three miles west of the T and T Mine, more than a mile west of Timmons's section seventy-five. He trudged down the opening slopes with the sun just over the western ridges and found a pair of wagons on the pass road below. One driver was standing by his wheel, the other some distance off holding the reins of Captain Keech.

"Hello," the near driver said. "Thought that was your horse. I guess he ran away."

"He certainly did," Charles Henry said with a nod.

"Have you by any chance been up at the Timmons camp?"

"I certainly have," Charles Henry affirmed, breathing deeply.

"Well, look," the man said. "We've been driving around this mountain with these kegs ever since noon, and I guess we missed the right road, because we can't get there. Can you direct us?"

"I don't know where the wagon road is," he said shrugging. "But I know where Mr. Timmons wants this powder. I heard him say."

"Good enough," the driver answered. "We'll take it there."

"He wants it buried," Charles Henry advised the man. "With a fuse to the surface plus four feet."

"Then we'll bury it. Lord, *anything* to get done with this haul."

"I saw where he wanted it buried. I guess I could lead you there. It's quite a way from here, though. Clear around on the east slope."

"Look," the man said with a scowl. "We did catch your horse for you."

"Yes, there is that. Very well, come on. I'll show you the hump."

The moon was high, and the valley lay still and silver as Charles Henry Clayton led the two wagoneers along the Denver road, a mile east and south of the Calamity City townsite. Ahead, across the wide bottoms of Covey Creek, Calamity Peak thrust a massive shoulder out to shadow the stream itself.

Charles Henry pointed across. "That's the hump. Right there on top of that slope, where it flattens. Mr. Timmons wants the powder buried there, with the fuse like I told you."

"I don't suppose you'd help us bury it?" the first driver suggested.

"I've had a long day."

"Tell me about it. Oh, well, I guess we can lug it up there and get it planted. Anything to get this job done. Will you sign for this stuff?"

"Sign?"

"Sure. Somebody has to sign for receipt."

"I'm not Mr. Timmons."

"That doesn't matter. I just need somebody to sign."

"Well, all right. Seems a bit odd, but I suppose it's all right. Just be sure you bury it like he said."

"We'll do it just exactly like he said," the man

328

assured him. "And I hope we're halfway to Denver before anybody decides to light that fuse. Lord, I'll never take another job like this one. Sign here."

"I saw those other three wagons going north this afternoon."

"Yeah, they were for a place up in the hills. Same order, for Timmons, but to be delivered at a different place. Something called parcel nine."

Charles Henry had been almost swaying in the saddle with exhaustion. Now he came fully awake. He backed away and watched as the drivers began urging their teams down the wide shelf of the Covey Creek bottoms. He watched as they dwindled toward the creek itself, saw them splash across it. It seemed shallower than it should be. The wagon climbed the far bank to angle up toward the hump.

"Captain Keech," he said then, "I hope you're not as tired as I am, because we're starting for parcel nine right now. I think it's time for me to inspect my property."

He stayed with the road for a few hundred yards, back toward the townsite, then turned north across rolling country bright in the moonlight. The travel-toughened blue roan took the new direction with enthusiasm, stepping out in a mile-eating lope toward the distant moon-bathed hills at the head of the valley.

Behind them a closed hack clattered up the road from Denver, trace chains ringing in the night, its driver starry-eyed and acutely aware of the precious cargo he carried. In his time he had been from Springfield to Santa Fe and from the Pecos to the Platte, but never anywhere had he seen a girl to match the one who rode now in his coach.

Miles away, on the outskirts of Denver, a clerk

named Emil Bencher leaned on a saloon bar and threw back his fourth shot of whiskey. "They fired me," he muttered. "It wasn't my fault, but they fired me anyway."

"But Emil," his companion pointed out, "you know federal land records are confidential. I just don't see how you could have broke that seal—how you could have just—just opened up the files like that to somebody that just walked in."

"I couldn't help it." Bencher rapped his glass on the bar, scowling at no one in particular. "She walked in and pointed that pair of thirty-eights at me. I think she prob'ly had a gun, too."

IV

Calamity City had quieted with the coming of night, but it was the quiet of temporary truce, just waiting for morning. The town-that-would-be had seen an eventful afternoon.

First had come the missionaries, three wagonloads of tired and dirty saviours who arrived over the old trail to descend upon the town with righteous wrath. "Go not into the heathen temples!" Brother Thorpe shouted from his wagon box. "The Day of Judgement is at hand! Strike from thine eyes the blindness that besets thee, and look about! For among you walks an Angel of the Lord, come hither upon His business! Find him, brothers and sisters! Find him and adore him, for in his wake lie the ruins of Sodom and Gomorrah!"

"Line up! Line up!" Clarence Nightingale shouted back, trying to drown out the strident voice. "Finest lots in Colorado! Prime commercial sites still available on Broad Street, just off Grand! Homesites of your choice! See the pi'cher here! This here is Calamity City as she'll be soon!"

Intermittent thunder rolled overhead, the mine blasting on schedule on Calamity Peak.

"Hear the voice of God!" Brother Thorpe shouted.

"Make way for the Angel of the Lord who walks among thee! Let his voice be heard that we may know his divine purpose!"

"Get in line! Prime housing lots at bargain prices yonder in Divine Meadows—I mean Rolling Meadows—mister, will you shut up that caterwaulin'? Do you want a lot?"

A substantial crowd had begun to gather to hear the shouting match, and bets were placed on who might last the longest.

"Wonder what them folks hollerin' 'bout," Aphrodite mused aloud as the bandana gang plodded along State Street, veering through Hopper's Dry Goods and Sundries, which wasn't yet in existence, to circle around the crowd.

Watson was looking around as he rode. "I've never seen anything like this. Do you suppose he has been here, and the whole town is just—"

"Never was a town here in the first place," Aphrodite declared. "They jus' fixin' to be one is all. I don' see no sign of his doin' yet."

"Neither do—" Watson started, then stopped and reined in his mount so suddenly that two grinning bandanas piled into him from behind. "Look! Look at that!" He pointed at the drawing of a city, displayed on a plank before the land office.

"Right nice," Aphrodite said.

"It's his! That is his work. I'd know it anywhere!" His spectacles fogging in his excitement, Watson climbed off his horse and pushed through the crowd in front of the land office tent. "Sir! Oh, sir! That picture there, where did you—"

"Make way for the Angel of the Lord!" Brother Thorpe was shouting. People hurried to get out of Watson's way, unsure just who the missionary meant.

"Line up! Line up! Goldang it, will you folks get in a

332

line of some kind?"

"Sir! Please, I must know about that rendering!"

"I have seen him! The Angel of the Lord, as he brought down Sodom and Gomorrah. Now he walks among you here!"

"Looks more like a schoolteacher," someone said.

"I don't think he means him," someone else responded. "I don't believe any angel ever had a Boston accent."

"Sir!" Watson had reached the table. "Can you tell me about that picture? I really must know."

"This here is a vision of Calamity City," Nightingale explained, pleased at the man's interest. "I gave a lot for it."

"I am so pleased to hear that," Watson said nodding. "But where is the artist, sir? I have been looking everywhere for him."

"Oh, he's around somewhere. Now you see, right here is the Grand State Hotel, which is gonna be over there on that corner. You're lookin' right down Grand Avenue here, you see. And notice the courthouse."

"A vision!" Brother Thorpe was proclaiming. "Mine eyes have seen a vision of glory! Fire and brimstone did light the very skies and the Angel of the Lord smote them one and all."

Watson hurried back through the crowd. "He's here!" he shouted at Aphrodite, still sitting tiny atop her mount, shotgun across her saddle and her mockingbird hat primly fixed atop snowy curls. "He is here somewhere! The man said so!"

"Another witness!" Brother Thorpe shouted. "Our brother has heard the word and seen the light! Glory Hallelujah!"

Many in the crowd had turned to watch Watson depart, and now they glanced at Aphrodite and the gawking bandanas. Some new arrivals peered closely from one to another. Aphrodite noticed the shift in interest and scowled. "Come on," she said. "I don' like this. Le's move along."

As they moved away, men in the crowd glanced at one another. "You know who them could be?" one asked.

"Not likely," another said scratching at his whiskers. "Sure matches th' description, all right. But that bunch is over in Kansas—maybe even down in Arkansas. Way I hear it, they don't work this far west. What would they be doin' out here, anyhow?"

"Never know," another said shaking his head. "Why, just this mornin' I'd of swore I saw that gunfighter Henry Clay right over yonder, big as life, top hat an' contraption an' all, walkin' along the street."

"What street?"

"That one over—well, where it shows a street in the pi'cher there."

"You mean the real Henry Clay? The notorious one?" a plump man questioned him. "That ain't too likely, seein' as how he was seen up in South Dakota just a week ago."

"Texas," another argued. "It wasn't South Dakota. It was Texas."

"Could have swore I seen him right here, though."

"It's the altitude. You'll feel better in a week or so."

"Line up! Goldang it, you people can't get a lot if you don't line up!"

"Angel of the Lord! Make way! Lift up thine eyes and hear the messenger of the Lord!" As Brother Thorpe lifted up his eyes by way of illustration another blast erupted on the mountain, a cloud of dust rising from the distant mine. "Ah! He has walked among you and now is risen on high to heal thee of thy sins! Make way! Make way!" He plopped onto the wagon box and flapped the reins. "Where he goeth there also must we follow, for he is the Angel of the Lord!"

The bandana gang had turned south on Grand. They rode between twine boundaries, past tents and lean-tos and beneath a suspended canvas sign that proclaimed in large, crude letters, Welcome Mining Committee. They pulled aside to let the missionary wagons pass, and Watson looked back at the land office crowd. "I think you're right. We are entirely too conspicuous, particularly with our companions. It would be better if we split up."

When they came to the bottoms where the combined Covey Creek spread its waters before curving around the base of the peak, Aphrodite nodded. She signaled the bandanas forward. "I wants you folks to take all the horses and supplies an' go on down there an' hole up. Me an' Mr. Watson got business to 'tend to." She and Watson dismounted, handed their reins to Jesse and Joe, and started back toward town.

Jasper frowned in puzzlement. "Wonder what kind of job they settin' up this time?"

Alexander grinned at him. "Must be somethin' real big, 'cause we sure come a long way for it."

"Wonder what the signal will be," Joe pondered aloud. "Did she say?"

Jesse shook his head. "Must be the same as before. She didn't say any different."

As they headed down into the bottoms Jasper scratched his head. "You mind if I ask you somethin', Alexander?"

"What?"

"What was the signal before? I've kind of forgot."

Walking up Grand Avenue, Watson remarked, "It is a little strange to see a place we know he has visited and no real signs of disaster."

"He still aroun' someplace," Aphrodite pointed out. "He jus' ain' happened yet." She stopped then, her eyes went wide and she pointed east. "Will you jus' look at that!"

Coming in on the east trail, just entering the tract that was Calamity, rolled a wagon piled high with luggage and boxes. It was driven by a soldier. Three other soldiers rode escort.

Aphrodite and Watson blinked at each other. "I done thought we lost that," Aphrodite said.

At the land office the sergeant in the driver's seat pulled up. "Beggin' your pardon, folks," he called, "but can you tell us who might be in charge here?"

Clarence Nightingale came around his table. "I suppose I am. What can I do for you? I have some real prime lots, special discount for servicemen."

"O'Shay." The sergeant saluted. "First Sergeant, Company B. These here are Corporal O'Malley and Privates O'Brien and O'Roark. We're to meet Lieutenant Grist and the rest of his patrol here, to escort the minin' committee. Orders of the territorial governor."

"Fine," Nightingale answered. "But what can I do for you?"

"Well, sir, this here wagon is civilian property and we need somebody to turn it over to. We don't know who it belongs to. Lieutenant Grist said deliver it to the local authority. And that bein' you, sir, here it is, delivered." He climbed down from the box. "Dismount," he told the others.

"What am I supposed to do with it?" Nightingale shook his head. "This here is a land office, not a warehouse. Now if it belongs to somebody lookin' for a nice lot—"

"It belong to Miss Emmalee Wilkes," Aphrodite said, pushing through the crowd that seemed to gather everytime something unusual occurred.

The sergeant tipped his hat. "How do, ma'am. Are you claimin' this here civilian property?"

336

"I sho' is. Where you all get it?"

"Just a minute," Nightingale protested. "I'm the authority here."

"Not on Miss Emmalee Wilkeses belongin's, you ain't. An them is her belongin's. Where you soldiers get this stuff?"

O'Shay looked down at her. "Well, we was on the way up here—Lieutenant Grist's patrol, that is—to report to the minin' committee, an' just inside the front range we saw this wagon hightailin' north with a pair o' Shoshoni braves on ponies leadin' it, an' directly behind them was an old fellow ridin' a buckskin, shootin' and hollerin'. Well, when they seen us them two braves left off the wagon an' headed for the hills, an' the old man right after them. So, Lieutenant Grist sent us on ahead while him an' the rest of the patrol went after the Injuns an' the old man. They had to, ye see. The Shoshonis is under our protection."

Aphrodite shook her head. "Chaos an' havoc. Lord, I feels his presence."

"Where do you want us to put this stuff, ma'am?"

Aphrodite waved vaguely with her shotgun. "Put it in the hotel. She'll be here direc'ly, if she ain' already."

"The hotel isn't built yet," Nightingale pointed out.

Aphrodite turned on him, glaring. "Well, build it! I ain' got time to argue wit' you!"

Through the afternoon, as the soldiers set up a bivouac area surrounded by State and Jefferson Streets and Grand and Washington Avenues, directly across State from the land office, Watson and Aphrodite proceeded with their related searches. More and more people arrived at Calamity. There was a train of wagons from Nebraska, a trio of hard-riding brothers from Tennessee, and a mixed and bickering group of families from Missouri and Arkansas. Trailing these was a nattily-dressed little man in a battle-scarred buggy who went first to the land office and then northward toward the distant hills across the valley.

In mid-afternoon a party of armed miners came down from the mountain to erect a cluster of tents in the cavalry's bivouac area, and Jason Trask himself, founder of the T and T Mining Co., with his lieutenants, arrived by surrey to prepare for the hearings that would ensue when the governor's mining committee arrived. The blasting on the mountain had stopped, and Trask wore a satisfied—almost smug—expression on his aristocratic face.

The expression soured somewhat an hour later when the burly Bull Timmons, surrounded by sullen dark-suited men, came down from section seventy-five to erect his own tent enclave behind Bedlow's Grocery Store.

"Decided to clear off my property?" Trask shouted across when Timmons passed. "Or do you prefer to be evicted by an officer of the court?"

"I'll make you one last offer," Timmons shouted back. "I'll take section seventy-six and your quit-claim to section seventy-five, and I'll pay you half what you have invested to date—cash money. That's twice what the operation will be worth to you in a few days."

"Nonsense!" Trask exploded. "Tomorrow—you watch! Tomorrow you will see the first operations of a high-grade, paying mine! You can't stop it, Timmons! I've found the vein, I have the ore, and it doesn't matter what kind of contest you lodge on section seventy-five—the entire operation is on section seventy-six! You can't touch it! Why don't you just go away and stop wasting the time of a lot of busy people!"

Still, to Trask's dismay, Timmons smiled across at him, and his smile was the smile of a winner who knows he has won. "Just remember, Trask! I made you a fair

338

offer! Whatever happens now is your own doing."

"Trask turned away, proud and erect, but sorely troubled. He could think of no way Timmons could interrupt the operation of T and T. And yet—the man seemed so sure. What could he possibly be planning?

Trask had invested a fortune in T and T. Some of it was his money, some from backers. The operation was simple. The ore was not high-grade enough to warrant freighting it to a distant smelter, but it would pay handsomely when crushed and smelted on site, and this was the key to the T and T venture. The ore would be produced at the mine, carted down to water-fed stamping and smelting operations at the base of Calamity Peak on Covey Creek, and the accumulated metal would be transported to Denver by armed caravan.

Project security was sound and total. Yet Timmons had come in with a questionable claim to the neighboring section, had boldly offered to buy out T and T at a ridiculous price, and had stated flatly that if Trask didn't sell he would break him. How could he?

Trask could think of no way. Yet the man's confidence was frightening. Timmons had not been idle since his arrival on Calamity. He had brought in men and supplies—and then the men and supplies had simply disappeared. No one knew where they had gone, or what Timmons was up to. But Trask had a premonition that he would know soon and would not like the answer.

He himself had requested the mining committee hearings, to put an end to Timmons's dispute of his ownership of section seventy-five. Now he felt the hearings somehow would become a trigger, and Timmons held the gun.

As the sun sank behind the western range, Trask brooded about it. But he could see no answer.

Two twine-demarked blocks west on State Street,

Watson and Aphrodite met.

"You find him?" she asked.

"Not a sign. A lot of people recall seeing him. He became quite a celebrity yesterday with his pictures. But no one has seen him since morning. How about your young lady?"

"I don' think she been here. People who sees Emmalee usually remembers, mos' 'specially the menfolks. But I got a hunch she ain' far away. Prophecy say, 'All roads lead to Calamity.' An' that sho' nuff where this is." Her old eyes were large and troubled. "Calamity. Jes' like it say, I is done come to Calamity. All's I can do now is jus' try to keep that girl away from your Mr. Charles Henry—an' I 'spect I'll do that, no matter what it takes."

"Well, I wish us both luck. I promised Mr. Powers I would find the young man, help him establish himself and keep him out of trouble."

"Tryin' times is comin' soon," she said fretting. "I feels it in my bones."

A lanky figure approached them in the dusk. It was Jasper.

"You want us to keep an eye out for things and tell you about 'em like we done when we was travelin'?" he asked.

"Can't hurt nothin' if you do."

"Well, we seen somethin' unusual an' we talked about it and we figured one of us better tell you if you wanted us to."

"What you seen?"

"Well, it's the creek. While ago when we first went out, there ol' Jesse was waterin' the stock an' he fell in, an' it was neck-deep an' we like to never got him out—"

"Is he all right?" Watson asked.

"Oh, sure. He dried out eventually. But then later ol' Joe, he was lookin' at a fish an' he fell in an' we got him

340

out a lot easier because it was only waist-deep. An' he ain't that much taller than Jesse."

Watson and Aphrodite looked at each other, trying to make sense of what the man was telling them.

"Anyhow, a little bit ago ol' Alexander decided to take hisself a bath. So he jumped in the creek an' all he got washed was his feet, 'cause that's all the water there was."

It was only a hundred yards from where they stood to where the two creeks joined. Jasper had a hard time keeping up with the two older people.

Big Covey Creek was down to a trickle, its rock bottom drying in the evening air, trapped fish floundering here and there among the rocks. The smaller stream, Clear Creek, was just a string of little pools on dry bottom. Just hours before, both had been full and flowing streams.

"Chaos an' havoc!" Aphrodite gasped.

"I don't know." Watson took off his hat and ran curled fingers through his hair. "I just don't know."

"What we was wonderin' was," Jasper continued, "if maybe we ought to move the saddle stock. Feller told Joe there's a springwater pond up on that hump over there, couple of miles south. Maybe we ought to go wait there. Looks like they've done used up these creeks."

In all, it had been an unusual day in Calamity City. Now, under a silver moon, the townsite rested, waiting for what tomorrow might bring.

A rented hack rolled in from the south, coming up the Denver road. The driver waved casually at the four men moving horses south along the road, eased his team right around a bend, and drove along a path bordered by stakes and twine until he came to several clusters of tents that seemed to be the center of town. He hauled in in front of a large lantern-lighted tent with a sign painted on it: Grand State Hotel.

The driver set his brake, looped his reins and climbed down to hold the door for his passenger. His eyes went round and moonshot as she climbed down. He had never in his life seen so lovely a woman.

"This doesn't look like much of a place, miss. But this is where you said you wanted to go. Calamity City. This is all of it there is, at least right now."

She looked around, her brow wrinkling at sight of what passed for a hotel, then her eyes lighted as she saw the empty wagon standing next to it. It was Mr. Underwood's wagon. "Oh, good!" she said. "My luggage has arrived."

The flap of the tent opened, and a small dark figure in a long, flannel nightgown appeared. "Miss Emmalee! That you, girl? You get yo'self in here this minute! Where you been all this time? Lord a'mercy, I never heard of such a fool thing, runnin' off like you done—I said get yo'self in here! Right now!"

V

With the moon to light his way and the winding course of Covey Creek to guide him, Charles Henry rode north across the rising, rolling valley. He held as nearly as possible to a straight line, due north, intending to reach the encircling hills from where the creek issued, and from there begin his search for parcel nine. Covey Creek had swung far to the left of him, though he could still see its course: a dark, ragged line on the silver of moonlit grass with occasional stands of trees. But as an hour passed, and then another, the creek edged closer to his route, its line pointing off into the hills where he was heading. When he had gone about ten miles, the creek was near at hand again.

He finished off the last of the sandwiches Sarah Smiley had made and swung left. He was nearing the hills now, and their silhouettes showed them to be a series of tall ridges like long fingers pointing at the gorge where Covey Creek issued into the valley. Little Clear Creek was nearer now, too, on his right, a mile or so away, its course mostly hidden by rolls and swells in the land.

He urged Captain Keech through rich-foliaged brush toward the bottom land along Covey Creek, came out on its high bank, and stopped, staring in disbelief. The creek was gone.

Where before had been a small river, leaping and laughing down its wide path, now there were rocks, rounded and bone-white in the moonlight, with here and there a still pool among them.

"What in heaven's name is going on?" he muttered. Then, more loudly: "What have they done to the creek?"

Suddenly an inspiration built in his mind, and he turned to gaze north, up the wide and drying stream. For hours he had been wondering about the conversation up on the mountain. For some reason those men wanted parcel nine, wanted it badly. There had been menace in the deep voice when it said, "If he'll sell parcel nine, buy it. If not, you know what to do."

Now, as he sat his horse above the empty creek bed, he had a hunch where parcel nine might be. He had some other hunches, too.

He led the roan carefully across the rocky streambed to a pool and let him drink, then returned to the east bank and remounted. "Let's go see what the other creek looks like," he said.

With a refreshed Captain Keech under him he headed east of north, and in a mile or so approached the willow-lined course of Clear Creek. He was not surprised to find it dry.

He looked north again, toward the dark ridges, now close and towering over their approach slopes. "I wonder," he mused aloud to the horse, "how far apart these creeks are up there."

Two more miles and he knew. As he climbed the sweeping apron of the north hills the watercourses closed in on him, one on each side, until his path was a narrow, rocky ledge between deep gorges a hundred feet apart and still closing. Ahead the ledge shrank to a rim of stone barely twenty feet across, a hard rock blade edged-up between two canyons that were almost one canyon. And at that point, where the double stream issued from a steep notch between finger ridges, whole flanks of ridge had been blasted away and dumped into the gorges, damming them nearly to the top with rock debris. Atop that someone had built a crescent dam, buttressed at its center in the living rock of the blade ledge, its wings closing the notch from ridge-end to ridge-end and rising nearly twenty feet above the banks of the gorges. Charles Henry stared in awe.

At closer range he could see how it had been done. The crescent dam had been completed first, a great wall of timbers high and dry above the crests of the flowing streams. Then the rock above it had been shattered, probably by repeated blasting, and let fall into the streambeds, choking them up to the base of the log structure. It was a feat of engineering. And the final damming had been done within recent hours. He remembered the three wagonloads of blasting powder that had gone north from Calamity. They were part of the picture he had painted up on the mountain.

He had to backtrack a mile to find a place where he could cross the Covey Creek gorge. Then he turned toward the hills again, pointing at the finger ridge that was the west wing of the closure. It took him two hours to reach the top of the ridge. Then he stood, holding the horse's reins, and simply shook his head in wonder. Behind the fronting ridges was a wild and broken land, a land of fragmented finger ridges standing above deep breaks and gorges, weird rock formations, spires and pinnacles, a place of seeming miles where the earth was shattered and all the pieces stood on edge. Ridges like the prows of longships clustered to point at the cut where the twin streams issued into the valley. Besides the ridge he was on and the one across the canyon, two others extended sharp rock points into the chasm. In two of the canyons between, water stood. Twin streams, Covey Creek coming in from the northwest, Clear Creek from due north. But now the water stood still, high on the shoulders of ridge rock and climbing higher.

Within a short time, the streams would overtop the ledge between their courses, and then they would be one lake. Beyond, past a narrow saddle of soft rock, a larger gorge—this one dry—pointed away to the northeast. And on that saddle were people.

Embers of campfires winked red in the breeze, while the bright moon showed tents and huts, corrals with stock, wagons, plows, and moldboards drawn up together, a sizeable camp that spread on the slopes above the saddle and focused its equipment there. On the narrow saddle itself, hardly more than a drift of earth blocking the rising waters from the dry wash beyond, were mounds of earth and piles of rock, where deep holes had been dug in the drift.

With sure intuition Charles Henry knew what he was looking at. This was parcel nine. *His* parcel nine. This was the land that man on Calamity Peak wanted, and the reason he wanted it had to do with what was being done up here. But what did it mean? Why would they block the creeks? Granted, if a person wanted to dry up the whole valley, here was the place to do it—for a time at least. Of course the streams would keep flowing down through the broken lands, and the lake that they had made would get deeper until it lapped at the top of that saddle over there and overflowed the log dam. Then its waters would flow again in the streambeds down through the valley just as they had before. So what was the purpose? Only so much water could be trapped, then it would flow again. What was being accomplished here?

The ridge ascended behind him and became a wooded hill with another crest beyond it. Leading the tired roan, Charles Henry climbed until he found a grassy swale. Then he stripped off saddle and packs and turned Captain Keech loose in the little meadow. He stacked portfolio, valise, easel, and saddlebags with his saddle under a clump of brush, then sat for a time trying to think it out. He dozed and awoke to starry darkness. The moon had set.

The stars provided enough light that he could see, but maybe not enough to be seen.

Stepping carefully where the shadows were deep he made his way back down to the finger ridge and out to its abrupt point where tons of shattered rock had been sheered away by blasting. The lake was rising, its starlit surface lapping high on the rockfall now, approaching the base of the crescent dam. From where he stood the top of that dam was thirty feet below him. He lowered himself over the edge of the sheered incline.

At the top of the log dam he braced himself for a moment, feet testing the rounded, uneven timbers, then tapped his hat firmly in place, spread his arms and danced with long, erratic strides out to the first upright buttress brace where he clung as he took a deep breath. It was still a long way to the other side. Two braces later he was on the center of the dam and frozen in a crouch, trying for invisibility in his exposed position. There had been movement at the other end, and now he could make out a man there, up on the butt of the ridge, holding a rifle.

For a time the man stood, outlined against the starry sky where faint dawn light was beginning to show. The man seemed to be looking not toward him but to the south where Calamity Peak raised its bulk above the valley. For several minutes he stood there, as though

347

waiting for a signal. Then he turned and walked away, out of sight.

Charles Henry expelled a hard breath, straightened, spread his arms and raced for the next upright.

At the base of the east ridge he listened carefully, then climbed.

The near end of the project camp was a short distance up the ridge from its point. Campfire embers glowed in two places, and there were tents and a pair of sheds. Most of the stock he had seen was in corrals on this side of the drift saddle. It was the saddle that he wanted to see. As the hours had passed an anger had grown in Charles Henry. He didn't know what was being done up here, or why, but there was a furtiveness about it that went against his grain. People were doing things they didn't want known, in a manner that could hurt a lot of decent people out there in the valley. And they were doing them on his property. They should, he thought, at least have talked with him about it before they turned parcel nine into an elaborate lake.

Keeping to the north side of the finger ridge, with its crown between him and the campsite, he crouched and ran the hundred yards to where the drift saddle began, sagging across to another ridge just north where the rest of the work camp was spread. Behind and below, the now-joined canyons of Covey and Clear Creeks were fingers of deep water with a common, rippling surface that was within ten feet of the crest of the saddle. The arms of the lake already spread upstream for miles, beyond canyon bends that blocked his vision.

From here there was no cover except the darkness, and that was fading. Soon it would be dawn. Looking around carefully for signs of movement and seeing none, he ran down onto the saddle and along it to its center where the holes were dug. Mounds of earth and rock testified to their size. Each was as wide as a grave is long, and at least twice as deep.

There were four holes, twenty or thirty fee apart. At the first one he knelt, peered down into darkness that was not quite complete. There were things there, three round things that were faint graynesses in the gloom. He couldn't make out what they were. Carefully, finding handholds, he let himself down into the hole. The things were squat casks of wood, not as heavy as liquid contents but bulky and solid. He had seen such casks before. Lifting one, he crawled and scrambled back to the top, climbed out and looked closely at the thing he held.

Blasting powder. And nearby, on a wagon bed, were boxes of fuse. He turned, almost tripped and discovered that the keg he held was fused, ten or twelve feet of waxed fuse extending from a sealed bung in one end.

The eastern sky was brightening, faint pink over the mountains, and he found he could read the legend on the keg.

Then he looked eastward again, out over the big dry wash that deepened into a shadowy canyon and reached away into the miles. That was what they were doing! They had dammed the water in the twin creeks. Now they were preparing to divert it entirely, into a new course, away from the valley. The anger that had grown in him became bitter purpose. He didn't want a lake on parcel nine, and he certainly didn't want a channel diversion. He liked the creeks right where they were. Whoever these people were, they had no right to be here and no right to do what they were doing to parcel nine and the valley below it.

Decision came with determination. Setting the keg down, Charles Henry let himself into the hole again and hoisted out the other two. Then he carried them to the slope of the drift saddle, aligned them one by one and set them rolling.

The splash as the first keg hit the rising lake seemed loud in the stillness, and he looked around at the two camps. No one seemed to have noticed. The other two kegs followed. Then he went to the next hole.

He had to duck down once, as the silhouetted man appeared on the south ridge, but the man again was looking south and did not see him. Long minutes passed and the light strengthened as Charles Henry worked, emptying the holes and rolling kegs off into the lake.

When the final keg had been floated Charles Henry surveyed his work, frowned and muttered, "Aw, no."

The kegs had neither sunk nor drifted away. They rested at the water's edge, in clusters of three, bobbing and bumping at the shoulder of the drift saddle. He looked around for a rope, found none and settled for a large coil of heavy fuse. Hurrying now, knowing that any moment the camps would come awake and he would be found, he waded into the icy water and tied the fuses of the first three kegs together, then tied his long fuse to the knot and towed them after him to the second cluster of bombs. With these added to his tow he tied the third, and then the fourth. By walking in the water along the new and rising shore, he found he could tow the fleet of kegs handily.

Moving as rapidly as possible now, plainly visible in the dawn, he waded toward the dam. He had one purpose in mind: to get the blasting powder away from here before it could be used to divert the creek—take it off somewhere and dispose of it—then to have a serious talk with whoever was responsible for the dam. How was he going to make a fortune from parcel nine if it was underwater?

Luck seemed to be with him. No one had yet stirred except the single guard who seemed to look only south. He made the end of the saddle, then had to lengthen his line and tow kegs from the top of the ridge, which was slower, but he was nearly at the sheered face where the dam began when suddenly the sky was bathed in brilliance. Startled, he turned and his mouth dropped open. There was a sunrise there—an instant sunrise—and it was due south. Far across the valley, on the left shoulder of Calamity Peak, white fire climbed into the sky, bathing the land in a glare that reddened even as he watched.

There were shouts from the camps, and a second later the sound of running feet. Charles Henry ducked, but it was too late. More shouts, more running, and then he was surrounded by surprised, sleepy men holding guns.

"Who the hell are you?" one asked. "What do you want here?"

"Look, Hurley! What's them in the water? Is those our kegs? By God, I do believe they is!"

Rough hands caught his arms, removed his revolver from its holster, relieved him of the length of fuse he was using as a towline. "Come on! Speak up! What's goin' on here? What was that flash?"

"I don't know what the flash was," he said, trying to explain. "But you're on my property and have no right to—" Someone hit him then, knocked him sprawling. When he got to his feet the men facing him were somehow different from the rest. There were three of them, all burly, sullen, dark-suited men like those he had seen on Calamity.

"So this is your property," one of them growled. "If that's so, then you must be C. Clayton. Are you?"

"I am." He rubbed a sore jaw, working it to see if anything was broken. By the expression on the speaker's face, he judged this was the man who had hit him. "You people are trespassing on my property!"

"Well," the man said, "we can fix that. We'll buy it

from you and then we won't be trespassing. I'll give you a thousand dollars for parcel nine."

"Don't be ridiculous," Charles Henry snapped.

The man looked at the others. "Did Bull say we had to offer more than once?"

"Naw," another answered. "He just said buy it from him if he'd sell."

"But the man don't want to sell," the third noted.

"That's too bad." The first one smiled. He drew a bright-plated gun from his coat. Trailed by the other two, he stepped toward Charles Henry. "Good-bye, Mr. C. Clayton."

Charles Henry was trapped, his back to the edge of the ridge, the crescent dam far below, a wall of logs with water on one side and rocks on the other. "Look," he suggested. "We'd better talk about this."

The other men, the ordinary ones, had backed off slightly, letting the three thugs take over. But now one of them objected. "Look, gents, if he is the rightful owner here, then—" He didn't finish. One of the thugs spun around, a fist lashing out, and punched him where he stood.

"The rest of you," he said, "you don't want to see this? Then turn your backs."

The incident had distracted the man with the gun, just for an instant, but Charles Henry was desperate. As the muzzle wavered he leapt and grabbed it, trying to force it to the side while he threw a looping left into the man's midriff, giving it every ounce of strength he had. The man doubled over, the gun shoved aside for an instant. But then he straightened, his face beet-red, and swung a roundhouse blow that whistled over Charles Henry's bobbing head, knocking his hat askew.

An aching wrist and a bent hat had confirmed two things: for a man who looked fat, the thug was astonishingly solid. And for a man of his size, he was amazingly fast. Charles Henry went for the gun again. He levered and pushed, using both hands, and managed to swing the man half around just as the gun roared.

The second thug screamed and doubled over, clutching his stomach. He fell across the body of the third thug who, Charles Henry noted with the odd clarity of panic, was lying on his back with an arrow protruding from his throat.

The man he was wrestling caught him with an elbow that sent him spinning away. He grinned again, brought the gun up, and glanced at his companions lying on the ground. His mouth opened, he backed an involuntary step—and was gone. Far below, there was a rattle of rocks before the crescent dam.

"My Lord in heaven," Charles Henry breathed, dazed. He had been aware of shouts and screams, seemingly all around him, but now those seemed to have dwindled into distance. He straightened, found his gun on the ground by his feet, and returned it to his holster. Then he looked around.

The Indians who faced him were not like the Indians he had painted in the Five Tribes territory. These looked a lot more like some of those who had chased him in No Man's Land, yet different from them, too.

There were five of them, carrying bows with arrows notched, four of them in draw position. In the distance, up the ridge, a lot more Indians were hard on the heels of men from the project camps.

Four of the five facing him had their bows up, pointed at him. Now one drew the string, but the fifth—a somewhat older man—raised a hand and said something. The warrior eased his draw.

The leader peered at Charles Henry, his eyes like ebony in a face right out of hell. He tapped the young man on the chest with a bony finger. "I know you," he said. "Falling Rock dream, see vision. See pan'monium, 'poc'lypse fall on white-eyes. See you, too. We watch, you drop thunderkegs in water. We watch, you try get away." He lapsed into a string of Indian, using his hands, speaking more and more loudly as Charles Henry stared at him blankly.

The warrior shook his head. He walked to where the dead thugs lay and kicked one of them. "Don' like," he said.

"I can understand that."

"Don' like you, too," Falling Rock continued. Then he pointed southward. "You go back. Pan'monium! 'Poc'lypse! Bullshit!"

When Charles Henry reached the center span of the bridge he clung for a moment to the upright and looked back. Falling Rock still stood atop the finger ridge, watching him. Several of the other Indians were fishing kegs out of the water, looking curiously at the fuses. One of them turned toward Charles Henry and an evil grin spread across his dark face. Charles Henry dashed for the other side.

He retrieved Captain Keech, saddled and packed him, strapped on his tripod and headed down the ridge. Circling to the base of the rockfall he removed his hat, straightened its crown, replaced it firmly atop his head and looked up at the structure in the cleft. A line of Indians was coming down the sheered face, each carrying a keg of blasting powder. Falling Rock stood on the east ridge, pointing downward to where the dam buttresses converged.

"I hope you've had a nice rest, Captain Keech," Charles Henry whispered. "Because we need to be a long way from here before they get across that gorge."

He had gone barely a mile, most of it at a dead run, when he saw a buggy coming toward him.

Weldon Hempley grinned in recognition and waved. "Mr. Clayton! I want to talk to you about parcel nine!"

Hempley grabbed his railings then and held on for dear life as the flying horseman thundered past him, dipping in the saddle to grab the buggy horse's lead, and headed onward at a gallop, the buggy sailing and soaring over rough ground in his wake.

VI

Dawn was pinking the sky when Aphrodite arose quietly, put on her boots, dress, and mockingbird hat, picked up her shotgun and slipped out of the tent that Mr. Nightingale had erected because she demanded it.

She wanted to take a look around while Emmalee slept. She had a feeling that Charles Henry Clayton was around somewhere, that events were closing in on her, that the prophecy had reached critical mass. And yet, the little town was quiet. All seemed in order. She heard footsteps, and Watson appeared from beyond the land office, his coat tidy, gray sideburns combed and his round hat horizontal on his head.

"You is up early," she said.

"Rather. I didn't sleep well. Thought I should get up and have a look around."

"I knows. I feels it, too." She looked around, her eyes large with dread. "Don' look like he been here, but it *feel* like he been here. Somethin' fixin' to happen."

"I dare say." Watson cleaned his spectacles. "The creeks are still empty. I looked. Strangest thing."

"I heard wagons an' people mos' the night."

"Yes. That mining committee the people have been expecting came in by coach from Denver. And a lot of

357

other people have been arriving, coming from out in the valley. There are going to be hearings this morning." His tidy features looked very pale in dawn light. "Aphrodite, have you ever heard of a person named Timmons? Did Charles Henry happen to mention him?"

"Timmons?" She thought about it. "Sound familiar. Seem like Miss Emmalee was ditherin' 'bout some gentleman name Timmons as was out to shoot Mr. Charles Henry dead. I tole her it might be a blessin'. But the gentleman never did show up."

"Well, he's here. I saw him. He is the one who has contested the mining claim up on the mountain. He is the one who has caused the trouble up there. That's his tent right down there—the big one. I can't imagine how he comes to be here, of all places."

"Maybe he gone shoot Mr. Charles Henry?" Aphrodite asked, hopefully.

Watson looked around, bleakly. "I wouldn't put it past him to try. He really is a rotten sort of person."

"That too bad. You know I don' hole no hate for Mr. Charles Henry. He ain' too bad, fo' a young white gentleman. It jus' that he carry chaos on him like white trash carries lice. He prob'ly cain' help it, but he do."

"Yes. He do—does."

"An' I feels it a-buildin' up. It fixin' to happen. I knows—"

Suddenly the town was bathed in brilliant light, stark and blinding as of a sun abruptly risen. As one they turned and saw the fireball on the east shoulder of Calamity Peak, just above the hump where the streambed and the Denver Road curved away around it. The light grew, flared and seemed to stutter as it was renewed and renewed again. In its blaze they could see tons of debris rocketing away in all directions, and the hump of mountain seemed to cleave apart, its lower end starting to slide downward. The sun-bright glare reddened, sombered and died, lost in a huge cloud of dust and smoke that grew above the crumbling slope. An instant later the earth beneath their feet shuddered violently. And as it subsided there came a roar that washed across the valley like the thunder of giant cannons.

There were shouts all around, people erupting from tents and wagons, many of them carrying hastily grabbed weapons.

Aphrodite clung to Watson's arm. "I knowed it," she whispered. "I knowed it! He here! Chaos an' havoc done come amongst us!"

Watson stared in open-mouthed awe at the stately black cloud of debris that now hid the valley to the east. "Incredible," was all he could think of to say.

In the sudden semidarkness a bugle blared and abruptly went silent. A voice shouted, "O'Toole, what in Sweet Mary's name are ye doin'?"

And others, overlapping: "Holy Christ, what was that?" "The mine blew up!" "Wasn't the mine, it was over yonder on that shoulder!" "What was that? Anybody, what was that?" "A volcano!" "It weren't no volcano, that there was explosives!" "Go back to sleep, Howard, I have a headache."

People thronged about in the dim light of dawn, rubbing sleepy eyes, shouting and shoving, thronging to stare at the cloud of dust and smoke slowly writhing in the breeze above the hump.

Emmalee burst from the hotel tent wearing a clinging night dress, her dark hair flowing around her shoulders and a large Smith and Wesson .44 in her dainty hand. Men in the gaping crowd forgot about the explosion and gaped at Emmalee.

"Here!" Aphrodite barked, "You men mind where you's lookin'! Miss Emmalee, get back in yonder an' put on some clothes!"

As the morning light increased and the cloud of dust drifted away up Calamity, it was obvious that the hump was shorter than it had been. Its downward slope was sheared away, and a great fan of rubble lay below it, standing above both the dry creek bed and the Denver Road.

Clarence Nightingale issued from the land office tent, looked at the crowd and set out to round up helpers. Within ten minutes they had fires going and pots on to cook and were setting up plank tables and restaurant signs. A number of men had headed down the road toward the hump. Now most of them came back, trailing along after four blackened horsemen with huge eyes and tattered bandanas. As they came into town Aphrodite met them. She stopped and stared. "Jasper? Jesse?"

"I'm Alexander," the front one said. "Ma'am, would it be all right if we take the horses somewheres else? We don't like it up there. We hadn't no sooner got a fire goin' for coffee and went to see about the stock than . . . than . . ." He seemed at a loss for words.

"Than Kablooey!" one who might have been Joe added.

"Kablooey is right," another said with Jesse's voice. "And Jasper here. Are you Jasper? No, Jasper back yonder, we had to fetch him down out of a tree he never clumb, an—"

"An' where we was campin' ain't there anymore," Jasper finished. "Kablooey!"

Six nervous members of the territorial mining committee convened their preliminary hearing shortly after sunup. Chairs and plank tables in a roped-off area within the bivouac perimeter served as the courtroom.

The committee sat behind one table, Trask and his superintendents at another, and Bull Timmons at another with several of his thugs. A sizeable crowd gathered beyond the rope cordon. Following yesterday's mystery of the dry creeks and this morning's exploding mountain, everyone was curious to see what might happen next.

Lester Magee, chairman of the mining committee, rapped a gavel for silence, glanced at a stack of briefs from which he and the committeemen had made notes, and called the hearing to order. "The matter in contention regarding the so-named T and T mining venture having been outlined by way of notarized affidavits prior to this hearing, we will dispense with the formalities of preliminary review and proceed with the statements of the principals. Mr. Trask, are you prepared to state your case?"

Trask arose from his chair, removed his hat and nodded. "I am. My name is Solomon Trask. I am the founder of T and T Mining Company, operating on section seventy-six of the Calamity Peak highlands sections surveyed by the Department of Interior and dispensed by the agents Forbish, Walker, and Boole. My company owns both sections seventy-five and seventy-six, adjoining slopes both bounded by the middle line of Covey Creek at the low end.

"My case is simple. T and T Mining is the legitimate and sole owner of all lands involved in the T and T mining operation, and can prove it—and, furthermore, is prepared to begin the treating of middle grade ore within a matter of days."

He replaced his hat and sat down. There was a buzz of conversation. It had been common opinion that Trask was an eccentric and that no worthwhile payload would ever issue from T and T Mine. But now, he sounded so positive, so sure, that eyebrows were raised in speculation.

Magee rapped his gavel again. "Mr. Timmons, would you care to state your case?"

Bull Timmons arose to his considerable bulky height, placed his hands on his hips and shot a malicious grin at Trask. "I certainly will. My case is that this man Trask has defrauded his investors, has defaulted on his claims and that as a rightful shareholder in T and T Mining—"

"What do you mean, sir?" Trask erupted. "You are no shareholder of mine!"

Magee rapped his gavel. "Mr. Trask, if you please, allow Mr. Timmons to state his case."

"Ah, but I *am* a shareholder," Timmons said with a smile. "I have documentation showing the acquisition of sixty shares from one Thomas Barnes shortly before that gentleman's untimely demise."

"So that's what happened to poor old Barnes," one of Trask's assistants whispered. Trask went pale.

"And," Timmons continued, "sixty shares entitles me to lay clam to the assets of T and T on the basis of default or fraud. As you gentlemen know, I already have filed my claim on section seventy-five. But now I arrive here and find that Trask has placed the entirety of T and T's capital investment on section seventy-six, which I contend is misappropriation of collateral, since only section seventy-five was put up as collateral to the shareholders."

One of the mining committee, who seemed to be a lawyer, interrupted. "There is no such thing as misappropriation of collateral. Misappropriation applies to removable assets and funds, but not to—"

Magee banged his gavel. "Hush up, Woodrow. This is a mining committee hearing, not a court of law. We understand what Mr. Timmons is saying."

"My contention," Timmons summed up, "is that

Trask should be evicted from that mine up there and it should be turned over to me."

Trask had half risen from his chair. "This is infamous!"

Magee's gavel chattered. "Trask, sit down!" Then, with order somewhat restored, he turned to the smiling Bull Timmons. "Mr. Timmons, you made two specific charges a moment ago. You claimed that Mr. Trask has defrauded and defaulted. Would you care to explain?"

"Gladly. Mr. Trask defrauded the investors when he claimed that he would mine ore on a mountainside, rail-cart it to the base of the mountain and there stamp and smelt it using power flumes to operate the mill and separate the slag. He has defaulted in that he, in fact, cannot do the things he said he would do."

"What do you mean, 'cannot do these things?'" Trask was livid now, pounding on his table. "Of course I can do these things!"

"Mr. Trask—" Magee roared.

"It takes water to operate flumes and separate slag," Timmons explained slowly and quietly. "You may have noticed by now, Trask, that there isn't any water. Both creeks are dry."

There was a long silence. The mining committee members stared at one another. Trask went pale again, and Timmons stood gloating. Then a man in the crowd asked, "You tellin' us you had somethin' to do with that, mister?"

Magee rapped his gavel. "Let's have some order here!"

"Sounded to me like that's what he said," another man said. "Listen, mister, I got a place out at parcel thirty-three that I spent everything I got on, and I have to have that creek across there. It makes all the difference."

"My place is the same." Tom Smiley stepped

363

forward to the cordon rope. "Without Covey Creek I can't make it."

"Order!" Magee rapped. "This is a hearing we're having, not a free for all!"

Another member of the mining committee pointed a finger at Timmons. "Is that what you're saying, mister? That *you* dried up the watercourses here?"

Timmons smiled and shrugged. "All perfectly legal. You see, I control the headwaters. There is no law that says I can't dam water on my own property."

At this the gathered crowd surged forward against the cordon rope, some shouting, most glaring at Timmons, and Magee rapped uselessly then shouted at Sergeant O'Shay: "You soldiers! Control this mob!"

"All four of us?" O'Shay muttered, then squared his shoulders. "O'Roark, to me! O'Malley, you and O'Brien left flank! Rifles ready!"

The cordon rope went limp as some of its posts were pushed over, and part of the angry crowd boiled into the hearing area, but those in front found themselves facing soldiers and stopped. Beyond the soldiers, Timmons's thugs had guns out and had formed a protective shield around their employer.

"Recess!" Magee shouted. "This hearing is recessed until this afternoon!" As the mining committee stood, he said to them, "I want to have a look at that mine. Tell Trask or one of his men to take us up there."

With daybreak more people began arriving in the Calamity Valley, families with wagons and supplies coming to find the promised land. But some also were leaving. Two wagonloads of missionaries plodded along the Denver road, tired teams transporting exhausted men who had somehow become separated from Brother Thorpe in their search for the Angel of

364

the Lord. Left without the reinforcement of Brother Thorpe's charisma for several hours, they had lost their zeal and were on their way home. Rounding the shoulder of Calamity Peak they came to a huge fan of rock and soil that completely blocked both the road and the creek bed to their right. The entire gap was solid fill, nearly twelve feet above road level.

As they sat and stared at the obstacle, a large man appeared atop it, looked down at them and began clambering down toward them. His clothing was tatters and rags, his shoes were ruins. He was bruised and battered, but there was a cold purpose about him that chilled the men in the wagons.

He approached them, stared at them, looked at their teams and walked to the second wagon. "Ged dowd," he told its occupants.

As he turned the wagon and started it toward town he left behind him a road full of bruised and dazed ex-missionaries.

The sun was quartering above the mountains to the east. The little townsite was full of people, puzzled mostly, some clustering in groups here and there to talk about the hearing, the dry creeks, the blast on the mountain, all of the odd and ominous occurrences that seemed somehow connected but not clearly.

Emmalee Wilkes, stunning in a gown of pale jade and matching bonnet with trim that accented her dark eyes, her proud chin high, had investigated the entire town in the past hour, looking for Charles Henry Clayton, but she had found no sign of him although a number of people recalled him. And through it all, Aphrodite trailed after her, complaining nonstop. Finally she turned to the black woman. "Aphrodite, you might just as well hush. I have come this far to find

Charles Henry, and I intend to find him."

"He nothin' but trouble, child. Tha's what I been tellin' you. What we needs to do is pack up an' go on back home."

"Aphrodite! Don't you understand? I love him. I shall never be apart from him again."

Aphrodite glanced at the brooding Watson, who stood slightly aside. She shook her head. "What we gonna do? I cain' let this happen."

Watson wiped his spectacles. "Miss Emmalee, I am afraid she is right. I don't fully understand it, but Mr. Charles Henry is what they used to call a Jonah. A jinx. Trouble trails him. He is my responsibility, and I promised Mr. Powers I would look after him. But after all I have seen—"

Her eyes widened. "Mr. Watson! You, too? I can't believe this. You sound just like Aphrodite. Certainly you can't believe such nonsense?"

"On the day when juices flow," Aphrodite chanted, "and th' virgin fires glow . . ."

"Aphrodite!"

"One will come to fan the flame . . ."

"Aphrodite, hush! Not in front of—"

"Chaos an' havoc be his name. . . ."

"Where have I seen you before?"

At the deep voice, demanding, they all looked around. Bull Timmons, flanked by a pair of his thugs, was staring at Watson. "You. Where have I seen you before? I recognize you."

"Timmons!" They all turned again. Solomon Trask was approaching with three of his mine guards. "There is something you have overlooked."

"Oh? And what might that be?" The thugs tensed, but Timmons relaxed. His smile was a goad.

"Your dam will fill and spill. You can only stop so much water, then the creeks will flow again. I suggest you withdraw before the mining committee returns. You can't pull this off, you know."

"I have overlooked nothing, Trask." Timmons's deep voice was a contented purr. "You see, where I control the water there is a third channel that does not enter this valley at all. Before the day is out, there will be an entirely new river flowing east, away from here. You can't stop me, Trask. I've won."

"I seem to recall," Watson said cleaning his spectacles and replacing them to stare owlishly at Timmons, "that you said that once before—in Boston."

None of them, absorbed as they were, noticed the tall young man riding into town on a lathered blue roan, with a buggy following, or the wagon approaching from the south with its tattered large driver.

At the corner of State and Grand Charles Henry swung down from Captain Keech and faced Weldon Hempley as he reined in. "I'll anchor your buggy for you. Over there somewhere is a man named Nightingale. Tell him what I've told you. He seems to be in charge, if anyone is."

Hempley jumped from the buggy and hurried toward the land office. Charles Henry glanced around, found the beat-down cordon rope lying in the dust and picked it up. "Careless," he muttered. Then with no obvious place to put it, he walked to the back of Hempley's buggy and tied it there. Twenty feet away, he saw Bull Timmons with a group of people, most of whom were hidden beyond the hotel tent. He strode toward the man.

"Mr. Timmons," he announced. "I have been to parcel nine and it belongs to me. I want your people off of my property. I do not intend to sell, and I will not be driven—*Miss Emmalee? Aphrodite?—Watson?*"

"Watson!" Timmons roared, remembering. "Watson! That was you!"

Charles Henry gaped at Emmalee. "Miss Emmalee! It *is* you!"

"Oh, Lord," Aphrodite breathed. "It's him."

"It was me," Watson assured Timmons. "Mr. Charles Henry! It's you!"

"It's him." Tom Smiley pointed from across the street.

"Who's he?" Solomon Trask asked one of his guards.

"It's him. From up there yesterday."

"Oh, Charles Henry." Emmalee's eyes were huge. "Is it really you?"

"It's me."

A large, battered man pushed into the closing crowd, saw Charles Henry and stopped. "Id's hib!"

Timmons swung around. "Luther? It's you!"

"Id's hib!" Luther repeated.

Charles Henry glanced around. "Hello! It's you!"

"Who?" Timmons asked Luther.

"Hib! Frob Bostod!"

"Hib? Him? Ah." It all came together now. "Him! It's him!"

"It's me," Charles Henry told Emmalee as their hands joined.

"It's you," she said.

"It's happenin'!" Aphrodite shrieked.

"Get him!" Timmons thundered.

"Sure." Luther nodded. He took a gun from one of Timmons's surprised thugs. At point-blank range he leveled the gun at Charles Henry.

VII

High on the face of Calamity Peak the mining committee, trailed by a pair of Trask's miners, inspected the T and T project. They looked at the piled ore collected in the clearing before the mine, took lanterns into the shaft to inspect the vein Trask was working, nodded appreciatively at the narrow gauge rails installed to move carts up and down the slope, and gawked at the arrangement of risers, cable, and grapples with which empty carts would be handled. "Damn good idea," one of them said. "If it works."

"Oh, it works, all right," Lucas told them. "I've rode them carts up an' down several times, checkin' 'em out. Rolled 'em right down to the dock where the stamp mill's goin' in, then winched back up here with them grapples. This ain't high-grade ore here, but doin' it thisaway we can process a lot of it."

"Not bad," Magee said. "Not too bad at all. But he sure isn't going to prove up unless he has the water down there."

"And if he can't prove up, another opined, "then I guess that Timmons fellow makes his point."

"That one is a real son of a bitch, you know it?"

"Yeah, but our jurisdiction doesn't extend to son of a

369

bitchery—just to mine claims."

"I'd like to see these carts work," Magee suggested.

"If you want to," Lucas told them, "we can ride them back down the mountain."

"Make way!" someone shouted. "Make way!"

They looked around. Six dirty men were making their way along the ledge leading from section seventy-five. The leader, a grimy man with whiskers and burning eyes, hailed them again. "Make way! The Lord has spoken on this mountain and His Angel walks among us on this day!"

The committee looked at one another. "Who is that?" Magee asked.

Lucas shrugged. "Some nut. He's huntin' angels. Was down to town yesterday."

"Have you seen him?" Brother Thorpe approached them. "The Angel of the Lord, have you seen him?"

"Haven't got any angels up here," Lucas assured him. "But you fellas are on private property. You better get off."

"It's the Lord's will," Brother Thorpe proclaimed. "For this is the Day of Judgement."

Magee shook his head. "We're just a mining committee," he explained.

A pair of mine guards came up to them. "We'll get them off the place," one said.

Lucas scratched his whiskers. "We might as well take them down with us," he suggested to Magee.

"All right. I guess we've seen enough up here."

Under the watchful eyes of the guards, Lucas got the missionaries loaded into the front cart. "You gentlemen climb into the middle one," he told the committee. "Wilbur and me will ride the rear one. That's where the governor assembly is, so's I can keep us goin' slow." He looked up, then looked again. "What in hell is that?" He pointed.

Far away, across the miles of rising valley to the north, a dense smoke cloud was rising from the hills. Huge and dark, it stood above the horizon.

"The Lord be praised," Brother Thorpe intoned.

"Explosives," Wilbur said.

"Crap," Magee told his committeemen. "He's diverted the streams."

"I guess that's that, then." One shrugged. "No water, no mine, is how I see it."

They clambered into the middle cart. Lucas and Wilbur got into the rear one with its massive ratchet gears and governing lever. Wilbur waved at the guards. "Be back in a while."

Lucas set his pipe aside, scratched his whiskers and glanced around to make sure everybody was seated. Then he leaned over the tailboard, uncoupled the restraining cable and released the brake. The three carts lurched and began their journey.

As they rolled away on the gentle slope one of the guards glanced at the base of a grapple stanchion, walked to it and picked up a long, tapered iron pin. "What's this?"

The other guard looked at it curiously, then his face turned pale. "Oh, Lord! I know what that is!" He ran out on the clearing, waving his arms wildly at the receding carts. "Hey! Hold up!" He fired his gun into the air, knowing as he did that it was too late.

Below and a little distance beyond the break of section seventy-six, four smoke-darkened horsemen reined in.

"Did you hear that?" Alexander asked.

"Sure did." Joe nodded. "That was the signal."

Jesse hauled on his reins, bringing his mount around in a rearing dance. "Let's go!"

As one they drew blackened bandanas across their faces, drew their pistols and thundered down the trail.

In the rear mine cart Lucas settled himself, grasped the ratchet lever and eased it back. It came free in his hand. The carts were picking up speed.

Eyes wide, Lucas flung himself to the side and peered down at the running gear. "The pin!" he shouted. "Where's the damn pin?"

Wilbur looked around, the wind beginning to whip his beard. "What pin, Lucas?"

"The governor pin! It's gone!"

In the middle cart some of the mining committee turned to look back, worry dawning on their faces.

With a yell, Lucas threw a leg over the tailboard, then changed his mind. It was too late to jump.

In the foremost cart Brother Thorpe stood and spread his arms to the wind. "Oh, glorious!" he proclaimed. "Glorious!"

The carts sailed over the hump and down the mountainside, wheels singing on their rails, the pitch rising to a whine then on, up and up to a shrill whistle.

"Oh, holy shit!" Lucas screamed and buried his face in his arms.

In the front cart Brother Thorpe turned, braced himself, turned his face to heaven and began to sing. The other missionaries joined him, their voices whipping back on the wind. "Glory, Glory Hallelujah! Glory, Glory Hallelujah . . ."

Gaining speed with each unhindered yard, the juggernaut careened through forest, screamed around a pair of switchbacks, hurtled past brush and mountain thicket and out onto a cleared slope, plummeting toward the waiting town below.

Captain Keech, ridden hard, pulled in wet and left ground-reined with his saddle and cargo still aboard, was on the verge of a temper tantrum. He nibbled at a

372

tent corner, pulled on the fabric and then waded through its guy ropes, collapsing it behind him. Inside, someone cursed and thrashed under the limp canvas. Captain Keech plodded on to where the chairs still stood from the morning's hearing. He nosed one chair over, went on to another, stepped on one and shattered it, and the cracking of wood startled him. He backed up, and a hind foot got caught in the slats of a fallen chair. He reared, plunged and lashed out. The chair sailed high, doing a lazy somersault, then landed on the back of Weldon Hempley's tired buggy horse which came awake with a snort and bolted. Posts snapped as the tied-on cordon rope came alive behind the lurching buggy. Another tent collapsed, and the rope burned through the rigging of still another. The flared-nostril horse careened left on Grand, and a confusion of rope, collapsed tents, furniture, cooking utensils, and supplies followed it, veering wide to flow around the hotel tent, destroying it a foot at a time.

Luther's gun had just come level when a loop of torn tent fabric closed around his feet and upended him. He crashed down atop one of Timmons's thugs. People were scattering and dancing to avoid the chaos in the buggy's wake. Aphrodite dodged a plummeting chair and started to shout at Emmalee, just as Charles Henry turned toward Watson, his hands momentarily leaving Emmalee's.

"Kill him!" Timmons roared. The remaining armed thug reacted instantly. Gun in hand he spun toward Charles Henry, hesitated as Charles Henry ducked a flying pot, then sighted and squeezed the trigger. Charles Henry bobbed again, and the gun was pointed squarely at Emmalee.

Aphrodite raised the shotgun and touched off both barrels. The thug went cartwheeling away, large parts of him missing. The recoil of the gun drove Aphrodite backward into Watson, and both of them sat down hard.

Timmons drew his own gun, his eyes on Charles Henry. At the motion Solomon Trask's guards opened fire, and Timmons ducked and ran, bullets singing around him. "Get him!" Trask shouted.

Emmalee was digging in her purse. Now she came up with the Smith and Wesson and looked around for someone to shoot. It had all occurred in an instant, and she was not sure what was happening.

Timmons dodged behind a wagon, scuttled the length of it and saw Charles Henry a few feet away, fighting with a piece of tent fabric. Timmons fired. His bullet singed Charles Henry's side and made him howl. Emmalee whirled and emptied the .44 in the direction of Timmons, its missiles biting slices from the wagon bed. Everywhere people were running, shouting, colliding, fighting blindly with anyone in sight. A line of wagons just entering Calamity from the east became instant pandemonium when three of the four teams, startled at the havoc ahead, reared, spun, collided and tangled. The woman driving the fourth wagon hauled hard on her reins, veering around the tangle. Her team leapt ahead, running. The man beside her, a sling on his arm and heavy bandages around his torso, flipped backward into the closed wagon and came up an instant later with a long rifle in his good hand.

"Yee-Haw!" he shouted. "Ride 'em out!" Then his eyes widened. "Pull up! Pull up!"

Solomon Trask and his guards dived for cover behind a pair of seed bins. "Over there!" he pointed. "That's Timmons by that wagon. Get him!"

Weldon Hempley and Clarence Nightingale ran from the land office tent, skidded to a halt, turned tail and sprinted for the cover of Nightingale's cook pits. A loose horse thundered over them, dragging a mass of twine and stakes behind it. Its rider, one of Trask's men, lay twitching on the bloody ground of State Street.

More Timmons thugs had run to join the fight. One of them tripped over Luther just as he was getting to his feet, and Luther swung on him, catching him square in the face with a roundhouse punch that flattened the beefy man. Another went for Charles Henry, who was just throwing off his shroud, but collided with Emmalee, sending her spinning. Charles Henry saw the collision. Before the thug could regain his balance the young man was on him. Two blows to the head, one to the midsection and another to the chin, and the man was out on his feet. Charles Henry shouted a war cry, grappled with the sagging thug, lifted him and hurled him bodily at one of his cohorts. Both of them went down.

Charles Henry raced to Emmalee, bowling over a pair of soldiers on the way. He scooped her up, crouched and raced to a supply wagon that had been turned on its side.

There were people behind it, but they were not his people. One of the Chicagoans saw him coming, raised and aimed, and fell back with a hole in his head as the unmistakable crack of a long rifle resounded. "Get out your gun!" a voice shouted from a distance. "Ye got Gittingses!"

Charles Henry dropped Emmalee unceremoniously, drew and fired the navy Colt, and the second thug behind the wagon fell.

Emmalee tried to struggle to her feet. "You might exercise a bit more decorum," she snapped.

He looked around, astonished and thoroughly confused at all that had happened so suddenly—that was still happening, building in violence and volume. At opposite corners of what had been State and Grand,

Timmons and Trask with several men each were shooting from cover, a full-scale shoot-out. Hot lead sang and ricocheted everywhere. Sergeant O'Shay and his men had taken cover behind a cabin foundation and were trying to decide which way to fire.

A bullet whined through the crown of Charles Henry's top hat. He stooped, scooped up a fussing Emmalee under one arm and ran, zigzagging between people and obstructions, toward a wagon that was just completing a smart turn on State. He dodged behind it and tossed Emmalee over its side. Virgil MacLootie grinned down at him. Charles was beyond being surprised at anything. "Take care of her, Virgil. She's mine."

"Congratulations," MacLootie said, admiringly. "What's all this about?"

"I haven't the foggiest idea," Charles Henry told him.

Suddenly there was a pause in the pandemonium as someone shouted, "My God, look!"

Everyone ceased fire to look. Roaring down the valley, still a mile away but traveling at tremendous speed, were two great crests of foam and spray, their voices like thunder, sheer walls of water roaring down the beds of Covey and Clear Creeks.

"Flood!" Someone shouted. "Flash flood! Get to the high ground!"

People erupted from barricades and cover and ran in all directions. Most of them ran in circles.

Behind a pile of luggage where the hotel tent had been, Aphrodite sat spread-legged on the ground pouring powder into her shotgun. Watson crawled around looking for his spectacles.

Emmalee's head poked up from MacLootie's wagon. She saw the floodwaters, saw the running, colliding, and rebounding people, saw Aphrodite. "Aphrodite!" she screamed. Then she was up and over the wagon bed

376

and running.

Charles Henry shouted, "Emmalee! Damn it!" And he took out after her.

Beside the luggage Aphrodite paused in her loading, raised her face heavenward and sat motionless for a moment. Then she frowned. "Gabriel, where in hell you been?" Then she listened again.

Watson perched his spectacles on his nose. "This is disastrous. Something has to be done. This can't be allowed to go on. Just look. And look there, and—omigod, look up there!"

On the mountainside, plummeting toward them, a string of three rail carts full of people veered into a switchback, shot out of it at a perilous cant and entered the straightaway toward the bottom. He had never seen anything move so fast.

"Yo' right," Aphrodite whispered, and Watson knew she was not talking to him. "This chaos an' havoc done got clean out of hand." He peered at her, saw a terrible sadness spread across her dark face, and blinked.

She got to her knees. "He'p me load this shotgun," she ordered Watson. "This got to be stopped." She was barely aware of Emmalee who was running toward her.

The heads of the two flash floods were nearer now, their roar deafening. In both creek beds, sheer walls of thundering water pushed a howling wind before them, heading for convergence in Calamity.

And just downstream, where animals stampeded from the bottoms, four sooty horsemen galloped across the wide wash and up the near bank, bandanas flapping, guns waving as they charged toward the town.

"Must it be?" Watson whispered as he helped Aphrodite load the shotgun. She held it upright as he labored to squeeze the load into the bore.

"It mus'," she said. "Gabriel say they ain' no other way. I hopes I put 'nuff powder in there."

377

"You poured powder?" Watson blinked at her. "So did I." The load had jammed briefly in the bore. Now it thumped home. Watson shrugged. "Well, it shouldn't matter all that much."

The Timmons and Trask forces had begun shooting at each other again, caught up in their battle, oblivious to all else.

Aphrodite lifted the shotgun. She and Watson got to their feet just as Emmalee reached them. "Aphrodite!" she panted. "Mr. Watson! We must run! Flood!"

"Hang on to her," Aphrodite said, and Watson caught the girl around her shoulders and held her still.

Charles Henry came at a run, crouched low and easel flapping, straight across the battlefield between the Timmons and Trask men. A bullet tugged at his sleeve, and he spun to shoot a thug, then ducked and ran. "Emmalee!"

"Charles Henry!" she squealed, struggling in Watson's arms. As he neared the luggage a large form separated from the shadows of a seed bin and hurtled toward him, a long knife upraised. Charles Henry tripped over a tent peg and Luther stumbled past, then turned cat-quick for another attempt. Charles Henry's gun leveled and clicked on an empty chamber.

"Now!" Watson shouted.

Aphrodite raised the heavy shotgun, took a bead on the center of Charles Henry Clayton's back, and squeezed.

Emmalee screamed, "Aphrodite, no!" But it was too late. The shotgun roared. The force of the charge, dead center between the young man's shoulders, flung him violently forward. He pitched past Luther, skidded on his face and lay there, limp.

Luther looked down at him, then across at Aphrodite, Watson, and the struggling Emmalee. "Shid," he muttered.

Trask's men had routed the Timmons thugs and

were in hot pursuit. Timmons, looking back over his shoulder, ran toward the convergence of the creeks. He passed Luther, and the big man spun around to shout at him, "Bull!"

At the voice, Timmons stopped in his tracks. He turned. They stared at each other across a space of ten yards, across the body of Charles Henry Clayton.

"Dow, you sud ob a bidge," Luther growled, "id's your turd." He started toward him.

Timmons fired, the bullet thudding into Luther's chest. The big man doubled over, dropped his knife, then straightened again. "Shid," he said. Timmons fired twice more, but Luther did not stop again. His hands closed on Timmons's throat, and the force of his charge bore him back and back. Thunder was in his ears, mounting as his throat was slowly crushed. Blood ran from Luther's mouth. Back they staggered, and another step—then they fell, over the edge of the creeks' high bank as roaring flood waters howled down upon them. In an instant they were gone.

Hoofbeats erupted, and suddenly strong hands lifted Watson and dropped him into a running saddle. Others reached for Aphrodite, but she flung herself to the ground, and they passed over her and were gone, splashing away in foot-deep water that was the wake of the flash floods.

Released, Emmalee ran to Charles Henry and knelt beside him, lifting his pallid, blank face above the rising water that washed across them both. "Charles Henry," she sobbed. "Oh, Charles Henry."

The waters flowed, mounted and then ebbed as the roaring flood raced on down the bottoms, on and on, to smash and backlash against the great dam of debris below the hump of Calamity. Water rose in the bottoms, filling them, splashing over the banks.

And across the sudden lake three rail carts shrilled out across the flat, soared over the stamping mill dock

379

and sailed a hundred feet over water before landing with a tremendous splash. One by one, people bobbed to the surface and began to swim.

All of the thunders died now, and in the town of Calamity a silence grew. Aphrodite stood ankle-deep in receding floodwaters, her dark old face a mask of fatigue and pain. She dropped the shotgun into the mud, then walked to where Emmalee sat sobbing, cradling the still form of Charles Henry Clayton to her breast.

"It over, child," she said. "It all over now."

An hour later Watson came back into town, the four horsemen trailing repentantly behind him. People were cleaning and patching, trying to restore order out of chaos. He dismounted at a standing tent, looked inside, then entered. Aphrodite turned to him.

"I was scare to death we put too much powder in that charge," she said. She held up a mangled contraption of bent metal and splintered wood. The tripod easel was a wreck. Near its crushed center and splattered outward, its lacquer finish was smeared with nameless substances. "Whatever was in that juju," Aphrodite said, "it sho' made a mess."

On a cot beyond, a pale and badly bruised Charles Henry lay propped on one elbow, oblivious to them as was Emmalee kneeling beside him. They were holding hands.

"You're sure it is over now?" Watson asked. "The chaos and havoc business?"

"It over. Juju done its job."

"But there is still the virgin's curse."

"Well, I got me a idea about that. I 'spect they got that preacher fished out of th' water by now. You go get him and bring him here. Man that loud ought to be good for somethin'."

VIII

Aphrodite had retrieved her shotgun. Now it lay across her lap as she sat in a slat chair in front of a canvas tent and watched evening colors play across Calamity Valley.

The song of saws and hammers, of trace chain and tackle brace, had subsided with the coming of evening as people retreated to wagon, tent, and cabin site for their suppers, their quiet talk and to make their plans for tomorrow. It would be a while before the townsite of Calamity was put back to real order, but the task was begun.

Watson had sat with her for a time, then had wandered away somewhere. Now another man approached, a man with a sling on one arm and a long rifle in his hand. "This where you put what's his name?" he asked.

Aphrodite nodded.

"He doin' all right?"

"Doin' fine. His back's all bruised, is all."

"Thought maybe I'd have a talk with him. Since I sold out to Samuel Gittings and got him to buy out Cousin Millicent too, this might be a good place for us to settle in."

"Sho' might," Aphrodite said. "But you gone have to talk wit' him some other time. Right now Mr. an' Mrs. Charles Henry Clayton ain' gone be disturbed."

Inside the tent, Mr. and Mrs. Charles Henry Clayton were beyond being disturbed by anyone. They had progressed beyond holding hands. Far beyond.

In the pleasant gloom she nuzzled his ear, nibbling at the lobe, and thrilled to the movement of his exploring hands on her body. She stretched and sighed, intensely aware of the hard tension building within him, the hard rasp of his breathing, the hard, quivering thrust of his desire.

"What are you going to do now?" she breathed, adrift in raptures beyond reason.

"I don't know," he whispered between kisses. "Aunt Samantha was never very specific on this subject."

THE NEWEST ADVENTURES AND ESCAPADES OF BOLT
by Cort Martin

#11: THE LAST BORDELLO   (1224, $2.25)
A working girl in Angel's camp doesn't stand a chance—unless Jared Bolt takes up arms to bring a little peace to the town . . . and discovers that the trouble is caused by a woman who used to do the same!

#12: THE HANGTOWN HARLOTS   (1274, $2.25)
When the miners come to town, the local girls are used to having wild parties, but events are turning ugly . . . and murderous. Jared Bolt knows the trade of tricking better than anyone, though, and is always the first to come to a lady in need . . .

#13: MONTANA MISTRESS   (1316, $2.25)
Roland Cameron owns the local bank, the sheriff, and the town—and he thinks he owns the sensuous saloon singer, Charity, as well. But the moment Bolt and Charity eye each other there's fire—especially gunfire!

#14: VIRGINIA CITY VIRGIN   (1360, $2.25)
When Katie's bawdy house holds a high stakes raffle, Bolt figures to take a chance. It's winner take all—and the prize is a budding nineteen year old virgin! But there's a passle of gun-toting folks who'd rather see Bolt in a coffin than in the virgin's bed!

#15: BORDELLO BACKSHOOTER   (1411, $2.25)
Nobody has ever seen the face of curvaceous Cherry Bonner, the mysterious madam of the bawdiest bordello in Cheyenne. When Bolt keeps a pimp with big ideas and a terrible temper from having his way with Cherry, gunfire flares and a gambling man would bet on murder: Bolt's!

#16: HARDCASE HUSSY   (1513, $2.25)
Traveling to set up his next bordello, Bolt is surrounded by six prime ladies of the evening. But just as Bolt is about to explore this lovely terrain, their stagecoach is ambushed by the murdering Beeler gang, bucking to be in Bolt's position!

Available wherever paperbacks are sold, or order direct from the Publisher. Send cover price plus 50¢ per copy for mailing and handling to Zebra Books, Dept. 1663, 475 Park Avenue South, New York, N.Y. 10016. DO NOT SEND CASH.

**FORGE AHEAD IN THE SCOUT SERIES
BY BUCK GENTRY**

#12: YELLOWSTONE KILL (1254, $2.50)
The Scout is tracking a warband that kidnapped some young and lovely ladies. And there's danger at every bend in the trail as Holten closes in, but the thought of all those women keeps the Scout riding hard!

#13: OGLALA OUTBREAK (1287, $2.50)
When the Scout's long time friend, an Oglala chief, is murdered, Holten vows to avenge his death. But there's a young squaw whose appreciation for what he's trying to do leads him down an exciting trail of her own!

#14: CATHOUSE CANYON (1345, $2.50)
Enlisting the aid of his Oglala friends, the Scout plans to blast a band of rampaging outlaws to hell—and hopes to find a little bit of heaven in the arms of his sumptuous companion . . .

#16: VIRGIN OUTPOST (1445, $2.50)
Tracking some murdering raiders, the Scout uncovers a luscious survivor, a hot-blooded vixen widowed on her wedding night. He'll try his hardest to please her between the sheets—before the raiders nail him between the eyes!

#17: BREAKNECK BAWDYHOUSE (1514, $2.50)
When a vicious gang of gunslingers sets up a hardcase haven—complete with three cathouses—the Scout knows the Sioux plan a massacre. Rescuing the ladies of the evening, the Scout finds it hard when he tries to convince them he came for business, not pleasure!

Available wherever paperbacks are sold, or order direct from the Publisher. Send cover price plus 50¢ per copy for mailing and handling to Zebra Books, Dept. 1663, 475 Park Avenue South, New York, N.Y. 10016. DO NOT SEND CASH.